You ca[...] [...] Instagram
@carolinecorcoranwriter.

By the same author:

Through the Wall
The Baby Group

FIVE DAYS MISSING

CAROLINE CORCORAN

avon.

Published by AVON
A division of HarperCollins*Publishers* Ltd
1 London Bridge Street
London SE1 9GF

www.harpercollins.co.uk

HarperCollins*Publishers*
1st Floor, Watermarque Building, Ringsend Road
Dublin 4, Ireland

A Paperback Original 2022
1

First published in Great Britain by HarperCollins*Publishers* 2022

Typeset in Bembo by Palimpsest Book Production Limited, Falkırk, Stirlingshire
Printed and bound in UK using 100% Renewable Electricity at CPI Group (UK) Ltd

This book is produced from independently certified FSC™ paper to ensure
responsible forest management.

For more information visit: www.harpercollins.co.uk/green

To my friends Zo, Suse, Vic, Hellie, Mike. The best decisions Teenage Me ever made.

Prologue

It's hard to know what to do with the yellow helium balloon you're holding when you discover your wife is missing.

Especially when there is something else that requires your hands: the newborn baby who is screaming from a cot in the corner of the room.

You hold on to the balloon.

You clutch it tighter, like it could lift you up, up and away from this, whatever this is.

You feel your chest tighten.

Your wife. Gone.

Missing from the maternity ward, a day after your daughter was born.

You stand there, looking around. For your wife, for somewhere to put this balloon, for someone to help, for something that can explain what is happening in this moment that shouldn't look like this, that should look like euphoria and newness and nostalgia and life.

You cling, cling, cling to the balloon.

The baby cries louder.

Your chest pulls tighter.

You cling.

The usual bustle of the maternity unit happens just outside the room you are in but it feels, then, like you are sectioned off from it. You know you should go to them, tell somebody, but that involves leaving this room and you can't remember how to do that. Can't remember how to move.

A bell rings and an exhausted midwife sighs, her sensible shoes bouncing a rhythm up the corridor.

Finally, you remember how to turn around. Go to open your mouth as she passes. But you aren't sure what to say because what if you've got this wrong? You know really though, don't you. You know.

Another dad smiles at you as he walks past the room, soft Stan Smiths moving as fast as they can towards a family that his chest will always twitch for now.

You stare at him, living your alternate reality.

You hold on to the balloon.

A shell-shocked woman is pushed past next in a heavy wheelchair, holding a doll. Okay, a baby, but surely a doll. The woman is wearing no bra, exposed, dressing gown open, whole self open. It is just minutes since she gave birth; the most vulnerable of times.

You stand still, still.

The balloon bobs.

The baby cries. Louder again. Piercing now.

And it's that that forces you in the end to let the balloon go, drift, and to move at wading pace across the room to pick up your daughter. You clutch her to your chest. You sit on the bed with her and wait for your wife to come back. The baby doesn't settle. The crying gets louder.

Your wife does not come back.

The baby roots around, pursing her tiny lips for milk she should be able to depend upon.

The tightness in your chest gets worse.

Still, you wait and you wait and you wait. But you have to know, don't you, when it's time to give up. The baby's cries tell you, if nothing else.

You walk to the nurses' station.

'Her mum,' you say as the baby screams even louder now, appalled at the absence of food. 'Her mum has gone.'

And they stare at you, mirroring your horror.

This is how I picture it happening anyway.

Who knows what the reality was but somehow, my husband Marc found out I was gone.

I go over and over scenarios. Flashbacks, they feel like, except I never lived through them. Doesn't stop them coming though; hourly, maybe more. Waking me up if I sleep. Making me long for sleep if I'm awake.

This one comes now as I walk in this mismatched black and yellow bikini to the edge of the lake to dip my feet in the water and try not to spear my soles with rocks and then, submerge myself. And in that first second, perhaps two, I am able to forget what brought me here. Water's always done that. I'm not religious but every time I submerge myself it feels like starting over.

Hundreds of tadpoles swim around my feet.

Look at you, tiny creatures, at the beginning of everything.

I think of those people who pay to have fish eat the hard skin from their feet and how it's the start of a process of being eaten alive and how weird we are, human beings, how weird.

I am as new as the tadpoles. If only the feeling would last. Instead, what has happened slowly comes back to me. It is fully remembered by my own body. Your mind forgets, briefly; your muscles don't.

When I am deep enough that I can't stand, I lie on my back in this lake hundreds of miles away from that sterile room and hundreds of miles from my newborn baby.

The tadpoles don't brave this part; fish swim around me.

I take a deep breath.

One of my expansive, milky breasts tries again to break free of its bikini top and I push it back in. Between my legs, I bleed. My stomach hangs loose like an empty plastic bag.

On the shore, a woman in her early twenties walks past, neat breasts fitted into triangles, leaking nothing but lake water, unlike mine. Her rucksack lies on shore.

My heart starts to hammer. Is that her? The woman I came here for?

But then I catch a glimpse of her face. No. This woman joins a group at the edge of the woodland and I hear the clink of a beer bottle. The smell of meat fat on a barbecue drifts over and makes me gag and I think of the signs on the drive here that warn of forest fires, but I feel no fear.

Not of forest fires anyway.

There is only one thing that scares me.

I feel the slime and rocks as I wade out of the lake. I don't have shoes on my feet like the other swimmers; there wasn't the time to think of it. The time, or the inclination.

I sit down on the shore, the rocks immediately digging into my thighs. I experiment, pushing them into the ground, feeling them imprint. Feeling them hurt. Harder. They *should* hurt.

I should hurt.

'You want a beer?'

It's the woman who just walked past. French, knowing automatically that I am English, as often happens. She is barefoot; has come down to the water to paddle her feet, cool down.

Her hand, outstretched, brandishes a stubby bottle.

I look up at her and want to laugh. Me? Really?

I have a baby face that has meant I am often mistaken for someone younger than I am. But everything from the breasts down surely now paints to weathered? My hand sits awkwardly over skin I could scrunch up like Play-Doh.

'No. I'm okay thanks.'

Perhaps she just feels pity for me; alone, no joy.

She shrugs.

'*Pas de problem.*'

As she walks back to her friends, she is framed like a picture, steep rocks behind her, lake to the side. Something ridiculous happens and three women on horseback arrive and head straight into the water next to me, the horses paddling, majestic, and the whole scene would be idyllic if I weren't living in it, if I didn't know that it is a hell.

She smiles at the horses, this other woman, wades out to stroke them and looks up, awed. And then she walks away, her already tanned body about to spend a summer outdoors, travelling perhaps, drinking at times, lazing in hammocks, on parched sand, in beach bars. It is May, and everything is ahead. Being young and wild is how it should be, but not how it is guaranteed to be, we now know. Not so long ago, we lived through a pandemic. If you can, you kiss and you dance and you share a beer. If you can, you live.

I watch her. Remember how that feels, to live. Twist the rings on my left hand, one at a time, like I'm fixing machinery.

I remember how it is to be her. How a tan and an ankle bracelet make you feel when you are young; a goddess, a myth, for those two weeks after the flight lands home, until September forces you into tights and your hair braid unravels and your tan peels off on your fingertips in front of *EastEnders*.

I look down at myself. Could she really have mistaken me for one of her own; someone who was working in a bar for a few months to save enough to head to South East Asia?

I look around.

If that's not her, where is the woman I'm waiting for?

I feel a tug of impatience.

The lake laps at my unpainted toenails, uncared for feet. It pushes it a bit, creeping all the way up to thighs that are now smarting from the rocks.

More young people arrive, carrying boxes of wine, picnic blankets and camping chairs over the rickety bridge from the patch of land that functions as a car park. Music comes with them, moving in their wake, like it's emitted from their pores when really it's just their iPhones. There is a strong smell of weed.

It's Friday, late afternoon, just slipping into evening. Friday at the lake means party time. Even the fishermen swig from those fat beer bottles as they finish up; the Gallic equivalent of the after-work pint.

Many of them put a hand up to wave. The world is friendly, since Covid-19. We like people more than we did.

All of them are framed by the rocks that climb up on each side like they are hiding the body of water from view. Perhaps they are: nature is smart; keeping a natural beauty away from the bulk of tourists seems as good a reason for the formation of some rock as any. I think of my sister Loll, then: a pharmacist, who would be exasperated if I said that out loud.

It hurts to think of Loll.

I press harder onto the rocks.

My thighs sting. My breasts throb.

The water is so clear that I can see my reflection in it but that's not something enjoyable.

My face without make-up looked young and bright not so long ago. Now it had a tendency towards sleep-deprived and drawn. Lots can change in a few months. Faces. People. Lives.

When other people walk by, they would think I have a hang-over maybe, or − if they had seen my tent, at a campsite round the corner − that I've been travelling for too long, in need of a hot bath and a freshly washed duvet. Similar to a lot of the people across the lake, whooping, shouting to friends to join them in the water. When they swim, they are lithe like fish.

I look down at myself. My limbs thin, contrasting with my middle.

If people asked, I would tell them my name is Kate, as planned, but they don't because I don't speak to them or I bat them away, like I did with the Frenchwoman and her *bière*.

I don't speak to anyone, as much as I can help it.

Sometimes in the evening, I see the wetness spreading outwards on to my T-shirt from my nipples. I glance down, clasp my hand

6

across my chest. I try my best to drift off so that I don't have to think about it.

And then, I *do* talk.

And it's always a version of the same thing.

'Please, I want to live.'

And with that line, every time without fail, I wake up.

Because I scream it so loud.

Day #1, 6 a.m.

The Husband

I don't mean gone as in to the toilet, or to wander the corridor to find someone to top up her water.

I mean gone. *Gone.*

Her things, her clothes, her phone. All of them. Gone.

Everything of Romilly's has been shipped out, in fact, except for the tiny speck of a person who lies sleeping in her clinical hospital cot.

I call Romilly's phone. Off. Shove my own back into my pocket.

I inch closer; approach this child, all seven or so pounds of her versus six foot, fifteen stone of me.

She feels like a booby trap.

The stock blue hospital blanket that was placed on her when she was born yesterday is no longer in place. In its stead is a beautiful cream one Romilly's sister Loll knitted for us. My sister-in-law started work on it as soon as we found out we were having a baby; it's been sitting in our bedroom waiting for its big moment for months. I presume it was Romilly who put it on her.

How long ago did she leave?

I touch the blanket, briefly, without realising what I'm doing. But it would be warm whatever time Romilly left; babies do that.

Peeping out from the top of the blanket is a mint green babygrow that I saw my wife, sitting cross-legged on the floor of our bedroom, packing in her changing bag a few weeks ago.

Our baby's tiny chest rises and falls, as dependable as a clock. I check that, and only that, before I walk fast out of the room to the nurses' station. Last time I was here was before I left yesterday evening, asking for some basic pain relief for Romilly.

'Excuse me,' I say to a midwife who looks vaguely familiar. 'Has my wife gone for some treatment? She isn't in her room?'

I speak louder as the midwife is distracted, checking a form. 'She's not there,' I repeat. 'She's gone.'

Emergency surgery, perhaps; complications not as rare as we'd like to believe in the Western world during and after labour. Romilly moved at speed, the baby left here under the care of experienced midwives? Do they do that – leave them alone in their rooms? Were they about to call me and let me know?

And yet, this doesn't feel like that. Emergencies leave something in their wake.

The midwife looks up, confused.

'I've only just come on shift,' she says. 'Let me check with someone else. What's the name again?'

'Romilly Beach,' I tell her. 'And I'm Marc Beach. Her husband.'

I pull off my hoodie, combusting. Stand up straighter with the formality of the word 'husband'.

She nods, calm.

'The baby is in the room though, yes?' she asks.

I nod.

However matter-of-fact she might have seemed then, the air shifts with her relief at the answer to that question.

I wipe the sweat off my forehead.

'Okay, go back and wait in your room with the baby,' she says. 'I'll find out what's going on.'

So she walks away and I return to the private room I had been surprised we were allocated after Romilly had our baby two days ago. The hospital was quiet; home births perhaps have become more common in a world that's retreated from Covid-19.

The balloon bobs on the ceiling as I stare at the baby who

now looks rudderless without Romilly there, and who frightens me a little. I circle her. Look from a distance.

Shortly afterwards a nurse walks in, looks around as though Romilly may be hiding under the bed, and says to me: 'Sorry, my love, but your wife hasn't been taken anywhere. She was perfectly fine on the last ward round.'

She looks at her notes.

'Didn't need any follow-ups, just a couple of paracetamol,' she mutters, half to herself. 'Shall we give her a few minutes?'

I shake my head.

'No,' I say, decisive. 'Don't wait. She's being monitored for postpartum psychosis. We need to track her down as soon as humanly possible.'

The midwife looks at me like I'm overreacting.

My voice rises. 'Her stuff has gone,' I say. 'She hasn't nipped to the café. Her clothes, her bag, even her phone . . .

'She has a risk factor for postpartum psychosis,' I repeat, interrupting myself, focusing on the important detail. There isn't time to waste, with this. 'Her mum had it. She is being monitored. Is that in her notes? Do you know about it?'

She glances. 'Not in here,' she says. Doesn't respond to my heavy sigh. 'Have you tried calling her?'

I bristle. Of course I have tried bloody calling her. But I try again. Shake my head at the midwife, who is staring at me hopefully. Did she hear what I said?

She takes out her notes. Scribbles something on them.

It's difficult to read upside down but I think it is, laughably reductive, *Mum. Gone.*

She looks up. Both of us glance around the room. Two sets of eyes reach their final destination at the baby. What next for you, then?

The midwife speaks. 'It looks as though she has just – like you said – gone.' She exhales.

How is this moving so slowly?

'Do you know much about postpartum psychosis?' I ask.

My heart is hammering.

'There is a very real risk that Romilly could harm herself. Even kill herself. Postpartum psychosis can be that severe. We need to act fast. *Now.*'

She swallows. 'Let me go and put out an alert,' she says. 'See if anybody knows anything.'

And while she is out of the room I put out my own alert, to Romilly's sister Loll.

'Marc,' Loll answers, brusque and alert when she answers even though she's probably making porridge for her kids in her nightie.

'It's happened, Loll,' I say. 'Romilly has gone.'

'What do you mean, gone?' she says, sharp.

I look around and the room is taking on that ghoulish quality: the one that comes with death or trauma or shock.

'What do you mean, Marc, gone?' she says again, voice louder.

'She can't have gone far, Marc. Have you spoken to the midwives, to the . . .'

'Her stuff,' I interrupt. '*All* of her stuff is gone.'

Silence.

I run my hand through my hair and even that is damp. I could wring my T-shirt like a flannel.

'Except the baby,' I say more quietly, looking at that fleck of a person. 'The baby is still here. Romilly wouldn't leave her baby. Not if she was in her right mind.'

Loll takes it in.

'Of course she wouldn't,' she says, snapping into action. 'Of course she wouldn't. Okay, Marc. Okay. Stay with the baby. I'll go and call the police.'

As I end the call to Loll, I realise I have been pacing.

I stop. Look around.

Not my normal life, but an episode of some drama I am watching on Netflix on a Friday night.

I speak lines from the script of a life that isn't my own.

Because come on; my own script is that of a mundane 30-something existence. A script of band practices and cheese sandwiches and we must remember to transfer that cash for the new driveway because it's been three weeks now.

We knew postpartum psychosis was a risk but my wife was being monitored for it; we were being careful. It wasn't really going to *happen*.

With an effort at a cry, the baby wakes up, unaware that her mother has gone.

I look at her.

How long have you slept for?

How long has Romilly been gone? Did our baby wake up and cry herself back to sleep, the midwives assuming her mother was there and would comfort her, feed her?

The baby's cry intensifies fast and the sound slaps down my thoughts.

I approach her nervously.

Seconds later the midwife returns. Her eyes go up towards the balloon.

'We'll keep digging but, so far, no one's seen anything, no one noticed her slip out,' she says.

'Her sister is on the way,' I say, kissing my baby on her cheek, gently. 'She knows a lot about postpartum psychosis. She can tell you more.'

The midwife nods, grim.

'And how is baby doing?'

I look down at my daughter.

Hello, baby. Some bad news since we last spoke. I've lost your mum.

'Okay, I think,' I say. 'Just waking up.'

'Well that's a good thing,' she says. She sounds chipper but her teeth come out to bite her bottom lip. 'Will you call the police?'

'Her sister's doing that on the way over,' I tell her.

12

A thought occurs.

'Did anyone hear the baby crying?' I ask, cutting her off. 'I'm just trying to work out how long ago her mum left. If the baby's been fed.'

I'm impatient now. These early minutes, hours are crucial when someone goes missing, right? If you don't figure it out now, you never do. That's the trajectory Netflix has fed to me at least.

'Oh, love, this place is *full* of babies crying,' the midwife says to me with kindness, sitting on the edge of the bed, taking the rare opportunity to hold a weary foot in its ugly slip-on shoe. 'We just assume their mummies are taking care of them unless they ring their button for help.'

I look at our baby, fitful now in my arms, and picture her crying, stomach empty, no one filling it and finally, finally, giving up. Concluding that this is how the world worked, in her earliest experiences of it.

Oh, my girl. I kiss her head again. Keep my mouth there.

The midwife looks at her too and for a second it's as simple as that, life at its start; tiny foot in tiny babygrow. The midwife lowers her own foot down to the floor.

'Let me get her some formula,' she says, decisive. 'Do you have a preference on brand?'

I shake my head.

Romilly wanted to breastfeed.

'You're taking your baby home today, right?' says the midwife, as she comes back in with a miniature bottle of ready-made Cow and Gate a few minutes later and takes the baby from me.

I don't object. I don't know how to do this. I don't know this baby. I don't know this scenario. Does anyone know this scenario?

I nod.

'Okay. Well. I'll give you a run-through of formula feeding, and you'll need to stock up obviously, or get someone to do it for you if you've got your hands full with the baby. And we'll do the usual discharge things . . .'

'And then?' I ask.

She stares at me. There is no precedent. *Mum. Gone.*

And then?

'Keep in touch once you've spoken to the police,' she says, pragmatic. 'And obviously we are here; I presume they'll want to speak to us. Here's the best number to get us on. And we . . . well, if anything comes up this end, we'll obviously let you know too.'

She hands me a piece of paper. I rip a bit off and write my number on it for her and it's like we're ending a date in a time before mobiles – a scene as simple as that.

'So I am still taking the baby home today?' I say, panic rising. I am eleven, being given the house keys and the alarm code and instructions to heat up the leftover hotpot.

'Sure are, hon,' she says, warm as she slips the bottle into the baby's mouth. 'We don't keep them in any longer than they need and you have a super healthy baby here. But we will absolutely keep in touch. Community midwife will be round at yours tomorrow for a visit.'

I am on mute.

'We'll tell you if we hear or see anything,' she carries on eventually. 'But I'm sure your wife will be home soon.'

Surety. Can I take some of that?

My phone beeps. Loll.

On my way, she writes.

'Right, burping,' says the midwife, sitting up my baby and holding her carefully with red raw over-sanitised hands and trying to normalise things that could never be normalised. I try to focus. But it's hard to concentrate on the rites of passage of a newborn when you're simultaneously fielding replies on your phone from friends that you've messaged asking if they've heard from your missing wife.

I put my phone away and try to exude calm while I fight an urge to scream the place down. Eventually Loll arrives, sees my face and steps in.

'Look, I think I can take this from here,' she says, from the doorway.

The midwife looks at her sharply. There is something about each of them that reminds me of the other.

The stare lasts a few seconds.

The midwife rubs circles on the baby's back for the duration.

'I'm not being rude . . . Julie,' Loll continues as she moves towards us, checking the other woman's name badge.

'It's just that I can tell him anything else he needs. I've had two myself. I'll be at the house helping with the baby too,' says Loll, gentler now, and God I am relieved by that news. I squeeze her hand. 'But right now I think we need to go, make some calls about my sister.'

She turns to me.

'I've given the police the details,' she says. 'They have my number so hopefully they'll have something for us soon.'

I nod.

Loll has already switched her focus.

Julie slips the bottle back into the baby's mouth.

'I'm sorry,' Loll says. She takes her sensible glasses off and wipes them on the sleeve of her blouse. 'This is not a normal discharge. This is not a normal day. Let's finish her feed and get her dressed and get her out of here. I can teach him how to get wind up.'

And she swoops in and takes her niece, finishing the feed, she changes the baby's tiny nappy on her tiny bottom before I've even noticed where it's come from. Julie sits next to her, quietly fuming. Eventually she stands, wincing and muttering about her knees as she goes.

Loll doesn't say a word.

Day #1, 7.15.a.m.

The Husband

When the baby has her nappy on, Loll wraps her in a blanket, stands up and rocks her.

'Hey, you,' she whispers, breath on her face. I realise then that it's the first time they have met. 'Oh gosh. Your cousins are going to *love* you. You are in for so many cuddles.'

I smile, sad. Don't miss out on that, Romilly. Please don't.

It's 7 a.m. now. An hour since I found out Romilly had left. It's a relief she is not with the baby, but postpartum psychosis means that there is a chance she can be a harm to herself too. Loll and I talk around that, carrying it in our deep frowns and shaky hands instead.

'Bring them round,' I say. 'Would be nice to see them when we get home.'

Loll's bottom lip is sucked into her mouth.

'It's just . . .'

Ah. Yeah.

'Bit intense?'

She nods. 'Sorry. But yeah. They've been through a lot, my kids, in the last few years with the divorce. I want to shelter them . . . Hopefully it'll all be over soon and they'll never need to know.'

I am envious. Her children can avoid this; mine has no choice but to be a part of it.

I pull out my phone.

'Okay, so postpartum psychosis then. Firstly – the timing. This usually hits straight after the baby is born.'

Loll's face stays buried in the baby. 'Marc, I know all of this,' she says. 'We don't need to go over it.'

My eyes are back on my phone.

'Feeling suspicious or fearful – could explain her bolting.'

Loll bites that lip again.

'Restlessness – well, she's not here so yeah. Pretty restless.'

Not even a wry smile.

'Confused. Acting out of character. Delusions.'

I look at her.

'It carries on and it all makes sense. And I tell you what else makes sense – *fuck all*. If you freak out when you have just had a baby, you have a cry, call your friend, post something panicky on Facebook. You don't *leave*. It has to be this.'

Loll puts the baby in the Moses basket. She wraps her arms around her own body like a blanket even though it's twenty degrees outside, the start of the warmest day of the year so far. We are only in May.

'I know,' she says, voice hard as set cement.

'Every symptom, every . . .'

She places a soft hand on my arm but her voice doesn't lose its solidity. 'You don't have to *convince* me, Marc,' she says. 'I went to every one of Romilly's meetings with her. And I saw my mum go through it.'

I nod, in my place. Defer. Loll is the expert.

After that, we get back to the baby.

Loll – a surrogate mother to Romilly often, as there is a ten-year age gap between them – takes charge. As I sit on the edge of an empty bed messaging and calling everyone Romilly is close to, Loll is rummaging through the hospital bag that Romilly packed, muttering: 'Going home outfit, going home outfit, the yellow cardy, hat.'

'I don't think she needs a hat, Loll,' I say, trying to find a purpose as I sit swinging my legs off the bed like a teenager, phone in hand. 'It's a warm day.'

She doesn't look up. Keeps rummaging. 'Babies always need a hat, Marc — it's a thing. Heat escapes out of their little heads.'

Is it true?

I'm embarrassed at my lack of knowledge.

Part of me wants to tell her to sling on the first babygrow she finds, that it doesn't matter what the baby wears; we are in the middle of a crisis.

But slowly, like a ritual, Loll starts dressing the baby in this soft tiny onesie that she has been looking for and something about it calms me for a few seconds. I stop looking at the messages coming in on my phone; look at this spindly doll instead.

Loll looks up at me. Pauses.

'Is it okay?' she asks suddenly. 'That I'm doing this? It doesn't feel right. It should be her parents.'

'Well nothing about this is right,' I say with a shrug. 'It's just clothes.'

And doesn't our baby deserve it? A nice outfit, some ceremony, the stuff the other babies have?

She is currently deprived of fifty per cent of her parents; the least we can give her is a thirty-quid John Lewis babygrow with a fancy collar.

Afterwards, Loll and I stare at each other.

'Ready?' she asks.

I nod.

And when we leave, nobody takes that picture — you know the one, me from behind, walking along holding the baby in the brand-new car seat.

Actually, nobody takes any pictures.

Nobody tells me from the back seat to drive slower, slower, slower all the way home because nobody is in the back seat with our baby, holding her hand.

Loll is in her own car.

In here, it's just the baby and me.

Silence.

But still, we head home, into a day that is the wrong shape and grotesque.

This can't be it for good now, I think, a sick feeling spreading across my middle.

Romilly has to undo this.

But I have a terrible feeling that she won't.

Day #2, 2 p.m.

The Husband

'Thanks, man.'

I take in a delivery of flowers from someone who has forgotten to put their name on and forgotten to check that the baby they had heard had been born hadn't mislaid its mother. Someone who must have had a text from Romilly or me telling them that the baby had arrived in those blissfully normal hours before this seismic thing happened.

But when I go to shut our front door the image of Romilly, there, transforming it into its current bright green, is so stark it winds me.

Romilly painted that door when we moved in last year.

When the delivery driver pulls away, thumbs up from the van, I stay rooted to the spot.

I picture my wife, kneeling on the step in her denim cut-offs and with bare feet, paint splattered all over her legs.

'Shouldn't you put on some overalls?' I had asked, leaning against the wall next to her with a beer.

'As if we have overalls, Marc.' Romilly laughed. 'Real adults have overalls. Loll probably has overalls. I'll just scrub it off in the shower. Put my shorts on a hot wash.'

'And the . . .' I had said, gesturing to the blob of green paint on our tiles inside the door. She waved me away.

'Shush, Marc, shush, it's part of the process. And it adds character.'

There was something about her expression in those moments that you couldn't argue with.

Outside the door: Romilly's royal blue wellies, upside down on the stand outside and still encrusted with mud from our last walk a few weeks ago when her belly ached and the baby pressed on her bladder so hard that she had to wee in the woods and we stopped on the way home for emergency crisps.

'I'm really into pregnancy Romilly and her diet.' I had smiled, as she walked next to me shovelling in a family bag of salt and vinegar.

'Not a word to the café lot,' she said, finger wagging. Threatened to deny it and tell them they were edamame. The café she manages has an ethos based on 'wellness'. Always been baffling to me, as a man who eats Coco Pops for lunch.

I stand at the door picturing our life before. Years have passed since then, surely. But no. It was alarmingly recent.

My own khaki wellies are next to Romilly's, about twice the size. Romilly is a shoe size three, in proportion to her minuscule frame. Pregnancy made her look as though she would topple over.

When I close the door, I shove the flowers on the kitchen table, no water, and think how often flowers are supposed to be a nice thing and all they are is a chore.

Fuck the beauty.

My wife is missing, with a mental health condition that could mean she takes her own life. Any second. This one. This one. Now. Then. Anything. Any time.

And someone thinks I want to look around for a vase; snip off the ends. Add sodding flower food.

Send beer, I think, if you want to send something. Send a bottle of vodka. Send me sedatives so I can sleep until this is over.

When I land back in the living room it is onto the sofa that Romilly and I have sat together on so many times that it is indented by us, moulded to our shapes. Where Romilly's belly had laid on its side so full of daughter earlier this week as she pored over a hypnobirthing book. Where a tiny stain is left on the arm from that time Romilly's best friend Steffie stayed over and a tipsy Romilly spilt red wine. This place drips Romilly, spills over with Romilly, oozes Romilly like an overly stuffed burrito.

Now she's not here in person, though, I want to contain these traces, scoop her up and put her in a cupboard until we fix this.

Seeing her everywhere is too much.

I bow my head low and cover as much of my face as I can with my palms.

It is 2 p.m. It was only one day ago we found out Romilly was gone.

My sister-in-law sits on the sofa next to me, holding the baby. I can feel her eyes on me.

Is he okay? Can he cope? Do we need to call for help?

At least she knows what is happening.

Without the context we have, I know what everybody else will think.

Is it his fault?

They will think I did something. Hurt Romilly. That I caused this. *Always the husband* and all the other taglines. I have a target on my back.

And when I see them, I will have to force my heavy head upwards to plaster on a smile and reassure them and hope they know that this time, it's nothing at all to do with the husband, actually: the husband is a good guy, give the husband a break.

'How's my girl?' I ask, looking over at my baby.

I lean down and stroke our white Labrador Henry, who is chilling out by my feet, finally done with investigating the baby.

I wrap my arms around his sturdy neck, the soft coat around it. Inhale. He has been bathed for the new arrival, the smell of old carpet eradicated. For a few weeks at least.

The baby doesn't have a name yet. It's the kind of decision

you make together, isn't it? With the baby's mother having disappeared, our baby doesn't get to have one.

Loll strokes the baby with no name on her nameless nose, smiles at her nameless face.

'She's good. Content baby. Clearly oblivious to the nightmare going on around her.'

The smile collapses.

More silence.

'She'll come back,' she says, softer.

I say nothing.

Instead, I stare out of the window into the day that 7 a.m. promised it would be. A toddler flies past on his bright red scooter, a flash of colour. The tulips we planted last autumn are showing off in the sunshine. The day's palette is bright; my insides are a muddy grey.

The atmosphere feels close, like it's holding its breath.

'Kids at school?' I ask Loll.

And then I think how ridiculous it is that I still feel pressure to make small talk when I am going through something like this. Small talk *is* small; a tiny speck of pointlessness.

'Dropped them with my neighbour,' she says, palm on her forehead, rubbing like a bad massage. 'She's a living legend, that woman. It's half-term – bad timing – and I would have taken them to Jake's but God knows how he would cope with a visit that wasn't scheduled four weeks in advance.'

No. No. I haven't got the headspace for bitching about Loll's ex-husband Jake right now. Not that that makes any difference when Loll decides she wants to bitch about Jake.

Not now, Loll.

I focus on being grateful that she is here.

Loll picks up the bottle of milk.

'She's such an easy baby,' she enthuses again – like having a good baby might make me feel better about having a missing wife – and tips a bottle back at an angle from The

Baby With No Name's mouth. Something about mimicking the flow from the breast. The midwife did go over it with me before we left yesterday but it was a lot to take in. I'm figuring out that this newborn part contains a lot of very specific practices.

I had nodded at Julie as she showed me the bottle and fed my baby and talked while Loll took over as my brain whirred: *your wife is missing, you have no idea where she is, this baby is now your sole responsibility.*

Now we're home, where I expected the answers to lie. But they don't. Nothing has moved on. Romilly hasn't been in touch. The baby has no mum. I look at Loll in her place on Romilly's indentation. Too big for it. Too not Romilly.

Out of the corner of my eye I see Romilly's nail file. There are fibres of you on there, I think. You are so very definitely not here and yet you so very clearly are. How can I marry these two things?

'No reflux or anything yet,' chatters Loll. 'Hopefully she will be *much* simpler than my two.'

I look at her.

'Nothing from the police yet?' I ask.

My sister-in-law shakes her head. 'They are checking hospitals; CCTV,' she says.

'And you still haven't heard from Romilly?' I ask. A bead of sweat runs down my forehead.

Loll's head snaps up and she puts the bottle down for a second; grabs her own ponytail and yanks hard, almost clasping it. When she speaks her tone is different.

'Marc, I would obviously tell you if I had heard from my sister.'

Do the words 'my sister' have some ownership to them?

I wipe the sweat with the back of my hand.

There is a pause.

She raises her eyebrows at me. Shakes her head in complaint.

I know really that she would tell me if she heard from her.

Loll has been irreplaceable for the last two days, feeding, changing, cuddling.

'I know this isn't easy on you, especially on your own with the kids,' I say, and Loll winces.

'Don't,' she says, pushing her glasses on to her head as she rubs one eye. 'I'm just trying to make an awful situation a bit less awful. This isn't about me.'

I should have known better. Loll hates being seen as a victim. It's one of the main reasons hate pours from her every pore towards her ex-husband; he made her the victim, stuck her on the receiving end of cocked heads and there theres and offers of paella nights with other couples all alone or worse, the worst of all, date set-ups.

I think at times she would have killed him, if she could have. Not for leaving her; for the embarrassment.

We sit in silence for a few seconds, Loll and I, as she feeds and pauses, feeds and pauses, mimics that AWOL breast. On the other sofa Henry yawns, the sound an exaggerated cat mew. He licks his lips. Settles back down. I think he's getting used to our newcomer.

When Loll's phone rings though, he leaps – supersensitive hearing.

Loll looks at the screen. Silently hands the baby to me.

'Mum,' she says. 'Thanks for calling us back.'

I had to badger Loll to call her mother Aurelia this morning. She protested it wasn't worth it; she wouldn't know anything, Romilly would never go to her, there was no point upsetting her.

'But what if she does know something?' I said, incredulous. 'Who might you go to when times are tough? Is your mum not up there?'

Eventually, she gave in.

Aurelia is only just getting back to Loll now, hours later. This

25

is the speed at which she moves through life; I envy the lack of urgency.

I watch Loll's face as she speaks; it gives nothing away.

Romilly and Loll don't have a dad; he is dead now but to all intents and purposes that happened to Romilly and Loll a long time ago; he left and picked himself up a new family soon after Romilly was born, is how the story goes. Contact was on and off when they were small; more off than on.

My own mum is elderly and in a care home in Sussex and my dad passed away three years ago. So Aurelia's belated return call is the nearest we are going to get to any parenting for the adults.

I am close enough to Loll to hear the other side of the conversation too, as Aurelia is shouting.

'Sorry, darling, am in the van!' she yells. She and Bill, a man in his seventies with a long white beard and loafers who is referred to as her boyfriend, are travelling through the Basque region in a camper van. 'But I got your message about Romilly. Goodness me! Do you need me to come home?'

Loll's lips are pursed. She sends her eyes skyward, like she doesn't believe the offer is genuine, or just thinks that it is useless, or both. Even from this distance, I would admit it sounded token. Not to mention reticent.

'No, it's fine,' Loll tells her.

'Ask her if she's heard from her,' I hiss.

Loll does.

'What's that, darling? From Romilly? We haven't heard from her since her text to say the baby had arrived safely, have we, Bill? But if she turns up here we'll send her straight back to you.'

My turn to pull up my eyebrows.

Loll winces too, interrupts.

'We'll keep you posted,' she says.

'Bad reception in the van, darling!' Romilly's mum shouts.

'But yes. I'm sure it's just a freak-out about giving birth. I remember being utterly horrified the first time I tried to put you to the breast. The agony! Like it was on fire! Maybe something like that?'

'Mm hmm,' says Loll, eyes rolling like dice. 'Yes, perhaps. Anyway I'm helping Marc to look after the baby.'

'Good, good, you're very good at that, the whole mummy bit. He's lucky to have you!' she shouts.

I see Loll cringe. 'Mummy bit?'

'I'd better go now, darling, but keep in touch, Lolly, and get Romilly to call me when she's home, won't you? Bless her, what an upheaval. She might need her mama there. We'll do some talking, some being together, even if it's just on the phone.'

Loll's face does not say good things.

'Right,' she says. 'Sure. Some being together, on the phone. I'm going now.'

She is about to hang up and then remembers: 'Oh, and Mum. Your granddaughter is a beauty, if you were wondering.'

'Yes I saw the picture – adorable darling!' yells Aurelia, distracted, already with her head in a map on the way to San Sebastián most likely, daydreaming about the fresh seafood platter she's going to order for lunch alongside half a cider.

I imagine worlds existing outside this one. Simple ones, with seafood specials and map reading. With art galleries and toes dipped in the sea and sun cream ready to be slathered on. It seems like fantasy.

When she puts her phone down, Loll throws her head back to the sofa and sits for a minute.

'Told you,' she mumbles. 'Pointless.'

I stare at her.

'Why didn't you tell her it's postpartum psychosis?'

Loll shoots me a look. She sighs.

'I don't know how much Romilly has explained to you – or even how much she really understands about our mum, because

I've always tried to protect her from Aurelia as well,' she says. 'But my mother needs to live in a bubble. She needs to be treated like a child. Like, the way I don't mention death in front of my three-year-old and pretend sex doesn't exist even to my ten-year-old, you have to do that for anything that will make her stress out. Just . . . pretend it's not there. That was as far as I could go. We don't talk about it.'

It's Romilly's mum who is the reason she was being monitored for postpartum psychosis. Aurelia, giving birth in the Eighties, was never diagnosed but Loll and Romilly are sure in retrospect that when Romilly was born, that's what she had.

Loll pushes her fingers into an imaginary mark on her forehead.

'But she might have *wanted* to know.' I pause. 'She might have had some . . . insights,' I say gently. 'Since she lived with it herself.'

'She wasn't the only one who lived with it,' Loll snaps. 'I was there too. And I was a lot more lucid through it than my mother was.' She sighs. 'Look, Marc, trust me − my mum cannot deal with this.'

She picks lint off her plain grey jumper.

'Not as in she doesn't like it, like the rest of us, but *cannot deal with it*. You have to keep it away from her. We all have to. This is no different. In fact it's worse − it'll bring it all flooding back for her. I can't do that.'

'But it's her daughter, Loll. You're a parent. You know what you sign up for.'

We stare at each other.

I nod. Don't trust myself to speak. I look at the baby and everything contracts.

'To be honest, Spain is the ideal place for my mother through this,' says Loll, dry. 'A couple of hours' plane ride away. The last thing you want is her turning up here. It would make the situation harder, not easier.' Her face is darkness.

'So if she's not with her mum, Loll,' I say, trying to push down the bubbling sensation, 'where would she go? Because that was about my best guess.'

I look at Henry. Lying down with that solid head of his between his outstretched front paws. Huge, sad sigh. Do you miss her, buddy?

'Will she miss him?' I ask Loll. 'Through the fog? Or is there not room with it to compute feelings like that?'

Like I say, she is the expert. I don't know how many things fit through the gaps with postpartum psychosis.

But if anything would, if even our baby is too unknown yet, the thought of Henry would. She *loves* that dog. She normally can't cope if we leave him for twenty-four hours.

Loll looks at me. Then at my hands, knotted into fists. I uncurl my fingers.

Something flickers across her features and she goes to speak but stops herself. When she starts talking again her face is reset. 'I don't know.'

And I must be imagining it because it's Loll and she's made of rock but I swear I see a globule of a tear.

Is it the chat with her mum that's done it? Or are the tears coming finally as a response to everything that has happened to our family in the last two days? We all have limits.

Loll coughs lightly then as she picks up a text. She slips her phone in her pocket. Heads out of the room. I hear her turn the lock on the bathroom door.

When she comes back in, my sister-in-law's arms hang awkwardly. Loll is so used to having her own children, Keira, three, and Lucy, ten, attached to her, feeding them, wiping them, cuddling them, that she looks incomplete without them.

The baby – my baby – usually fills the space but I hold her now so Loll's arms are empty. Maybe – looking at how awkward she is – for the first time in ten years.

Instead, Loll fills them with dirty plates and cups, with rogue bibs and dirty nappies. She hoovers up Henry's ever-moulting coat. By the time there is a knock at the door, the baby is asleep in her Moses basket and Loll has found a can of Pledge and is dusting furiously, the air sharp with cleanliness.

'I'll go,' I say. 'It'll be Steffie.'

Or I hope so. Yesterday was like being at an elongated version of my wife's wake. Those close to Romilly, but no Romilly. Neighbours popping over to see the baby, turning up at the doorstep with facial expressions so perfectly one-dimensional they are like emojis. Their words are similar: bland reassurance. I suddenly realise what Loll must have gone through with the break-up.

I don't blame her for hating it.

I don't blame her for wanting to rip Jake to pieces.

When I open the door, Steffie flings her long arms around me and I let her, relieved to see someone who's less tense than Loll, less active. Steffie will sit with me, talk; she won't need to dust the top of the TV while she does it.

'Oh, Marc, my love,' she sighs. 'How are you doing?'

I nod. Shrug. Bite my lip to stem the sob. She puts her arms back around me.

Romilly is a hugger and Steffie is the same. She and Romilly always have an arm slung around each other's shoulders, a hand at the other's waist. They clutch palms, kiss each other on their heads. It's absent-minded because they spend so much time together.

Steffie works at the café that Romilly manages (usually; Steffie is managing it when Romilly is on maternity leave) and they glide around each other all day, handing over green juice, drizzling over the chilli oil, taking away the plates.

It's a version of cohabiting; it contains the same comfort, the same ease, exacerbated by the fact they have known each other since school days. In our bedroom there are drawers stuffed with postcards they wrote to each other when they were away at university, two or three a week, like a diary, and the odd more detailed letter too when a small rectangle wasn't enough. Their minds are used to sharing a space, and their bodies too: when they go away together, Romilly tells me they are frequently naked. That's what long-term friendship can do, apparently.

Sometimes, to me, it's different to that: it's like my wife is one half of another marriage.

But the Goodness Café is Romilly's other home, Steffie is Romilly's other partner and by extension she and I are comfortable in each other's company. Steffie has been in constant contact today. Now she is in tears.

As Loll starts scrubbing at the windows, Steffie and I get on with our hug, her sinewy arms bare in a running vest. There is a slight musk of sweat. I pull her closer.

'Sorry I asked how you're doing,' Steffie says, pulling away finally and whipping her waist-length ash hair up and into something I think is called a topknot. I notice the stubble in her armpits. She slips off her trainers. 'Stupid question.'

Fingers rub across her eyes, angrily. When she takes them away, she looks like she's suffered an allergic reaction. She picks at the corner of ragged nails.

'Are you still thinking,' she says, nervously, 'that this is to do with what happened to her mum?'

I look back at Loll and she turns to face me. Breaks for a second.

We both nod.

'That's what we think, yes.'

I glance into the living room at our baby dozing in her Moses basket; Loll has changed her nappy and her babygrow is brand new, the folds from the packet still down the front. She has a decent crop of black hair, the baby, the colour of Romilly's.' No trace of my strawberry blonde. It is still disconcerting how tiny she is, but I long for her to stay tiny enough that she has no idea what's going on. The idea that we get to a point where that baby becomes a small person who can understand the concept of absence and who can ask about Romilly is unfathomable.

I shake my head. No. I can't race ahead like this. For the sake of my own sanity. Romilly will be back while we are still putting on brand-new babygrows with folds down them. When the baby's face is still wrinkled. When Romilly's breasts still spurt milk.

She has to be.

The doorbell rings again.

'You're serious, mate, the police have *nothing*?' says my own best friend Adam, ambling in behind Steffie as he ambles everywhere, emergency or no emergency, new baby or no new baby. The fact that his body language is identical now to how it was in the pub in the heady, innocent days of two weeks ago at the baby shower he insisted on throwing for me ('Mate, why CAN'T a guy have a baby shower?' he protested for a long time and I capitulated but when I showed up it was just us and three mates having a drink, which was fine but, you know, not a baby shower) is reassuring.

Adam is Steffie's boyfriend. He and I met through the girls.

I realise that he is staring at me.

We are bunched together with Steffie and Loll now, in our narrow hall.

I am staring at the wall behind him.

I snap out of my daze.

'Well, they'll look at some CCTV, check hospitals but other than that there isn't a lot they can do,' I murmur, trying not to wake the baby.

I glance at Loll.

'Yep,' she confirms. 'She's an adult. They will bear our comments on postpartum psychosis in mind but with no official diagnosis, it's tricky. She's just a grown woman who left of her own accord.'

Steffie is crying again now, standing in the doorway to our living room. Loll is still too, head bowed low.

'Tears aren't going to help, Steffie,' she says, a little snappy.

Slowly Loll raises her chin and she's pale, I think, paler even than usual, her shoulder-length dark hair much shorter than Romilly's used to be before she had it cut into a crop. Easier for the wild swimming that she loves apparently. Loll sighs. 'I don't mean to be harsh. But they aren't helpful. To any of us.'

I think about that rogue tear though. It's in there.

I put an arm around Steffie, marking myself out as being in her camp, the camp made up of the emotional wrecks; the people who cry at a wedding reading and get goose bumps at a beautiful song and are singed with life's highs and lows.

Loll likes to keep to room temperature.

Romilly, I know, would stand with Steffie too. Mutter about her sister and her pragmatism as Loll turned away from us and fogged the mantelpiece with Pledge.

But Romilly isn't here.

The baby wakes up.

I go to swoop in but Loll gets there first and I don't argue because in my pocket, my phone is ringing.

I pick it up. See the name.

I nip out to the kitchen. I shouldn't answer this, not when they are all here, but how can I not?

So we talk, in hushed tones, me pacing the kitchen with my head down until I glance over at the half-open door and see the bottom of Steffie's leggings standing just outside the kitchen and then her long feet in their trainer socks quickly walking away.

Steffie leaves to pick up something from work soon after. Her hug is half-hearted. She doesn't make eye contact with me.

Day #2, 6 p.m.

The Husband

In the early evening, Adam leaves too and it is just Loll, me, the baby and Henry Dog: a wonky, pseudo family.

Loll goes to call her babysitter to check on the kids and I take my T-shirt off and put the baby, just in her nappy, on my chest.

'Lots of skin-to-skin,' the new midwife said at the hospital. 'It's the best for bonding, especially in the, er . . .'

'Absence of a mother,' I filled in.

'Quite,' she replied quietly.

We went through another half an hour of awkward chat before we left, trying to fill in forms that are always answered by the mothers. Attempting to bend questions to be dad-shaped. But they weren't malleable. I didn't fit them.

An absent mother: I am bewildered, applying that description to Romilly.

A laugh, loud, penetrates my thoughts.

Loll. She is still on the phone, listening presumably, to a story of something one of her children did today and it's so warm, her laugh, so full, that everything in me tenses. I forgot that Loll existed outside of this. I forgot other people could feel that kind of total joy from their children. When I look at my child, I can't help but see an absence.

Henry lies in his spot on the sofa, wags his tail with the little kink in it. I reach out for him, then back to the baby.

'Hey, baby,' I say. I feel self-conscious. I think it would help if she had a name.

But the baby sighs lightly, fed, content, oblivious, not unlike the dog.

I look at my phone for the thousandth time, and still nothing. I know Romilly's phone is off but try and call it again anyway. Nothing.

'What do you think, Henry Dog?' I ask. I hear my throat make a noise, something akin to a croak.

An absent mother looks less like Romilly and more like her own mum, travelling around Europe in a camper van with a new boyfriend and a newer tattoo of a bird on her ankle when her youngest daughter was about to give birth. Aurelia wouldn't let something as unimportant as a new grandchild change her plans.

Though to be fair, her children are grown adults.

I picture Romilly not long before the baby arrived, such a thin layer of skin between them by then, my wife stretched to her limits. Their team. I watched, that tiny bit removed. It's hard to admit it but there was even a little envy.

No. Not Romilly. An absent mother looks like the ones in Channel 5 afternoon movies, wrapping babies up and depositing them outside hospitals.

I feel my stomach deep-dive.

Romilly is thirty-five, married.

I've seen her with Loll's kids. She wanted her own.

I picture Romilly when she was pregnant on our local beach one day, taking her hoodie off, tying it around her still-slight waist. She stood still and tipped her face to the sky even though there was no sun that day in Thurstable, our little scribble of coastline in the north-west of England.

'Bright and fierce and fickle is the South. And dark and true and tender is the North.'

She was pleased with herself, remembering the Tennyson. She loved nothing like she loved a brutal northern beach.

Loves.

Romilly blends avocado into her smoothies. She bakes cakes with sweet potatoes. She tries to eat as many pulses and seeds as she can. She walks everywhere, swims most days. It had not sat well with her that she had to at times bow to her body's wants during this pregnancy: crisps, even – and she is a vegetarian – ham, lying on the sofa for hours at a time able to do nothing but guess what they're going to do with the prawns on *Australian MasterChef*.

That day though, she had had a burst of energy. We walked for a couple of miles along the coast, wellies on, weaving in and out of rock pools, the edge of the water, around hardy kids building wonky sandcastles.

'Let's sit down for a bit,' I said, and we weaved back towards the cliffs, to drier sand.

She took her phone out. Showed me a picture of a grapefruit.

'Fifteen weeks,' she said. 'That's how big our baby is.'

I kissed every part of her face.

Henry – tired out from his sea run – came and sat with us, looking interested. *What's this now? A new brother or sister?*

Romilly heaved with sobs then; nerves, joy, hormones perhaps so that a dog walker glanced our way and frowned at me. Had I just broken up with her? I smiled at him, shook my head lightly and put my arm around Romilly.

I reminded her to calm down, to breathe in the way she was always advising other people to, because she had a baby in there.

I had said the same thing on our wedding day, which had been five months earlier.

Now, I stare at the baby with her warm skin on mine thinking about all of it, everything we have been through since then, Romilly leaving, and my throat makes the sound again.

Loll comes back into the room and I am conscious suddenly of having no top on. Embarrassed at the belly that's sprung up in the last year.

I'm only thirty, I think, too young for middle-aged spread. But when am I going to get the chance to get back to the gym now, as a single parent of a newborn? Romilly doesn't get why I don't go for a run instead – easier, quicker, and she would always choose to be outside over in – but I like the routine of the gym. The air con. The sense of order. The fact I can't step in a pile of dog shit.

What follows my feeling of self-consciousness in front of Loll is a flicker of irritation. We should be a house full of nudity right now, bathed babies, feeding breasts, skin on skin, barely leaving the house, split apart from the world in a warm home that cocoons us like a womb.

No boundaries because we are us, the Beaches.

I look up. Instead, this other person – even if she is Romilly's sister, she is still, in this setting, an other – is here and I have to cover up, to feel sheepish, to take my phone calls to the kitchen and scream into my hands in the bathroom so she doesn't see, and hide the private parts of my life. Yes, I am appreciative of her being here. I just don't want her to have to be.

I pick up my phone, looking for something, anything, to take myself out of this room for a few minutes.

Loll takes the hint and heads out to empty the dishwasher.

Online I see people we know, living their normal lives, posting their normal drivel. I wince and realise that in the giant tub of emotions I'm working through, I've just grabbed hold of another one: embarrassment at being the odd one out. The one to pity.

And it gets worse. Because on my email is a request from Sal, who runs our local news site.

Hello, Marc, it reads, oddly formal like it might be the word 'hi' that tips me over the edge. *Hope you're well. So sorry to hear about Romilly. I wondered if you wanted me to run an appeal for anyone who knows anything about where she has gone? To help try and find her?*

How does she know anything about Romilly being missing?

But I am being unfair. Sal has run stories on promotions at the café or gigs my band is doing so many times. People talk about people they know. We're well known, Romilly and me. Everyone in our town has chatted to Romilly when they've popped into the Goodness Café for a matcha. Everyone has booked my band to play at their wedding or their thirtieth or their anniversary do and flung their beer-soaked bodies around to our 'Mr Brightside'.

I message Sal back. She's only doing her job. Doing her best, like we all are. Sure, she can run an appeal. Maybe it will help.

Loll brings me a cup of tea.

'Message from our local news site,' I tell her, nodding to my phone. 'They want to run a story about Romilly.'

She winces. Loll recoils at the concept of living your life in public. Keeps the thousands of pictures of her and her children, their tight little unit, faces squeezed together, on every wall and every surface of their house instead, behind closed doors.

'Do you want me to deal with it?' she asks, soft, and I shake my head. No. I'm her husband. I want Romilly's story to be in my words. To be the narrator.

When Loll leaves the room again, I turn the TV on but can't concentrate; thoughts keep meandering in. I point the remote control at it and hit mute.

The baby gives a light snore.

I reach for my phone. On Instagram my last picture is the baby's tiny hand in Romilly's.

I stare at the picture. At those hands, joined. One now gone.

'She was happy about having you,' I tell the baby. 'I promise.'

It might have been me who steered it – us having a baby when we had been together for so little time; we only met eighteen months ago. But if I was happiest at the news, she was a close second.

Our life was being formed.

From our tiny house by the sea, we can walk to the beach

in ten minutes and Romilly sighs with relief every time her toes touch the water, no matter how freezing it is. 'I don't care how small the house is,' she said when we had been searching for somewhere to live. 'As long as it's by the sea.'

She always meant to get that quote – 'As long as it's by the sea' – in a frame.

Will she get the chance now?

I look at Henry and I know our dog is missing her too; I hear him cry for her. They spend a lot of time together. She works so close by, she can nip home to walk him on her break.

I picture her cuddling our giant dog into her pregnant belly.

He makes Romilly look even smaller, this dog, when he pulls her on his lead – half-heartedly a lot of the time; he's getting older.

Fuck.

I look at that purple helium balloon, bobbing around my living room. I nearly asked Loll to get rid of it but it seemed unfair, somehow. The baby was still here. Her arrival was still a celebration. And there is already enough we are missing out on. I stroke the baby's head, skin that hasn't felt sun on it, has never bruised, never bled.

And I can't help it: I'm angry with Romilly because of the hours she's losing with this baby, the breaths, the tiny rises of this chest. Of how when – if – she gets back, the baby will already be a bit less raw, a bit less innocent.

Loll comes back into the room and my T-shirt is still off but I have stopped caring.

'I called my neighbour,' Loll says, eyes darting away from my naked chest. 'She's okay to keep the kids overnight again. Adam's coming back in a bit so I'll nip round and see them and grab some bits while he's here then I'll come back and stay over.'

I protest.

'It's fine,' she says, waving her arm in the air. 'I'm used to being up with babies. You look like you could do with the sleep too. I'll sleep on the sofa and keep the baby downstairs with me tonight.'

She walks back through the door at 10 p.m. Baton passed by Adam.

I hand her the baby with a feeding update, then head upstairs and climb into the big double bed that just houses me now, Romilly gone, the baby missing from the bed on the side, where she slept – a couple of hours at a time – last night too. I am about to put in earplugs and leave it to Loll, who will sleep in the living room next to the Moses basket.

Loll, who is quickly becoming the baby with no name's surrogate mother.

But I can't do it.

There is something I can't stop thinking about.

Something that feels off.

Super mum, I think: that's Loll. Picking up a third child like it's no big deal. Taking our baby now, overnight.

As though Romilly never existed.

I roll over; try to ignore it and sleep.

My brain skips, image to image, thought to thought, refuses to take a break.

I bury my head in the pillow.

But sleep isn't happening.

Or is it? Was I asleep?

It was something about Loll's ashen face when she came back from home.

Something about her distracted, puffed-up eyes.

Staring, losing focus.

But I am half asleep. Was that a dream?

It's no good. I kick the covers off and head downstairs, two at a time.

A sense of foreboding.

Shit.

Had something happened, since she left for home earlier?

Something even worse than what has happened to us already?

I pick up the pace.

Run down the stairs now.

When I fling the door open into the living room, Loll screams. I glance at the Moses basket. I can hear the baby breathing. I exhale.

She's there. The baby's there. I don't know what I expected but for some reason, it wasn't that.

'Jesus, Marc, you scared me,' she says, stage whisper. 'What the hell's the rush?'

'I don't know,' I mutter. 'I panicked. Nightmare, perhaps. I don't know.'

Then I notice that Loll is still in her clothes. Sitting upright. The duvet I had given her for the sofa is on the floor at the other side of the room. And she has her shoes back on.

It's midnight.

'Couldn't sleep?' I ask.

She glances at her shoes, as I do the same. Then she looks up and meets my gaze.

'Was just giving her a few minutes to settle,' she says, after a beat. Looks away. 'You okay? What are you doing down here? I thought I was on duty for the night?'

And I tell her that I'm not ready to hand the baby over yet. Not for the whole night.

'You sure? You could do with the sleep, Marc, and I'm here anyway . . .'

But I shake my head.

'You may as well go home, to the kids . . .' I start but she scoffs.

'God no, with all of this Marc and a newborn! You need some support. The kids are fine.'

Okay. I nod.

'I'm just down here if you need help. If you want to leave her with me and get some sleep at any point.'

The baby scrunches her face up as I pick her up in her blanket, tuck her in tight and step towards the door.

'I mean it,' she says. 'I'd love to have her.'

'Night, Loll,' I reply, baby up on my shoulder.

But something comes into my line of vision.

I glance to my left.

Loll's bag.

Packed and lined up at the front door. When earlier it had been with her in the living room, ready for bedtime, stuff spread out everywhere.

Shoes on, bag packed.

Where were you going, Loll?

And were you about to take my baby?

Day #3, 8 a.m.

The Best Friend

Work is a confusing concept, isn't it?

We complain about it, celebrate like we've been released from a long jail term when we have some time off from it, but sling us a bad time in life and it is stabilisers on a toddler's bike, the only thing that keeps us upright.

My days need the café and its chatter so much to counter the buzzing silence at Romilly's house. Here feels open, airy. There the bathroom tap drips, drips, drips. There it feels like I can't breathe.

I need work so I have a reason to leave there, and so I can recharge myself enough to head back.

So I can think.

So I can work stuff out.

Who was Marc speaking to yesterday on the phone?

The words might have been too muted for me but his tone wasn't. Panic. Desperation.

Pleading?

I put the soy milk back into the fridge.

Give the granola on the counter a quick stir.

I see table five looking around irritated and muttering about their wait for their breakfasts. The chef we employed a few months ago moves at bloody snail's pace. I make a note to myself to have a word, the manager now in Ro's absence, even though confrontation is my idea of hell. I laugh: it's hardly like my best friend is any better at it.

And then, I stand still. Look around. Try to see the world – our little dot of it – through Romilly's big brown eyes. What did my friend look at, in those months before she gave birth? What was she thinking?

I feel for Marc, you know.

I know he thinks that whatever we know about her mental health, everyone always suspects the husband.

But the truth is that I don't.

Everything about the explanation he is offering of postpartum psychosis does – terrifyingly, given what it means for Romilly's safety – make sense.

I don't believe Marc has any involvement, even after that phone call.

I just don't think he's telling me everything.

More crucially, I have no idea – when we are all on this team together and so focused on getting Romilly back – why that would be.

Day #3, 8 a.m.

The Husband

The morning is a barefaced cheek of a day, daring to call itself spring.

Wind howls like a wolf.

When the baby wakes at 8 a.m., I grab my dressing gown and pull it around me tight, shivering with tiredness as much as cold.

I take her downstairs. My eyes fly straight towards the front door. The bag has moved.

In the living room the curtains are open. It's light, technically, but so grey it barely makes a difference. I flick on a lamp switch on the floor with my bare toe, as I hold the baby.

No Loll.

I find my sister-in-law in the kitchen, leaning back on the kitchen worktop as she reads something on her phone while the kettle boils. The radio – always tuned to a local station in our house – is playing Classic FM.

It unsettles me. It's still our house, mine and Romilly's.

'The story's up,' she says, passing me the phone. She takes the baby off me as a trade.

'Bloody hell,' I say, as I scan the link she's showing me from our local website. I had sent the details to Sal last night.

The jolt, when I see that picture of us that I sent to them, taken in a restaurant on our honeymoon in the Lake District. I'm not sure why I picked it. It seemed to strike the right note.

Happy, not flash – no one could think we deserved it like they might if we were posing with champagne in the Caribbean?

I look up. 'That was quick.'

She raises her eyebrows.

When I finish reading the story, I check on the baby who Loll has put in the Moses basket in the living room, eyes open, learning to focus.

'Hey, you,' I say. Little kiss on her head.

In her mouth is a dummy.

I walk back through to the kitchen.

'We'd made a decision not to use dummies,' I say, holding it in my hand. 'It was only in the drawer for emergencies.'

Loll makes a noise that sounds like her nose is blocked. Takes her glasses off and wipes them.

'I'm sure you'll change your mind at 3 a.m. one morning.' She laughs.

In the other room, the baby starts to cry. Loll puts her glasses back on. Redoes her ponytail. Her face says: told you.

But I can't put the dummy back in now.

I stalk off to my daughter.

'Shush, shush,' I say and inhale her as I bounce her in my arms, walk around the house.

'Want one?' says Loll, nodding at her mug as I pass the entrance to the kitchen. 'This is my second.'

I get it: you're shattered from sleeping on the sofa. Is there anything more irritating than someone who offers something then makes you feel shit for taking it? Plus I was up four times last night with a newborn baby. Is she kidding me playing tiredness wars?

'I'm sorry,' I say. 'About how much you're doing for us.'

She cuts me off.

'Marc, I offered,' she says. 'Stop saying sorry.'

I pull my dressing gown tighter around me. Loll pours the kettle over instant coffee.

'Oh, there's a cafetiere,' I say. 'If you want to . . .'

She is scowling at me. I've crossed a line.

'It's fine,' I mutter, chastised, parched; whatever, just give me the caffeine. 'I'm going to message Adam. While it cools.'

As I walk away, like a child, I whisper the words 'fuck off' from behind a wall.

'Don't listen,' I tell the baby.

In the living room I close the door and my daughter has fallen back asleep on my chest. Fine, fine, I did put the dummy back in. But that crying. My poor girl was distraught. Clearly Loll's given her a taste for it; what am I supposed to do?

I might go to look for her, I type to Adam. *I can't sit here drinking instant coffee and making baby small talk with Loll all day again. I'm getting grumpy with her and it's not fair. I'm losing my mind.*

I look at the wall. A photo I took of the sea where Romilly swims – her body in its wetsuit a dot in the distance – hangs on the wall. There you are, Romilly, everywhere and nowhere.

Adam replies straight away. Everyone replies to me straight away at the moment. I'm an emergency. They are my 999.

You can't take the baby? he types. *PS Loll's coffee is shit though, you are right.*

I laugh, despite myself.

I am desperate to get out of this house, its walls coming closer, closer. Could I take the baby?

Could I leave her with Loll?

I think of last night. That packed bag. No. Not alone, not with my baby.

And anyway, both parents gone? That isn't fair. I feel a heaving swell of desperation to speak to Romilly. None of this is fair.

At some point too – and my stomach dives at the notion – Loll has to go back to her family. Not to mention her job. Compassionate leave only lasts so long, even in a freak situation like this. And with a jolt I realise: she isn't the only one. Two weeks' parental leave is my lot at the music shop I manage. Eleven days left. I make a mental note to call my boss.

Maybe I could take her? I type to Adam.

Is that possible? Me and a newborn. And starting where? How can my tiny newborn baby and I traipse around, trying to find an adult who presumably doesn't want to be found, with no clue where she is, what she's doing, to drag her home?

I think of Romilly, sitting at the kitchen table, little bump, bigger bump, balance-threatening bump.

I think of how soon after that she would leave us – me and that baby who was spreading out inside her – and how we could never have seen this coming. Unless it was building? Did that happen, before the birth? I make a mental note to ask Loll, who knows far more about the condition than I do, what was likely.

I look around at our home.

Any updates from the police yet? Adam types.

'Nothing but I've had to just let Loll deal with them,' I voice note him back. 'You wouldn't believe this newborn thing could take up every second but Jesus, it does. I can't make a phone call, I barely have time to eat. And the sleep deprivation . . .'

'Loll is a good one,' he says. 'Thank God you've got her for support.'

Yep. Saint Loll.

I stare at the hand cream of Romilly's on the coffee table; the baby name book she had been highlighting.

It's relentless, the ache of being in a Romilly museum.

A few hours later, I reach for the baby name book and pick one I have liked all along. If my daughter and I are going to bond like we need to, to make up for this chasm, then I need to be able to call her something. This baby is missing enough; she shouldn't be missing a name.

'We'll find her,' I say to the seven-pound baby, frog-like on my chest. 'We'll find her because we have to find her.'

Name decided, I absent-mindedly check my email.

And just like that, we know where Romilly is.

Day #3, 1 p.m.

The Husband

There are some messages that make you sit up straight immediately. This is one of them.

The message has been forwarded from Sal, who runs the news site, at the writer's request.

I saw someone getting on a plane at Manchester airport, it says. *Hysterical and in tears.*

I am holding my breath.

I only realised when I read about her going missing in the local news. But I am 99 per cent sure it was your wife.

From a woman, if that matters. Name of Susanne.

You read a thousand descriptions in your life of your heart thumping in your chest and then it happens for real and you should be able to describe it another way, as your body, horrified, pushes out from its insides.

Thump. Thump.

But no. That is what happens.

Thump.

She was on the same flight as me and I saw her get off the plane too – the flight was to Nîmes, in the South of France, she says. *Lost sight of her after that, I'm afraid. It's a small airport though. Not that many places you'd go if you fly there. So hopefully that will help.*

A sign-off and a number to call if I want to, but there is no need: I have my information. I reply to Sal to say thanks.

When I sit back against the sofa, I smell the coconut oil

49

Romilly used to smear on her bump; I see the smudge of it on a cushion, another bit of her left behind. A reminder too of just how recently she was here with a baby in her belly and a smile on her face.

What is certain now is that Romilly got on a plane to France. However much it upset her, however hysterical she was in that airport, she went through with it.

And then a sentence I scanned over jumps out.

It was this morning, about 6 a.m.

I stare at it.

Because if my wife only got on a plane this morning, where the hell has she been since she left the hospital?

More than forty-eight hours earlier.

Day #3, 2 p.m.

The Best Friend

After the lunch rush, I give the coffee machine a wipe-down. Next to it is our café pinboard: photos of us all at the Christmas do, quotes we like, a thank you card from a customer who had her fiftieth here. We all shoved stuff on there regularly; it's supposed to be a kind of inspiration thing. I know, I know, but we love it.

My eyes fall on a piece of paper, slipped mostly underneath it.

I wish I had longer nails — hadn't picked them all off over the last three days — for some purchase. But eventually I get it.

Just three words, in Ro's handwriting: *Lac de Peiroou.*

I frown.

Was it meant to go on the board? Did it fall off? Unlike the other stuff on there, the note has no context. No beauty.

When my phone rings, I leap on it as per current emergency rules.

'Stef, I think she's in France,' Marc tells me, breath ragged with excitement.

I dart outside.

And suddenly the note means everything. I dig it out from my pocket.

'Yes, Marc . . . that makes sense.'

'What?'

'I found this . . .'

I reach into my bag. Take out the crumpled paper. I feel myself pause.

What if I've just exposed something of my friend's life I wasn't supposed to expose?

He hears my doubt.

'What did you find?' Gently mocking, he adds: 'Don't worry, Stef. I don't think this is the time in her life that Romilly has gone off to have an affair.'

There's a beat.

'And to be honest, even if she has it's the least of my problems.'

I hear the baby stir.

He tells me what the email said. Then, daring: 'Now you.'

I sigh. Of course I need to share. What am I thinking?

'There was this note in the café that she wrote, that I think she was keeping for some reason.'

'What did it say?'

'Just the name of a lake. Lac de Peiroou. I've looked it up. It's in France.'

He googles.

'Fuck. Near Nîmes airport.'

Silence at both ends of the phone call but there is a charge between us. News. Information. The start of something. Dots connecting.

'And you haven't heard from her?' he says, and I am thrown.

'No, Marc, I would clearly tell you if I had heard from her.'

Something occurs to me.

'Don't you have family in France?'

A pause.

'No.'

'It's just . . .'

'The C in my name. Yes.'

'I thought you said you had . . .'

'They're distant,' he snaps, dismissing. 'Second cousins or something. No one Romilly knows.'

52

I smirk then and suspect his spelling of Marc is, actually, an affectation. A hangover from a time he thought it was cool. But how can a thirty-year-old man with a paunch admit that without cringing?

I hear Loll walk into the room. He fills her in on the note. Puts her on speaker.

'How about your mum, Loll?' I ask. 'There's no chance *she's* in France?'

'Nope. Spoke to her yesterday – she's in Spain.'

I hear a thump, thump, thump. A rustle.

'Marc! What the hell are you doing?' shouts Loll.

And then the phone goes dead.

Day #3, 2.15 p.m.

The Husband

I hang up the phone to Steffie and take the stairs two at a time. In our bedroom I head straight for the drawer where Romilly keeps all the important stuff. I try to open it but it won't give. I yank harder. A birthday card from her colleagues falls out. Some old bills. A roll of sellotape. I mutter to myself. *Important stuff.* Right. Classic Romilly.

I hurt then for grumbling about everyday stuff. For arguments. For bickering. For telling her off about her important stuff drawer; the 'Romilly trail' of stuff she leaves everywhere. For the mundane.

'What are you doing?' asks Loll, as I fling it all one by one on the floor. Finally it is empty. 'Marc! What the hell?'

I try Romilly's underwear drawer next. Her bedside table. 'Marc!'

Instead of answering Loll, I call Adam.

'We think Romilly is in the South of France,' I say. 'And I think her passport has gone.'

He sucks in his breath. Loll, standing next to me, does the same.

I fill him in on the rest. The sighting, the lake.

'Mate, what if I go?' Adam says straight away, as Loll's phone rings and she goes downstairs to take the call. 'It's somewhere to start, at least? I can go to the South of France, go to this lake, see if she's there.'

I laugh.

'Yeah, man,' I say sadly. 'That should do it. She's probably there, swimming laps around it twenty-four hours a day.'

But he's determined.

'We can make a list of campsites to check,' he says. 'If she's there overnight, she has to be staying *somewhere*. And then I'll start looking around, get speaking to people. Do some digging. Perhaps it's good for her wild swimming? Could that be the appeal? That's her thing, right?'

I interrupt him.

'Just one issue, Adam. Romilly just had a baby. I don't think she's going to be doing a triathlon.'

There's a defensive silence.

'No one said a triathlon, mate,' he says. 'But a little dip would be manageable, no? Just being in the water.'

'Just being in water,' I concur. 'In any way she can. Yep. That's why we live here. But then again her other thing is usually not running away. Her other thing is living at her own house, with me. It's a long way to go for a swim.'

I kick the chest of drawers in front of me.

A picture pops into my mind suddenly. That moment Romilly gave birth to our baby into a pool; this slippery bundle scooped up quickly by the midwife. It had always been the way Romilly wanted it but she was realistic enough to know it wasn't always possible; that babies choose their own way. Man, the joy on her face when it did happen.

'You did it,' she whispered to our daughter. 'You did it.'

'You did it too,' I whispered.

She kept her head down. Didn't look at me.

Adam speaks, bringing me back to the present.

'Got to be worth a shot? It's somewhere to start with at least. And got to be better than you going with the baby. You can't do that, mate. And we need her back. We've got to get her back.'

Downstairs, I hear the baby cry and I head down to get her.

I hear a tap dripping in the bathroom.

I think about changing a newborn nappy in an airline toilet. What if the baby needed a doctor? What if something was wrong? I think about travel cots. I picture the bag Romilly packed for the hospital; the chaos in the baby's nursery when Loll doesn't tidy it for a few hours. The sheer volume of *stuff* this baby needs.

I need to get to Romilly. But I need to do it from here, on my sofa, with formula in the cupboard and a steriliser in the kitchen.

No matter how much I need to get out from between these walls.

Adam, on the other hand, has no such restrictions.

I pick up the baby.

'Oh, mate, sorry, did us talking wake her up?' says Adam and I can hear him making a coffee, know he has the phone tucked under his chin.

'She's got a name,' I say. 'Her name is Fleur.'

'Awesome!' he says. 'Love it.'

And I am about to tell him that no, he can't go to France, that this whole thing is ridiculous, I got carried away, it's insane.

But then I think: what the hell else are we going to do?

I can trust Adam to tell me everything. To take me to her. He's the right one to go. My friend.

'Put Fleur on speaker,' says Adam.

She has her eyes open now and is rooting around for a bottle.

'Be quick, man, she wants the milk,' I say.

'Hey, Fleur!' he says. 'Uncle Adam here! We've got you, baby, we've got you. And you look out for your dad for me, right? We're going to find your mum!'

I wince at how fraudulent his positivity is. This is based on finding a reluctant needle that's buried itself deep into a dense haystack. Then persuading that needle to up and leave.

'Right, I'm on Google Maps,' says Adam. 'Let's find this lake.'

I leave him to it. Dial off because Fleur needs milk and because I might lose it again and beg Adam to come and move in and be here and I know I can't because it's time – overdue perhaps but never that necessary before – to be a grown-up.

But Jesus, all I want is a beer. All I want is oblivion.

Loll walks into the room.

'Calmed down now?'

I fold the wipe over, get into the crevices.

I am still holding the baby's – Fleur, Fleur, Fleur, remember – spindly legs. Feet that are the size of my thumb.

'Are you sure you have no idea why Romilly might be in France?' I say, ignoring her question. 'Childhood holiday spots? Old friends out there?'

'Not that I can think of,' she mutters, distracted. 'Sorry, Marc.'

I look at my sister-in-law, in her middle-aged jeans and ballet pumps, such a world apart from Romilly. Taut, rigid, when Romilly meanders around the place like a river. There is no symmetry to Romilly: when she accepts defeat on her flip-flops around the end of October and wears socks, they are odd. One boob is a little bigger than the other; she has rings on every finger of her left hand but wears only a bangle she's had since she was a teenager on her right arm, fingers bare.

'Loll,' I say. 'Do you remember the email said that Romilly only flew today? This morning.'

Nothing.

'So where did she go before that?' I push.

Loll?

'What was she doing?'

But Loll is silent. Like the rest of us, she doesn't have an answer.

Odder though is that, for once, she doesn't have an opinion.

Day #3, 4 p.m.

The Best Friend

In the café, I hear them, mouths half full of flourless chocolate cake, half full of gossip.

'You never know what's going on in someone's head and you can't blame the woman until you know the full story . . .'

I am at a table in the corner with my laptop, emailing our meat and fish supplier. Trying to block out memories of Ro floating around the place; of Marc sitting in the corner with his coffee and his iPad.

But. But. I wait for it.

This woman, Stella, a regular, is without a doubt setting up for the main course of her sentence, the part she really believes in, with this weak kindness starter.

I try to block it out and type: *48 chicken breasts.*

'But leaving a newborn baby. How *could you?*'

Two whole salmon.

A story was posted on our local website asking for anyone with information to come forward. Marc's doing.

But even without that they would know.

Small town, small conversational topic pool.

I keep my head down.

Keep typing.

Two whole cod.

'I think about when I had Ray – I know it was a long time ago now but you'd do anything for them. They are so helpless, they are so . . . God. I mean I know anything could be going on in that girl's life. And I'm not one to judge, I'm not. But a newborn baby. How could you?'

There it is again.

How could you, Romilly?

It's a question I ask too, albeit in a less accusing way.

What I mean is how could you, Romilly, practically? Let me rephrase: how was it possible? How did you get yourself out of hospital and spirited away when you had just given birth? That's what's bothered me, as I sipped tea or coaxed Fleur to sleep in those hours at Marc's yesterday. That's what's weighed on my mind. How did you do all of that, and stay safe?

I feel a shiver run through me.

Thanks, Sanjeeta, that's all for today.

I shut my laptop. Stand up and head over to their table.

'Is that finished with?' I ask Stella, gesturing to her coffee cup. It's only then that she registers me and it is like she has just plonked a little cream blush on the apples of her cheeks, forgotten to rub it in.

'Oh, Steffie, I didn't see you there,' she says, exchanging a glance with her sister Rose.

I smile. Not a word.

She takes that as meaning that all is well, perhaps I never heard her conversation, and places a hand on my arm. I am meant to feel comforted, warm, but that hand belongs to the same body as that mouth.

'That'll be £15.75,' I tell her, snatching my arm away.

There is some counting out of coins and wrangling over who had what before the exact change goes down on the plate. I remember: they're not tippers.

When it's done, the hand is back.

'How are you, petal?' she says.

I hear the gentle chill-out music playing in the background, a playlist of Romilly's, and see the bowls of salad up on our counter, and I feel at odds with this place that normally reflects my whole demeanour. It's calm, focused. Today I want to scream at a seventy-year-old woman. Slap her and her sister around their faces. Kick chairs. Throw urns of cereal across the room.

Get a grip, Steffie.

She goes again.

'Any word yet on your friend? The most awful thing that, the most awful thing.'

Rose echoes her: 'Terrible. Just terrible.'

She shudders. 'Doesn't bear thinking about. The husband must be in bits.'

Must he? I thought anything could be going on in her life? Sounds like you've painted one clear picture actually and that you are planning to stick with that one.

'We all are,' I say. 'Just trying to focus on getting her back.'

I pause. Fuck it. I love this place but I love my integrity more. I hate confrontation but I hate being a doormat more.

'For the record, Stella,' I begin, and I feel my heart charge in after me, 'Romilly is a good person. That type of nasty comment you were making before isn't helpful to anybody. There are parts of her life you have no idea about. And I also imagine you are the kind of thing she worries about when she thinks about coming home and that could put her off, which is the last thing we want. As you say, we need her back.'

Stella has the indignant face of the person who has decided she is too old now to beat around the bush; that she has earned the life years to 'tell it like it is' even when all that means is that you can be a rude, snide bitch.

Finally! I've been on the earth long enough that I can *truly* enjoy myself, being a rude, snide bitch.

'So from now on, when you're in our café, can you please exercise some more kindness?' I add, trying to bring it down a notch.

She inhales. Aggrieved.

'Steffie, I don't know what you think you're talking about but

I have nothing but Romilly's interests at heart, nothing,' she sniffs.

She looks pointedly at Rose. 'And that of the baby of course.'

Rose raises an eyebrow. Do they think I can't see facial expressions that are formed from the nose upwards?

Respect your elders, they say?

Nah.

Don't think so today, Stella.

'Of course.' I smile. 'In that case, do try a little harder not to be such a rude, snide bitch.'

Day #3, 4 p.m.

The Husband

I am flat out, the baby bridging the width of my chest, when I wake up with a start. Shit. I fell asleep on the bed with her. This is bad when Fleur is so tiny; there is a chance of her suffocating. I poke her, check her and she curls in on herself, furious with me for disturbing her sleep. My heartbeat slows back down to normal.

But my daughter is awake from her nap now and wants milk. We head downstairs.

In minutes, Loll puts an instant coffee and something that smells of sugar on the table.

'The police called me,' she says.

My head snaps up.

'CCTV footage. At Liverpool airport. Backs up the woman's story.'

She takes Fleur out of my arms; cuddles her in close as she feeds her.

I nod. Good, at least the police are being some use; the random passenger's story corroborated.

I lean against the chair back and shove half of a cupcake into my mouth. When Steffie comes you get falafel wraps from the café; with Loll it's carbs from Tesco, and I know which I prefer.

'Anything else?'

She shakes her head. 'That's it. But it's good. Important.'

'Have you seen it?'

She nods. 'It's definitely her. Want me to ask if you can go and see it too?'

I nod. Yes. Absolutely. Break off another piece of cake and shove it in my mouth.

Loll has to all intents and purposes moved in. Despite her cynicism about his parenting, Jake has stepped up in a crisis and, after two nights at her neighbour's, the kids have now gone for a stay at their dad's.

And I'm relieved. I'm still not sure what we would do without the emergency procedures of a sister-in-law on the sofa and a revolving front door.

The idea terrifies me. Not to mention exhausts me. It must be what it's like when people you live with die and the furore stops and the funeral passes and everyone else slips back to the office, to their families, to life, while you sit staring at a gap on the sofa where they used to drink tea in their pyjamas and mark the *Bake Off* bread week contestants out of ten.

I feel my stomach flip.

I block the thought out. Because never seeing Romilly again is not an option. Fleur not having a mum is not an option. We have a lead, we have information: this is a lot more than we had a day ago. And we have something else: Adam, willing and eager to get out there.

'You look like you could do with that.' Loll smiles as I neck my coffee in one and eat the last of the cake and for a second it's a normal picture.

Tired dad, sister-in-law coming to give some respite.

I need to lie down again.

'Shall we go into the living room?'

I pull my hoodie sleeves over my hands and sit down on the sofa, chaos all around us; Loll follows after me with the baby. I let my head loll back on a cushion; feel my eyes droop.

'Why don't you go back upstairs for a proper sleep?' asks Loll, the baby with her back to me as she burps up on Loll's shoulder.

I shake my head.

'It's fine,' I say. 'I'll just rest my eyes here.'

I look around.

'I promise I'm not normally this messy,' I say, sheepish.

Loll eye-rolls. A flash of darkness.

'This isn't as bad as Jake used to be when he was left alone,' she says. 'Trust me. And not just when we had newborns.'

There is no chat that Loll can't turn into an assault on Jake's character.

Me? I like the guy, to be honest.

Not that I plan to ever voice such blasphemy.

Both Romilly and Loll would lynch me. They may not be similar in many ways but they both treat sibling loyalty like a vow.

I miss my old life deeply at that moment – all the parts of it – as I nod and talk in stock responses to Loll. Man, I want it back. Not sofa small talk. Not Jake-bashing. Not politeness. Not instant coffee. I want Romilly's home-made soup, the Romilly trail, I want her chill-out music blasting, her incense burning. I want this house to feel like my house and it hits me that with Romilly missing – and all these other people added – it doesn't feel like my house at all.

'Loll, I think we need to talk about it, the psychosis.'

I hear the tap dripping in the bathroom. Again and again, starting to feel like it is coming from the inside of my brain.

Loll looks at me.

We sit without speaking.

It is so quiet that when Loll puts Fleur in the Moses basket and takes a large gulp of her drink, I hear the insides of her throat and it sounds so intimate, I squirm in my chair.

'The idea of Romilly sick, ill, not in her right mind and out there all alone?' I say, pressing on. 'I'm terrified of that, Loll.'

But Loll shakes her head, raises her eyebrows in frustration.

I pick up my phone, brandish something at her from Google.

'There are some very concerning stories of women with this,' I say.

I don't mean concerning. I mean horrific. Seismic. Life-changing.

Loll knows that. She looks away.

She is panicking. But about this? Or something else?

Loll cups her coffee in both palms. The baby pink on her nails is chipped. A little dab of mascara is on her knuckle.

Drip.

Drip.

Drip.

For fuck's sake, *this house*.

I plough on.

'If she does have postpartum psychosis, it's a medical emergency. Time is crucial. Are the police still looking into it? They haven't drawn a line now they have the CCTV?'

She takes her glasses off; uses her sleeve as a wipe.

She sighs.

'In truth, Marc, I don't think they know what I'm talking about with postpartum psychosis. The guy I'm dealing with is a dinosaur. The CCTV is all I could get. But I am on it, and I promise I'll keep chasing and chasing them. In the meantime though, I think we're totally right to chase our own leads. Especially as it tallies with theirs anyway.'

She pinches the skin between her eyebrows.

'She'll be okay,' she says, putting her coffee down and starting to tidy; right angles and piles, sweep and stack. 'I know Romilly.'

I bristle. Loll knows a mental health condition negates what she knows. Why is she answering me like that? And why does *every person* in this house think they know my wife better than I do? I think of Steffie, when her note backed up the CCTV.

I had bristled then, for some reason.

Loll stops at the Moses basket and leans down; touches Fleur's smallest pink nail. She has pushed her glasses up onto her head.

She rubs her eyes. Underneath them are rims so dark they look like they have been sketched in.

'You do still think it's postpartum psychosis that's done this, don't you?' I ask, irritated now, poking at her.

She nods. But says nothing.

'Because you're not saying much about it. And I'm trying to work out what else you could possibly think would drive someone to do this,' I say. 'What could drive Romilly to do this?'

Loll puts her head in her hands.

And when she looks up, her expression has changed. She studies my face like a textbook.

She stares at me and raises her eyebrows.

'What indeed,' she says.

I look at her, a question.

Day #3, 4.30 p.m.

The Best Friend

I am shaking with adrenalin as I walk away from the table and back behind the counter, watching Stella and Rose's pinched faces as they leave the café.

At least they've had their minds taken off Romilly.

Ten minutes later, my phone rings.

The owner of our café, Davina.

I am the manager now, so what I have done is even worse.

'Steffie, what happened?' she says, voice soft. 'I just had the most awful phone call from this woman called Stella but the things she said. You can't have . . . it's so not you . . .'

'Yep, I did,' I say, deadpan. Still simmering. 'I said them all. She was being a *dick* about Romilly.'

Davina sighs.

'You know I'm going to have to give you a warning, don't you?' she says. 'So I can tell this woman I did something? No matter what's going on, the manager can't speak to any customer – especially an old woman – like that. We all miss Ro, love. But you can't put the weight of this square on your shoulders. And you're also going to have to be non-customer-facing as much as possible, for now. Stick to stocktaking, get the rota sorted . . . We can't risk this happening again if you're feeling all wound up. Oh, Steffie. This isn't like you.'

I nod even though she can't see. I know I should feel sorry, grateful that she's not sacking me, but I feel nothing but fizz, a vibrating rage.

Later, as the adrenalin fades, I shake at something else: the shock of feeling myself unravel, lose control. I felt like I could have hit an elderly woman. Easily. And enjoyed it.

I am the least violent person you could meet.

But maybe we're all only the versions of ourselves that exist within the parameters of our lives. Move those, and you move our limits.

Maybe, when it comes to it, we are all capable of anything.

Day #3, 4.30 p.m.

The Husband

I change the subject.

'Adam is going to France,' I say, my voice treading carefully. 'I think it's the right call.'

Loll nods. 'I'm sorry,' she says, and the moment between us has been covered in cement. 'I should have offered . . . it's just, the kids . . .'

'Loll, shush,' I say, and despite whatever just passed between us then, I reach for her hand. 'No one would expect that. You're a single parent.'

She pulls her hand away. 'And work too,' I say.

'You have so many responsibilities. Let Adam go. He wants to do this. He can sling a few T-shirts in a bag, jump on a flight and not even think about it. All he has to do is square it with the office and he can work anywhere with a laptop.'

God, work.

I realise I forgot to check in with Linds.

I still haven't been in touch since I told her Romilly had had the baby and we signed off for my two-week paternity leave, my replacement managing the music shop sorted.

The baby, the police, the house . . . There is just too much to keep track of.

'I'm sure they have Wi-Fi in the South of France,' I carry on. 'I'm quite sure that he can design websites in other countries too. A lot easier than you trying to relocate your job.'

Or is it, truthfully, the fact that I trust Adam more than Loll? To be fully in my camp? To not be point scoring with me over who knows Romilly better?

To not tell me a lie?

I squeeze Loll's palm again.

But I think of that bag packed, the shoes on.

'I have so much guilt . . .' she mutters to herself. She looks stricken.

'Guilt?' I move my hand away. It's clammy.

'Do you not feel the same?' she asks quietly. 'The guilt?'

I clasp my hands together. 'Should I?' I say. The words snap from my mouth, brittle. *Always the husband:* is that what this is?

Wrong tone.

I sigh.

'There's nothing you could have done and nothing I could have done,' I say, and I try to take a deep breath to remove the snippy edge from my voice; to ignore something that sounded similar in hers. 'Adam is going. He'll bring her back. This will all be a grim memory. Fleur will have her mum.'

I grin at her, upbeat. A little wired, suddenly.

Why am I comforting you though, I think. This is the wrong way round.

When Loll looks up then, her face is changed and things are back to normal; she is Old Loll. Practical. Focused.

'So what's the plan then?' she says. 'When Adam goes out there.'

I pick my coffee up from the table to buy a few seconds.

There is no plan.

Romilly – by nature of what she has done – doesn't want to be found. She doesn't reply to anybody's messages; hasn't posted on social media.

The place Adam will head to in France is a loose steer, based on a vague notion of Steffie's and an airport from which you could travel for miles. I called the woman who emailed in the end but she knew nothing else. Had lost sight of Romilly once they got off the plane; thought no more about it until she got to her Airbnb and checked her email, saw the local news round-up. She had no more of an idea where my wife had gone than we did.

Loll looks at me expectantly.

And then . . . what?

My cheeks burn. Not only can I not keep my wife by my side at what should be the most special moment of our lives, but I am behaving like the kid that everyone accuses me of being even when it comes to getting her back. I stare at the wall. Fight the urge to punch a hole in it.

I look back at her.

Loll would have a plan, I think. She wouldn't bring this to the table so partially formed.

Her eyes are on me but mine stay resolute on the deep mud of my coffee.

And then Fleur cries, and I'm saved. For now.

I rock my little girl to sleep alone in the other room for some quiet.

Her body relaxes into me. Her breathing makes my own slow to its pace. I stare at every millimetre of her face. I hold on to her earlobes. I kiss her eyebrows. I marvel and marvel and marvel at her.

And then I tell her: 'I'm sorry, Fleur. I am so sorry.'

Day #3, 5 p.m.

The Best Friend

I have to trust him.

Don't I?

Now, my shift at work ended, I sit on a nearly empty Thurstable beach, looking up at that sky, with this thought spinning round and around. It is late afternoon and May but the day couldn't look more different to yesterday, the heat of the last week about to break. Now it is monstrous; black like a warning.

It has to have been the right thing, telling Marc where I think Romilly is. Romilly has postpartum psychosis. That means it's imperative we get her home.

That means there's no one to blame.

No hidden element to this.

Nothing to uncover.

I am looking to solve a mystery that's not a mystery.

But I think about the phone call I heard him make yesterday.

I think about my guilt; like I've just betrayed the most important person in my life.

I think about how something niggled me so much about telling Marc what I knew that I called a customer at the café I manage a bitch.

I mean it was true.

But still.

What difference did I make, anyway, I reason? The lake focuses things, sure. But the email would have alerted him to the area anyway. Not to mention the CCTV from the police.

Why, then, is what I did sitting so heavy in my insides?

I message Ro repeatedly but no reply comes. It's devastating when habits of a lifetime change; when the most present voice in your life becomes absent.

So I keep trying.

I don't tell Marc the content of the messages.

Yeah, they're married. I have never been married – even if Adam and I have been together longer than Marc and Ro, who got married eight months after they met – but I'd hazard a guess that often female friendships include bonds that run just as deep. We don't have sex to complicate things; all we signed up for was the talking. And now the talking is what will bring her back. I'm sure of it, even if it is currently only going in one direction.

Like she is in a coma, though, I believe it: if I keep going, eventually she will respond.

I lie on my back on the sand. Put my phone away.

In the distance thunder rumbles.

It's clear why I haven't told Marc about the messages.

What's less clear is why I haven't told Loll. Loll who I have known most of my life. Loll whose team, right now, I am so firmly a part of.

Perhaps a gut instinct? Hug my friend close; lock out everybody else.

A pin dot of rain drips onto my forehead. I wipe it away. Take my phone back out. Hesitate. Should I? I don't want to spook her. But also, I need something. This might do it.

I think I know where you are, I tell her.

Nothing.

If there is anything you want to talk about, just to me, I am still here. I still exist even if you can't see me, I tell her. *I can keep it between us.*

Another.

I mean it. A private conversation. Pick up the phone.

I take it further.

I can come, Ro. Pretend I'm coming to look for you, not tell anybody else. Just be with you. We can have a wine, sit around crying, figure this out, whatever. I hate the idea of you being alone.

Is she alone?

More than anything, I want to make her feel like a person. Like the person I know. Like my Romilly.

Yeah, she is a mum now but she isn't only a mum: she is my friend. If she feels like she needs to do something as extreme as this, there is a reason.

Is it the one Marc believes? That Loll backs up?

Either way, I will not dismiss her. As I worry, sometimes, she might do. Because Romilly is hard on herself, always. I try to pull her back from an imagined place. Because if you denounce yourself, where the hell do you go from there?

That's what I worry about, in the darkest parts of the night.

That's what scares me.

The reason I'm not sleeping.

The reason I exploded at Stella.

That, and the other thing.

Because there are times, awake under that duvet, when I think that this whole thing is more sinister, more dense, than it looks.

Times when I wonder why Marc – even after he hugs me so tight – will not make eye contact with me.

Times when I notice that the same is true for Loll.

Times when I am even suspicious of my own boyfriend.

Times when I wonder if anybody in that house is telling each other everything.

If anybody in that house is telling the truth at all.

Day #3, 5 p.m.

The Husband

Her eyes droop, she is almost asleep and then there is a loud bang on the front door. Fleur is on high alert, eyes wide. What is this madness?

The midwife.

For fuck's sake.

You'd think, as occupational skill sets go, a quiet knock might be something you'd master when a lot of your job involves visiting people who have just had a child and who are desperate for them to sleep.

Fleur screams.

I go to answer the door.

'Oh, petal, missing Mummy?' says the midwife, sweeping past, then she looks at me. 'Sorry I'm late. Snuck you in at the end of the day. Any news?'

I glower at her. Internally, of course; externally I am serene.

Loll sticks her head round the door.

'Nipping to the shop while the midwife is here,' she says. 'Give you some space.'

Please don't, I think. For all of her irritating ways, space to have a one-on-one chat with the midwife about everything I don't know and all that has happened sounds terrifying.

'Well,' I say to the midwife as she starts to strip Fleur off for a weigh-in. 'Yes, some news – she has a name. Fleur.'

'Ooh!' she says. 'That's sweet. But I meant any news on mum?'

I blush. Of course that's what she meant. Jesus. That's what everybody means. I touch Fleur's face. My poor baby. Nobody asks the usual questions; how much did she weigh, what's she called, how was the birth, because they are far too focused on the situation we are facing.

'Yes,' I say quietly. 'We think she is in France.'

Her eyebrows zoom upwards.

'France,' she replies, peeling off Fleur's nappy and placing her on a towel on the scales. 'Well. Seven pounds six. Lovely. Putting it on nicely. She'll be back to her birth weight in no time.'

Then she pauses.

And I realise: I can't remember what her birth weight was. How bad a dad does that make me? Then again, since I was told that news, we have mislaid her mum. The figure has been superseded by others: number of hours since we last saw Romilly, pounds of panic I am dragging around the house.

The midwife starts to put Fleur's nappy on as she turns to me.

'Who on earth has she gone to France with then?' she asks.

'No one,' I reply. 'We're going out there to get her – well, my friend is.'

She nods, impatient. She is on the floor expertly buttoning Fleur into her babygrow.

'That's good,' she says. 'Yes.'

She holds my daughter up as if she's examining a pretty vase.

'Sooner we have you back with Mummy, the better – hey, petal?'

She hands her back to me and climbs up to standing.

'But, Marc,' she says. And she is kinder then. Puts a hand on my arm.

'What I'm trying to say is that when women have babies, it's a huge undertaking, physically and mentally. Childbirth, especially the first time round, drains women. Exhausts them. Makes the most basic tasks about as much as you can manage. When it's your first, even a relatively simple birth like Romilly had is mammoth, emotionally and physically.'

I nod. Mmm hmm. Yep. I get that. What is her point?

'The whole thing is also such a shock. To the mind and to the body.'

She sighs, but it's kind. Building up to something. Feeling her way around it.

'Marc, in my experience – and that's twenty-five years of helping women have babies – there is no way that whatever she was experiencing, Romilly came up with a plan to go abroad, got out of hospital and away all by herself when she and her body had just been through the huge, life-changing experience of having her first child. I'd argue we're not saying unlikely. We're saying impossible.'

Day #3, 5.15 p.m.

The Best Friend

I take my phone out of my bag again.

'On my way over to your house,' I say into my phone.

It is still your house, I think, even if you appear to have sublet your life to your sister and a giant bottle of Pledge.

I am trying a different strategy.

Remind her what her world looks like. Her people.

Remind her what human contact looks like, potentially.

More than anything, I realise, I am using these messages like a diary, an outlet, a record of a time that I already know in the midst of it I will never forget but that I may lose the details of, amongst the headlines.

Depends how things end, I suppose.

'Unofficially,' I tell her, like she is on holiday and I'm updating her on the news in a postcard. 'Loll has us doing shifts.'

And it's true. I sometimes think I see Marc exhale when the anxiety of Loll's shift ends and she puts the bleach back in the cupboard and Henry is allowed to move without her vacuuming around his bulk.

I arrive with a hug and a tiny hint of lightness in a house of heavy burdens.

Loll – and I say this with love and a knowledge of the chart that covers the wall of her kitchen and informs her that she will eat chilli con carne (mild) a week on Tuesday – has never known lightness.

I stand up. Dust the sand off my bottom; pick it out of my hair. Slip my grubby feet into Birkenstocks. And then I message her again.

One last try.

For this afternoon at least.

'I pick over it, again and again, the run-up to what happened,' I ramble. 'And here's what I think. For a while now something has been off but not in a way I could put my finger on.'

She wouldn't talk to me about it. I didn't know why. The distance hurt.

I felt uneasy about her behaviour while she was pregnant, wondered whether I should flag it to somebody. *Antenatal* depression? Concern about the birth? I knew as well that there was something she was being monitored for, something potentially genetic related to her mum, even if I wasn't sure on the details. She was oddly reticent on them. For once, with Romilly's pregnancy, we were diverging. Maybe, I thought, that was why.

'Just something they've got to make sure of,' she said, cheeks rosy, headscarf over her crop, whipping a cloth across a table at work. 'But it's nothing to worry about.'

And what did I know to question?

In the end I didn't; she didn't want to talk to me about it, for whatever reason, and that was her choice.

'I nearly mentioned it to Marc the other day, that feeling I had over those weeks, to see if he felt the same,' I say in a new voice note to Romilly. 'But I didn't.'

What, though, would make me hold things back from Marc, at a time when we are transparent with each other; an odd little unit? Marc, Loll, Adam, Steffie and Henry the dog: the Famous Five, with fewer pork pies and a lot more sterilising.

Others drop in, sure, with vats of tagine and batches of brownies and tilted heads like people do to gossip while they dress it up as care – apologies. I'm not normally so cynical – but we are a team.

79

Though that may build up my part a bit. Because it's not me who leads things but – of course – Romilly's formidable big sister Loll. Is it wrong that sometimes, for all of her skill at running a house, I wish she could step back? I feel bad for even thinking it. But sometimes . . . Let Marc be a dad. Let me be an honorary auntie. Adam may not have the experience with babies but honestly, look at the love that pours out of my boyfriend; give him a chance too, Loll. But she sweeps in, arms open, mouth closed, and takes the baby, ticking off all the things she needs and rendering the rest of us embarrassed at how little we know.

Sometimes I think it helps her not have to look at me, at any of us, this hive of activity.

I shouldn't complain.

What could I contribute really? Thanks to Loll, I know that Fleur has a new nappy, clean bottles lined up in the cupboards, washed babygrows, fresh sheets. I know Loll will tuck her blankets in right, wipe down the surfaces. I know she can administer medicine if Fleur needed it; apply cream to a red bottom.

And that's reassuring. When the worst thoughts kick in.

If the baby needs to – however devastating the idea is – she will survive without Romilly.

We could all survive without Romilly.

We just don't *want* to.

I am standing on her doorstep by the time I send her the next message.

'Not a word, Ro. To anyone. Nothing is off limits. Talk to me.'

I think again about the way I flipped at those old women. How I've never felt so angry, every second. And then I try to work out: who am I angry with?

The Husband

I stare at the midwife.

She looks sheepish. Knows I am embarrassed.

I want to slam a fist into the wall.

Because it's obvious, isn't it, now that she is spelling it out to me.

I take Fleur off her and my baby starts to cry. I don't reach for the dummy that I know is in the kitchen because I don't want her to think I'm failing; that I'm bad at this too, as well as at realising the most basic of concepts when it comes to my wife being missing.

Someone helped Romilly run away from me and from our baby.

And for Romilly to trust them with that, it must have been someone close.

I think of all of Romilly's friends, messaging, checking in, leaving bags of shopping outside the front door.

I think of Loll, out picking up supplies for us. Earlier I saw her sitting at the kitchen table. She didn't know I was watching her and had her head down. She was silent; her shoulders shaking. The back of her neck was pink like sunburn.

I don't have siblings. Don't quite get that dynamic. But I do know how much this hurts.

The same thing happened to Steffie yesterday; as we hugged she erupted like a volcano.

I know that feeling.

Someone close.

Someone close helped my wife to leave me.

Someone close helped my wife to leave her newborn baby.

I look at the kitchen table. Think of Loll's heaving shoulders.

The vegan carrot cake Steffie brought me yesterday sits on the kitchen counter, where I will it to morph into a KitKat. The light in there – the day so dark it is turned on already – still flickers.

A message pings in from Adam.

I take a deep breath.

Someone close.

The man who checks in constantly; my best friend.

The woman who hugs me and brings me sustenance.

The one who weeps at my kitchen table.

How close is close?

Day #3, 5.40 p.m.

The Best Friend

I stare at the bright green door Romilly painted on a whim one day – the reason she has a notable blob of green on the thigh of her favourite shorts – when Marc answers, smile thin.

'Sorry,' I lie, putting my phone in my back pocket. 'Just work, checking shifts for the week. How are things?'

And then I sketch a smile on my face and rejoin the team. I find a task for myself as I go out to the kitchen and put the kettle on to make Marc a coffee.

I put the carrot cake I brought him yesterday on a plate. Shove it at him.

'Eat,' I say.

But he is holding Fleur and an overwhelming stench suddenly drifts upwards.

'I'll be at the changing table.' He smiles, but his brow is furrowed. The exhaustion of repetition is showing. 'Hold on to that cake.'

I nod, distracted. Then while he leaves the room, I lean against the kitchen worktop and stare at my phone.

A face appears around the door.

'Oh!'

'Sorry,' says Marc's head only. 'Didn't mean to scare you.'

His eyes travel down to my phone.

I shove it into my pocket.

Something odd passes across his face and I roll my eyes.

'Work again,' I mutter. 'You'd think that place couldn't run without me.'

His thin smile is now emaciated. But it's still in place.

The kettle boils.

'Was just going to say could you make mine black?' he says through those tight lips, nodding towards it. 'Thanks, Stef.'

He looks old, I think, as he walks away.

His stomach bulges; the lines around his eyes are deeper.

A bald spot I never noticed before retreats and leaves the room. And when it does, my smile immediately fades.

I hide behind the kitchen door and send one last message to Romilly, typing this time instead of voice notes for the silence.

Then there was the night you gave birth, that message you sent me.

Ro and I were messaging on the evening she went into labour, just before things started. It was unlike her, she usually called, but when I had phoned her earlier she hadn't picked up.

In the middle of our text conversation, the messages paused for half an hour.

When she came back with one last message, it was odd.

Everything is a lie, it said.

Made no sense. I didn't pick it up for a couple of hours; I was at some birthday thing at a pub with Adam but when I saw it I went outside, tried to call her. Nothing. Minutes later though, I had a message from Marc: *Romilly is in labour, on way to the hospital!*

Everything else was forgotten. That's what brand-new life does.

Fleur arrived, the delivery was safe, Romilly was healthy and I put that message down to her perhaps having been in early labour, delirious with pain.

To the nerves, the excitement, that feeling of oh fuck what is about to happen to my life. To a unique situation where you must feel like you're standing in a queue about to access the next part of your existence.

Everything they tell you about being in labour is a lie?
Perhaps.

I don't know. Not my area.

But then Romilly went missing.

And I kicked myself for ignoring that message and not digging deeper.

I know that logic says this is a moot point: she has a mental health condition, so all other theories are null and void.

But the feeling that I missed something that night – something that could have prevented this – won't go away.

I can't drop it.

The thought drips, drips, drips like Marc's dodgy tap. I hear it in every step I take in Romilly's slippers around her house.

If anything, it is getting louder. My thumbnail stings and I realise I have picked it so far down, the skin underneath is exposed. I wince.

Something happened in that window between Romilly's flurry of messages on the night she went into labour, and that final one: sad, scared, desolate.

Whatever made Romilly leave, I feel sure happened then.

Which means that it happened before she gave birth.

And suddenly, something painfully fucking obvious occurs to me.

I google whether you can get postpartum psychosis before a baby is born.

Feel stupid even typing it.

The clue is in the name, surely. *Post*partum.

And Google nods in agreement with a clear answer for me.

A resolute no.

Postpartum means post-baby.

If whatever happened to Romilly happened before she had her baby then it's not postpartum psychosis that is to blame. it's something else entirely.

Day #3, 6 p.m.

The Husband

It's a tricky conversation, the one where you ask for extra paternity leave because your wife has abandoned you and your baby.

Not standard-issue.

No template available on Google.

'Linds?'

My boss, the owner of the shop, has been quiet now for about ten seconds. I thought she might have seen the local news story. Clearly not.

Then she rallies.

'Jesus, sorry. God! Sorry. Marc, I'm so sorry.'

My hand forms a tight fist. Sorry. Isn't everyone? If I could fund a search for Romilly with sorrys, we would have no problem here.

'I mean hopefully she'll be back by next week and this won't be a thing and . . .' I hurry out.

'Well even if she is, Marc,' and she sounds appalled, 'I think you'll have some stuff to . . . sort out?'

My barrier goes up.

Everyone has their thoughts now. On our marriage. On what must be going on behind the scenes.

As if any of them has a clue about what has happened to Romilly and me.

'Take the month, Marc,' she says. 'I'll sort cover now. Then we'll take it from there.'

Now comes the awkward part.

'Will I . . . get paid?'

Linds sighs. The music shop where I work is her business. This comes out of her pocket. There is no government grant for people who misplace the mothers of their children.

'I'm sorry to ask,' I say quietly. 'But there's a baby and stuff to buy and . . .'

Linds cuts me off.

'Let me see what I can work out, Marc. I'll be in touch. In the meantime, take bloody care. I can't believe this has happened to you. It's like something out of a film.'

Helpful.

'Yes,' I mutter. 'I'd file it in the horror genre.'

I dial off.

Next, Macca.

I stab the keys on my phone to my friend.

Can't come to Andy's stag. No babysitter.

I have slipped from my standard-issue abandoned victim husband character role because I am sulking. Loll had offered to babysit – encouraged me to go even – but I knew what it would look like. A stag do, while my wife was missing? Guilty, guilty, guilty.

I shake my head. No more sulking. No one is going to help you if you sulk.

So I can't go because I am – I am reminded – the only parent here. The feeling is one of being tethered, but at my own choosing. I wouldn't leave Fleur, even if I could. Not now.

Whoa, wouldn't expect you to at the moment, bud, he replies, which makes me feel even worse. Is this my life now? Guilt if I expect to do anything, as the sole parent? Would they all have looked at me weirdly anyway, the absent dad doing a vodka shot in the corner while his wife swims across a French lake?

Steffie comes into the living room.

'Another coffee?' she asks, and I nod while typing.

I've barely finished the last one but all the rules of the bad times live in this house and we exist from hot drink to hot drink, clutching mugs close to us like candles at a vigil.

I look up after she leaves.

Stare into the space.

There's a wariness that's settled between Steffie and me that wasn't there before. A distance. Fewer hugs. Do we just need fewer, as we get used to this situation? Now we're moving on from the initial shock, is it too odd for adults to stand there with their arms around each other?

No. It's something more.

I know Steffie heard me on the phone. And lately, she's been pretty attached to her own phone too. Generally, Steffie is someone who replies to messages three days later and can't remember the last time she logged on to social media. I know she is using it to update people about Romilly. But still. The thing is sellotaped to her palm.

Many times, Steffie has told me that Romilly hasn't been in touch with her since she went missing.

Every time her phone beeps though, I stare.

In life, Romilly would rather speak to Steffie than anyone else. She sits in our tiny patch of garden and talks on the phone to her straight after they've been on a shift together.

Someone close.

As Fleur sleeps in my arms, I follow Steffie out to the kitchen.

'Steffie, the midwife pointed something out to me earlier,' I say.

She looks up as she spoons coffee into the cafetiere. Another bonus of her being here over Loll.

A tiny contented snore comes from Fleur; Steffie smiles in her direction, pure love.

'Yeah?'

I choose my words carefully. I need them not to sound accusatory. Because Steffie, who *told* me Romilly was in France, who held my hand, who makes me proper coffee when my skin crawls with exhaustion? She can't have steered this. Cannot have made this happen. Surely.

'She said that this would have been difficult for Romilly to do alone,' I say. 'In fact she didn't use the word "difficult", she used the word "impossible". Getting out of hospital. Boarding a plane. At that time.'

Steffie shrugs. Pours the water into the cafetiere. Puts it down and twists a ponytail that could do with a wash around her index finger.

'She ain't no ordinary woman,' she mumbles in a weird fake American accent. It sounds like it's something she says a lot; a catchphrase. Maybe something her and Romilly say to each other.

I nod.

'Yeah,' I say, irritated but trying to sound calm, patient. Sling in a laugh. 'Sure. We'd all agree on that. But she's still human. She had still just given birth.'

Steffie's unreactive.

But of course she is; she hasn't been through childbirth; wouldn't get it.

She stands still, considers.

'Well, I guess none of us can understand what it must be like to have . . . postpartum psychosis,' she says. Nervous of the term. Out of her depth. But with an edge? 'Mental health conditions can change the rules on a lot of things.'

I wince. The idea of Romilly dragging her tired, bleeding body abroad rather than coming home, getting in her own bed, cuddling her baby and eating peanut butter on toast in a clean dressing gown?

I feel the bile come up again.

I walk out of the room then before I am tempted to snap at Steffie.

As I head out, she plunges the cafetiere, hard.

Day #3, 6.15 p.m.

The Husband

I drain my coffee and think.

Maybe this conversation will be more pertinent to Loll, who has given birth herself twice.

And then I realise something else that would probably have been clear much earlier if I'd had more than two hours' sleep: if Loll would understand more than anybody how impossible a solo mission like this would be after you have a baby, why the *hell* – in the hours we've talked this through and analysed the situation – would she not have brought this up herself?

I message my sister-in-law.

Can you come straight back? Need to talk to you.

On my way, she types back.

A few minutes later Loll lets herself in; I have given her a key.

'Left the stuff on the checkout,' she says, out of breath as she walks into the living room where Fleur and I are on the sofa, the baby still snoozing. 'What's happened?'

She slips off sensible shoes. Stands, in black tights so thick they are like trousers, staring at me.

I realise in that second that she thinks I have had some news about Romilly.

'Has something happened?' she prompts, impatient for the news. 'Has she been in touch?'

I stare at her. Then shake my head. No, no. No news.

She lets out a breath. Her sister is not dead. Or no more dead than she was yesterday, at least.

I sit down on the sofa but Loll stays standing and then starts tidying up around me, putting letters and bits of paper into piles and taking coasters from the side of the sofa. Muttering about a mug of Steffie's that's been left on the floor; Steffie does it all the time as she likes to sit down there, cross-legged in her leggings. Less than seventy-two hours and we know each other's habits; even starting to be irritated by them like true housemates.

She goes to move a side table out to get underneath it and I jump.

'Can you leave that?' I snap, and she looks shocked. Understandably. I have been letting her dust my living room without saying a word for the last three days and now I've just summoned her back but moved the goalposts.

It's suddenly irritating me though that Loll is treating this like her house; treating me like her child.

She still stays standing. Her hands are now clasped together to stop them from tidying.

'Do you think Romilly could have done this alone?' I ask.

'What do you mean?'

I start ticking the movements off with my fingers. 'Gives birth, for the first time. Shell-shocked. Bleeding. Gets dressed. Packs. Leaves hospital. Sneaks past medical staff.'

I carry on. 'Books a flight. Gets to an airport. Gets on a plane. Buys whatever she needs. Gets to bloody *France*.'

Loll stares at me and it's like a stand-off. She pushes her thick dark hair off her face, then takes a bobble, coated in hair, from her wrist and ties it around her hair.

'I don't know the details,' I say. 'But there is physical stuff, right? Bleeding. Discomfort.'

I think of the antenatal classes we did when Romilly was pregnant.

Loll looks at me like she's issued a dare.

91

'Even pain,' I say.

She still stares.

When Loll breaks, it's to start tidying again.

'Are you going to answer me?' I ask, louder than I intended. My heart is taking on the rest of my body now, booming. What am I asking her? What am I getting at? She is here, isn't she? Not with Romilly. And she backs up my thoughts, all day, every day: Romilly has postpartum psychosis, we both believe it.

So what am I getting at?

'Please can you *stop fucking tidying*,' I hiss at her.

She stops, with a dummy and a blanket and a TV remote in her hand, and I snatch the remote control out of her hand and throw it across the room. The back falls out; the batteries scatter.

Loll stares at me.

'People can find strength they didn't know they had when they want to, Marc,' she says. There's an edge in her voice; an accusation. 'You know, when they are at breaking point.'

And suddenly it dawns on me that she and Steffie – they are reading from the same script.

Because they worked on it together?

Steffie sticks her head through the door.

'Everything okay?'

She looks at Loll.

And a new thought comes in.

Loll and Steffie: they are trying to set me up for this.

Day #3, 7 p.m.

The Husband

Is sleep deprivation making me paranoid? Disjointed since Fleur was born. Barely an hour straight since Romilly left.

I weigh it up.

Don't turn on the only people in the world who are changing your baby, feeding her, covering her gently in a soft blanket. Who sing to her and read her books even though she is less than a week old. Who make you coffee that may be the difference between you being sane and losing your mind. On the one who stays over, despite having her own kids, just in case you need her.

Don't be an idiot, Marc.

I nod. Loll nods too, briefly.

Agreed then.

As we were.

Don't turn on your allies.

But I can't help it, something is scratching at me like a mosquito bite.

I leave the room so Loll can finish off her tidying but she shouts to me a few minutes later.

'I'm popping home now, Marc,' she says, voice neutral. Steffie has just gone too. 'I can see Adam coming back up the drive so you're all good and I'll be back before he leaves.'

She pauses.

'Let me know if you need anything bringing back,' she adds.

And the words are a tacit agreement: we will carry on as we were, say no more about the conversation we had earlier.

I'll stop asking questions, she'll keep burping my baby.

Why rock the boat, I think, when it has already capsized and disappeared under water anyway?

But while I keep quiet, the thoughts won't.

What do you know, Loll?

When I glance at the coffee table after she leaves, the batteries are back in the remote control. It is lined up, neatly, alongside the others. I am fairly sure it has been dusted.

'So I'm doing this, right?' says Adam as he walks through the door, swapping quick pleasantries with Loll in the hall as she puts her shoes on.

I look at him.

Adam would board the plane now if he could. He is hopping from foot to foot like a child at a party having to speak to the adults when there's a bouncy castle and ten classmates on the other side of the grass.

He's fired up on adrenalin; of the joy of being able to do something when you have been frustrated by inaction. He's also fired up on sleep and a trip to the gym this morning; I recognise what used to be normal with a shot of envy.

'Let's make a plan,' he says, following me as I close the front door behind him.

'Can I talk to you about something else first?' I ask.

'Sure, mate,' he nods. Small frown.

He follows me into the kitchen.

Leans down to kiss Fleur, who's flat out in her Moses basket.

I sit down at the table; Adam heads across to the kettle to make coffee. People do that in our home now, Romilly, I think, as I talk to her sometimes in my head. Help themselves.

I watch my friend as he makes a drink.

The bulb in the kitchen spotlight flickers on, off, on, off. No one mentions it. I guess it's my job to replace it.

I can't be bothered.

Let's face it, this is barely still a home that you tend to so much as a Marc and Fleur support system; a tent that has been put up to deal with the suffering and the needy.

Loll's not the only one who recoils at victim status.

When I made myself some toast at 11 p.m. last night there was a brand of butter I've never seen in our fridge before. I took it out, stared at it for ten seconds and then slammed it against the wall before crying, quietly, until my eyes hurt. I look now at the pale blue paint of our kitchen and feel the memory of the anger. A little grease remains on there where the wrapper had come open a touch and I picture Romilly spotting it in a year, tiny finger touching it lightly. *What's this?*

Would I be angry then too? Or just too grateful to have her back to care? Or is this a picture that can never really happen anyway, us all slotting back into our positions? Not after everything.

God, I miss her.

Now, Adam is looking in the fridge.

'Just going to make us a sandwich,' he says. 'You've not got any butter?'

I laugh, sort of. Shake my head.

I had thrown it away straight after it slammed into the wall. Decided I preferred no butter to pity butter, placed into my fridge wordlessly without people telling me along with vegetarian sausages I don't eat, my short-lived attempt at being veggie long gone, and cheese that's too strong because I prefer mild cheddar with the texture of rubber. There was also something purple and pickled in a jar that Steffie brought over from the café.

Adam opens the cupboard and takes out some cereal instead. 'Want some?'

I shake my head. Whatever other problems she brings, the catering is better when Loll is on a shift.

Adam sloshes milk into his Rice Krispies then sets down our coffees.

'Right, mate. Sorry. I'm good to go. Talk to me.'

I lean forward.

And at that moment, of course, Fleur wakes up with a cry.

I pick her up and pull the blanket around her tighter; stand up to rock her gently as she curls into my chest.

'Is it possible that Romilly could have done this alone?' I whisper to Adam.

Back, forth, back, forth. Fleur's eyes droop.

Adam looks confused as he shovels cereal into his mouth.

I sigh.

'After childbirth, women are . . . you know, they're in pain. Losing blood.'

Adam picks up his mug.

'Go on,' he says, back down low to the cereal.

'They're also physically, mentally exhausted,' I say. 'Beyond any sort of tiredness we can imagine.'

I feel my own eyelids sag.

'Sure, mate, yeah,' he says, nodding slowly.

I think of the irony that Romilly would be impressed by my empathy. By Adam and I speaking openly about childbirth.

She'd appear behind Adam at this moment, give him a squeeze. She adores him.

She would try to switch his cereal for home-made granola though.

'The midwife brought it up,' I say. 'Not necessarily that Romilly has been with someone all the way along. But that it was impossible that she could have done this without any help at all.'

Adam nods.

'Okay,' he says, still eating. 'Wow. Yes. That makes sense. I feel stupid for not thinking of it. I just thought . . . with the psychosis . . . that it was all about her, nothing to do with anyone else. Sorry.'

I feel my cheeks heat up. My chest feels hot too, with the warmth of a second heart close to my own.

I look down at my girl.

'Man, if I didn't think of it – and I'm her bloody husband – you shouldn't be expected to.'

He dismisses me.

'You're exhausted, mate. In sole charge of a newborn. It's inevitable you'll miss stuff.'

I feel even hotter then, like I'm a fake because *am* I in sole charge? I think of Loll, and how often she feeds Fleur. Of my baby's little space on Loll's shoulder, my sister-in-law stroking her back like a ritual as they pace, rock, then come to rest.

How I already feel like Loll knows her better than me, somehow; that she's the real parent here and how sometimes I hover in doorways awkwardly when I enter a room, feeling like I have no idea what to do; suspecting I am interrupting a sweet moment between Fleur and Loll that is at its essence maternal.

Does Fleur know there's a difference? Or to her, is that voice that coos into her ear, that warm body, simply her mum, the end, done? What's the definition of a mother?

'Does this mean though . . . are you discounting the psychosis?'

I shake my head. Firm.

'Not at all. I'm just considering that when she made the plan to leave, someone helped her on her way.'

I kiss my daughter on the head. Still getting used to her smell, her shape.

Adam puts down his spoon into an empty cereal bowl. Takes a swig of coffee. Winces.

'Sorry, mate, I've made that a bit strong,' he says. 'Though we probably all need it.'

We sit in silence.

'Someone she trusts then,' he says. '*Really* trusts. And someone who would do anything for her, always put her first. Even above Fleur. Because otherwise you'd stop her, wouldn't you?

Tell her that she had to stay with her baby? That you can't leave a newborn?'

I nod. Yep. These are all thoughts I had as I have sat with this today, changing nappies, making up bottles, trying and failing to get in the shower.

I sip the coffee. Feel the zing of the caffeine.

Adam shifts in his seat. Then he stands up, takes his cereal bowl to the sink. Fills it with water.

'Not many of us have people who would go that far for us,' he says. 'They're the "drop everything at 4 a.m. if you need them" people. There can't be many people in Romilly's life who would do that for her?' He stays there, leaning on the sink.

'Not many at all,' I say, holding my mug.

We make eye contact. He turns the tap off. Looks at me.

Then he says it, at the same time that I am once again thinking it.

'Two, maybe?'

Day #3, 8 p.m.

The Best Friend

What if she isn't alive anymore?

That's the thought that keeps creeping in.

Would I *know*? Would I feel it?

I push the thought away. Of course she is alive, of course. She was getting on the plane. Upset, yeah, but no coercion.

Does there need to be coercion?

Probably not, when the biggest threat to Romilly is Romilly.

And that's the thought that won't leave me alone. If the biggest threat to Romilly is Romilly then it is constant, there at every second.

It is early evening now, Adam at the house with Marc. Later, Loll will head back to stay over so tonight, I am not needed.

Instead, I am back on the beach, Ro's spot, and as the sea swells and waves, the same thing happens to my eyes.

My socks are off, tucked into my trainers next to me.

The tide is high and I walk to the shore in bare feet. Dip my toes in. Wince at the cold.

It wouldn't bother Romilly, of course, the iciness. Never did. She'd be fully immersed in there now.

The tears won't stop but I shove them off the edge of my face and try to think, instead.

I've stopped focusing on that final message though, instead going further back, the weeks, even months before.

There is no doubt that her behaviour changed.

I picture my friend, heavily pregnant, her belly heaving down onto its tiny frame. Still she insisted on working.

It is bloody physical, running a café. And though she pared back her shifts, and I was the one who lugged stock in or up from the cellar or did the thirty-fifth run up the stairs again that day, she still looked exhausted.

'At least take a lot of breaks,' I begged her. 'Sit and drink tea with those customers who love you so much. It'll be like they get a celebrity guest with their lunch. Take it easy. Be here in a cake recommendation and sampling capacity only.'

She laughed. 'I can do that.'

'Look,' I told her, serious. 'You make this place run seamlessly. You stay late every day. You clean even though we have a cleaner. You make cake to bring in in your own time. You find new local suppliers every time you have a conversation with someone. You don't need to prove anything to anyone. I love having you round. But you need to look after yourself.'

She nodded. For the last few months, I had tried to drag her to yoga, sound baths, walks on the beach, anything to unknot her shoulders. Most of the time she had an excuse not to come; on the rare occasion she did, it didn't work.

In those last weeks before she had the baby, Romilly *was* hard to be around. I feel guilty for even thinking it now, when I would take her presence in any form. But it was true.

In retrospect I credited it to nerves over the birth, to the discomfort of the belly-to-frame ratio that she had going on. To frustration. She was constantly having to ask us to do things for her: carry that box of wine up from the cellar; heave the milk delivery up to the kitchen. It was getting harder.

But it was more than that: she had an air of tension about her that was like nothing I had ever seen in her body before. I know the angles of her body. We weren't tense people, Romilly and me. Aren't.

Suddenly though, she did everything differently.

The way she would half-dance around the place to playlists she was constantly tweaking when she remembered another song, that one from last year's Bestival, the one she used to listen to when she watched the sun come up island-hopping in Greece, that tune she heard on the way into work, was gone. Instead she was laden down. I don't even mean by the bump, which was neat even with the ratio, but by shoulders that drooped, a head that looked too heavy for her neck.

I pull my top lip over my bottom lip, remembering. When I snaked an arm around her waist, in those weeks, she would stiffen.

'Is everything okay, Ro?' I asked of course, many, many times in those weeks. As she tweaked the board, as she cleaned out the fridge, as she turned on the coffee machine in the morning and stared at it, in her own world, before I interrupted and she jumped, like it was midnight in a dark alley.

She gave me different answers. Mostly she was fine; sometimes tired. Occasionally – previously unheard of – she snapped at me.

I was irritated by her, and now we are here in a disaster zone, that seems like such a privileged emotion.

You know what I thought, in truth? I thought that it was the start of Romilly moving away from me.

That Romilly was crossing – as many friends had before her – to 'the other side'. That *of course* I couldn't understand that shift in behaviour. Not when I wasn't that holy grail of basic womanhood: the mother.

I felt like I *could* understand, whether I'd been pregnant yet – whether I ever was – or not. But maybe I was deluding myself. Maybe that's the reason she isn't speaking to me now too. Or maybe there's another one.

I think of that final message before she gave birth.

I think of how we are crediting everything to postpartum psychosis but how if she is in France she must have taken her passport with her, to the hospital before she had her baby.

Planning.

Knowing.

Jesus. Imagine what was in her head.

And where does that leave the theory of postpartum psychosis? The theory that has morphed, thanks to Loll and Marc, somewhere along the line into fact.

I look around.

I'm not sure why I'm retracing Romilly's steps again but it keeps happening.

I look at my phone. My evening shift at the café starts soon – a private party booking – and I slip my Birkenstocks back on and walk up the path from the beach playing Café del Mar in my headphones and thinking about bringing up those changes that happened to Romilly in those months to Marc.

But I don't want to ask Marc.

And I realise: I don't *have* to ask Marc.

I turn the corner to the street that the café's on.

Outside the Goodness Café, I pause. The smell of roasted aubergine charges proudly out of the door and I would normally inhale it deeply. But today I hold my breath.

I lean up against the window.

Look around.

Another day where the air is tense; like it contains a secret. I fan my face with my sleeve.

You still have your phone, as far as we know, I type to this lost pen pal of mine. *You don't reply. But messages are getting through. Perhaps I just have to ask the right questions.*

But I don't; not straight away.

Instead I tell Romilly how I noticed that change in her. How odd it made me feel.

You know what else I've thought about, Ro? That note, in the café. The name of the lake that I found under the board.

I keep typing.

Anything to get a reaction.

I am alone outside our second home, inhaling the scent of aubergine swirled in with the sea air, and I am staring at the screen. I have to get this right.

I look up at the arch that marks the entrance, framed by spring flowers, and I try to make myself feel the beauty but it's too hard at the moment; it's too hard to feel much at all.

I am starting to cry now, as I type.

I told you the other day that I know where you are, I say. *If I am sure, if that's true, would you want Marc to know now? So he could come and get you and make this all stop?*

And something happens.

Words on a screen.

Romilly is online.

Romilly is typing.

Day #4, 7 a.m.

The Husband

I spread over to Romilly's side of the bed last night to make a point. To find a silver lining in all of this, even if it is only to do with big beds and long limbs.

Four wake-ups and feeds later, muscle memory has taken over and I have made space for an imaginary Romilly and curled up on my own side. Turns out: there are no silver linings.

My head throbs.

Fleur wakes.

I go downstairs, opening my eyes just enough not to fall and to see the time on the clock – 7 a.m. – and the formula box but not wasting any energy on unnecessary eye opening. I can hear Loll stirring in the living room.

She insisted on staying over.

'You don't need to,' I told her yesterday, approximately seventeen times.

She nodded, each time. 'Don't need to; want to. Just in case. It's a lot, Marc, by yourself. Good to have some back-up in these first days.'

Silence, then. Would replacement back-up return soon? How long would these solo days last?

I saw Loll pop into my room during the night. Checking on Fleur. Putting her dummy back in. Laying a hand on her chest.

She thought I was sleeping.

Loll needs to be in charge.

Now, I race back upstairs with the bottle as Fleur's cries get more horrified; as she gets more panicked that she may never see food again.

The second the bottle is in her mouth Fleur's little body sighs with the relief and she sucks hard, snuggled into me. I'm awake now, the adrenalin of the pace back up the stairs kicking in and I am twitching with the need to get on with something, to do *anything*.

I think of the conversation with Adam yesterday.

Of those words.

Two, maybe.

We are both aware who those two are: the evidence is in the way they know where the mugs are in my house; in the way they quietly place another bottle of Sauvignon Blanc in the wine rack, ready for their next visit. Put the empties in the right recycling bin.

I take Fleur downstairs. Hand her over to Auntie Loll while I make a coffee.

The light flickers on, off, on, off.

When Adam arrives at 10 a.m., Robin the midwife is heading to her car and I am at the door saying goodbye to her in pyjamas that have an obscene hole in the crotch. Fleur is clutched close to my chest.

Adam and Robin nod hello to each other as they pass in the driveway.

I groan, audibly, like a toddler doing an impression of a T-Rex.

Adam doesn't notice.

He is looking at his phone, which is ringing. He turns it off and flips it to silent.

'Steffie?' I ask, trying for normal.

He nods. 'I can call her back later. You, my friend, have my undivided attention. And a . . . massive fuck-off hole near your balls.'

'Bye, Robin!' I shout after the midwife.

'Bye, Robin!' echoes Adam.

'Could have made an effort for her, mate,' he says as I shut the big green door behind him.

I shake my head, wince.

'Don't,' I say. 'We slept in. I feel sick. What if she writes it down somewhere? That I basically exposed myself? Thinks I'm not coping? She says no one gets dressed for the first month after they have a baby but I'm not sure. Suspect she is being nice. And also that she means wholesome mums breastfeeding in their pyjamas, not dads in their crotchless pants asleep on the sofa.'

Adam laughs and our house now is so desolate that the noise sounds odd and tinny and out of place.

I don't smile. Nothing is funny.

We walk into the kitchen.

'Did you ask her about CCTV at the hospital?'

He had brought it up with me yesterday.

I nod. 'Yep. She's going to ask someone on the front desk. But Loll asked already on the first day and she keeps getting passed back to the police. It's infuriating.'

And whenever I start to turn on Loll, I have to remember this. Chasing the CCTV, educating everyone on postpartum psychosis, changing my baby, dealing with the police.

Any paranoia directed at Loll is exactly that: paranoia. Surely.

I hold Fleur with one arm and drape the other in front of my trousers for decency, as I did for the entire duration of Robin's visit. But I can't stop pacing.

'Oh, she's forgotten her scales.'

I scoop them up with my spare hand, run out barefoot and give them back to her. Hoping to claw back a few points.

When I come back in, Adam is standing in the centre of the kitchen, staring.

'Jesus,' he says before he can stop himself.

Loll arrived last thing to sleep here and left first thing to see the kids before school: she's had no time to tidy.

Which means that the odd version of a boys' night in that Adam and I had last night, which involved two beers and a lamb balti each, Fleur on alternate laps, is still spread out, scent and all, across the kitchen.

Adam scrunches up his nose.

Unlike most boys' nights in, last night also took the form of a planning session on how I would find my absent wife and a scouting of a lake in the South of France, using scant information from a scrawled note and a radius that seemed reasonable around Nîmes Garons airport.

I fell asleep twenty minutes into *Toy Story 4*. We decided on that in case Fleur was taking it in. A *Breaking Bad* rewatch felt risky and in truth, I prefer Woody and Buzz.

Now, last night's foil cartons of congealed goo and empty beer bottles have joined half-drunk bottles of formula and crisp packets. Despite its low-key nature, it is somehow giving the impression of us having had a party. Albeit a strange one.

'The midwife didn't come in here,' I tell him quickly – when did I get so paranoid that I am worried about being judged even by Adam – but he knows it too. Eyes are turned my way a bit more often than for your average new parent. The midwives are awaiting news of Romilly but their focus, their responsibility, is Fleur. 'I don't even think Loll did.'

'I've got an hour before I need to leave for the airport,' Adam says. 'Want me to help?'

I nod, beaten and unable to be stoic. I look around and it's too much.

So Adam clears up while I hold Fleur, and then he makes us both a coffee in mugs that Steffie had designed for Romilly as a Christmas present when they were younger, adorned with a selection of pictures from their school days together. They met when they were five.

I look at the snapshots of the two of them on there, Steffie towering above Romilly, tucking her into her armpit in school uniform. Both in eyeliner that stared you down at a gig in the early Noughties. Eyes closed on matching Lilos in a swimming pool. Face masks on in sleeping bags, twelve perhaps, or thirteen.

Romilly, Romilly, everywhere and nowhere.

I sip my coffee.

Fleur is in her rocker on the floor, dummy now a familiar sight. We sit down. The silence isn't that comfortable, for me at least: I am trying to build up to something.

Adam drinks fast. 'Is there anything new from the police I need to know before I head off?'

I sigh. 'Not really. Loll is hammering away to make them grasp that she has a mental health issue, so it's different to another adult leaving. But it's awkward. They say she doesn't have a diagnosis. It doesn't go to the top of the pile. But they got that CCTV from the airport. That's something. We know she was alone then.'

Adam nods. 'Good that it backs up the woman from the airport too. She says Romilly was definitely alone. And she saw her at both ends of the journey.' Adam opens the cupboard and hands me a packet of biscuits. I shove in a custard cream, whole.

'Still,' I concur. 'It's lucky we have this eyewitness. The police have been pretty shit. Loll is going crazy with it. Did you hear her losing it on the phone yesterday? They just don't comprehend postpartum psychosis at all. Have no grasp of the severity.'

I see a shudder run through Adam. We all know what we mean, when we talk in code like this.

Romilly could already be dead.

A bang makes me jump.

'Right,' he says. 'Goodbye cuddle.'

His coffee cup, on the table. That's all. What is wrong with me?

Adam leans down to unclip Fleur from her rocker and to

snuggle her in. She sighs, happy as ever to be next to a body. 'Won't be long, girl. I'm going to bring your mamma back.'

But he doesn't sound convincing; instead he looks distracted, staring out of a window.

There is a lot of footfall outside our house, a regular stampede to the beach in muddy wellies in autumn, winter, the tread lighter in its sandals by summer, buckets and spades clinking as they go.

I am convinced more of them look to their left at our window now than they used to, now we are intriguing, now tragedy lives here.

And when they look, I think, as an old guy catches me at the window and glances back down at his whippet, we appear like prisoners. One or other of us is always at that window, staring out like we are locked in.

I feel like I am, often.

What would Loll do if I put a sign up in the window?

Help me, help me, help me.

'Adam, am I right to trust Steffie?'

I blurt it out before I can change my mind. Before he can leave.

Slowly his head turns back to me, brow furrowed.

'What?' he answers. I glance over my shoulder on autopilot but she isn't here, she's at the café.

'Of course you are,' he says, an unreal laugh. 'She's Romilly's best friend. Mate, she's my *girlfriend*.'

There's a pause. No laughter now. Adam looks awkward.

'In the end though, her loyalties are with Romilly, aren't they, not our family?' I push though I know it might be the wrong choice; that though Adam is my friend, he is Steffie's boyfriend first. 'It isn't like Loll, who loves Fleur just as much, who knows she needs her mum. Steffie is Romilly's friend. That's where her attention is. She isn't exactly maternal. So who's to say she didn't help her? And who's to say she isn't still helping her? She's always checking her phone. Always.'

I can hear myself and I know I sound paranoid, but I am sure there is something in this. That I was wrong to turn on Loll but in this, I am right.

'Well,' he says. 'By that score, my loyalty is to you and I don't care about this kid either.'

Adam snuggles down into my baby. I see three of her fingers cover a small part of one of his. In Fleur's limited world, Adam is one of the most consistent figures. But by the same score, he is right, so is Steffie.

'And that's obviously not true,' he pushes on, and am I being paranoid or does he sound irritated now? 'If you'd done a runner I would want you back here with your family because I'd know that's where you belong and that's what would be good for you. Mate, Steffie . . . no. You can't say this to me.'

I look up from Fleur. Meet his eyes. But we all know that Steffie and Romilly's friendship runs deeper than Adam's and mine.

'What if you believed that coming home wasn't what was good for me?' I ask.

He raises an eyebrow in silent question. He's singing a lullaby under his breath. When I look at her, Fleur's eyelids are drooping.

'You're getting pretty good at that,' I tell him, in an almost whisper so I don't break the sleep spell.

We sit in silence for a few minutes until Fleur is in a deep nap, crumpled into Adam's stomach. A stomach that I used to tease him about, little beer belly, but now looks like a gym body compared to mine.

'Whoever is supporting Romilly clearly thinks that this is the right thing for her,' I whisper. 'Even if it's for a reason we haven't figured out yet.'

'Either that or they felt like they had no choice,' he counters, hushed tones too. 'Like they had to support her. No matter what. *Because* of her mental health. Or because they love her, and you always support the people you love.

I nod my head. True.

'Fuck!'

There's a loud knock at the door. I am so in my own head that I jump when it comes. Again.

'It'll be my taxi,' he says.

As he hands Fleur over to me, he speaks again.

'I know we said someone close, but there has to be someone else. Not those two, mate. Loll and Steffie . . . there's just no way.'

He's right. If Steffie had helped Romilly, he would know, wouldn't he?

I watch his face.

It ducks away from me as he picks up his bag to head for his taxi.

'I'll be in touch when I get there,' he says, standing up.

'Don't forget to keep me in the loop with everything,' I tell him. 'However small it seems. *Everything.*'

He reaches up to rub me on the head at the crown. He examines it. 'Yep, you've definitely lost an inch or so there.'

Then he smiles, but sort of grim, and picks up a backpack and tent that normally go on camping trips and did a month in South America with Steffie last year and now are going on this odd, odd rescue mission, over his shoulder.

He would know.

He slips out of the front door.

And I stand in our big bay window in the living room and watch his cab pull away.

He doesn't see me there, Fleur in my arms. Has his head down.

In the last second before the cab pulls away, I see Adam with his phone to his ear.

Come to think of it, he's been attached to his phone a lot too.

Day #4, 10.30 a.m.

The Best Friend

By the morning, she has stopped typing and no reply has actually made it to me and so I think she's changed her mind. But then she starts again.

Romilly is typing.

The reply, when it finally comes, only contains one word.

But one word is all I need.

No.

Then, though, comes more.

Don't trust Marc, Steffie. Do not trust Marc with anything.

Oh my friend: I'm sorry.

I have given Marc the information and sent him – via Adam – straight to Romilly, when Romilly does not want him near her.

Fuck.

But I stop myself.

Calm down.

Romilly is experiencing postpartum psychosis.

We are all sure of that.

Aren't we?

So whatever Romilly thinks she wants, doesn't mean that's the right thing for her.

Post, post, post.

I think of Marc making that phone call. I think of the word *post*partum; of whatever went on with Romilly before birth, pre, pre, pre.

If we have this wrong, the only way I can change things now, the only way I can make this up to Romilly for giving Marc such a focus as the lake, is to cut off his source.

At least until I figure out what's going on.

Outside work, I slip my phone out of my pocket and call Adam. I can hear the noise of a bad local radio host shouting in the background, something Adam – slave to a Nineties indie playlist that expands constantly but that he plays at all times – would never have put on himself.

He's in a taxi. To the airport.

'Ad, listen,' I say, walking round the corner towards the beach. My breath sounds as loud as my voice. 'I know this sounds crazy. But please if you find out any information about where Romilly is, don't pass it on to Marc. Come to me first. I'm probably being ridiculous but I'm not sure we should be telling him—'

He interrupts me.

'What do you mean?' he says, careful. 'This is the *entire point* of me going. To get Romilly back to her family.'

I sigh. How can I explain this to him when this is so difficult for me to comprehend too? When I don't know why yet.

It's been our sole aim, our only focus, to find Romilly.

'Okay, okay,' I say, trying to take the conversation down a notch, keep him with me. 'Don't tell Marc this either. But there are a few things that have started to not add up for me, with this postpartum psychosis thing. And then . . . Ro messaged me.'

There is a beat.

I walk back on myself, towards work.

Pace.

'She messaged you?' he says. 'And you kept this to yourself?'

'It was short.'

'Oh that's okay then!'

The radio sounds even louder.

'And you didn't say?'

'It was only an hour ago, Adam, and I'm saying now.'

113

'Not to the police.'

'No. Not to the police.'

'Not to Marc.'

I am quiet. 'No. Not to Marc either.'

'He thinks she could be *dead*, Steffie.'

Silence.

How to answer that?

I've betrayed the team. Am potentially doing something torturous to someone who doesn't deserve that.

Adam is – I know him well enough to establish from his breathing alone – boiling with rage.

One of the waitresses, Meg, sees me outside the café and knocks on the window. Arms and rolled-up sleeves out in question. So much for being non customer-facing: my shouting at customers is suddenly forgotten when there are tables crying out for their micro salad.

'Give me a second, Ad,' I mutter.

I hold up two fingers to the glass. 'Two minutes,' I mouth.

'So what exactly did she say, in this message?' he says.

The tone is more Loll, no messing around, straight to the point; not Adam.

The mood until now has been kindness; compassion. An understanding that for somebody to do this, something must be very wrong.

I make this point.

'Exactly,' says Adam. 'Something *is* very, very wrong. But that thing is happening *inside her own mind*. One thing I do know is that the only way to make it *right* is to get them all back under their family roof. Get her medical help. We won't make it right by leaving Romilly floating around Europe with undiagnosed postpartum psychosis.'

It was *a theory*, I think, a theory. Since when did this psychosis become fact? Or is that often how facts become facts, simply by being repeated until they're accepted?

'She's not exactly floating around Eu—' I start but Meg is in my vision again, pointing at a watch she isn't wearing. I can hear the pre-lunchtime rush of plates and voices and teacups on saucers starting now.

I sigh.

'Anyway, Adam, we're veering off the point,' I whisper, quieter now as I am conscious of people walking past, on their way into the café, hearing. 'She didn't say much. She disabled her phone straight afterwards. But she did say that it was crucial that we don't tell Marc anything.'

There is an angry silence, a disbelieving one, a silence that contains hundreds of words, a shouting match, maybe even a hug at the end as we make up but have to agree to disagree. All of it's there but none of it as well as I listen to tinny music on the other end of the phone, see the face of an angry waitress.

We can't do this now.

'Adam?'

'Yeah, mate, that's great,' he says to the cabbie. 'Steffie, I have to go. I've just got to the airport.'

And he hangs up. When I call back – ill-advised, given the work situation and the fact I am now so late but I need him to understand this – he has turned his phone off.

I shove my phone into my pocket.

Trust me, Adam. Trust me more than Marc.

Marc carries a tiny baby in his arms in his pyjamas. He gulps coffee in desperation. He pushes his hair back with two hands and ages weeks, months in hours.

He does not appear like a guilty man; if he's acting he's gone method.

Do I believe he is a threat?

Especially when he is telling me that Romilly is experiencing postpartum psychosis?

Can I trust her judgement?

Can I trust his?

I dart behind the counter, serve a couple of customers. It is getting busy now, the lunchtime rush on. But I am twitching to be somewhere else.

'Pol, can you cover for a second?'

She looks mad but she doesn't have the confidence of old-hand Meg, pointing at imaginary watches even though I'm her acting manager. Polly has only been here six weeks. She won't say no.

I go outside. Call Romilly. Come *on*. Tell me something else. Tell me anything else. Tell me what Marc has done. Or what, at least, you believe Marc has done.

But her phone is still disabled; I can no longer contact her. That is all I will get to work with. All I will get to make decisions that will change people's lives. All I will get to persuade Adam with.

Inside, I say sorry to Polly.

'Can you refill the coffee machine?' I ask her and she goes to grab a bag of beans.

I turn to the next customer.

'Right, what was it?' I ask. I make sure I am friendly, no matter what's going on in my head. Fake it, fake it, fake it.

Two wraps, a brownie, a lemon drizzle, and she wants a pot of the kimchi to take away.

'Good choice.' I smile. 'The kimchi is incredible.'

She hands her card over.

As I wait for it to go through, I feel sweat on my back and it's too much suddenly, the heat of the coffee machine. Too much.

The sweat streams now. I stumble slightly as I step. My smile feels like it requires effort. My head is light. The card machine seems to take forever.

Do I overrule Romilly? Trust to the people whose mental health I am not concerned about? Or do I go with my gut, as I have always gone with my gut?

'That's gone through for you,' I say, pulling my grin up at the sides. 'Do you want a receipt?'

'That's okay, love,' she says, and walks away to her normal life, her everyday decisions. I stare at the spot she's left behind.

It's too late anyway.

Adam has gone now, moving across that blotched English sky to the more straightforward pastel blue of the South of France. Towards Romilly. Ready to find her, call home and report back: passing on everything he knows directly to his mate.

I head out to the tables, take an order. Fail to write any of it down.

Back at the coffee machine, I stare. Was it a cappuccino and an Americano?

I look at our giant rose gold metal mood grid, just next to the coffee machine. Touch a tiny bit of Blu-Tack. Think about that note.

I looked it up, of course, the lake. There was a sense of solitude; a vastness to it. How deep you could tell it was, even on a Google search.

It didn't do moderation. Bodies of water never touched me like they touched Loll, but still I got it: there was something special about this one.

On the other hand, you could drown in it. Easily.

When I take my finger away, a bit of Blu-Tack comes away on the tip.

I press the button on the coffee machine. Two Americanos. That was it.

I picture Adam, on board the plane now, researching, crossing places off a list, narrowing down his targets.

How short is your list, Adam?

How quickly will you find her?

'Argh!'

It cascades; boiling water that I have split all over my arm and I have it under the sink trying to take the sting out of the burn, prevent a scar.

I think of Adam, delivering Marc to Romilly, partly because of my hunch; my lead.

I think of Adam rescuing her, in the nick of time.

I stumble again, even as I stand still.

Oh, it hurts.

I look up.

Nothing.

The hum of people being social is too loud for anyone to have noticed me scald myself.

How much pain can happen in clear sight, because people are too distracted by their coffees, their conversation, that app they're scrolling on their phone.

It gets worse. Hangs around as a sting. More sweat meanders down my back now. Springs up in my armpits.

And I realise what this other feeling is. It is the horror that comes with the realisation that I could have put my closest, oldest friend in danger.

That I no longer believe Romilly is ill.

And what does that mean, then?

The pain gets worse, and worse, and worse.

The Husband

I turn from the window.

I try to open it again but it's still sealed shut.

Fuck.

I look around.

Adam might have tidied the kitchen but the rest of the house is chaos. Piles of stuff everywhere – babygrows, bottles, washing up, post I never asked for, never wanted – and I don't know how I'll ever get on top of this. It feels like it is all taken on human qualities and is plotting to smother me under its weight.

I put Fleur down in the Moses basket.

The kitchen spotlight flickers at me again: on, off, on, off.

I kick at the door. Kick at the wall. Shout so loud I wake up Fleur. Loll is due any second, picking up the baton as they all do.

As I go into the living room to settle Fleur I picture my best mate's face again.

It sounds dramatic, I know, but there is only one word for the expression that came over him when he took that phone call.

Tortured.

Am I right to trust Steffie? Now the paranoia puts on weight: am I right to trust *a single person* who claims to be on my team?

I suspected Loll and Steffie of being in some sort of alliance but are *Adam* and Steffie working together? They're a couple: that trumps everything else, however close my mate and I are.

119

Fleur sleeps again, finally and I put her back down in the Moses basket.

I shut three doors between us and scream the fucking place down.

When the midwife comes back later to drop off some cream for the baby's eczema, I am prepared this time and ready in jogging bottoms and a fresh T-shirt with a little product in my hair. Casual enough that it doesn't look forced – I am, after all, home with a newborn baby, living through a nightmare and spending 90 per cent of my time on a sofa – but not the crotch-revealing situation of earlier.

I don't feel warm towards Robin.

Not when I remember how she kept digging about Romilly. Pushing it. Pushing me.

Not when I think about what she said when I ran after her in my slippers to give her the scales she had left behind. Trying to get in her good books. Adam keeping an eye on Fleur back inside.

The window was down.

I stood next to the car holding the scales.

Before she saw me, I saw her, speaking into a hands-free phone.

'Someone in that house,' she said, clearly, 'knows something more than they are letting on about why that mother left.'

And then she looked up. Spotted me there.

Hung up on the call and opened the door.

'Everything okay, Marc?'

Did she flush a little?

Neither of us acknowledged the conversation she had just had.

I handed the scales over silently and walked away with a racing heart. Who was she speaking to and what power did they have? Was my guardianship of my daughter being looked at? Was I a suspect? How long did I have to get Romilly home before this was escalated?

I was about to tell Adam. But who wants to mark themselves out as suspected, even to their best friend?

Now, as I see her again, fear floods my body.

But when I answer the door, it's not Robin after all.

I don't have a chance to even say hello before a voice behind me yells.

'What the flying FUCK are you doing here?'

I turn, wide-eyed with Fleur in my arms, to see Loll standing behind me holding her can of Dettol spray like a weapon. I have never heard Loll swear before and I fight the urge to giggle like a child realising its parents are human.

The woman at the door reaches out and takes Fleur and despite the circumstances, I don't object.

How can you, when she's her grandma?

Or rather, MawMaw.

'Come to MawMaw, gorgeous girl,' she says, waking Fleur up with an enthusiastic cuddle. She looks at me.

'Grandma doesn't feel like it reflects me. I've got visions of knitting needles and slippers and such things.'

She shudders.

'So! Bill and I read up on some alternatives. MawMaw is lovely, right?'

She doesn't wait for an answer.

'French,' she chatters on as she comes in through the front door and Loll and I move aside. 'They're very taken with it in Louisiana.'

I lag behind her, mute.

Romilly and Loll's mum Aurelia heads into the living room, sits down on the sofa and takes a selfie with Fleur. She busies herself with her phone for a minute or so.

'Just sending this over to Bill,' she says. 'He wanted to come but he's a little tired from the flight. I've told him – get over it, Bill. You can sleep when you're dead! There's a life out there to grab and we are *not* on the right side of things, time wise.'

Loll and I watch Aurelia talk. My eyes blink. Her outfit features all the colours of the rainbow, varying shades, swathes of material and she is *a lot*, when I have stared at these walls now for so many hours. When life has been muted; coloured in shades of grey.

I glance at my sister-in-law's face but can't read it. Her can of Dettol is still poised.

Both of us wait for a pause.

'Come and give me a kiss, darling,' Aurelia says, very definitely not reading the room but Loll stands up, robot-like and does what she is told, pecking her mother on the cheek before returning to her place on the other end of the sofa. I am standing in the doorway, ready to escape if the air in this room becomes too unbearable. Or if Loll starts throwing things, the can of Dettol looking like it could be the first shot.

Or if anyone needs a cup of tea.

'Does anyone need a cup of tea?' I ask.

'Would love one, darling,' she chimes. Big smile. It is as though she has completely forgotten the part about her daughter – Fleur's mother – being missing. Or the part where we thought she was still in Europe until five minutes ago.

I nod, pleased to have a task, one that involves me leaving the room. I'm about to pour milk in. Nip back in to check if she has sugar.

And I get to the door of the living room just in time to see Loll hissing at her mum. Though I don't catch the words. Or the ones apart from 'Romilly'.

As I walk in, Loll slams the handbrake on her sentence and looks up.

'Oh. Hey, Marc.'

Far more slowly, Fleur still cuddled into her chest, Aurelia looks up too. And if she's chastised by her eldest daughter's words, she doesn't appear to be. In fact the look on her face would be described as Zen.

'Sugar?' she asks.

I nod.

She mirrors.

Most people would know their mother-in-law's tea order. But this is only the second cup of tea I've made Aurelia in the eighteen months Romilly and I have been together.

'No thanks, darling,' she says. Voice the same as ever.

It comes back to me, as many things about Aurelia are coming back to me.

It feels wrong to be here: like I have walked in on something intimate, despite being in my own house.

Aurelia looks back at her daughter. I wouldn't bet on either of them to back down, whatever this is. Aurelia cuddles Fleur tighter, like a human shield, but Loll won't go for her mum with Dettol cans. It'll be a sharp tongue firing long-held word missiles.

They have the same stare, the same dark eyes: Aurelia, Loll and Fleur. I feel Romilly's absence again then: she, of course, has them too. They seemed more intense, once she cut her hair.

Romilly's slippers are just there, next to Aurelia's feet.

'What's going on?' I say to Loll.

Loll ducks her head; Aurelia too.

Neither of them speak.

'Seriously?' I say. 'In the midst of this, you're not going to elaborate?'

Aurelia shakes her head. When she looks up at me, she appears in pain. I remember then: Aurelia can't deal with stress. She needs the positive spin; the happy outcome. When you're in the thick of a shitstorm, Aurelia stays in her camper van and ploughs on across the wine regions. She turns her phone off and her music up. She oms on Dartmouth.

The fact she's here, in the middle of this, is something. I try to go easy; treat her like the child Loll says I should. Even if she isn't practising her own advice.

Loll walks towards the window. Yanks it hard, but it won't budge.

123

'How can you stand your window not working?' she mutters, pacing like an animal. 'So claustrophobic.'

I sigh.

'It's no use turning on each other,' I tell them, chief mediator. 'Adam has gone to France now. Romilly's there. He'll bring her back, and we can get her treatment.'

Aurelia's face crumples. No make-up. Hair crinkled in blonde-grey waves. She is childlike, I think. I don't quite get how she can be when she is seventy-two, but she is.

'I'm sorry,' she says. 'I'm sorry this came from me.'

So she does know now. I wonder when that happened.

Loll flicks a quick glance in her direction.

'You can't blame yourself for Romilly getting postpartum psychosis,' I say.

Aurelia's face says nothing. She stares out of the window.

Loll won't look at either of us.

Eventually the silence is too much.

'Let me fetch your tea,' I say, and nip out to the kitchen. Go easy, go easy. I hear Fleur start to make noise in the living room and make her up a bottle.

When I come back, I sit next to Aurelia on the sofa and take Fleur from her, slipping the bottle into her mouth.

'Just because postpartum psychosis is the reason Romilly has gone away,' I say. 'That does *not* mean it's in any way your fault.'

Loll folds her arms over one another. She turns to Aurelia. 'It's the theory that makes sense, Mum. We are sure that's what it is.'

We all sit in more silence then, layering it so it sits thick and dense, loaded with as much feeling as the hissed conversation I walked in on a few minutes ago. I had come in here to comfort Aurelia; the situation and her demeanour have changed so quickly I haven't needed to.

'And you said the police . . .?' says Aurelia, voice cracking before she can carry on.

Loll's face darkens. 'Do not even get me started. Another conversation this morning, round and round the houses. Passed between departments.'

'Do you want me to take over?' I say, though the idea of anything else to deal with feels untenable. A newborn and a missing wife at the same time has me at capacity.

I feel my eyelids fold downwards.

Loll softens. 'No, Marc. You have plenty on your list. Let me tackle that lot. And in the meantime, at least we have our own lead. Our own focus.'

We tell Aurelia about the woman on the plane, the note with the name of the lake on. About Adam going out there.

Fleur suckles and pauses and suckles and pauses and after a while I sit her up and she manages a loud burp, and it's a sound that would be funny in any other quiet room but not this one.

'I think it might be best if I go home,' says Loll eventually. 'Try the police again. Leave *MawMaw to* bond with Fleur.'

Her voice rolls its eyes.

'Don't worry about coming to the door, Marc,' says Loll. 'Keep Fleur settled. And keep me posted on any updates from Adam too, although I'm sure he'll send them to the group.'

Yep. We now have a WhatsApp group in which our reason for being is not that we play a sport together or have children in the same year group or all lived together when we were twenty-two but that we spend a lot of time in this house, trying to work out why Romilly has left her baby.

Steffie created the group.

It's named *Romilly* and every time a message comes through on it – usually something practical about times that people will be here or if anybody needs a latte or can somebody pick up a new dummy for Fleur – I see it and for one second, one second, I think this is it, this is fucking *it*. A message from Romilly. And every time, that gut lurch when I realise my error.

I say goodbye to Loll and turn to Aurelia.

'So now we're alone, Marc, without my daughter who has fled the country,' she says, and her normal gentle let's-talk-about-this-over-a-tofu-bowl voice has been replaced by something grittier. A tone I've never heard. 'And without my other daughter too. Is there anything you want to tell me?'

I look at her. Perhaps a look she's never seen from me before, either.

She doesn't push it.

'I could take Fleur for a little walk?' she offers. 'Give you a break? You look shattered, Marc. Utterly exhausted.'

'Fleur is tired, Aurelia,' I say, calmly. 'I think maybe it's time that you left.'

Day #4, 11 a.m.

The Best Friend

One will be navy, one will be black.

Odd socks, like he always wears, the big idiot, in the visual I get of him padding without shoes through the gate at airport security.

Old battered iPad removed from his bag and then – lastly – his phone.

His phone in the basket too, still turned off.

Still ignoring me.

I have been accused many times in life of being 'too laid-back', which honestly when it's delivered by someone who feels their heart rate quicken over their neighbour chopping a hedge too low or a ten-minute wait for a pizza bill gives me great pleasure. Long may I lay back.

Now though, I find it hard to imagine ever being laid-back again.

Turn your phone on, Adam. Answer it.

Since Ro messaged me I haven't stopped calling him.

I picture him staring at his phone as it moves away from him on the conveyor belt, knowing that I will be calling him, not caring, focused on what he is going to do.

I know he'll have to turn it on eventually, to speak to Marc if nothing else, but even then I suspect he will ignore me.

'Screw you, Ad,' I mutter now as I plate up a couscous salad, pour out a red juice for a regular who works from here on her laptop three days a week. My palms sweat.

He will feel bad, I know. Adam is a good person; not the type who ignores calls or warnings. But, he will reason, it's *Marc*. The guy you'll recommend to play at your wedding. Who he goes for a pint with. How can Marc be a threat? He trusts Marc. He needs to reunite Marc with his wife. The rest – at this juncture – is white noise.

Give me a break, he'll think; I'm trying to fix my best friend's life here; trying to heal a family. He will sort everything else, including his relationship with the woman he has lived with for three years, after he has done that.

It's not that he'll think he is some sort of saviour – that's not Adam either. But just that it'll be a relief to *do* something when we've had these days of limbo, Loll in charge of the baby, him with little to do but watch Marc's face and hear the news come on the radio and realise another hour has passed and feel redundant.

I get it.

I've struggled too. Upbeat, free-as-a-bird me, suddenly dealing with an atmosphere that makes you speak in whispers, like we're grieving, coupled with the trials of a newborn and cries and mess and anxiety. Sometimes I am desperate to leave too. Anyone would want to walk away from that environment. It traps you in its claustrophobia and winds you with its sadness. When I walk out of the front door, I suck the air.

Loll taps our legs when she wants to vacuum beneath us. She makes us stand up while she plumps a cushion or tucks a blanket. Ten years, there are between Loll and me and yet she feels like my mother.

'Give her a break,' I say though when Marc complains about her. 'It's the only way she knows how to be. People can only be the way they are.'

And then there's Marc himself.

Most of the time Adam is happy hanging out with Marc; few beers, night at a gig, meet up at the gym. They settled into an easy friendship when we introduced them. But right now even for Adam it's hard. Marc is in a different place to all of us, getting to know his newborn baby in circumstances that should never exist. He is unpredictable. He veers between sadness and a rage that neither I nor Adam have seen in him before. Yesterday I walked into the kitchen and he was kicking, repeatedly, at the back door.

'What are you *doing*?' I asked, static in the doorway.

'Sorry,' he muttered. 'Sometimes you've just got to erupt. We're all volcanoes at the moment, Steffie.'

And then he left the room without another word.

We haven't mentioned it.

But isn't it fair enough that he would be angry with the world? Scared? We all know what the risks are to Romilly with this thing, and they are the worst kind. It's the one thing I feel bad about: I know Romilly is alive. I could give Marc that. But how can I without betraying her?

People are different, in the bad times. I am seeing sides normally reserved only for people we live with.

The ones reserved specially for Marc's wife.

What does he kick when you're here, Romilly?

I consider, for the first time, the idea that Romilly feared Marc.

But the thought disperses quickly because, if she feared him, she wouldn't have walked away and left her newborn baby with him.

What about that message though?

Don't trust Marc, Steffie. Do not trust Marc with anything.

I thought I was getting it right, being there for her family, figuring it out from the inside: now I don't know if I've just made everything worse.

My mind is catapulted back to work via a hand on my arm.

And the customer looks at me as I hand her salad over, face scrunched up in my own thoughts.

'You okay, Steffie?' says this smiley young woman as she looks up from her laptop. 'Thanks, yum – the hazelnuts on top look amazing.'

'It's so good.' I smile. 'I took a bowl home last night. Could have eaten three. Oh I'm fine, yes. How's your toddler group going?'

And she regales me with information about her new business, eyes giddy with success and positives and focus and the day-to-day minutiae of life not being a disaster zone.

I feel a pulse of envy.

'So glad it's going well,' I tell her, then I back away before I can offend anyone, before they can offend me, before I can erupt out of nowhere. I am customer-facing out of necessity but I know there are no more chances. And I no longer trust my own reaction, if someone says the wrong thing.

I run two at a time up the stairs and head into the office, check there's no one else around.

And I kick a wall too, then wince at the pain in the toe beneath my thin Converse.

Like Marc did.

So perhaps this *can* be a moment of pure frustration, and that is all.

I head out of the office and into the kitchen.

'Where have you been?' asks our chef, Jane. 'The bell rang two minutes ago. That's getting cold.'

I mutter an apology.

Pick up a plate of aubergine curry and two soups and head back down the stairs, imagining once again what Adam is doing. Picking his bag up, flinging his rucksack over his shoulder . . .

'Enjoy,' I say, serving the food then slipping my phone out of my pocket as I walk away.

It's all he will have brought, that carry-on, not knowing how long it will be before he finds Romilly. We must have been on twenty-five, thirty flights together. He travels light.

My pulse quickens.

The smell of Jane's curry – delicious, hearty, spiced to perfection – makes me feel ill.

I tell myself to calm down.

I might have given Adam a loose steer – aided by the woman who emailed, I caveat, not to mention the police, not all me – but we don't have a location pinned down, do we?

Maybe I shouldn't feel guilty at all.

I think of that message Romilly sent before she went into labour. Of the conversations that Marc and Loll have over Romilly's mental health. How it gets brushed under the carpet when I walk into a room and they are discussing it. How I bury my head on that front sometimes; in truth, it scares me.

One time though, I googled.

Behaving out of character. Why else would Romilly leave the country if it weren't because of postpartum psychosis? Causing her to make decisions she would never make; choices that are inexplicable?

I saw another word too: *delusions.*

I shudder. Every time I think of it.

Think of her distrust of Marc.

And then, the ante upped. Words that ground you.

Self-harm.

Suicide.

And suddenly, it felt like we were dealing with a ticking time bomb.

I hear it in that tap.

Feel it in the flicker of the light.

Every pick of my nail, even.

Tick, tick, tick.

What if I *have* done what's best for her? What if the help she needs from me doesn't take the form that she thinks it does?

But my gut battles those thoughts.

Hands free for a few seconds, I nip outside the café and call

Adam again. His phone is on now but rings out anyway. I throw it into my bag.

'Fucker,' I mutter under my breath.

He knows what I am going to say. If he isn't answering, he isn't buying it. There is no point in him speaking to me.

He needs to stay focused on what he's doing. My paranoia about Marc and refusal to accept that Romilly is ill will, for now, have to wait.

And so he lets his phone ring out.

It rings out as he finishes the last of his tuna sandwich, picks up his bag and checks the screen above to see which gate he is heading to.

It stays off as he walks there at his Adam ambling pace, searching in his bag for his mask as he goes. Finding it screwed up at the bottom.

Eventually, he will step onto the plane. His phone will still be off.

And then, a brief flight, the one from Manchester to Nîmes Garons, and Adam will make his way to Romilly.

I head back inside. Glance at the clock.

Think about that ticking time bomb.

I tidy up a table, smile politely.

Seconds later, the plates I am holding clatter to the floor and when Polly falls to the ground next to me and holds on, I wonder why she is doing that at first and then I realise it is because I am sobbing, uncontrollable with the burn, the hurt, with the loneliness, with missing Romilly – unsure, sure, everything tumbling out, guilty, scared, responsible, out of control.

And she clings hard to contain me, to hold my parts together, like we do to Fleur when she can't settle but we know she needs sleep.

I am definitely no longer a laid-back person.

How can you be laid-back when you don't know what has

happened to your best friend and when she is nowhere close to find out?

How can you be laid-back when you think the man who is looking after her daughter might be a liar?

The weight of it all is too much.

I picture the look on his face as he kicked that wall.

What if something has happened in that house that means that man is not the man I think he is, at all?

Something bad enough to make a woman leave her newborn baby.

I google again.

This time it's not about Romilly.

One word, Marc. One word.

Sociopath.

Day #4, 12.30 p.m.

The Husband

Fleur, in her Moses basket, has dozed back off into a post-milk sleep so that she looks like me after eight pints. I smile at her, touch those wisps of hair lightly. I'm sure Loll would tell me it's not physically possible, but she makes my heart hurt.

Right now, I am that specific mix of exhausted and wired and completely in love, as Fleur naps.

I nod off on the sofa and each time I stir, I sit bolt upright and check my phone for news from Adam, even though the second I am awake I know it's too soon.

As I check that Fleur is still gently snoring, reach over to touch those wisps of hair, I drift off again.

Over and over it goes.

In my half-asleep state, my mind starts exploring the before.

Walking into the Goodness Café on my day off to say hello to Romilly at work and grab a free coffee. I think I was partly checking up on her that day; making sure she wasn't overdoing it. She was three months pregnant: the day before we had been at her twelve-week scan.

I sat down and looked over at her in her black Nikes, right hand on hip, left holding avocado-smeared plates, chatting to some regulars with a big smile on that tiny face, bump beginning to jut out into the world.

She hadn't spotted me yet and for some reason I didn't want

her to for a little longer. I wanted to watch Romilly, in her natural environment. Didn't want to spike the bubble.

God, I loved her.

An older man handed her a glass with the remnants of something orange in.

He had what looked like a grandchild on his lap. He squeezed the child hard. 'They're the best, kids.'

He glanced at her middle; I saw her hesitation to bring up her own 'baby' at this stage.

I was standing next to her before she noticed me and when I touched her on her arm, she jumped.

When I hung around she offered me her polenta and pistachio cake but I pulled a face and asked if they had any sticky toffee.

I remember looking around then as she went to check and thinking this was her world: a Morcheeba album played that I knew she had picked; the music was her soundtrack. On the wall was a chalkboard scrawled all over in Romilly's writing: yoga class times, painting workshops, calligraphy courses, the monthly walk and talk.

The place was more than just a café; a community hub. Romilly, as the manager, had made it that way.

My wife booked local artists to run sculpture classes and chefs for Korean cooking courses. She knew everyone's name and she thought carefully about what they'd like, what would make this place work just that bit harder for them.

Lots of people came to do their jobs at the Goodness Café at 9 a.m., set themselves up in the corner, didn't leave until 5 and considered the other regulars their colleagues. Romilly worked long hours. It wasn't her place, but it might as well have been. She longed for the day that it could be. There, or an equivalent.

'Daydreaming about that café again,' I said to her once as she plotted with Steffie in our garden.

'I think the word you're looking for is planning,' said Steffie. She was smiling but her tone was short. She never likes being treated like she's silly, Steffie. She certainly doesn't like being patronised by men.

Romilly and Steffie joked that there was only one thing it can be called, when you live by the sea with the surname Beach. Beaches Café would happen, they said. It was just a matter of when. I looked at our finances and knew otherwise: if people said I was a dreamer, these two were worse.

'Hey, Bob, we're starting a book club next month,' Romilly said that day as she walked away from the café table. Took some chalk out of her back pocket and wrote the book club onto the schedule. 'You love your historical fiction, right? You should come. This author's being called the new Mantel.'

And as she made this man smile, I stared at her, looking as radiant as all the clichés would describe, even though I knew she had had to eat a whole ham pizza for breakfast that morning to stem the nausea that was persisting, when she was usually an unwavering vegan.

'Desperate times with these cravings,' she had muttered, as she shoved in the final slice. 'Bloody good job you had that in the freezer.'

It was 8 a.m.

I had laughed, kissed the top of her short black hair. The sight of it still surprised me sometimes. But she pulled off anything, Romilly: you do, with eyes like that. With a face like that.

'Always happy to oblige with emergency supplies of morning pig,' I said. 'Though most people would prefer a bacon sandwich at this time but whatever works, right?'

She retched. 'I know it's a terrible thing to be in denial about what meat is, and that if I ate it I have to face that, but just . . . can you not call it pig again? At least not while I'm pregnant?'

She stood up and hugged me and groaned into my chest.

Now, Fleur wakes and I pick her spindly body up, hold her close to me, in this half and half state of awake, asleep, past, present.

Loll puts her key in the door; out of breath. It's been fifteen minutes since Aurelia left, and that's the longest Fleur and I have been left alone.

My eyes droop again.

However the midwife spoke to me.

However Loll catches my eye sometimes.

Whatever Aurelia hinted at.

However I feel like even *Steffie* has started to look at me.

That one thing is true: on that day, in that moment, Romilly and I were happy.

Always the husband is reductive.

There's no such thing as always and what it really means is: look close.

But I am not the only one who is close to Romilly.

Look at the sister, I think.

Look at the mother.

Look at the best friend. Even look at *my* best friend. I've started to.

Look at them all closely.

And don't blink first.

Day #4, 5 p.m.

The Best Friend

Henry is getting older now, seven, and most of the time he walks more slowly than I would like. If I had my own dog, I'd get a puppy, matching me like for like for energy levels, for enthusiasm, for silliness. I'd be one of those irritating people who runs with their dog on a lead, carefully knotted bag of poo jigging along on my jog.

Right now though, the slower pace works.

I hold Henry's lead in one hand, my shoes in the other, bare feet on damp sand.

At points I try to break into a slightly faster walk, speed him up. He doesn't take the hint.

Henry's a guy who moves at his own pace.

Doesn't everyone in the end?

Eventually we stop, and I sit, staring out at the vast space of beach with a tide so far out it's hard to believe it could lap at your feet, that you could jump in and swim. But you can. She could. She did.

I stroke Henry's head and he backs up into me for a leg tickle. I smile. Happy to oblige, my friend.

I've always thought Henry's mentality is how we should all live our lives. His first thought cynicism-free; 'how much fun would that be' as a default. No preconceptions about people. No grudges. Just a desire to be a friend.

I sigh. When did it stop being so simple?

I try Adam again. He was due to land three hours ago but so far, still nothing.

Still, I think, she's a lost wedding ring in the long grass; impossible, surely to find.

I shift in the sand.

'Steffie!' shouts a voice I don't recognise immediately but associate with a reaction and it's one of deflating, slowly but surely, a birthday balloon the week after a party. It's a feeling that effort is coming; effort that is not worth it. I know what this is: it's the looming presence of an acquaintance.

'Leonie, how are you?' I say as a shadow falls above me but then she sits down, places a hand on my arm, tilts her head slightly to the side like she is stretching after a particularly gruelling run. She ignores my question.

'How are *you* doing, babe? I heard about Romilly.'

You heard, but not as much as you'd like to hear, I think. And honestly, the babe thing for a woman in her thirties you see around once a year? Not working.

But her eyes are bright. She's waiting.

Leonie went to school with Romilly and me. In a class of twenty at primary school, we were – an anomaly of a year – the only three girls. While Romilly and I stuck close, our bare legs sticking out on the school carpet, one long pair, one short, next to the practical trousers of the boys, those lucky fuckers, the dynamic with Leonie never worked. She would be at the other side of the carpet, outside of our world. I don't know why. Nothing wrong with her. Just didn't work.

Now, her bare legs are back, stretched out next to mine on the sand. She is looking at me, I can feel it, but I continue to stare out to sea. Will myself to say something. The seconds go by. She starts to shift, uncomfortable. I surprise myself by not mirroring her reaction. But I don't care how awkward this is for her. I'm good with silence. And I don't have this conversation in me.

'I'd better go,' I say eventually. 'The dog needs to get back.'

As I head away from her, she shouts. 'Romilly's dog, right?'

I nod my head but I doubt she sees and I keep moving away from her, away from a world that thinks my friend's disappearance is gossip.

I imagine her getting home to her boyfriend. 'Those two always were a bit weird,' she would say, but perhaps I am turning her into more of a bitch than she is. Were we weird? We certainly didn't care about making friends outside of each other, if that's the definition. Our twosome didn't shift, like friendships normally do in school days, to encompass a third, a fourth, to replace each other even. Instead we stuck and stayed, content with our choice, knowing it couldn't be bettered. Hushed voices, heads close. We had our secrets, Romilly and I, always.

I walk as fast as Henry will let me, off the beach now, in between stopping to smell his favourite lampposts; a deep sniff at each like he's just sat down in front of a glass of fine wine.

I have Leonie in my ear, Adam in my head, but Romilly drums the hardest, right in my chest even though I have gathered no real pace.

Henry stops again. His favourite bush this time. Little dig at the grass close by.

Eventually, we move on.

A couple of minutes from the house, I see someone turn onto the pavement. A man. Early twenties perhaps but you know what, I am reaching that age where that could mean he was fifteen. Hands tucked deep into jean pockets. A flash of red hair. Nike trainers break into a sprint and then he is gone, round the corner. On foot; not a delivery driver.

Did he come out of Marc and Romilly's drive?

I frown.

'Home, Henry Dog,' I mutter as we turn into the path.

And I am barely through the unlocked door when Marc appears, triumphant.

'Adam just called,' he says. 'He's landed. Gone straight to the lake. We're getting closer, Stef, we're getting closer!'

The drumming intensifies.

But now it feels like Romilly is pummelling my insides, telling me to hold him back. *What did you do Steffie, what did you do?* And I do not blame her.

What *did* I do?

Day #4, 6 p.m.

The Best Friend

Oblivious to the horror that I feel etched on my face for the few seconds before I catch myself and reorder it, Marc picks me up and scoops me round. My trainers hang in the air, my arms dangle like a scarecrow.

Or a limp, dead body.

'We're going to find her, Stef!' he says. 'We're going to find her!'

He is on fire. Set alight.

The dog wanders away from me as I let go of his lead. Marc keeps hold of me even though I go to pull away, his grip a little too tight.

It's a humid day – another one – and my body drips sweat.

He doesn't know that Adam isn't communicating with me. Why would he? To know that he would have to know what I told Adam. And there's no way my boyfriend has thrown that into the mix.

No, instead Adam has decided to plough ahead with his initial task and block me out. He presumes I'll fall into line later. That I am overreacting.

You didn't *see* the message Ad, I think. If you had, you would get it.

'Marc, you're hurting me,' I say, and when he pulls away I can see indents on my upper arms.

But he is too distracted to say sorry.

When we walk into the kitchen, I get some food out for Henry and fill his bowl. He eats like Adam, face down in cereal.

I look at Marc and he is stretching his arms above his head, doing tiny little jumps up and down. Like he's warming up.

Marc is high. High on news, high on hope, high on something finally moving on.

It's why he hasn't noticed my reaction. I don't matter. He's got his own buzz.

'Henry's sandy,' I say. 'I'll take him round the back and hose him off.'

He looks irritable then, Marc, and I know it is because he wanted to deliver a monologue to me and I haven't allowed him to, and now he has no audience.

No one to share his joy at potentially getting his ill wife home safely, you mean? says a voice in my head, probably Adam, giving him the benefit of the doubt, reminding me that Marc isn't a bad guy. He isn't.

Is he?

Round the back of the house, as I spray the hosepipe at a delighted Henry, I take my phone out and stare at it, willing it to beep. Come on, Ro. Talk to me again.

My hands shake with a responsibility that is paired awkwardly with a lack of any control. The hosepipe slips out of my grasp.

'I wish I could see her,' I murmur to Henry, who is in the middle of a full body shake.

I get the hose back on him.

I could tell what was going on if I saw her. How are you supposed to judge this over two texts and guesswork?

I sit on the grass, still hosing long after the dog is clean. I feel sweat tickling in my armpits.

I turn the tap off and Henry barks in complaint. He is currently trying to drink the water direct from it.

'Sorry, pal,' I tell him. 'Greater good, save the water and all that. It's never just about us and what we want, sadly.'

He gives one final, almighty body shake and my clothes are soaked.

Guilt picks at my insides like a toothpick and I feel that niggle that comes with time pressure; with not being able to mull something over until it's clear in your mind, until you know your answer.

I don't have that luxury.

If Romilly is ill, or a danger to herself, then I have to act.

If Marc has done something so terrible that it means Romilly has needed to flee, then I have to act.

My decision on which of those two I believe will have lasting consequences, for people I love, for a baby that I have surprised myself by already adoring.

It's clear that Adam believes Marc and Loll. And why wouldn't he?

When Henry is dried off, I take him back inside.

Marc smiles at me, the oddness of before abated.

'Coffee?' he asks. 'No, let me dig you out a fancy herbal tea.'

When the kettle is on, he comes over, hugs me. He is happy, for the first time since his wife disappeared. And how can I begrudge him that?

But nothing in me feels the same. My fingers pick at nails that are as low as they can go.

The dodgy bulb flickers on and off. I have started to become obsessed with it. Why won't he just *change the bloody bulb*? I squeeze my eyes closed.

Tick, tick, tick.

'I appreciate everything you're doing, you know,' he says, voice loaded suddenly with emotion. 'Juggling work, being here all the time, all that you do for Fleur, walking Henry, picking us up food.'

He lets go. Holds my hand.

'I know you're Romilly's friend but I love you too, and I couldn't do this without you.'

He hugs me again, even tighter this time and full and I feel that same feeling again, like I can't breathe, like I need to open the door and gasp.

He's saying all the right things.

And my gut instinct tells me to not believe a word of them.

Day #4, 6 p.m.

The Husband

I watch Steffie, walking around my house, unpainted and bitten fingernails spread out across a mug with the string of a herbal tea bag dangling over its side.

I suspect she was close enough to home to see the guy leaving my house, but she hasn't mentioned it or asked who he was.

Why, Stef?

'Are you wearing Romilly's slippers?' I ask, but it's not a question because I know what my wife's slippers look like.

And that's them on feet sticking out the back of them, two, three sizes too big.

She looks down, like she's forgotten she had them on.

'Yes. Sorry. Is that not okay?'

I shrug.

Where are the boundaries now anyway?

The familiar smell of peppermint and liquorice permeates the air. Romilly's favourite. Of course that's what she chose.

When two people are as close as Steffie and Romilly, and have been that way for so long, it's inevitable that there will be many similarities. But sometimes it's like I'm still living with her, and it's too much, at moments, too much.

She bites a carrot, whole.

Tilts her head back to stretch.

Stop being Romilly.

Stop it.

Stop.

Irrational, I know.

It's not her fault. Not really.

Today is a good day. Ten minutes ago I was euphoric.

But now I've crashed.

I need to get outside.

In everyone's efforts to help, they've stripped my world down to existing almost completely within these walls. I have no purpose to leave. Shopping – with its wrong brands, its random items – is piled high in my fridge again before it's had time to dwindle; the dog is walked regularly.

Are they *trying* to keep me inside, imprison me?

Well if they are, they won't succeed today.

It's a hot day. I need the air. I need the space. I need to make a call, alone, urgently.

'I'm taking Fleur out,' I tell Steffie. 'We might be a while. If you leave, can you lock up and put the key under the black bin?'

'I'll take her,' she says, and I shake my head, firm.

'No,' I say. 'Like I say, you've done so much. I appreciate it. But it's my turn: I will take my daughter for a walk.'

'But Loll says . . .'

I stop. Interesting.

'Loll says what?'

Steffie shrugs. 'Just that we should try to take the pressure off you. Be around.'

When I go to set the pram up I realise I don't even know how to do it and I know then that it's true, they *have* clipped my wings; made it impossible for me to function. I wasn't being paranoid.

'Can I help?' asks Steffie, but I snap at her that I'm fine, I can do it. Then I wrestle with it, swearing, kicking it into submission.

Five minutes later though, Fleur is in her pram, tiny feet covered by a blanket, and I am about to open the front door when my phone rings.

'Hey, man,' I answer. 'How's it going?'

From the hall I see Steffie's shoulders lift on the sofa where her head is buried in her phone, her jaw stiffen. What's that about?

In the background of my call to Adam, I can hear crickets, whisking me away to walking home with Romilly from a Spanish restaurant, the sangria having loosened our limbs and tongues on a trip to Barcelona soon after we met, our shoulders tinged with the day's sun. Sunglasses on our heads from when we'd still needed them at the start of the evening. Clothes sticking to our bodies. We would fall asleep to the sound of those crickets; windows wide open even though no breeze could cool our bare skin; the nights were too still.

'Mate,' Adam says back. 'Can you hear me?'

Was I dreaming then? Barcelona felt real. Was it just an intense daydream? Fuck, I am losing it. The sleep deprivation of a newborn, man. That and your wife leaving you in the midst of it.

'I'm not sure what just happened. Sorry, Ad,' I say. 'Go on.'

I feel dazed. Fleur makes a noise like she is irritated by the delay to our walk and I slip a dummy into her mouth.

'Okay so I feel like I'm making progress,' he says. 'I went to the lake, spoke to some people about accommodation close by. Lot of fancy places by the sound of it but a couple of people brought up the same campsite that's a lot cheaper than the rest. Bit out of town and a faff to get to but I'm going to head there next and hope it's where she's staying.'

I nod. 'Mmm hmmm.'

Disinterested in the detail. I'm not booking a holiday: I just want news.

He carries on.

'Just hoping the campsite has availability tonight. Not to mention Wi-Fi and somewhere I can work . . . Like I say, it's quite pricey round here and it's getting into holiday season . . .' he says.

There's a pause that's loaded some weight onto the conversation. Am I supposed to offer to pay? I still don't know whether I'm getting paid myself after next week. And how much this search and whatever comes next is going to cost. There's no way I can pay for Adam's trip.

I stay silent. Ride it out.

'But it'll be fine,' he says, sounding like it won't be.

I glance up. Steffie is watching me talk. I step back. Look down. She is still wearing Romilly's slippers.

'Okay, man, right I'm going to go now – I'm just taking Fleur out for some air.'

'Can't Steffie take her?' he asks.

I bristle. Wipe sweat from my forehead.

'I can do some things for myself. She is my daughter.'

Marc Beach, always seen as a big kid. Even now.

Adam is quiet. 'I was only trying to take something off your hands, mate.'

Yeah. But you've all taken so much off my hands that my hands are *desperate* for something to do, only they can't push a pram or hold a pint in the pub because I am supposed to be too traumatised to go out and so I sit here, in this house, hands empty, no use to anybody, just going over and over and fucking *over* how the hell this could have happened.

I sigh.

'I know, man. But it's fine. I need some air. Keep me posted when you get there.'

He clears his throat then and I know what's coming next makes him feel awkward; more awkward even than asking for money.

'Listen, mate, don't mention any of this to Steffie, okay? Let's wait until we get firm answers.'

I look at Steffie. Watching the conversation unfold even if she can't hear Adam's side of it; even if my contribution has been minimal.

I scrunch my forehead. Nod. 'Sure. Not a problem, man.'

My eyes rest on Steffie's. I don't *think* she could hear anyway. Why would Adam not want her to know?

Is there a dynamic I don't understand here?

'Any updates?' asks Steffie as soon as I hang up. She is fanning her face with a food magazine.

'Nothing yet,' I say. 'Hopefully soon. I'll be about an hour with Fleur. You may as well head home really, Stef – we'll be fine for the rest of the day. I'm planning on doing some more reading about maternal mental health as soon as Fleur sleeps. I want to know what we're dealing with, so we can get it sorted as soon as possible when we do get Romilly home.'

She goes to speak but stops herself.

There is a barely visible nod.

'I'll get my stuff and go now,' she says, and steps carefully out of Romilly's slippers. Puts Romilly's favourite mug down next to the sink. Hands back Romilly's life.

She stops just before she leaves.

'You know there are more storms coming? The rain has just started, I mean, for your walk . . .'

I don't answer.

In her hand is a rain cover for the pram. She hands it to me wordlessly.

As soon as I step outside, the rain quickens and begins to pummel me. I fit the rain cover while muttering to myself on the drive. A white van emblazoned with the logo of an oven cleaning company drives past too fast and soaks me.

'Fuck you!' I shout after them. 'FUCK YOU! FUCK YOU FUCK YOU FUCK YOU.'

I walk.

Faster.

Lightning marks the sky.

There was an odd mood as we walked out of the door and Steffie headed one way, Fleur and I the other, I think, as I put

150

one foot in front of the other through the rain, a large drip falling off the end of my nose. Fleur screams, furious, and then is so still that I have to take the rain cover off to check she is breathing. She starts to scream again.

Faster.

Break into a run.

There was no touch, I think, breath coming faster now as I hear thunder crack loudly despite the puffa jacket hood that is pulled up around my face and over my ears.

There was no eye contact.

A sense, suddenly, of the team disbanding. An end-of-term vibe.

And maybe that's a good thing.

I keep walking, keep running, until finally the rain relents.

Everything needs to end, Steffie.

Day #4, 7 p.m.

The Best Friend

And *still,* Adam declines my calls. Even as I am there to witness him phone Marc and fill Marc in on whatever is happening. As I watch him, clearly, ask Marc to keep me out of the loop, while I sit there redundant in Romilly's fluffy slippers.

We have divided down gender lines. Even though I have been in a relationship with this man for four years. Even though Marc only *knows* Adam because Ro and I introduced them.

I feel it again; a flash of furious scarlet.

When Adam finally speaks to me, he will say, I know, that this wasn't about me. That he had to focus on Marc. I'm collateral damage.

But the utter disregard for my opinion, for what I believe is happening . . . I feel a rage that hasn't come to me often in life. Stella level.

Because for the first time, as I change back into my trainers and walk away from Romilly's house and break into a run to clear my head and feel a fog lifting as I move, faster, faster, I am able to elucidate it.

The rain begins.

This is what I think.

I think that the reason Marc is so fixated on making us believe that Romilly has postpartum psychosis – handed to him on a plate as he had attended Romilly's appointments with her – is because he is using it to cover up something else.

Something that he did.

Heavier, now.

Something that is the reason my friend is so adamant that I don't trust him.

Something that affected Ro in those months before she gave birth.

I think that whatever he did, something even worse happened just before she gave birth, when she sent me that message that alarmed me so much.

The rain pounds down, means business.

And this time, that thing was so bad that it made Romilly leave the country, just after her baby girl was born. Made her feel she had no choice.

All of which means that Marc is not the man I thought I knew.

Here is what Google tells me about sociopaths:

Sociopaths lie. They are aggressive. They don't make long-term plans and they blind people with their charisma.

I picture that big kid, up there on stage with his band.

Sociopaths don't feel guilt if they have harmed others. They could carry on as normal.

They could make you a cup of tea.

They could take a bite of carrot cake, smile and tell you the cake tasted good. They could say they loved their wife or their child. But that would be fake.

My stomach plunges.

I speed up, heading towards a sprint as the rain gets heavier, as lightning strikes the mid-afternoon sky.

What I still haven't figured out is whether Loll genuinely believes that her sister has postpartum psychosis too. And if she doesn't, why she is going along with it. She knows so much about this condition; she would wade through freezing seas for Romilly. So where does she fit into whatever has been going on?

My breathing gets shorter. Droplets of rain drip from the end of my nose.

Marc has, I realise, given himself the perfect get-out. Even if Romilly gets in touch with me, by now he thinks he has convinced me that she is ill.

And so whatever she tells me, I will not trust her words.

My trainers pound the pavement.

The thunder comes; the rain torrential now.

Marc is betting that the risk is too great. That it is precisely *because* I am her best friend that I will help to bring her back to him.

He is banking on that fact, more than anything.

Like I'm a jury. *Beyond reasonable doubt.*

I am fit but my breath catches as I move faster, faster through this furious storm.

What he's not banking on is what happens now, as I turn into my road on the way back from Romilly's house and my phone – finally, finally – rings with Ad's name on the screen.

'You fucker,' I say, panting hard and slowing to a walk. Inside my hood, I try to keep my phone dry. 'If you think we will ever speak again after all of this is over, if you think you're staying in the flat, you're mis—'

I am putting my key in the door of our home and shaking the rain from my face, still going, thinking about how much I want to punch him in the face – my newfound violent streak gathering pace now – as I hear it.

'Steffie,' a voice that I know so well but that has snapped apart, broken away from itself says.

'It's not Adam. It's Romilly.'

Day #4, 6 p.m.

The Woman

I am in the water when he arrives.

I have swum a slow breast stroke as far out as I can go, exhausted, legs jelly, a deep ache across my middle.

Running out of steam and treading water until I can muster the energy to swim back to shore, I look up.

And there he is.

Adam.

Standing on the edge of the lake.

He is barefoot. Trainers and socks on the sand next to him. He's been waiting for me to pause.

My chest tightens.

I scan the shore for Marc.

Eyes back to Adam.

No.

He confirms it with a tiny shake of his head: Marc is not here.

I realise then that I can reach the bottom of the water. Put my feet down. Scan around for an exit. The fight-or-flight reflex hasn't fully departed, even with Adam's assurance.

Is he round the corner? Waiting for the nod from his friend?

'I'm on my own, Romilly,' Adam shouts, as I take tentative steps over stone to shore. A few people turn. 'I'm alone!'

And that's when I lose it because empathy is what I didn't expect to receive ever again, after I did this: the most awful thing.

I stand there in the water, unmoving, except for the sobs that make my body convulse. I wait there as Adam wades in still clothed, scoops me up and carries me back to shore.

'Thank you,' I whisper as it starts to subside. We sit alongside each other on shale. My breath is shallow. 'I know you will call Marc. But can you wait and hear me out first? Please. If you could just give me . . .'

Inexplicably, he nods.

Puts his phone back into his bag.

I see the screensaver: a beautiful close-up of my best friend Steffie.

Adam and I are silent on the drive back to the campsite along the narrow, one-car road.

There will be a time for talking, we know, but it is not now.

Instead, air con ineffective in a cheap hire car, we open the windows and the crickets do the chatter for us.

I lurch to one side as Adam pulls over for a much faster local driver.

'Sorry,' he mutters.

I shake my head. That's all we can manage.

When we get there, Adam and I sit outside my tent under the shade of the awning with a beer each. I am still in swimwear, dry now with the heat though; a towel wrapped around me. The pool is closed, the bar too, even the long-running early evening games of petanque have come to an end. Most people are out now, exploring the nightlife of the region, eating rare steak, making plans over fish stew and a rosé to be up early tomorrow to see the Pont Du Gard; hop on a boat at the Calanques.

'Is no one else here with you?' Adam says eventually, glancing into my tiny one-person tent, picked up when I arrived here. There had been no planning, of course. 'We didn't think . . . Well, the midwife suggested someone must have helped you. That you couldn't have left the hospital alone.'

I take a deep gulp. 'Oh. Oh right. No, I didn't do it alone.'

Adam frowns. A woman walks past the tent, in her sixties, a little tipsy, waves at us.

'*Bonjour!*' she yells. '*Bon Vacance!*'

I see us then as she sees us: a quiet British couple, having a quick drink on our holidays.

I smile back, no joy. Reach up and smooth down some frizz that I can feel springing up on my forehead. Not quite.

She carries on past to her tent.

'There's no one in France with me,' I say. 'But I did get help before that.'

He raises an eyebrow for more. I don't elaborate. Other things are more important.

'Is the baby okay?' I ask Adam. I note the pronoun I choose; I don't deserve *my*.

Adam leans back in the camping chairs the site provided. I was lucky, to find somewhere to stay at such short notice. I needed it last night. And by the time I had done what I came here to do today there were no flights back until tomorrow.

'She's awesome.' He smiles, speaking slowly, like too much emotion or noise might break me. Afraid of poking me now, scared and unsure of what the hell I will do next. If she could do *that* . . .

'Do you want to see some pictures?'

I shake my head, my heart racing, looking away. Panic sets in. No. No. The only way this has been okay is by blocking out the baby. I took a long route to my tent earlier to avoid the play area; looked away when I saw those toddlers splashing their little fists in the pool.

'How did you find me?'

He tells me about Steffie finding that scrap of paper.

I remember then, how I wrote the name of the lake down when I saw it on Instagram in a quiet moment at work. Shoved it there when someone came over with an order.

'Steffie knows me back to front and upside down.'

I'm pretty back to front and upside down now, as it happens.

But when he tells me about the local news sighting, the police CCTV, he throws me. I have been so consumed by the impact on my family that I hadn't considered this reaching wider.

Adam puts his beer down. Leans forward, interlacing his fingers.

We sit in silence, realising how loud that white noise of the crickets has become here too.

After a few minutes, I look at him.

'I will talk, Adam,' I promise him. 'But get us another drink first, hey?'

He grabs the beers from the cool bag – no joy, like we're topping up the morphine drip, a necessity for what it accompanies.

And then, I start to speak.

It's messy.

This won't be easy.

But here is what drives a person to walk away from their family. From their home. From a human being who was attached to their insides only hours before. Here is what drives a person to do what I did: that most awful thing.

Day #4, 7 p.m.

The Woman

It was two days before I would, unbeknown to me then, go into labour and I was at the dentist. I stepped out of the door, bump first, when Marc's bandmate Macca appeared behind me.

'Romilly! Thought that was you. Here, let me help,' he said, getting the door. 'How are you doing?'

'Not seen you for an age,' said Macca as I turned to him on the pavement. 'Wow, nice hair.'

I touched my growing-out crop, self-conscious. It was nearly at my bum the last time he saw it.

'Well, you rock stars tend to keep the family away from the scene, I suppose,' I said. 'What goes on tour to your shed at the bottom of the garden stays on tour in your shed in the bottom of the garden, right?'

Macca laughed. 'Exactly right, Romilly, exactly right,' he said. 'In between fillings and X-rays on my back teeth, I am quite the rock star. Not that we're heading for much fame soon until we get a new guitar player of course.'

He looked at me.

'That shed at the bottom of the garden is missing your husband,' he said, mussing up his hair lightly. 'Still can't believe he left us. We were on the brink of something big!'

Macca was taking the piss out of himself, and the others, when he said they were on the verge of something big. But I tell you who would say they were on the verge of something

159

big all the time, and believed it? Marc. Marc was going to be a rock star. Which made what Macca was saying all the odder. I stayed silent, because I was embarrassed that I didn't know what he meant. Because I was confused. Because I thought silence could be the best route to finding out what he meant, without shaming myself and my marriage.

'Four months since he handed his notice in and we can't find anyone half-decent,' Macca ploughed on. 'It's music's loss, Romilly, music's loss.'

My stomach would have lurched, if there wasn't so much else going on in my insides.

Instead my throat did the work, filling up with bile.

Four months. Four months since Marc started lying to me.

As Macca carried on talking, I started to back away, muttering something about my belly needing a sofa.

Marc hadn't been in the band – the band that he formed his identity around – for four months. When we met strangers at weddings, Marc mentioned his day job managing a music shop as an afterthought. The band, his guitars, were the headline. His passion. And Marc was nothing if not passionate.

If he was doing something else when he said he was at his weekly practice at Macca's, it was something he loved more than the band.

A phone beeps, bringing me back to the campsite, to France, to now.

I look up, Adam glances at it.

Looks at me.

We both know who it is.

Adam's hand doesn't move towards it though, and it sits there, too far away for me to read but lit up, a little bomb.

I look around me. See two French teenagers bringing a stack of pizza boxes back for their family, an eight-pack of stubby beer bottles in their other hands. They smile over at Adam and me.

'*Bonsoir!*'

I smile. Raise a hand. When I look at Adam, he hasn't even bothered. His face is preoccupied. Looking at me with expectation.

I keep talking.

When I left Macca, I went to the beach, so many steps down that they put most people off from bothering and I still can't believe I did that; I was nine months pregnant.

But if you made that effort, the reward was how much beach you got to yourself. How much silence you got to yourself. A few dog walkers in their wellies. Not much else. It was starkly juxtaposed with the tourist beach a mile up the coast; buckets and spades for sale, six different options for an ice lolly.

'When I was there, I called Loll,' I tell Adam.

His phone beeps again.

He puts it away in his pocket without looking at it.

'There is no one more honest than my sister,' I tell Adam. 'Loll is a straight talker. When I told her what had happened with Macca, she must have asked me twenty times why I couldn't just *ask* Marc where he was going.'

'And why didn't you?'

'Because I was heavily pregnant and I didn't want to deal with it. Pathetic, eh?'

At the beach, I thought hard.

Before I got pregnant, I did all of my best thinking as I swam in those freezing Thurstable waters that made my heart slow and my mind fizz. Moving, that determination it took, cleaned my mind like a glasses wipe. I would have done anything for that feeling that day.

But I couldn't go in the water. Not then.

Instead, I watched the people in wetsuits on their paddleboards, in kayaks. That's the kind of beach it is: you go there to be active; it's too cold to stay still.

I tucked my chin into my coat collar.

When the wind blew, the cold was sharp.

I wiggled my bum forward, inched a little closer to the sea's edge. Dug my fingers into the damp sand. I thought of my old frame, wading easily out to deep waters from the shore.

A slimy lake. A toad-green pond. I'll get in any outdoor water I can find. But mostly it's been there, on our local shoreline where I grew up paddling in the water, thinking thirteen degrees was balmy.

It's not a boastful coastline, ours. Not showy. It's not the Faux France of the South Coast; there's not the drama of Scotland. But it's mine. I see beauty.

Any window I could, I pulled on my wetsuit and I swam.

'Not being able to do it that day, when I needed it the most,' I murmur. 'That was hard.'

Wetsuit on, a woman about my age pulled a paddleboard out, wading until she was deep enough for the fin not to catch. She was experienced, on in seconds, graceful as she knelt, her paddle digging into the water. I was far from her chest but I could still see her breathe out. Leave her day behind. Work through whatever she had to work through.

It's a meditation, whatever you do in the water. In, out, forward, onward.

I sighed. Lay on my side on my elbow on the sand and watched. My stomach was being punched rhythmically from the inside; hey, baby. They would be on the outside soon; I could trace their outline through my belly.

Over the next hour, the paddleboarders moved further and further away. Above me the noise from the microlights that always hovered above this part of shoreline became louder, only rivalled by the unembarrassed squawk of the gulls.

That night, funnily enough, was band practice. At 7 p.m., I was in my regular position in the only spot I could now get comfortable in on our sofa. Pregnancy pyjamas on.

Marc bounded downstairs and pulled on his Converse. No guitar in his hand; normally I'd have assumed it was in the hall, or he'd put it in the car already. Now I noted its absence.

'Heading to Macca's?' I said, finding my bump a shelf on a cushion.

The look he gave me was odd.

'Course,' he said.

I knew there had been four months of them but this one, this outright lie to my face, still came as a shock.

I stared at him.

'What?' he asked. Eye contact too. Nice.

I shook my head: nothing. Turned on a bad dating show. Slipped my hands under the cushion to hide the fact that they were shaking. Said goodbye.

When he left I turned the TV straight off and sat in silence, picturing him in various scenarios.

I'll have this baby, I thought, at first – then we'll come back to this. But while he was out, I thought fuck that: I'm not scared of being a single mum. But I am scared of being lied to for my whole life.

I am scared of the man Marc has become.

I turn to Adam.

'It wasn't out of the blue, Marc behaving weirdly. The band practice thing was a shock but there had been things in our life that had happened that no one knew about, Adam.'

Adam moves his sunglasses up off his eyes and looks at me.

'Including me?' he says.

I nod.

'Including Steffie?'

And again.

I was scared of drifting further from who I was. Being pulled away from friendships. Craving junk food like I never had, shovelling it in for comfort. Being stalked around the café with his impromptu visits. Told my career is pointless; *don't build up*

your part with all this 'community hub' shit, you're a fucking waitress.
Reminded that I am stupid, stupid, stupid. Made to watch Marc's
band play on YouTube over and over and fucking over, so I
understood how good he was: so I understood that it was *my*
fault he didn't make a career out of it. I wasn't supportive enough,
see. That's my problem. I never am.

I was scared of all of it; of that drip-feed being my life, of
what it would do in the end to my soul.

I felt a surge.

Touched my hair then, as I sat on that sofa and wondered
where my husband was, and remembered.

The next thing I remember are fingers that pressed, and pressed,
and pressed.

It's 1 a.m. Marc just home from wherever he had been instead
of band practice.

I was finally asleep; the discomfort of late pregnancy meaning
it had taken this long to manoeuvre into position.

I woke up to my husband pulling at my thick pyjamas.

'I'm scared, Marc,' I whispered, curled childlike, tired deep
inside my bones. 'The baby feels so low.'

I was nervous. All I wanted was a hug.

He carried on pulling.

My body tensed.

'Marc, I'm scared,' I repeated. 'I'm scared for the baby.'

I twisted my body away, not tired anymore.

A beat.

And then he stood up. Slammed the door behind him.

The baby had saved me, I knew. I was under no illusion.

Downstairs, I heard a bottle smash against the wall.

The noise made me jump so much I was scared again, for
the baby, and counted its kicks for hours. When he came back
up, I had finally dozed off.

I was shaken awake.

'D'you know how humiliated you made me feel then, rejecting me? Why do you do this?'

Gin on his breath made me gag.

I apologised, to make it end.

'No,' he breathed. 'I want to *explain* to you how it made me feel. You're my wife. You are supposed to listen if I'm upset.'

My eyelids sagged.

'In the morning . . .' I whimpered. Begged.

He shook his head. Heaved me out of bed. This couldn't wait. He pulled me out of our bedroom.

'I'll make you coffee. That'll wake you up.'

I was pregnant and couldn't even have coffee; he knew that. Didn't matter. He was in a zone that didn't incorporate the real world.

'I was so tired that I stopped to get myself together. He shoved me, told me to keep moving.'

I inhale suddenly now. Or gasp.

'Are you okay?' asks Adam.

I nod. But the humidity makes me feel like I can't breathe. That, or the remembering.

I try to breathe deeply.

I was wrong to think my pregnancy would protect me. In the end, he couldn't stop himself.

'Adam,' I say. A beat. 'When Marc pushed me, I was right at the top of the stairs.'

Day #4, 8 p.m.

The Woman

Does Adam's sharp intake of breath mean this is going in?

I take a swig of water, gulp it down, and watch his face.

When I'm done, I pick up my story.

'You know our stairs – they're steep and I went fast,' I say, quiet, the first time for these words, so alarming even to me.

But they are tumbling out now.

'Marc sobbed and sobbed, wept that what if he had hurt the baby, but I had no time to comfort him. I didn't want him near me. He was in no fit state either, drunk on the gin he had swigged before he threw that bottle. So I drove myself to hospital at 2 a.m. for a scan, ignoring the aches, the pains, the bruising, to check my baby was okay.'

I should have told them, of course, what had really happened. That's a huge regret now. Then it would be on record.

I didn't. I told them I had tripped. My pregnant body toppled over with its imbalance on the way for a glass of water.

Heavily pregnant, my body had expanded, swollen, magnified but sitting on that plastic chair, alone in the middle of the night, I felt like half a person. As I lied to doctors. As I murmured to my baby to please be okay, please be okay. As I thought that I had put this baby in this position, me, by staying with Marc.

'Next time, get your husband to get your glass of water,' said the sonographer, with a tut, an eyebrow raise. 'Men, eh? Where is he now, too?'

I murmured something about work.

Men.

She had no idea.

As I drove home, I wept from exhaustion. I was due in work in a few hours, knew I would have to call in sick. And then what – could I *leave* him? What would he do? Where would I go?

All these thoughts were buzzing around when the car swerved and I looked up suddenly to see something that seemed wrong.

A fence. Right in front of me.

Shit.

'Oh, Romilly,' murmurs Adam.

I look up at him. Shocked by his presence for a second. Brought back to the now.

'I fell asleep driving home from hospital,' and the tears start to fall. 'I had been up all night.'

They roll down my face.

'Nine months pregnant, and I fell asleep at the wheel.'

Day #4, 8.30 p.m.

The Woman

On the campsite now, I have pins and needles in my foot from sitting cross-legged for so long and I stand up and stamp it out on parched grass, as much as a flip-flop allows. I wipe away tears I hadn't noticed that have smeared my cheeks.

'Luckily I swerved at the last second. Luckily the roads were quiet. Luck. Just luck. That's how we made it. The only reason we are here.'

Not quite here. Oh, my baby. We were one entity that night. Now look at us.

'Once I got home from hospital, Marc was his best self,' I tell him. 'Oh God, the difference. The relief not to be battling. He had sobered up from the shock of it all, in tears with how much he loved me, loved our baby.'

He made me a hot water bottle. Called work for me and told them I was sick. Tidied the house while I slept. Brought me herbal tea and scrambled eggs in bed when I woke.

'I thought this had done it, given him a wake-up call.'

I laugh: ridiculous me.

'He didn't even know what had happened in the car. Didn't give me a chance to talk. And I thought, what was the point? But the panic about me falling down the stairs had flicked a switch. He was obsessed with being a dad. Of doing it better than his parents had. A new version of him, one who could start from scratch. I thought that maybe now, and with the baby coming, he would stop being so angry with me.'

I pictured it. All the trimmings of a thirty-something new start. A family car. A roof rack. New towels for the bathroom.

I look at Adam.

I'm not sure now if it feels good to finally, finally get this out, or terrifying. I have stopped identifying feelings, just know that something in me is heightened.

'Did you never notice anything?' I say.

I hear it: desperation.

Adam stares at me like he is taking an eye test.

Reaches for my hand.

'Marc told me you're experiencing postpartum psychosis,' he murmurs so quietly I can barely hear; he is deliberately gentle like he's easing a gun from a terrorist. 'And it feels . . . Romilly, it feels from the stuff you're saying, like that . . . like that would make sense. This isn't Marc you're describing. You know it isn't. Maybe this story is something you've read somewhere?'

It's a frightening sensation to go from focused and ploughing forward to being punched, slam-dunk in the gut and grounded like an aeroplane.

'If you're experiencing postpartum psychosis, it means you would have delusions.'

Beat.

'Paranoia.'

Beat.

'Suspiciousness.'

He believes it.

He is checking the symptoms off now on his fingers.

'I know what it fucking is, Adam. I've been monitored for it throughout my pregnancy. I have read papers on it. Whole books. Everything the internet has to give me.'

'And are you . . .'

I stiffen.

'Am I experiencing postpartum psychosis?' I interrupt him. 'No. I am not. But the problem is, as I'm sure Marc knows, that if I *was*, I wouldn't believe I was, so it is quite likely that no one will believe me when I deny it anyway.'

I hear my voice plead.

'He is *trying* to make me sound crazy, Adam. That's the point.'

Postpartum psychosis.

Of all the things, Marc.

But aren't I playing into his hands?

Adam can't hide his frustration with me.

'The thing is, Romilly, that even if this were true and weren't a delusion – no, hear me out – even if it were, then it still wouldn't make sense that you come *to France* when your newborn baby is lying in hospital. Would it?'

I twist the rings around my fingers, round, round, round.

'So why would you have done that, Romilly?'

'There is a woman,' I answer, as I look up at him. 'A woman I thought could help me to prove the truth about Marc. Ella, she is an ex of Marc's.'

Round.

Round.

Round.

'But she didn't?'

I swallow. Another thing that went so wrong. 'No. She didn't.'

Round.

And even as I am talking, I know I am handing it to Marc on a plate. I *sound* deluded. Of course Adam doesn't believe me.

He doesn't even bother to ask more about Ella or find out who she is. He thinks she is fiction.

'I've spent a lot of time with Marc lately,' he says instead, careful with each syllable. 'I can see how much he's hurting. And you as well though, Romilly! You've been through a lot.'

I stare at him. My friend. Sitting in front of me, looking me in the eye.

'You're acting out of character, Ro.'

'I'm acting out of character because of what he did to me, Adam.'

'But Ro. I know you. And I know that you would never leave your newborn baby, *ever*, whatever Marc did. Unless you were going through something that took you out of your normal headspace. This is the only explanation, Romilly, the only one I can believe.'

I feel my fists ball up.

God, of course. Of course. That's what he thinks I did.

'Adam, this wasn't me leaving the baby!' I tell him, voice raised though he is inches away from me, even though the teenagers eat their pizza close by, the adults have another vin rosé. 'This was only me leaving Marc.'

I picture it – how wrong it went – and it still makes me want to wail. The sadness of the irony.

'I didn't leave the baby, Adam,' I repeat. 'She got me out, and then she went back for the baby. But when she got back to the room, he was there. It was before 6 a.m.! There was no way he was supposed to be there then. He wanted to keep an eye on me, I suppose. As always. But it meant she couldn't bring the baby.'

I can hear his breath.

I can hear my own.

'She's been trying to get the baby back to me ever since.'

There is the distant splash of someone jumping into a pool in the distance at what must be a private house, holidaymakers fancying a post-dinner dip. A yelp of joy, or drunkenness, or both.

Their joy hurts when I am burning in pain. When this has gone so wrong. When all I want is my girl.

'Who?' he asks, an odd note in his voice. 'Who is she?'

And I realise he is terrified. Terrified that his girlfriend has been lying to him the whole time, and about what that means for them, their future.

The Woman

'My sister,' I reassure him. 'Of course, my sister, Adam.'

'Loll knew?' he says. 'But she . . .'

I think of my sister, who doesn't watch films or read fiction because she doesn't understand suspending your disbelief. Why would you waste your time, she says, when there are so many facts to learn? My sister is literal; a pharmacist who deals in fact and truth with everyone who walks up to the counter in our local chemist.

And yet, there she has been next to them on the sofa, lie after lie after lie.

I can see how this would be baffling to anyone to learn. But something else about Loll: she is thorough.

'She's been trying to stay on Marc's side – or to seem that way – so she could be his confidante and that way she could be alone with the baby,' I say quietly.

His chest rises and falls too quickly.

'So she could get her out and to me. I couldn't think straight to make any sort of plan but Loll could. The problem is that Marc never leaves the baby alone. Maybe a hunch that he'd better keep her close or somehow I'll come back for her.'

I twist my bangle now, around and around my wrist.

'He's good with her,' says Adam, a little defensive.

I nod. Not surprised.

'It's always been that way, Marc is brilliant with his nieces and nephews. Was far more into the idea of having kids than I ever was.'

I know how this stacks up in the public eye too: extra points for Marc for doing some basic parenting; minus points for me for being something so unnatural as an absent mother.

No wonder I am struggling to be believed.

Our baby was very much planned, steered by Marc. Wasn't everything? He had a handy little app for me; installed it on my phone one day when he was on there anyway checking my messages.

Carefully removed my underwear when the app told him he should.

I lay there the first time hoping it didn't work quite yet, that we had a little longer. We had only been together nine months.

I didn't get my wish.

But that's fine, I thought. That's fine. Didn't Loll shriek with joy when I told her I was pregnant, so soon after our wedding?

Didn't she tell me how rare it was to meet a man these days who *wanted* to settle down, wanted to have a family? And he was so good-looking too, wasn't he, she nudged me. Win win win win win.

So who was I to whine about wanting to wait a little longer? Me, a woman in my thirties, who'd had exes who wouldn't commit. How petulant! How ungrateful.

I come back to the now. Think, Romilly, think.

'Adam, did Marc tell you he sent me messages, after I left?'

Adam nods. 'Of course. Asking where you were. Begging you to come back. Reassuring you. He said he sent them constantly, the same as we all did.'

I laugh, kind of.

'Not quite the same,' I whisper.

In the distance there is the sound of dance music. A club up in the hills; the type that is a pilgrimage for any teenagers in a twenty-kilometre radius, deprived of cities, Marseille too far away, too young to appreciate their beautiful village and a rustic bistro. Still craving sweat, beer, chaos.

'Adam, the messages told me, over and over. Told me I would lose my baby because of this. That he would get me arrested or sectioned. I thought if I saw him again, it was one or the other.'

And that's why we're here, isn't it?

Those messages were an assault. By the end, I might as well have been unconscious in a ditch.

'It was too big a risk to take. I needed to get her back another way.'

I wipe a palm across my brow. My chest feels tight like it's wrinkled.

Adam puts his own head in his big familiar hands; knuckles dry as a bone. I look up, see the exact moment that the sun dips behind the mountains. And then to my side, at his face. Cheeks you want to pinch and kind eyes.

He still needs convincing.

'I thought if I went back, he would have her taken off me for good,' I press, repeating the point so he gets it. 'If I stayed away, Loll could bring her to me. Do you see?'

An emotional decision. A panicked decision. A parental decision, perhaps, even though I'm not naïve enough to know how many would question that justification.

Adam moves from the chair to sit on the floor, knees to his chest.

'No, Romilly, I don't see at all,' he says, patiently repeating. 'All I see, like Marc told me, is a woman experiencing a mental health condition who has lost sense of all reality.'

I hear his phone vibrate in his pocket.

See his fingers creep towards it.

I feel myself holding my breath.

Day #4, 9.30 p.m.

The Woman

I move down to the floor with him. Gingerly. Less than a week since I gave birth still. Everything hurts.

I grab his hand.

'Just listen to me before you speak to him,' I beg. 'At least do that. I'm in front of you. I can't come to any harm. Just hear me out and then you can do whatever you feel is right. You don't lose anything.'

Barely perceptible, but it's there: a nod. I cling to that. Something is stopping him telling Marc where I am. Even if it's as simple as the fear that I'll run.

His phone stays in his pocket.

'The first time it crossed over to being physical was on our honeymoon,' I say at a level barely beyond a whisper. My own knees are pulled in, a mirror to my friend. 'I mentioned in passing that Stef got on well with my ex. He lost it.'

He bows his head down low.

'How would this have happened without me knowing?' he says, without looking up. 'I can't have missed this. I know him too well.'

I don't want to sound world-weary; it's not a good look, not my vibe, but sometimes you can't help it and the world wears you down.

'I think that's a story we tell each other, Adam. About friendships, relationships, marriages. Does anyone see everything?'

In truth, the world has two layers, the ones we all share and let exist on the surface and the hidden ones that we ignore when we're asking if anyone wants the last spring roll or telling them about the new taps in the kitchen, all the while consumed with the lump in our breast or the brother who is suicidal. The real stuff rarely gets let out of its bag.

I need to get this out now.

'Did you know Marc had a bad time growing up?'

Adam sighs like a huff. 'Oh, Romilly, we all had a . . .'

I hold a hand up.

'Don't do that, Adam. Don't dismiss it. We all have our stuff but not like this. He carried it. What happened to him at school, the belittling, the torture from the other kids, has never gone away for him. I have tried to help. He didn't think he needed it. He is very, very good at hiding it. There can be long gaps between anything physical so that I'll convince myself that's it, explain away all other stuff, the mocking, the manipulation.'

Adam winces.

I remember it then; that conversation with his mum, in the early days of her dementia last year. We were meeting for the first time; Marc hadn't been keen but I had badgered him. It was important – me meeting his mother.

I combed my hair, which tumbled then all the way down to my bum. Ironed a pair of jeans.

'Well well well,' his mum boomed, louder than her frail frame would make you expect as we walked into the care home. 'You finally found someone who wants you. Just don't show her any of those pictures from high school. I'm not sure she could cope with that obese strange little man you used to be before you reinvented yourself. God, that skin! I couldn't eat my dinner if you were in the room.'

She shuddered. Pretended to gag.

Her grin, a second later, was wide and cruel.

His *mother*. I was shocked into silence.

I clutched Marc's hand. It smeared onto mine as he snatched it away.

I found my voice, then. Muttered some things. *None of us look our best as teenagers. I'm sure he was beautiful anyway. Et cetera.*

She leaned in so close I could smell her breath.

'Trust me,' she whispered. 'He wasn't. The only way he could get girls to go near him was to get them so drunk they didn't know what they were doing. So drunk they couldn't see those seeping spots, the pus, the . . .'

A nurse came along then. Spoke to Marc about upping his mother's medication.

On the way out, she shouted after me.

'It's spelt with a K really, you know! Don't let him pull the wool over your eyes that he's all exotic. He's just regular over-fat spotty Mark with a K!'

The laugh boomed and roared as we exited.

We did the other things we had planned to do on our trip to Sussex: headed to the beach, had dinner, before crashing out back at the hotel.

But there was a film of barely suppressed fury over my then fiancé for the rest of the day. I trod carefully. Held my breath.

I tell Adam the story.

'I imagine his mum has contributed,' I say. 'To how much he truly, truly *hates* women.'

Day #4, 9.45 p.m.

The Woman

'Okay, so if this were true,' says Adam. 'If we didn't see it, why didn't you tell us? We're good friends to you, Romilly. We wouldn't have ignored it, however we feel about Marc.'

I nod. I've asked myself this, a thousand times.

'I know how idiotic it sounds now . . .' I murmur, embarrassed.

Adam shakes his head. 'Nothing does. Just tell me.'

'I was convinced a baby would be a reset. That we'd have a new start. This would all fall away.'

It's hard to explain to Adam how all-consuming pregnancy was.

'I thought . . . we would be *parents*. How can you not have your shit together when you're parents, right? Ha. How naïve I was.'

In fact the more pregnant I got, the worse my husband became.

The bump grew and so did the anger The exposing of parts of Marc's personality that had peeked out from under the covers before, but tucked themselves back in. The resentment. The drip, drip, drip of comments and instruction during the day; roaring, heaving rage at night. The love bombing that had happened when we first met and used to rear its head every now and again was like a first hit of a drug and I tried to get back to it, if I could just say the right thing, do the right thing.

Everything shifted.

I wanted to find out what gender the baby was but Marc

wouldn't let me and a part of me thought *good, good. Put it off.*
Because if I knew I was having a girl I would have to face up
to something. While I never feared he would hurt a daughter
of ours as a child, once she grew up, became an adult woman
who could answer him back, stand up to him, get it wrong. . .
Yes. I feared that.

I look at Adam. Try to make something ring a bell.

Does he remember times when we weren't ourselves, Marc
and I? When he phoned Marc and his friend's voice was hoarse
from the way he had screamed at me, furious about this thing,
that thing, and I was too drained and scared for my baby to
argue back?

Does he remember that I ignored Steffie's calls, often – Marc
telling me our dependence on each other was odd, that she was
too clingy?

Does he remember that row Steffie and I had when she made
that flippant comment about my engagement ring not being the
one she would have thought I would pick, and I didn't speak
to her for a week? She was right, see. It wasn't the one I would
pick: it was the one Marc would pick. Sometimes I stared at it
and wondered if he had picked it before he met me even, for
someone else entirely.

If he picked it for Ella.

Another thought I blocked out. You had to block out a lot
of them, to survive.

In our house, where the sound used to come from Marc's
old record player blaring David Bowie on vinyl, now it came
from doors slamming, from glasses smashing. From Marc, forcing
his fist through the wall.

And then, silence. As I bandaged up my husband, as I cried
as quietly as I could, as I counted kicks again, lying on my left-
hand side and making sure that the venom that was growing on
the outside hadn't penetrated. Hadn't got to our baby.

But of course he didn't notice. Any energy I had left went

into painting a picture for the outside world: all is fine here. Fine, fine, fine.

In reality, I was living in a private hell that I – a talker – couldn't share at a time everyone thought I was happiest.

Now, here, I can't believe how much I managed to convince myself that the stuff Marc did during my pregnancy wouldn't follow us through into having a baby. And that the last person I would need on my team would be this man.

Steffie has always commented on it; the way society holds up parents as the real adults; every other over-eighteen simply play-acting, consumed with the frivolity of a non-parenting life.

I did that. And look where it led me.

'I grew up with a single parent, Ad; I told myself that *none* of this was important, compared to keeping my baby's family together.'

Do I say this, what comes next?

'Not even when he crossed uncrossable lines.'

Day #4, 10 p.m.

The Woman

I look at Adam, and I start to tell a story I never wanted to tell.

'Adam, being in that lake out here is the first time I've been swimming in seven months.'

Not because I was pregnant.

God, that wouldn't have been enough to stop me.

'So why?' asks Adam.

I bite my lip.

When it happened, we had been together for almost a year, married for four months. I went for a swim at the beach. It was a pretty cold afternoon, early evening really, and there wasn't another soul around.

Except suddenly, there was.

'Marc had turned up at the beach and was wading in after me. He was angry with me about something – spending too much time at the beach, yep the man could even be jealous of sea water. I tried to swim away from him but I was close to shore and had to wade and he reached out. Grabbed me.'

The air has tightened.

I swallow.

'There was no build-up, Adam. No warning.'

I try to breathe.

'He was already angry when he arrived.'

Twist my rings around, again, again, again.

'I didn't even have time to ask a question, to say something to snap him out of it.'

Twist.

Twist.

'He grabbed my face.'

I realise I am whispering. Shocked by my own words.

'He shoved it down with this *grip* . . . this grip that felt unmovable, Adam. I've never felt anything like it. It was unrelenting, like stone. That's the only way I can describe it.'

A whoop then, and a splash, as someone leaps in a distant pool. But I can barely register it. Now I've started, I have to finish.

'And then came the water. It felt like it was inside my brain. I tried and tried to turn my head but it was impossible.'

I look up at Adam. The whisper is even quieter.

'I had pretty much given up.'

I keep looking at my friend, this good man. I know it must be near impossible for him to comprehend such a bad one.

'So why did he stop?' Adam's voice is ice.

I sigh. 'He stopped because of what I did.'

I had to point to my stomach. I was under water and couldn't say the words: I'm pregnant. So I angled my finger down in the air and hoped he got the message.

Hoped that meant he would let me live.

Why hadn't I told him when I found out I was having a baby in the first place, the week before?

Because his rages had been getting worse.

Because I knew that once I said those words, *I'm pregnant,* to a man who had always wanted to be a father, there was no untangling myself. I couldn't be his ex Ella, who I knew from my searches had a new life in France. No. I would be tied up with Marc, like chains in a messy jewellery box, and there would be no unravelling us.

When he pulled me out of the water, he screamed at me for

not telling him and then wept as I lied and said I had only just found out; was waiting for a special moment to share the news.

Did he believe me? God knows. But there was an apology. Tens of them. Hugs. Excuses: he'd had a bad day, he never really would have done it, he was about to let me come up anyway, and at least maybe now I wouldn't be so *obsessed* with the water.

A towel wrapped around me and careful arms guiding me up the beach to home. I saw his face when he found out there was a baby.

I had been right: I was protected now.

'Or so I thought.'

You need more, Adam?

If you need more, I have more.

Uncomfortable, I clamber back up to the camping chair. Pull my knees up to my chest; my flip-flops dropping to the ground. I feel a mosquito on my big toe. Swat.

I reach to my right and sip from my water bottle. Tonight the weather is so close that even that feels like a major effort; I want to keep as still as I can to be able to bear the heat.

I look down at him, this friend of mine. Of ours. Or am I kidding myself? Marc's friend. Do I not stand a chance?

Adam moves round so he's facing me without cricking his neck. Says nothing.

I picture – as I have done so many times lately – Marc and me on our wedding day. Adam on his wing (was there something odd about that, in retrospect, that his best man was someone he had only known for a few months?), Steffie on mine. A field on our local farm overlooking North Wales; the place we picked up eggs from every week, sticking £1.50 in the honesty box and checking in on their veg cart. We had become friends with the farmers, Alicia and Jim, and their girls Trixie and Anastasia who roamed around in their wellies as they sold their giant cauliflowers and home-pickled beets. When I told them we were getting married, it was Alicia who suggested we did it there, even with the short notice. It was a dream of a suggestion.

The official ceremony was done and dusted at a registry office with little joy. But here, we went for it. My dress was vintage, its skirt the shape of a bell, bare feet on the grass. I had wanted to be pressing my toes into sand at the moment I said I do but the logistics of a beach wedding in the UK were too tricky, Marc said, and it was best we did it quickly; why hang around, he wanted to get on with having a baby.

Grass it was then, and it wasn't a bad second.

As the humanist minister said her words, I looked across at the view we had in Thurstable to the dramatic Welsh mountains. *This place*, with its hundred shades of blue, ink spilt, open fountain pens thrown carelessly across the sky.

I looked back at Steffie. Downwards at my feet, specks of mud across the big toe.

As I said 'I do', I looked right in the eye of an alpaca. When Marc echoed me, a horse brayed loudly like a cheer. You could probably hear us laughing across the estuary; my grin was as wide as the aisle.

It would all be okay, I thought. Any hints of what were to come were just what life entailed. No one could be perfect all the time. So what if Marc sulked sometimes; so what if he had a temper? So what if some things I did irritated him? Did I think being an adult was all eggs Benedict for brunch and long weekends in Barcelona?

I look down now at Adam, still on the ground.

I see his phone sitting next to him.

I hand my water bottle down to him. He swigs. Passes it back.

I plough on, my grim, grim story unfinished.

The phone lights up again.

I know messages are pinging in from Marc.

And I know I am running out of time.

The Woman

'Two days after I fell down the stairs and had the accident, I went into labour. Three weeks early is pretty unusual for a first baby. Probably the shock.'

My whole body starts to shake at the memory. The last one before things went so badly wrong.

Adam paces a few steps across the campsite to put our bottles into the recycling; quick glance back at me over his shoulder. He thinks he is being subtle but I know that he is keeping eyes on me at all times. Monitoring me on Marc's behalf.

When he comes back he opens another beer.

'Want one?'

I shake my head. Two has already had an effect, after nine months sober.

I need to be lucid.

The day I went into labour was a Saturday. I was sitting on a birthing ball in the kitchen with my hospital bag spread out on the table in front of me, vests and tiny nappies and bottles of Lucozade spilling out everywhere. Repacking, again.

Fixating on all of those tiny details you fixate on at that point in pregnancy. My head had never been so consumed by two behemoths simultaneously. It hurt. They flip-flopped. Pushed each other out for a front-seat place. Did I really need gardening mats in my changing bag? Was my husband cheating on me when he said he was at band practice? If I left him today, where would I take my baby home to? If I didn't leave him, would I be safe?

The bulb in the kitchen flickered.

'We must change that,' I thought, the last moments when the mundane mattered to me, before Marc walked in and the whole thing was set in motion.

'Hello,' I said.

He looked up. Grabbed the cafetiere. 'What's with the gardening mats?'

'To kneel on during the birth,' I said, embarrassed as I often was talking about these details. Boring me. Unsexy me. 'They mentioned it at NCT, remember? That it can be useful in some positions. Doesn't matter.' I laughed awkwardly.

'I think you've remembered that wrong,' he said, a scoff. 'I doubt she meant actual gardening mats.'

The adoration that had welcomed me home from the hospital had become boring to him now. I kicked myself for being so naïve, thinking that might be permanent. It hadn't even lasted the weekend. How often had this happened?

My cheeks reddened. I wished I was standing up; authoritative, proud.

But the baby was heavy and bearing down by then and I was sitting down most of the time now, bouncing a light rhythm that I had stopped noticing.

Something in me had switched; I knew I needed an answer, to bring this to a conclusion. I knew I needed to leave him, and if I was doing that, what was the point of staying silent?

To my annoyance, my voice shook.

'Marc, where have you been going when you said you were practising with the band?'

I shudder, remembering his facial expression as he looked up slowly from making his coffee. A smirk. An arrogance. A knowledge that it didn't matter what I knew; I would never leave.

Back in the now, I break from my story and look at Adam. I can see the darkness of sweat in the armpits of his T-shirt.

The complacency was the worst thing. Marc could barely make himself sound sorry.

'It's not like you care where I go,' he muttered, sulky, a child.

'You're right,' I said slowly. 'I don't care. I don't want to be with you anymore. I want a divorce.'

I hadn't left him when he tried to drown me in the sea but the stairs had been the final straw. The threat to my baby tangible. I thought back often to what his mother had said that day in the care home: yes, she spoke through the fog of dementia but hadn't some of it rung a bell? This raging man, rejected by women for years and now desperate to show them who was boss.

And now, the limited amount of protection my pregnancy had given me about to be gone.

I thought back to that beach.

What reason now would he have to pull my face out of the water? What was I waiting for here, other than death?

I stopped bouncing the rhythm.

He burst out laughing.

'Divorce! Even your family knows I'm the best you'll get. So don't fucking speak to me like that again.'

And then the usual trajectory began. Marc sneered at me, about what I had done wrong, how I had ruined our relation-ship and he came for me. I felt the baby move; his fingers trace a line on my neck as I was forced backwards off the ball and up against the door.

But this time, something new.

'All this band business, you're acting crazy,' he said then, and it was the quietness that gave me the goose bumps. The calm. Like he had just thought of something. 'You do know that imagining things is an early sign of losing your mind?'

He walked away from me.

'Not surprising,' he muttered. 'Crazy is in your genes.'

I hated him for lying. It had happened. Macca said those things. Didn't he?

But I hated him for everything else too. For the sneer in his voice. For the flippant way he talked about mental health, void of sympathy. I hated him on my mum's behalf. When she went through her postpartum psychosis, the worst thing that had ever happened to her, he would have laughed and called her 'crazy.'

I imagined that future daughter again.

The baby felt so low now, I thought it would burst into the room. I tried to breathe.

Are you a girl? And if not, is that any better; a boy, learning to be a man with an example like this?

'What?'

'In your genes,' he repeated. 'That's why they're monitoring you, right? Because you're genetically predisposed to be crazy?'

I hate you, I hate you, I hate you, Marc.

He hopped up, large frame on our kitchen worktop; dangled his bare feet like a teen. Dared me. Would I really oppose him now? I touched my hand to my stomach, held it up. Moved my fingers to my neck, sore from my fall.

Something surged in my insides. Not now. Not now. But the baby wasn't interested in my timelines.

In seconds, I was bent double on the floor, then flopped over my pregnancy ball like a rag doll, rasping for breath. It couldn't be happening now, could it? I still had three weeks. I glanced at my phone, up on the table.

I looked up at Marc. When people say words can hurt more than physical pain, they aren't counting labour. Nothing he said in that moment could mean anything. Bring it on, I thought. Whatever.

But I was wrong.

'You break up with me or start telling anyone any lies about me,' he said, eyes on my belly, 'and I swear to God I will take that baby off you. I will take that baby and let them know how crazy you are. So that no one in their right fucking *mind* would let you near them.'

I looked up from the floor.

I was wrong. There were words that could penetrate.

Breathe, breathe, breathe.

Breathe.

When Marc, still smirking, went to the toilet, I had time to send a message to Steffie. I typed as my breath came short and shallow, knowing labour was coming soon, that something worse may be coming even sooner, typing against the clock, before it wasn't possible anymore and my body insisted on my full attention.

'Everything is a lie,' I messaged Steffie then, as I accepted that I was in the early stages of labour; pain I had never felt, meaning I typed fast, with errors and random letters in the middle of it.

Send.

I was bringing a person into existence. I was doing that with just my own body. I was strong.

I was about to start a second message, to try and explain better. I knew it would be a shock: all the Jekyll and Hyde clichés were true with Marc. People thought he was a character, a joy, a gem, a big kid. A romantic, an old-fashioned guy. A traditionalist, buying me that big expensive diamond that we couldn't afford and I didn't even like and that I would never in a million years have chosen.

But they would see.

Breathe, breathe, breathe.

I started typing.

But then he came back from the bathroom and, in between contractions, I slipped my phone away into my hospital bag.

My husband sat down on the floor against the wall. Locked eyes with me. I braced against the ball. The wave started to build again. He didn't even register. Our baby was coming; he was too focused on threatening me to pay it much attention.

'You're not in control of your own mind, inventing all this stuff about the band,' he ploughed on. 'As if anyone would let you keep a baby if I told them that.'

These are contractions, I thought: I should be timing this. But to do that I would need someone who could press a button on a timer. Who wasn't — as ever — too focused on themselves.

'My mind,' I gasped. 'Is fine.'

One eyebrow rose. 'You sure?'

And the truth? He had ravaged it so thoroughly by then that no, I wasn't sure. I was no longer sure of anything.

The Woman

I tried to find some words to respond to him.

I tried to reach for my phone to call for help, to finish that message.

I tried to know, for sure, that he was lying. To believe that other people would know.

Wouldn't they?

Breathe.

Except my waters broke and things started progressing fast, then even faster, and I had no choice but to let the husband who had just threatened to take my baby from me, who was trying to convince me that I wasn't in control of my own mind – who I was realising for the first time was an abuser, as simple as that; there was no romance; there was no loving me too much; there was only false kindness extreme enough to make me tolerate the cruelty – drive me too fast and hyped and still threatening to take my baby the whole way, on a loop, to the hospital.

Where we would welcome our first child, labour progressing at a terrifyingly fast pace, in less than two hours to the backdrop of a drip-feed, whenever medical staff left the room: you're crazy, you're crazy, you're crazy.

I will take this baby from you, came the soundtrack to my labour.

You are crazy.

When they went to the other side of the room.

I will take this baby from you.

Whispered into my ear, as he wiped my brow.

You. Are. Crazy.

Say a phrase three times and it's yours, they say. How many times do you have to hear one to internalise it so deeply, it repeats itself in your own brain too. Until it becomes fact.

You are crazy.

You are crazy.

You are crazy.

I can still hear it now. A nasty word. A thoughtless word. A word that is cruel in its lack of nuance and understanding.

You. Are. Crazy.

Day #4, 10.45 p.m.

The Woman

I try to take a deep breath but talking about it is catching over and over in my throat and I can't, however I try.

'Are you OK?' Adam says. 'Romilly, are you . . .'

I can't speak but nod, squeezing his fingers, just give me a second, a second.

I want to be home. I want to be ripping up my wedding pictures. I want to be with my baby. I want my life back. I want to sleep. I want to be still.

A second, just let me figure out how to stop this.

Eventually it passes.

'All right?' he says.

I nod.

Pull my knees into my chest. It happens on the street, in my bed, when I am talking about something else and think I am fine. Sometimes it wakes me up, a bullet, and stops me from sleeping again even though it is only 2 a.m.

It's not just panic attacks that do that. My husband does it too. He wants to talk. It doesn't matter if I am in the third trimester, exhausted. There is a list of my faults to run through.

I take my hand away from Adam, picturing those long nights. Picturing myself in work trying to lift a brownie into a paper bag and realising I was too tired even for that. Looking up to see Steffie frowning at me. Avoiding her gaze again.

Adam stands up then, paces away from the tent.

When we meet back under the awning, he's coloured in the last part of the picture.

'So you're saying . . .' he begins, patiently. 'You're saying you were so terrified of Marc, that when you had a chance to run in hospital, you took it, even though you had just had a baby?'

I nod.

'I realised that family picture I'd been holding on for was impossible now. I lay in hospital with what he'd said going round and round. He would take my baby. Tell people I was crazy. I believed him, Adam; that man would do anything.'

And she was a girl. All night, I thought about that. A girl, who would become a woman. What was I setting in motion for my daughter?

Adam's fingertips rub at his forehead.

'We had to go, before he had the chance. I called Loll from hospital.'

He pushes harder at his skin.

'If Marc finds me, after I've done this . . .'

Adam doesn't ask me to finish the end of the sentence. Pushes his fingers into his forehead like he is kneading dough.

'Go back to this woman,' he says, frowning. 'The reason you say you came here.'

Does that mean it is going in? Do I have a chance?

I look around. It's dark. Teenagers stumble past feeling the effects of the first beers with mums and dads who are loosening their rules for the holidays. Soon, the adults will sleep before morning comes and they head for chocolat chaud on the terrace in their shorts and sandals.

'Her name is Ella.'

I wait for recognition to cross Adam's face. Nothing. But why would there be? Marc and Adam only met when we did.

At first, I had looked up Marc's ex Ella like anyone does; he hadn't told me her surname but I had cobbled together enough information

195

to find her on Google a few months after we met. It was casual; an innate human curiosity about the one who came before.

But Ella was significant; I knew that. She was the only ex he ever mentioned – and only when I pushed him, wanting to know the past, wanting to fill in the gaps. When he did, his face changed shape in a way that unsettled me, even in the early days. When I asked how things ended between them, he was vague.

Later though, when things turned dark between Marc and I, I messaged her.

I know it's odd to be in touch, I said. *But I am having a baby with your ex Marc. We are married. Is there anything I need to know about your relationship?*

What was I looking for, really?

Shared experience. Someone to identify with. Someone to confirm I wasn't losing it: your husband trying to drown you was bad, wasn't typical. But keeping everything inside all the time, plastering on a happy face, was making me doubt myself; worry I was overreacting.

Whatever I wanted from Ella though, I didn't get it.

She blocked me without replying. Every online trace of her was set then to private. Some even disappeared afterwards.

When I left my baby in hospital, and the threats from Marc started, I knew I had to try again. She was the only person who could prove it wasn't me; it was him, as he started to tell everyone I had postpartum psychosis.

And hadn't her reaction when I first got in touch confirmed that I was probably right about what happened between them?

'She's the only person who knows what he's like,' I told Loll, the day I left hospital.

'Not true,' said Loll. 'We all know now. You've told us.'

But my narrative wasn't enough.

Marc's version of events worked. Him? A bad guy? When all he had tried to do is look after his baby and protect his wife from a mental health condition?

I messaged Ella from Loll's account. She blocked that one too.

I called the school she now worked at, in the South of France. They agreed to pass on a message. When I called back they told me to stop calling. The third time they put the phone down on me.

I started to pack a bag.

Loll stood over me, unpacking it as I packed like I was a runaway child.

'You can't be serious,' she said, trying hard not to raise a voice that was desperate to shout in frustration. 'You're going to travel hundreds of miles away from your baby? As if this mess isn't bad enough, Romilly! At least if you're here, round the corner, we can get you back with her fast. This way you're putting so much distance between you. And for what? This Ella won't speak to you anyway. She's shown that already.'

I touched my hair. Stopped packing for a second. Turned away from her so I was in profile.

'Do you know why my hair is this short, Loll?'

Like I say, it used to be down to my bum.

Two months earlier, I had woken up and found it chopped off and scattered like confetti all over my bedroom.

Day #4, 11 p.m.

The Woman

It was long enough to sit on, my hair. My thing. Everyone I met commented on it. I loved its hippy vibe, its flow.

I loved it.

The night before, confidence up after a 'good' week – for us – I had made a flippant comment about Marc losing a little hair. He was still handsome, carried it off – who cared?

It was a mistake.

Loll sat down on the bed. Held her breath.

'You're serious?' she said. 'He cut your hair off?'

'I know you try to understand what I'm telling you has been going on,' I told her then, sitting down on the bed. She sat next to me. 'But the truth is that some of it, you can't. This sort of thing . . . I stopped realising it wasn't normal.'

Pause.

'I think Ella might get that.'

Why did I think that?

A gut instinct. Her extreme reaction to me getting in touch. A curl of his lip when her name came up. A belief, the longer time went on, that this was dug so deep into his inners that he couldn't *not* behave this way in a relationship.

'It's different blocking a faceless person,' I told Loll, standing up, throwing pyjamas into a bag. This time she didn't put them back in. 'But when I'm there, and I'm a human being, and she knows what I am going through, I know she'll speak to me.'

'So what?' said my sister. Her patience was at its edges. She had been through a lot too. 'Even if she does? What will that achieve?'

'She can help me prove it.' I was defiant. 'When he tells people he did nothing to me, that this is all in my head. He will do that, you know.'

I looked at her. Wondered if she had any doubts. If any part of her believed the brother-in-law making up bottles for his baby over the wild-eyed sister throwing pyjamas in a bag.

'And how will she help you prove it?' asked my sister.

'She's been through it herself,' I insisted. 'So she will have evidence. She can help me build a case.' It was the first time I had said it. 'A domestic abuse case.' I paused. 'If I don't go, Loll, I honestly believe that I won't see my daughter again. He is that fucking vindictive.'

I was deadpan, a simplicity in the statement as fact. I needed something to tip the balance in my favour. Marc was smart; he was playing this well. Ella was the only card I could think of to play.

Loll scoffed. 'Of course you will see your daughter again. Romilly, as if we would ever let that happen.'

But she didn't get it. Didn't know his malice. Hadn't heard his threats. If he cut my hair off when I teased him about his hairline, what would he do when he realised I'd tried to snatch away his child?

What revenge did that require?

'Oh for God's sake, let me come with you at least then,' begged Loll.

But I needed to do this alone.

'Besides, you have to get my baby back,' I told her.

So we booked flights and Loll dropped me at the airport, broken, belonging in a bed, a giant sanitary towel only just stemming the constant flow of the blood childbirth brings with it.

'I can't change your mind?' she said, when I got out of the car.

'You can't change my mind.'

People tried to chat to me on the plane.

I tried to shrink myself.

They looked away, like people do when you don't paint a picture of normal.

Shortly after I arrived in France, I vomited next to a tree at the airport, in shock at what I had done. How far I was from my girl. But I believed what I had said: this was the only way.

As I climbed into my hire car and headed off, thoughts dripping of the baby, the baby, the baby, I drifted away from reality and then back, so that the whole journey had an unreal quality. The signs showing the wild white horses of the Camargue as fantastical as unicorns. Later, I wondered if I had dreamt flamingos so pink they were almost luminous when I woke up with the loose skin that had been stretched around my baby girl lying defeated in front of me.

No baby cried; it was like the silence of a death.

I went straight to the English language school I knew Ella worked at but she wasn't there. I left a message, no one connecting me to the woman who had called previously. They smiled, wished me a happy holiday. Hoped I got to catch up with my friend Ella.

At the campsite later, I got a message. She would see me, since I had come so far, but she warned me: there was nothing to tell.

'Meet me at Lake Peiroou after work tomorrow, 5 p.m.,' she said. I smiled. Before she blocked me, I had stared at that lake on her Instagram. She was a swimmer, too.

My sleep that night was fitful.

At one point too I dreamt I was on a boat, bobbing, and the waves waved and the tour guide spoke in French, as I clutched my translation. Something about the egrets. The woman next to me peered through binoculars. Mum asked if she could borrow them for a quick look. I stared at her, baffled by all of this. I was not even sure in the dream if she was real, this Romilly, that any of it was real, and maybe I was nineteen, and I was having an adventure and my nipple felt wet only because it had been splashed slightly when I climbed off the boat and waded through the water to walk onto another terrifyingly beautiful island, a million miles from anywhere. Maybe. Maybe. Maybe.

I gasped awake. My top soaked; my breasts full.

I left the tent to get some water and looked around at other women I passed on the campsite. The stomachs unlived in. The faces with no need to wail; the mouths with no urge to vomit. I realised what I missed the most: being a blank canvas.

I glanced down at myself. Stomach, jutting. Legs unshaved since before my baby was born. I could smell my stale breath. The wetness of my constantly leaking nipples.

Not a blank canvas but one inked over with black. I was chargrilled inside too, burnt out.

We met at the lake, Ella and I. Full circle: it was the way I had tracked her down in the first place, a deep dive into the local area sending me eventually to her school.

I drove my hire car up the dirt road. No sign, of course, no one knew it was there but the locals – she had told me that – so the swing to the left in my hired Peugeot was sudden and sharp. I held on to my tender belly. Cupped a palm between my legs as though holding in insides that felt like liquid.

I headed for the unkempt shade of the woodland further back from the water, the edge of it next to a large field of horses.

Early. Of course I was. I had walked for as long as I could in the hills but I was aching now. And I had nothing else to do here, nowhere else to be.

I took my loose jersey dress off and left it where it fell and I walked across the stones in bare feet to the water. Nothing tentative, despite the pain. Despite how I'd felt about water by then for months.

But the panic didn't come this time. The flashbacks stayed away. Something had shifted and I was desperate to be submerged.

In the lake, I glanced down at my chest and saw a small wet patch developing around my nipple and the fleeting feeling of calm faded.

When it was deep enough I flung my body hard into the water, like a slap. In seconds I was immersed.

When I swam though, I felt like I was swimming in a post-card. It was as unreal as that; life could have been a rectangle of paper, sent in the post.

I stayed in there until she arrived, slipped her espadrilles off and came in with me. To the edge at least, sitting on the shore with her legs out in front. I swam to her.

'Come in?'

Anything to make you stay.

She pulled her knees up to her chest. Shook her head. Didn't speak for a good minute.

She looked around. I sat down next to her.

'Thanks for coming,' I said. A smile. She didn't respond.

'I don't go in the water any more,' she said eventually. 'The mistral wind was attacking me the last time, I remember.'

She put her face up to the sun.

'Hard to imagine, isn't it, on a day like today. But it is brutal.'

I saw her hands shaking.

My skin was dry in seconds.

Whatever this mistral had up its sleeve, the sun in early summer was just as determined and my shoulders burned with yesterday's lack of sun cream.

Protecting yourself from sun damage is self-care.

I had abandoned my daughter.

I didn't deserve self-care.

I didn't deserve anything.

'I'm sorry you've come all this way,' she said eventually as we sat at the edge of the water. 'But I have already told you that I can't help you. That hasn't changed.'

I felt my heart harden. This had to work; it had to. I had moved further from my daughter. Left the country.

'But you were with Marc for a long time,' I said, I could hear the desperation. 'The way he talks about you isn't normal. I need someone to back me up. Someone who understands. Someone who can prove this isn't me, but him. Someone who . . .'

She shook her head. 'No, you have that wrong,' she said, pity in her eyes but her voice hard. 'It was a brief relationship. Not a major part of my life, to be honest, Romilly. I am married now. I have absolutely nothing to tell you about Marc. In truth, I barely remember him.'

And she stood, walked across the stones with grace in bare feet, carrying her shoes.

'I came all this way!' I shouted at her, and it turned into a guttural sob. 'My baby isn't even a week old! And I am here, with you! That is how desperate I am, Ella. That is how desperate!'

I thought I saw her hesitate.

'Please!' I shouted, and I tried to head after her but everything still ached and I moved slowly over the stones. 'I know you're lying! I know, Ella!'

But she disappeared into her car, skidding on the gravel as she pulled away sharply.

The French twenty-somethings murmured to themselves; giggled. One checked if I was okay but I couldn't reply.

Half an hour later I still sat on the shore sobbing. It felt like Ella had slung my last bit of hope in her boot and driven away with it.

The entire reason I left the country when my baby was days old, to find somebody else who had been through what I had with Marc, someone who could back me up, and she says it was a brief relationship. Barely remembers it. It meant nothing.

It didn't happen to her.

Then why – when you live in a hot climate near a beautiful lake that you visit all the time, when I know you were a swimmer, once at least – do you not go in the water, Ella?

Is it for the same reason as me?

I reach over to the cool bag. Get Adam another beer. Take one for myself too.

'I know it's hard to hear about your friend,' I say, as he takes the bottle from his mouth. Swallows hard. 'To hear that he treated me like this.'

Adam says nothing.

I look at him. Expecting to see the pain of betrayal, the horror of the lies.

But when I look up, what's in his eyes is none of that; only pity.

'So she told you Marc didn't do anything to her?'

I nod. A light sigh from Adam.

'Didn't that ever make you wonder?' he says gently. 'Whether, if it didn't happen to her, it didn't happen to you either?'

Day #4, 11.15 p.m.

The Woman

'The problem I have, Ro, is that if this were true, you could have just left him,' Adam says with a sigh. 'You're free to do that. Why not just wait until you were out of hospital and do it *normally*?'

I shake my head, frustrated. 'Our world isn't normal. It hasn't been normal for a long time.'

Adam looks up. His face drains of colour.

'And now there is a baby, no matter what else, Marc wouldn't let me take her.'

I wonder if it's a good thing or bad, how long we go then without saying a word.

It is finally late enough to be chilly for most people. I am only in a T-shirt and shorts now, slung on over my bikini, but Adam is shivering in a hoodie. He turns down my offer of a blanket.

'Look, Romilly.' He sighs. 'I have to tell you something.'

What now, what now, what now? I am exhausted in my bones.

'Loll agrees with him,' says Adam, still easing that gun from me. 'She says it too, that you have postpartum psychosis.'

Oh shit.

'She doesn't.'

He protests but I shut him down.

'She's faking,' I insist, shaking my head hard. 'She's been faking so that she can get him on side, build his trust then be able to get the baby out of there to me. I told you, she helped me. She's on my side.'

Adam is shaking his head now, no no no no no. He has his narrative, three days old, bedded in from Marc. My newcomer isn't welcome.

'The fact is that you need to come home, Ro,' he says, decisive, a little impatience creeping in. 'Fleur needs you.'

Punch. Punch. Punch.

'Fleur?'

'He was always going to name her, Romilly,' he apologises, gently.

But it was a name that he had suggested when I was pregnant and had seen me pull a face about, eyes down on the baby name book as I ticked a plethora of options that I *did* like.

Fuck you, Marc. Fuck you.

Fleur.

My daughter.

My mind scans back over the last four days.

I know how it sounds, for me to have left my baby, believe me. I know it's the most awful thing. The unforgivable.

The truth is that when you're terrified and you're lost and something goes as wrong as that did, hours roll on and on and on and somewhere along the line you are encased deep in thick mud and it is impossible to pull your boots out.

And then those messages started coming. Confirming what he had already warned. He would call me crazy, take my baby, make sure I never saw her, done.

Threats about my safety as a mother: the final thing he'd need to justify to himself that it was reasonable to take the baby from me. He could do that; there's enough cruelty running through his veins, enough bitterness.

I was an unfit mum.

If he took the baby away from me? He would simply be doing the responsible thing.

Adam interrupts my thoughts.

'So what happens now?' he asks.

'Well,' I say, 'I ask you not to tell Marc where I am. And then you probably do anyway?'

Adam puts his head in his hands.

'Romilly, man, how can I not? There's a baby there at home who *needs* you. There is a man begging me to fix this for him, telling me you are ill. But then there's you, telling me that if I *do* fix it for him, it will ruin your life. There's my girlfriend – who I think must have a hunch that she doesn't trust Marc at the moment or something – agreeing with you . . .'

I thought so many times about telling Steffie what Marc did to me. But I was too worried. Worried she wouldn't be able to keep it from Adam. Worried Adam would tell Marc what I'd said. Worried what that would mean that night when I walked through the door after a shift.

I trust Steffie.

But who was I to ask her to keep things from the person she loved?

I thought about having to make sure we never spoke about it via text, in case Adam saw her phone next to the bed.

Adam hits a mosquito that lands on his arm hard. Harder than necessary.

I jump.

We sit in silence then, letting the last few hours sink into our skins.

And then he reaches out, cuddles me so tight. Strokes that hair that still shocks me in its sparsity. Cares for me like I'm a child. I am close to falling asleep on his shoulder.

So tired.

So exhausted.

It's hard to take that it's then, when I feel so soothed, that he says the thing that destroys me.

Day #4, 11.30 p.m.

The Woman

'I know that even *you* believe what you're saying to me. But this is all *part* of it; it's a . . . a delusion.'

He sighs.

'The more you speak, the more you check the symptoms. *Everything* points to it. Everything.'

I have no cards. He's right: everything I have told him ties in to Marc's narrative.

'I was there on your wedding day, Ro. I *know* you were besotted with each other.'

'We were! Infatuation or something. But things changed.'

'That fast?'

I grab Adam's shoulders then. He jerks away. Looks alarmed at my physicality. I mutter my apology.

'Look,' I tell him, eyes on eyes, pure desperation. 'You know *me*. But what you decide is happening here is up to you. There isn't a lot I can do to influence you. And if you do tell Marc then I'll have no choice but to face him.'

When I speak again my voice sounds steelier. 'Make no mistake though.'

He looks up, shocked again, this time at the change in my tone.

But I am fighting now.

'This is on you,' I tell him. 'If you tell Marc, what happens next, what he does is *on you*.'

Adam bites his lip. Pulls his hoodie sleeves over his hands. Even I can feel it now. The cool has set in.

He doesn't say a word.

Then he reaches up from his place on the ground; hands me his phone.

'Call Loll,' he says, putting his head in his hands. 'Tell her all of this. See what the hell she thinks I should do.'

But when I call my sister, she doesn't answer.

Adam looks confused.

'Try her again,' he says. 'There's no way she'd miss a call from my number when she knows I might be with you.'

But she misses the next one and the next one and after six tries, we give up.

Something eats at my insides.

Where would Loll be?

She never switches her phone off, especially at the moment when she is staying at my house to keep eyes on Fleur; her own kids with Jake.

'Speak to Steffie then,' he says. 'I need someone else to hear this story.'

Story. But still, I do. It's my only shot.

By the time I've told Steffie everything I've told Adam, I am weepy with the need to sleep.

'Can we carry on talking in the morning, Romilly?' asks Adam, wiped out too. I stare at him. Try to gauge things.

I believe he won't tell Marc where I am; not yet anyway.

I've bought myself some time.

At 7 a.m., I am wide awake and alert.

When I crawl out of the tent, the sun is up and so is Adam, dressed and waiting for me.

I blink into the day; so bright already. This time of year when daylight always wins.

Adam shouldn't be up this early. Not after how late we talked.

What's he doing?

209

And then I see his face and in my insides, something expires.

'I spoke to Marc,' he says.

Marc told Adam last night, of course, that we were happy. Excited about our baby. That he is broken by this; by the idea that he would hurt me, belittle me. Marc *loves* me. Poor slandered Marc wept down the phone, inconsolable.

I have a dull headache from a lack of water and three beers as I listen to Adam tell me this.

I look away from the sun, just risen.

'He was sad, Romilly. Devastated.' He sighs. 'But he understands. Knows you're not . . . in your right mind.'

Across the campsite, people are starting to rise. Tents unzip. Cars are packed. Paper bags come back filled with buttery croissants and rich pain au chocolat. Kids couldn't wait; faces are already smeared with flakes.

My heart's snapped open, again.

It begins to hammer, hard.

'You didn't believe me.'

Adam holds my hand and I remember now, him doing it the same way at points last night too, the lightest touch, wary of me, tentative.

He bites his lip; pulls at it.

'Romilly, mate, it's not that. I think that you 100 per cent believe what you're telling me.'

He puts his hands to his face, rubs an angry patch of a few days' old stubble.

'I spoke to Marc, and he explained how postpartum psychosis works. It's . . .'

'I know how it works, Adam. We talked about it last night. *It's not that.*'

'But very few women can diagnose themselves, Romilly!' counters an exasperated Adam, the least likely amateur psychiatrist you could ever imagine and now here, diagnosing me.

I stare at him. Yes, *I fucking know.*

'Do you want to speak to my mum?' I say. Epiphany. How did this not occur to me before? 'She had it! She's why I was being monitored. She knows I don't have it.'

'But she doesn't know Marc,' he says. Quiet. 'How many times has she met him, living abroad? Two, maybe? I *know Marc.*'

'No, you know a *version* of him,' I say, snapping now, going over and over this. 'He deletes my playlists, my films on the planner. He cut my hair off *while I slept.*'

I hear it: desperation in my voice.

'Sometimes it feels like he's trying to fucking delete *me*, Adam. And I don't want to be deleted.'

Nothing.

'You've been living with him this week,' I beg. 'Have you *honestly* not seen glimpses of anger, of a rage that was a bit too much?'

'What's too much, Ro? He had just lost his wife. He was looking after a newborn alone.'

'What about Steffie?' I say, desperate. 'Did you speak to her after I did?'

He nods. 'Of course I did. I wanted her opinion on what she thought was true.'

I see it again in his eyes: pity.

Oh.

My *best friend* believes Marc over me. Even after she spoke to me. Even after I told her the whole story.

And it's then that I know it's over for me. There is no point trying to persuade anyone anymore.

How can I do it convincingly anyway?

Because if Steffie doesn't believe me, and Adam doesn't believe me, I have to face up to something: doubt is creeping in; everything is feeling foggy.

I don't know now if I believe myself.

The Night Before

The Best Friend

On the phone, I listen to my normally calm friend sob like she is grieving.

Her narrative starts coherent. Soon loses its way. It takes tangents; swerves back and forth, trips up, stumbles and crashes. This woman cries so hard at certain points that I can't hear my Ro inside the tears. At other moments there is a rage I don't recognise either; a ferocity that is almost animal.

Nothing I say can calm her down.

It is difficult to keep up.

But the parts I do get?

They aren't from Romilly's world of wetsuits drip-drying over the bath and popping round on Saturday night for a Pad Thai.

'I used to be normal!' she cries to me. 'I used to be normal.'

I shake with fear, even as I try to console her. I am out of my depth. Because while I don't doubt that Marc has behaved badly – and that something *did* happen before the baby was born – Marc's version of events afterwards are ringing true.

Romilly sounds – yes – delusional. Paranoid. Very far away from herself.

Finally we end the call, and my boyfriend comes on the phone, promising he'll keep her safe, promising he'll call me soon, promising he'll get her home.

'Thanks, love,' I whisper, before we hang up.

Our own issues are out of the window. Romilly and this mess are all that matters now.

'So now what do you think?' Ad says an hour later, when we finally speak alone.

Romilly, he tells me, has calmed down and is sleeping. He is right outside; she is in the tent. On watch.

I sigh. The trauma has passed into my own skin and I feel bleak. I have a terrible fear of what is coming next.

'I think that she doesn't sound like Ro,' I say. Though I don't know exactly what that means. 'I'm worried for her. I'm scared. What do *you* think?'

Long exhalation. 'I think she got more emotional because she was talking to you,' he says.

'But . . .' I steel myself.

'But you are right. She isn't herself. And that story is . . .' he replies, and as he struggles to finish I think I hear him stifle a cry.

My brain is working overtime. I have to get this right.

We talk for ten minutes until Adam's battery dies.

And by the end we are in agreement. Awful as this is to realise, Marc is right. Romilly is experiencing delusions. Marc has done things wrong, sure, and maybe they were unhappier than we realised but he isn't abusive. The accusations are without foundation and wild and could do serious harm – to both of them. To their daughter, too.

We need to think about Fleur.

I climb into bed, eye mask on, half a ton of lavender on my pillow. But nothing works. I cannot switch off.

I take out an old basket of photos – Romilly and me in feather boas at our sixth form graduation, Romilly's long goth stage having only recently come to a dramatic and floral end. Me visiting Romilly at university, some long-forgotten and brief friends on either side of us. Seven or eight of us in unflattering shoes at a bowling alley. In unfilled bikinis on a beach in Cornwall; Romilly on holiday

213

with my family and me, as she always was, my mum hugging her close, me on her other side. I can't stop crying as I read a pile of our old postcards.

Postcards were what our friendship was made from for so many years.

We even sent them to each other when we went on holiday together: Romilly's family didn't do trips away. The relationship between Loll and her mum was strained and, her mum and dad divorced, it was a lot for a single parent; holidays were seen as an upheaval. They also involved a little too much prescribed time together.

Instead, just as she was the fourth person digging into the lasagne in our family kitchen, an honorary sibling, Ro was the fourth person on our holidays too, feet in my face as we top and tailed in a caravan in the Lake District, trying out our first bikinis on the beach on the Costa Dorada, our first cocktails in a bar we'd sneaked out to in Zante.

We wrote each other postcards as we sat next to each other on the beach.

'It would probably make more sense to write them to someone else,' Ro would mutter.

'Who else would I write them to?' I would mutter back, mid scribble.

I meant it.

I stopped sending them when we got home from university and settled in the same area but Romilly carried on. I have postcards from her from the Natural History Museum, with additional scrawl from her niece from Legoland, from her honeymoon. From a new café up the road. From home, when she just felt like writing.

And as I read them now and hear her teenage voice and her young adult voice, and the world goes quiet for its sleep, my mind slows down and I slot things more clearly into position.

And it's then that I start to doubt myself.

Go over things that are long past.

A jumpiness that had never been there before, if you appeared behind her. Sometimes all you had to say was hello. Bags under her eyes. Shovelling in junk food in a way that didn't seem like she enjoyed it but that it was a hit, a necessity. That extreme shock of a haircut, like she had removed a limb, out of nowhere, when her hair was the essence of her. No discussion about it; no enthusiasm for the crop. She stopped swimming too, when I knew friends that had still gone way into their pregnancy. When I thought Ro would swim until she rivalled the hump-backs for size; knew that's what her plan had been.

I put it all down to pregnancy. Now I wonder if it was down to something else.

A conversation Romilly and I had when I asked more about outdoor weddings – a friend of mine was considering it and I wanted to be able to pass on any wisdom – and she shut down. I frowned as she walked away from me: it had been such an odd moment for a woman who always wants to help, always wants to share an experience if it can help someone else. For someone who had *loved* her wedding.

Further back.

I think about seeing Marc put his arm round her one day, and a look cross her face that I didn't recognise, but it was something closely related to hate. They never did that; they weren't one of those couples, you know the ones, who simmer at each other privately too often for it not to spill out occasionally in public. I tracked back: it must have been two or three months before Fleur was born.

There were the strange conversations, the comments. A weird expression here, there. Phone calls made too quietly; more privacy than we'd ever had. A lack of detail, when Romilly *dealt* in detail. The row we had over her engagement ring. The distance between us for weeks and weeks at a time.

I was surprised by someone I knew too well to be surprised by. You do, after thirty years.

I stare at the pictures in front of me.

But if Ro is telling the truth and Marc is lying about her having postpartum psychosis, one issue stands tall above the rest: why is *Loll* so adamant that it's that too?

Jesus.

Loll in Marc's camp.

The blonde hairs on my arms stand up.

But for what purpose?

No. No.

I picture the way Loll looks at Marc sometimes, when his back is turned, like she could stab him in it, then her eyes flick back to normal and I doubt what I saw. Presume I am imagining things.

You easily could, existing within those walls.

The flickering light.

The dripping tap.

The stuck window. No air.

I pick at my nails; pick at the thread.

That phone chat I heard Marc having behind closed doors; the panic, the pleading.

His insistence that we believe his version of the truth – the one that focused on Romilly's mental health.

The fact that if he really believed Romilly was experiencing postpartum psychosis, he would have been hammering down the door of the police station, making sure they knew how serious this was. That they knew the danger Romilly could pose to herself, whatever he said.

That he would have looked tortured.

What the hell was going on?

The thread comes looser.

That conversation.

Looser.

This conversation.

And out it spools.

I got this wrong, I think, panic surging. I got this wrong. Fuck.

I call Adam, but he doesn't answer, his phone probably still dead; he had no idea where to charge it on the campsite. It was pitch-black there, all shut up: no one to ask.

My heart hammers in my chest.

I look at the clock. Midnight here; 1 a.m. there.

I sit down hard on my mattress.

What next?

And of course, what next is that I call Loll. Unlike Adam, she keeps her phone always charged; answers day or night. I suspect she is only ever 90 per cent asleep anyway, Loll; 10 per cent of her ready to leap out of bed for a crying child or a broken-hearted friend or in case someone, somewhere can help bring her sister home to her baby.

Except this time she doesn't answer.

I try again.

Odd.

The walls of our small flat come too close and I pull on some leggings and a sports top and grab my trainers. I'll run this out, until I can talk to Loll. Round here I feel safe any time; it's that kind of place.

I slam the door behind me, my phone clutched in my hand in case Loll calls back. I speed up. Hear footsteps behind me, faster and faster, and I feel my heart echo their pounding as they come up on my right-hand side, pulling out into the road.

Despite my confidence, I never normally see anyone else at this time and I hold my breath, clutch my phone tighter.

But they pass me, Asics pounding, headphones in, just another late-night runner. We've become more commonplace since the pandemic, everyone still in the habit of trying to find a quieter time on the streets.

I slow down again to a walk.

What next?

I could call the police and tell them that I think my friend's husband is putting her in danger. But what evidence do I have? And wouldn't they reach the same conclusion I reached last night, backing Marc and then starting to look more closely at Romilly and why she fled the hospital and left her daughter? The last thing she needs.

I can't risk the police.

I think about that phone call Marc made. The man I saw leaving the house. Loll, backing his theory.

What is this?

I run faster, harder until I can barely breathe.

Day #5, 7 a.m.

The Woman

'I'm sorry. But the important thing is that we get you home. Get you some treatment. We can fix this! You can get your family back.'

I look at him.

Who would *make up* a story like that? Someone experiencing delusions, I guess. Someone paranoid. And Marc is convincing. Convincing enough to persuade two of the closest people in the world to me that I am lying.

Hope fizzles out; a fire without kindling. I am out of ways to change this.

Until something occurs to me.

'Wait here,' I say and I go into my tent and dig around in my stuff.

Marc, I'm sure, is banking on me having got rid of my phone, chucked it in a lake somewhere so he can't trace me. He's wrong. It's switched off, but it's there. You can't fully exterminate your ties to the world, you see, when you've left part of yourself behind in it. Every parent knows that. Even bad ones like me.

Knowing I could turn it on, call the house where my baby – *Fleur* – lived at any moment: it got me through.

Now, it can serve as evidence.

I scroll through a plethora of unread messages, try not to take in the names but pick out Steffie, Loll and my mum before I get to the thread I want.

Marc.

I hand it to Adam.

'Scroll through,' I tell him. 'Scroll through as far back as you want.'

As Adam does, his cheeks going paler and paler and paler despite the sun rising to a beaming heat already, I twist and twist and twist my bracelet round my wrist. A present from Steffie, when I turned thirty. Twist, twist, twist.

Start on my rings.

This has to do it. Why didn't I think of it earlier? For a moment it makes me doubt myself again. Because I am delusional? Not in my right mind?

But they are right there in front of me. Proving it to me, as well as to Adam.

Yes!

I watch my friend take them in too.

More likely I didn't think of it because I am exhausted, broken, emotionally at my limit. Have just given birth.

What I am not is psychotic.

I slap my hand against my leg, a persistent mosquito circling.

'Adam,' I say as I rummage in my bag for mosquito spray. 'I know this is difficult, I know it goes against all of your instincts and loyalty, but please *do not tell* Marc where I am.'

He doesn't say a word.

Instead he just carries on looking at the phone. At the threatening, terrifying messages that Marc sent me when I first left. At the put-downs. At worse. At the apologies in between, before the whole thing started again. Our life, in miniature.

'Romilly,' he says, rising panic in his voice.

I stop twisting. Look up.

'I already told him where you were. I told him hours ago. I was convinced you needed help.'

Fuck.

'It will take him hours though,' I say. I am speaking to myself too. Calming myself. Talking myself down from catastrophising. 'He can't get here that fast.'

Adam pushes me inside the tent.

'He was already in France when I called him, Romilly. He got on a flight last night, got a hotel near the airport. Said he'd had enough of doing nothing. Was coming out to join me.'

Inside the tent, I stumble and fall to the ground.

'Start packing,' he shouts outside. 'You need to start packing *now*. I'm going to go and pay our bill and then we'll get out of here. Seriously. Pack quickly.'

I shove in my pyjamas. Sanitary pads. Painkillers.

He runs towards the campsite office.

Underwear. Shorts. Toothbrush.

But I have no sooner started to fold my sleeping bag than a new voice is coming under the canvas and into my ear.

I crawl out of the tent in silence.

Am still on the ground when I look up.

And there, holding our tiny newborn baby close in a babygrow I bought for her, murmuring a name I did not give her into her hair, is my husband Marc.

Day #5, 7.10 a.m.

The Best Friend

It took a while but finally I slept, though only for a fitful couple of hours before my phone rings early the next morning.

Adam. He must have found a charging point.

'Ad, I've spent all night thinking about this and—'

He interrupts me. I hear his breath rasp.

'Romilly showed me some messages . . .' he says, urgent. 'Stef, he's lying.'

I go to reply; to tell him I had reached the same conclusion anyway and that we're on the same page now, no word to Marc.

He interrupts me.

'It was too late,' he says, desperate. 'I had already told Marc. I thought it was my . . . responsibility. To do the right fucking thing. To be an adult. To think of Fleur.'

I feel fear, true fear, in my thighs first, and now they collapse like jelly.

There is no time to comfort Adam.

'Get her out of there,' I tell him. 'Just go. Wherever. As fast as you can.'

I suspect it is coming with the regret that hangs in the momentary silence, but it doesn't make it easier when he says it.

'Stef, she's left,' he says, and the sobs come thicker, harder. 'I left her for a few minutes to settle our bill and when I came back . . . she was gone. A woman who works here said she got in a car. With a man carrying a baby. Marc was already in France when I called him. He'd decided to come out here himself.'

I sit up in bed, in quiet rage.

'How. The. Fuck. Could. You. Leave. Her. Alone?'

He had to pay, he says. He couldn't leave without doing that. He thought if Ro packed at the same time; they could get out of there sooner rather than her wasting time standing in line with six other tourists trying to pay their bill with him when the card machine had broken.

I don't shout at him anymore. What's the point?

He is as sad and scared as I am. He has the guilt to bear on top.

Instead I dial off. There is only one thing left to do now. And that is to get there, to my friend, and hope that it is not too late.

Day #5, 7.10 a.m.

The Woman

'Good that Adam's not around,' he says, not moving his eyes from mine over Fleur's shoulder. I am still frowning into sunlight. 'This is between husband and wife.'

He dips his forehead low onto our baby's crown. 'And our daughter.'

I move in a daze.

Everything else is pushed aside as I walk towards my baby, take her from Marc and inhale her scent, soapy, fleetingly like biscuits, then oddly familiar.

She's a magnet.

That sensation overwhelms me, of wanting to push her back into my insides; to put my skin between her and any threat. I look at Marc's mouth, set.

To start again.

I hold on tight.

Marc comes at me, arms outstretched, eyebrows raised in a question. Can I?

Can he?

I don't react fast enough with a no and I am encased in a hug from my husband, Fleur too, as she sleeps in my arms.

When he moves away, he takes our daughter as well.

I know it's not in my interest to object.

'This has all got out of hand,' Marc says gently, the baby with her tiny back to me on his shoulder.

He glances at me. Puts a placating hand up.

'Look, maybe I haven't acted my best at times,' he says. 'It's a confusing time, being a bloke when your wife is pregnant. End of an era. So much responsibility. You're pushed aside. We did everything very fast, you and me. Everything has a context, Romilly.'

You were the one who wanted a baby so soon. *You.*

'But you *know* me.'

I feel my surety wobble again.

'We need to be alone to sort this out,' Marc says. His voice is gentle. Kind. 'Just – and I am sorry to be rude but he doesn't have kids; he isn't married. Adam doesn't get this, the magnitude of it all – our family.'

He strokes our daughter's downy dark hair. I stare at the back of her head.

It's just like mine.

He raises his eyebrows at me in question. Yes? I don't know the answer. I just know I have to follow this girl, wherever she goes.

Seeing Marc has made me confused. The monster I had built up in my head has a receding hairline and Nike trainers and bags under his eyes and screws his forehead up to squint into the bright day because he has forgotten his sunglasses.

I think of Ella, denying everything.

But I saw the messages.

Didn't I?

There is the problem too with simple brain space; I am so consumed now with looking at this tiny girl who nestled in my womb for nine months that I can't process much else. Maybe it's simpler than I thought. Maybe it's just me, him, her – a triangle. Maybe I have made this more of a squiggle than it needed to be.

I am so tired.

Steffie thought it.

Adam too.

Would I *know* after all if I were experiencing delusions? Or would I feel exactly like this: *it can't be true; what is he thinking?*

A hand on my back, and he moves me towards the car, murmuring quietly into my ear as we walk.

Nothing can scare you like that thought, back again: that I cannot trust my own mind.

Day #5, 8 a.m.

The Best Friend

'Stef?' she says, sharp.

We answer all calls in emergency mode.

'Aurelia, are you OK?'

'What's happening?' she says, dazed like it's the middle of the night.

She echoes my own question back at me.

'Is everything okay?'

'I'm not sure,' I say. 'Can you talk?'

'Yes,' she says. 'I'm in the hotel room. Bill is still flat out.'

And while I'm not sure it's the right thing, I don't know what else to do. So I tell her everything. And then I wait for the monologue; for her to decree I leave them alone, leave them to it, trust in the family unit.

I know what I am expecting to hear from her. That mums belong with their babies. That Marc is right to bring Romilly back. That Romilly has postpartum psychosis and that is not something to be messed with. That come on, *please*, Marc isn't a danger. Marc is a big overgrown kid but in this instance he's right: whatever the circumstances Romilly needs to be home, slippers on her feet, nipple popped into her baby's mouth.

But then Aurelia speaks, and it's not like that.

'They're alone? *How?*'

An adult is involved now and I feel guilty; ashamed. Between us, overnight, Adam and I let this happen.

'Stef? Stef? Where did you say they are again?'

'The Alpilles. Near Les Baux?'

I hear a laptop turn on.

'Nîmes flight won't go soon enough, only once a day, even from London. Okay, right, yes . . . Okay. You book us two flights from Manchester to Marseille. ASAP. It's not much further away from where they are. Call me back when you're done.'

She puts the phone down and I stare at it for half a second. But there's no time to be shocked.

There's only time to click the EasyJet app on my phone, find Manchester to Marseille, and book us two tickets.

The flight leaves in six hours.

Hold on, my friend.

Hold on.

Day #5, 7.15 a.m.

The Woman

Come on.

I'm embarrassed, suddenly. Filled with panic.

Marc loves Nineties indie music. Parties. Mild cheddar. *Toy Story*.

A threat? Have I got this right?

My husband smiles, slips an arm around my waist. So in sync. A little team. I see a couple with a tiny baby strolling past registering the mirror of a picture: neat, solid, familial.

I am holding my daughter now and I pull her in close. She is back and I follow her now, wherever she goes.

'Look, at us, a family of three.' Marc smiles at me and it's warm and filled with love but his arm grips.

I stiffen.

But Adam believed him, Steffie too.

Perhaps their initial judgement was right.

And perhaps this once, I have to trust it more than my own.

Marc's arm tightens again on my waist. I wince but keep it from showing on my face.

He keeps moving me towards the car.

'Shouldn't we wait for Adam?' I say, glancing back over my shoulder. 'So he knows where we are.'

'All okay, guys?' asks a woman who works on the campsite.

'We're fine,' Marc says, voice firmer now. Smile. I repeat it. Fine, fine, fine. My baby is here. How can this not be fine? I feel foggy. But that part is clear.

'Leaving now, back to the UK. Our friend is settling our bill. Thanks so much for the stay.'

She smiles back at me.

Marc's grip is firm. He doesn't reply to my question about Adam. Thirty seconds later, we are alone in the car.

A click – and the car door locks all come down.

We head upwards, into the mountains.

Day #5, 1 p.m.

The Best Friend

Aurelia and I don't meet up until we are through security and at the gate and so we speak through our masks, Aurelia's glasses steaming up so that every few minutes she has to take them off and wipe them on her jumper.

Those flashes of her eyes are enough to know her fear.

As I hug her, her whole body pulls taut.

She looks even younger, today. Her normal spidery mascara is missing; her blonde-grey hair hangs in loose waves around her face.

Folded in on herself.

I look down and see her fingers clutch and claw at each other.

As we walk through the airport, I keep glancing at her. It's making me nervous.

'Have you heard from Loll?' she asks. 'She didn't call me back last night. Not like her.'

Something sparks.

'Yeah, same,' I tell her. That's why I had called. Second choice, Aurelia, sorry. 'Early night, perhaps? It has all been a lot for her.'

We are sitting down in seats below the screen. We both try Loll again. Nothing. Aurelia's face stays constricted into a frown; I suspect mine is doing the same.

'How come you're not staying with her?' I ask.

She raises an eyebrow without looking at me as she types. We haven't established yet how much the other knows.

'It's a lot,' she says. 'In one house, with the kids. Besides, Loll and I are better with a little space.'

She sends the message with a prod.

'I'll get Jake to check on her,' she murmurs. 'Just to make sure.'

She pauses. Does an awkward laugh.

'I can't have two bloody daughters going missing on me, darling.'

The woman on the seat next to me looks up, alarm in her eyes.

I say, more quietly. 'She'll be fine though, Loll, won't she?'

And we conclude that yes. Where else would Loll be – with Marc and the baby gone now to France – than at home, consumed with the next round of peanut butter and toast, some maths homework, a living room that needs dusting.

But when I grab Romilly's mum's hand, it sticks to mine despite the air con. Shakes slightly as I clasp it.

'You find out where this campsite is,' she tells me as we walk to gate seven. 'I'll book us a car at the other end.'

We stand in line at the gate, heads buried in our phones.

'Will she . . .?'

I look up.

'Should we . . .?'

Again.

Each time Aurelia shushes me. Get our shit done, then we will discuss everything. Until then, it's not the time.

On the plane, I try again.

She holds a hand up.

'Just need to write a message to Bill,' she says. 'Before we have to turn phones off. Give me a minute.'

When she's done, Aurelia glances at the young woman next to me who is cordoned off: large, expensive and effective head-phones pair with her mask as she ducks down towards an iPad to render her faceless.

I'm relieved. We can talk.

I tell Aurelia everything that Romilly told me then. The way Marc treated her. Everything coming to a head that night as she went into labour. The messages afterwards. The threats about taking Fleur away.

Her hair.

Aurelia winces.

The time he tried to drown her.

She nods, slowly, yes.

This isn't new to her.

When the seatbelt sign goes off, the cabin crew come round to offer us drinks.

'Two gin and tonics, thanks, darling,' requests Aurelia.

'But we're driving at the other end,' I protest.

Aurelia waves her hand, flips my table down.

'Just one,' she says. She looks at me. Takes off her glasses again. 'God knows we need it.'

She wipes her glasses on the bottom of her blouse. Reminds me of Loll.

'Loll called me as soon as they got Romilly back to hers,' she says. 'Told me the whole lot. Romilly and I had been talking on the phone a bit while she was pregnant. I had thought there'd been something going on, something not quite right with her.'

She takes a second. Grimaces.

'I thought maybe stress over having a baby, some anxiety . . . worry about leaving work even,' she says. 'I never thought in a million years that what was bothering her was to do with Marc. This. God! Marc is charming. Marc came along when Romilly was low, sick of being single, wanted to be in love.'

'The endless messages though,' I murmur, remembering. 'Telling her he loved her after one date. The speed of the wedding, the baby . . .'

I sigh.

But it was romantic. Without the new context, compared to

233

the erratic and inattentive men of Ro's past, we all thought it was romantic.

We didn't know about Ella. We didn't know he had trodden this path before. We didn't know about where it would take her.

'I wish I had gone to find her,' I mutter into my plastic cup. 'So I could have seen her face. I would have known then, for certain.'

I didn't go for stupid reasons. Work, no one to run things. But who cared, really?

She shakes her head. Cuts me off.

'I'm not sure Marc would have let you be the one to go anyway,' she says, firm. 'So don't beat yourself up like it was your decision.'

I take this in.

'Do you believe her?' I ask. 'All of it?'

Aurelia looks at me, mask on.

Most people read the eyes for emotion; I love a mouth with its dips and upturns, its pursing and its opening. But this is post-pandemic. We're used to travelling this way.

As the trolley moves down the aisle away from us, she picks up her gin, slips down her mask, gulps hard and says: 'Remember, Loll spent a lot of time with her. Romilly stayed at her house after she left hospital.'

So many secrets. So many parts to this mess. So many lying people, smiling at each other over another round of milky tea.

Rom's mum tips her head back onto her chair.

'Loll didn't want her to go to France. She was inconsolable and desperate and worried about her out there without her baby and she didn't think that Ella would help anyway.'

She shakes her head.

'She was livid that it had taken so long – until she had just given birth – for Romilly to tell her what had been happening. She's like her second mum, Steffie, and she had no idea anything was wrong.'

234

She blushes when she says that, and tears threaten.

I reach out, squeeze her hand.

Her eyes glaze over.

'When we dropped Romilly off at university when she was eighteen and off to study her history of art degree, Loll cried all the way home.' She adjusts her mask, as though that will make her voice less muffled somehow. 'I know she has two children of her own now but honestly, I think Romilly was her first experience of parenting. She was so much more stressed than me.'

She laughs.

'I kept asking her, "What on earth is the matter, Louisa?" and I remember her crying so loud, I could hear it over the engine of my battered ten-year-old Volvo. That car wasn't meant to do over seventy, ever.'

I laugh too, for a different reason.

'I didn't know Loll's name was Louisa,' I tell her. We're gentle now with each other.

She rolls her eyes. 'Blame Romilly for Loll,' she says. 'She started it when she was a baby; it just kind of stuck.' She looks nostalgic. 'Like those things do with sisters,' she says quietly.

A pause.

When she speaks again, her voice is laced with sadness.

'I know I'm not a very good mum. But I love them, you know, Stef, I love them such a lot.'

As the offer of a bag of mini cheddars permeates our conversation, Aurelia gets herself together.

I clutch her hand tight like I am pulling her to safety. It's all I can do until we're free to speak again.

The thought of Loll comes back to me too; an unsettled feeling.

I think of her loyalty, kindness, the traits we didn't think were sexy enough to value when we were young. Before crises hit. How we need them now. How we need her.

Someone behind us loudly crunches Pringle after Pringle. I remember where we are.

'Loll's been there for everything,' she says, her voice cracking. 'If this was happening, why did Romilly never talk to her before?'

The woman next to us takes her headphones off and rummages around in her bag for two minutes. Aurelia and I don't speak until she puts them back on.

'I guess she thought she was protecting her family,' I say. 'Future family.'

My voice is now barely a whisper.

Aurelia nods. 'She phoned Loll from her hospital room, when Marc left after they had the baby, telling her all of this in one go, it all spilling out with a newborn baby clamped to her breast, over the phone, wild. Saying he was going to take the baby off her. That he'd tell people she was an unfit mother. That she had a daughter who would become a woman, and how could Marc not hate that woman the second she answered back?'

Wild? Marc of course would cite that kind of characteristic as evidence that postpartum psychosis had happened.

I am unnerved.

'Loll said she just had to get her out of there,' says Aurelia. 'She couldn't wait.'

Here we are, at the crucial part.

'Rom and the baby were fine, ready to be discharged, just waiting. So my Loll wasn't doing anything irresponsible . . .'

I raise an eyebrow. Jesus. She is defending her daughters, of course, but nothing irresponsible?

She registers my expression. Lowers her voice even further.

'Okay, well not dangerous anyway. They were safe, healthy. Romilly told Loll what time Marc was due back and her sister told her she was coming for them right away; they would figure the rest out later.'

I wince. Imagine the guilt, when it went so wrong.

'Loll would get her sister and the baby out and back to Loll's and away from him.'

She offers me some hand gel. I hold out my palm. She's putting it on her glasses now.

I still don't get it. How did Fleur get left behind?

'Loll couldn't take them both at once,' she says and her voice changes at this point. There is a bleakness coursing through it. 'Romilly was recovering well, had an easy labour compared to a lot of people but still, first births are gruelling whatever, and she was bleeding heavily. She needed support. There was her stuff. Loll got her, grabbed her bag, took her to the car. Then went back for the baby, sleeping on her own in the little room. Except by the time she got back Marc was there – apparently he had decided to bring Romilly in some pyjamas.'

She rolls her eyes. 'Lies. The man was checking up on her. She said it was common, for him to do that.'

Something hits me. At the time I thought it was sweet, him hanging out with a coffee while she worked. But he was turning up at the café just to watch her.

'Anyway Loll backed up and he didn't see her and she ran back to Romilly in the car park. Romilly was hysterical, trying to get back into the hospital but Loll knew then. If he knew she had tried to leave and take their baby, what happened next would be dangerous. She promised her she would go back for the baby. They just had to get her away for now.

'When they got home Loll was under the duvet whispering to her like they were kids to come out, to talk to her, but all Romilly would say was that they had to get the baby. She was hysterical.'

I look over at her for a second too long.

'No, she was still rational,' she says, vehement, knowing what I am asking. Was there any sign of postpartum psychosis then? If there's any doubt, Aurelia, give it a voice now. 'Loll got her list out of postpartum flags. Watched her. But it wasn't that; it was just how anyone would be if they were suddenly without their newborn baby.'

'So when Loll said she thought it was postpartum psychosis too . . .?'

'Yes,' she confirms. 'A lie. Loll needed Marc to think she was on his side so that she could get the baby back to Romilly. Unfortunately – and I suspect deliberately – Marc never left Fleur's side.'

I think of us there sipping tea, passing Fleur between our laps like an old-school village of parents. I think of Loll making Marc cheese on toast. Telling him to put a jumper on because he looked chilly. Of her gently encouraging her brother-in-law to eat his pasta, mothering him as she mothered Fleur. I think of our team. Of everything that was going on within it, on the seams.

'The whole time, she hated him,' I say. 'Didn't believe a word of it.'

I see Aurelia's breath get shorter behind the mask, pulling the fabric in towards her mouth.

She nods.

There's a moment then, where she has to reset herself and calm down. I see the mask pull in less frequently. She has done this before, probably in Marc's living room, just before Marc brought her in that tea and plastered on a smile.

I sigh. The thing is that he was such a good dad, Marc. I know it was a short window. But that's the part I can't reconcile: how that man has behaved with Fleur for these last five days.

Aurelia leans down, takes hand cream from her bag and rubs it in hard, like the pressure is reminding her body of something. Stay relaxed, lose the anger, be calm.

Then she looks up.

'If you're asking me if I believe her . . .' she says, firm. 'If I think Marc is trying to persuade us that Romilly has postpartum psychosis because he thinks it takes the blame from him and his psychotic fucking behaviour then yes. I do.'

She shakes her head in sadness slowly, right, left, right, left.

'She says he's dangerous, Stef, and hurts her. And all I saw was a handsome man, good bet for settling down, keen to have a family. What sort of mother does that make me?'

I put a hand on her arm. What sort of anything does that make any of us? But he didn't make it easy to see it. I picture him again, burping his tiny daughter up on his shoulder.

That man?

Then I picture him kicking that wall.

That man.

Aurelia slips her mask down under her chin and swigs the last of her gin and tonic like it's the first drink at a funeral; the last party before lockdown.

My heart pumps hard.

There are still forty minutes of the flight to go. For most of them, we sit in silence.

The Woman

He is right about one other thing, my husband: we do need to talk.

I wish my mum were here, and the thought is one that shocks me. It rarely happens.

But my mum, like everyone, is in England, summoned over from Spain after I left hospital in a desperate attempt to prise the baby away from Marc when Loll wasn't succeeding.

'This couldn't be called kidnap, could it, darling?' Mum asked nervously when she first arrived.

I bit her head off. *My* child. *My* right. No it wasn't bloody kidnap! Loll and my mum exchanged a glance; never said the word again.

I look at Marc now, his hands loose on the wheel.

'We need to figure stuff out,' he says, forcing a smile. I picture myself, holding my belly and crying out as I lay at the bottom of the stairs. Opening my eyes at the wheel. As I remember the water – my lifelong love – becoming terrifying to me after Marc shoved my face down into it. The panic attack I had when I first tried to swim after what he did to me; the thing that had always calmed me now a horror. I ball my hand into a fist to stop it from shaking. But this needs doing. There is no running away; him here next to me proves that. 'Adam will realise that.'

'But we could have left a note, a—'

'He's not stupid. He'll figure it out. He told *me* where you were, remember.'

I nod. Reassure him.

I feel a hand on my shoulder. A warning.

I nod again, more convincing.

Day #5, 3.15 p.m.

The Best Friend

I am restless, picking at already ripped-off fingernails. Aurelia flicks through the in-flight magazine, turns the pages too fast to be reading anything.

When I look up though ten minutes later, I see tears flying down her face and I am almost relieved I can't see her mouth, the mask is affording privacy on something that's too exposing. The woman with the headphones looks up but quickly back down.

Then Aurelia starts speaking, barely audible. I lean close to catch her words.

'How are we not there yet?' she says, hands in the air. She looks at me. 'I have to protect her. It's my job.'

She slams her hands down on the armrest so hard that the woman next to her feels it. Looks up. I apologise with my eyes.

If all of this is right . . . Romilly. Alone with Marc.

I shiver.

Twenty minutes until we land.

Day #5, 8 a.m.

The Woman

I stare at Marc as he drives the three of us to some unknown place. His phone is on his lap; he is following directions being spoken from its screen.

I keep glancing at him.

Who the hell are you? I think. And whoever it is: were you always him, on some layer of your Marcness?

Markness.

I know there were bad times when he was young. Severe bullying. The kind that forms you. Being laughed at, mocked, mercilessly by girls who wouldn't give him a second look.

And then there was his mum, who was supposed to fix it, instead compounding it.

Laughing too. Laughing harder.

'What are you looking at me for?' Marc smiles. His tone is light.

I look away. Out onto a road that winds sharply but then falls with grace; dipping down low onto the olive groves, the grapevines.

'Beautiful, hey?' says Marc dreamily. He glances out of the window.

I grip the seat tightly so that Marc can't see my hand shake. I focus on the kestrel that's policing us from above. I try to remember what the word *miel* is declaring to me is available from a handwritten sign on the side of the road. Anything,

anything, anything to quiet my mind. Avoid another panic attack. Keep Marc calm.

I glance back when we get stuck behind some cyclists and I am winded by the sight. A baby, asleep in our back seat. Yes, he has even sorted the car seat. You can't travel with children without a lot of planning, I know that from Loll. The fact he has got himself here is a miracle to me. But wasn't he ready to be a dad? Didn't he tell me this was all he wanted?

Marc mutters to himself. I don't ask him to clarify, knowing it is an irritation based on the mountain bikers in their Lycra who are up ahead of us, slowing us down, the bends far too tight here to take them on. I shiver, imagine him swerving out around them on a blind bend. I remember myself that night, eyes closing. Opening only just in time to swerve away from the fence.

And then I imagine sitting on that bike. Flying down the hill, away from him. The blast of air, the blast of freedom.

Finally, we get round the cyclists and pick up pace.

It's at the very last minute that he takes a sharp left into a dirt track. And here we are.

'I knew we would need some space,' he says, upbeat. 'You can't deal with something like this in a tent. We were lucky this place had last-minute availability when I decided to come last night. I guess it's not peak season yet.'

I don't answer but he answers himself. Loquacious, a monologue about how pretty the house is, the area, a potted history for me.

I drift away. Picture trying to reverse this.

I picture me zooming backwards out of that queue in the airport. I picture my feet going back back back to the taxi, and to Loll's house then in the lift up to the ward and I picture that long, wailing chunk of time starting with sunset and ending with pitch-blackness, just me and my baby as I took in what lay ahead for me.

What he seemed to be taking in his stride as he messaged me to ask if I wanted a bacon McMuffin sneaked into the hospital tomorrow morning. To see if I'd had any more thoughts on those names he had suggested for the baby. As though everything was normal. As though our relationship hadn't become the most toxic, cruel state of being. As though we weren't now about to bring another person into that. As though I hadn't been crumpled in a ball at the bottom of our stairs a few days ago. As though I hadn't hidden the truth from doctors. As though I wasn't a broken form of myself. As though he hadn't tried to kill me. As though he hadn't threatened to take my baby away; to lie about my mental health to keep her from me.

I had lain there that night in hospital and tried to block it all out.

But instead of subsiding, the reality grew so big that it filled the room.

The baby stopped crying eventually and I laid her down in her hospital crib. And then I stared at her.

How can I show you, tiny woman, that living like this is okay? Will I even get chance to, if your dad does what he threatens?

And he does most things that he threatens. I have learnt that.

I was establishing too that there was a pattern in who Marc hated. From the ones who had laughed at his skin, his belly when he was sixteen, to his mum, to Ella, to me. We had something in common.

My daughter had it in common too.

Too young to answer back now, what happened when she did?

A midwife popped in.

'How are you doing?' her soft, kind voice said. She glanced at the baby. 'Looks like your window to sleep. I'll leave you to it. I'm clocking off now so I'll maybe see you tomorrow night.'

She grinned.

'Hopefully not though. You'll probably have been discharged

by then and be off home to start your new life as a family of three.'

My stomach lurched.

Two, I thought. What if this family had two people in it? I preferred that picture. That picture didn't frighten me.

'What if I need help?' I asked.

'Oh, you can call your community midwife, lovie,' she said. 'And you and your husband will figure it out between you, most of the time. A little team.'

I didn't mean help with the baby.

She smiled. I knew she was picturing that man who spurred me on through labour; cracked jokes with the midwives. Who knew where the snacks were and got them out whenever I needed a boost. This enthusiastic new dad, eyes wet when he held his baby for the first time. Eyes bright when he bounded back down the hall with a coffee. My Marc. Big kid, lover of life.

My eyes widened at his duplicity.

And then it went wrong.

My baby, trapped with the man we were meant to be fleeing. In the end he hadn't needed to do anything to take her from me; I simply handed her over.

I lived inside my grimmest nightmare.

The worst irony.

I stayed at Loll's and I healed, physically, a little. I rested. But my mind was torture.

I knew I couldn't be away from my baby any longer, no matter what the alternative was, so I packed my sad little bag and I changed my giant pants and I was about to go home, I was, I was, whatever I would walk into.

Then my phone beeped.

You abandoned our baby, the first message said. *They'll put you in prison. Do you realise what you've done?*

He followed it with a link.

Baby dumping: When a mother or father leaves a child younger than twelve months anywhere with the intent of no longer taking responsibility for that child, it said.

This falls under child abuse statutes and is punishable as a felony. Following charges, this parent gives up their parental rights over the child, ending their relationship with them.

It sounded like American wording but surely I thought, heart thumping, the principles would be the same.

I had lain in a bed that wasn't my own, reading that over and over.

But I didn't do that. I didn't abandon her.

Did I?

Marc messaged again. Tens of them, possibly hundreds. Links. Warnings.

About this. About my mental health.

Who the hell would believe me about anything he had done, when I was the woman who abandoned her baby?

I needed something. I messaged Ella from Loll's never-used Facebook account but she blocked that one too. Nobody in their right mind would believe me – the woman who abandoned her baby, who everyone thought had postpartum psychosis, who had never said a word about it to anyone before – that Marc had abused me. But if there were two of us? And I knew there *were* two of us. I knew in the mist that came over Marc when her name came up. I knew in the way she shut down when I contacted you. I knew, and I was desperate.

That's why it didn't matter that she lived in France.

From my phone in Loll's bed, I booked a flight.

One day, one conversation, and I would have an ally, a team. Someone to take down Marc with. A route to get my baby back. A route to get my life back.

Day #5, 6 p.m.

The Best Friend

We go the wrong way twice when we come out of the hire car depot, and everything about Marseille – even this distant outpost of the airport where they send the cheap flights to – intimidates.

When we drive out of the airport there is roundabout after roundabout after complicated road system and any calm I was hoping to imbue from a journey through the Provencal countryside is a fantasy.

This is not the Marseille of lunch at the port and plates full of rich, steaming seafood. We don't see the markets heaving with sacks of North African spice. Instead it's just the edges of a city, the part no one heads for, the part people just get through. Large and looming.

I see no vineyards.

No olive groves.

Just those roundabouts and a massive branch of Decathlon.

I press various buttons to figure out where the air con is.

Even without it though, it's less claustrophobic than Marc and Romilly's house.

God, that house.

I think of the window I tried to wrench open. The light that flickers on, off, on, off in the kitchen.

I shiver with the relief at being out of there. Even when I am here, biting my lip while I sit still at another fucking roundabout.

Aurelia reaches in her bag for hand sanitiser.

I look ahead at the road. Recalibrate to driving on the right.

I think about the story she told me on the plane. There is a part of me that feels envious of the trust Ro put in her sister that night; why didn't she come to me? She moans about Loll all the time. It's a standing joke that I'm the 'sister she never had'. But I've never realised that Romilly not seeing Loll as a sister just means she sees her as her mum.

Loll's closed lips; Romilly's open heart. Romilly didn't dislike her sister. She just didn't always get her.

I would have been too much of an equal and from the moment she left hospital, Romilly wanted parenting.

The car is small and Aurelia and I are physically close enough to each other that I can feel her body tense. She shakes her head like Henry after a soaking. Reaches into her bag to change her glasses for prescription sunglasses.

'Where now?' I say as we move towards a junction.

She clutches her phone with the map on it.

'Left when you get out of the exit and then first right,' she says.

'Anything from Loll?' I ask.

She shakes her head. Nothing.

Loll would lose her shit when she knew we were out here without her. But what choice do we have?

Aurelia picks up the story that's been on hold since we got off the plane, went through passport control, picked up the hire car.

'Loll thought it would be a matter of hours. She thought she could tell Marc to go for a sleep or something, and get the baby out of there to Romilly.' She shudders. 'But he wouldn't leave Fleur alone. It was a nightmare.'

'Did he know, do you think?' I say. 'That she was helping Ro?'

She shakes her head. 'I don't think so,' she says. 'Not at first, for sure. I think he's just obsessed with control. I think he's paranoid. Even if he doesn't know what about.'

'First exit at the roundabout,' she mutters. 'Where that yellow car is going.'

What I'm about to say next makes me tentative. 'He also *loves* the baby though.'

Aurelia's face whips round to me.

But I feel like someone has to point this out. Marc won't leave the baby alone because of control, fine. But I have watched that man's face. His hands as he's slipped cream onto a tiny red bottom. His eyes if he nods off and wakes up and for half a second, is unsure where she is.

They are Ro's family so they are going to view him now as all bad. But that man is completely in love with his little girl.

And where does that come into all of this?

Aurelia ignores me.

I flick on my indicator. Remind myself again which way to go round a French roundabout. I'm nervous. Aurelia hasn't noticed.

'When Loll told me what Marc had done to her, I got straight on a plane.'

I reach over to hold her hand but she is folded in on herself, consumed in a one-person hug.

'I had *two* daughters in bits too. Loll had just wanted to help. And she felt like she had made everything so much worse.'

I reach out again then and this time I make contact with Aurelia's hand, soft from the hand cream, small like a child's.

I hear something guttural in the base of her throat. She gulps it down.

'You're on here for a good few miles,' she says, brusque, as I indicate to pull onto a motorway. I take my hand from hers, flick into fifth gear and try to relax into the drive.

But I don't think Aurelia can stop speaking now she's started.

'Marc called, of course, and told Loll she was gone,' she says. 'She told him she would come. Straight away.'

I sigh. 'She must have been nervous leaving Ro.'

'You've no idea,' she says, and the tears gather momentum.

She shakes her head to move on.

'When I got to Loll's, I moved Romilly's flip-flops out of the hall when I left, so if anyone came round suddenly there was no sign of her.'

'Didn't Loll's kids ask what was going on?' I say, suddenly remembering their existence.

A car beeps behind me. I pull into the middle lane. Put a hand up to the mirror. *Pardon, pardon.*

Aurelia rubs at her temple like it hurts.

'God, Lucy,' she says. 'I forget how grown up she's getting sometimes. Ten now. She asked where the baby was, why Romilly was here alone and Loll realised what she thought – that something had happened to the baby. She'd been so caught up in Romilly she hadn't thought about how the kids might be processing this. What was going through their little minds.'

She moves her glasses off her face and rubs at her eyes. Turns to me, pointed. Addressing what I said earlier, I think: the love that emanates from Marc to his daughter.

'Romilly never thought he would harm the baby, Stef.'

Then she mutters, almost to herself.

'Such a line drawn, like that makes it all okay, what he does to my daughter.'

Aurelia bites her lip.

'Loll was terrified anyway, of leaving them alone, of anything happening to the baby on her watch. That's why she stayed every night while me or Jake had the kids. Why she got you and Adam to do shifts. She used to stick her head in at night, set the monitor up. She's barely slept, Stef, bless her.'

I am on the inside lane, wanting to take it slowly through my own nerves but every second matters for Romilly. I indicate and pull out in the direction that feels unnatural, to the middle lane. Focus on the driving. But it's hard.

'What did she tell Lucy?' I push because I need to know, more, more, more.

The outside lane clear, I pull out again. Aurelia seems completely oblivious to the journey; to what is happening outside of this car. Outside of her story.

She laughs. 'That the baby was fine but it was a "long story". Then she berated herself for being "the worst kind of adult".'

She puts her head in her hands and I want to speak to Loll then; tell her she's not the worst, she's one of the best actually, even if I didn't always realise that.

Where the hell is she?

'Keira put a hand on her hip and stopped in front of the door. Apparently she said: "Oh, we know ALL about long stories."'

I smile. Check my mirror. Keira is three.

The clock on the dashboard flicks to the next minute.

'Message Adam again,' I tell her. 'Tell him we're on our way.'

Aurelia nods. Sends the message. But what difference will it make?

I think about that gin and tonic on the plane. Wish hard I could have a second, or even the last dribble I had left undrunk, worrying about being over the limit or feeling tipsy on a French motorway.

Every second we are in this car, Ro is at risk.

I put my foot down, despite my nerves.

I picture them, Loll and Romilly. I want to climb into that picture and pull the duvet up over all of us, grab the sugary tea and block the rest of this out.

Aurelia's shoulders heave. She has carried so much herself.

'She could have asked me,' I say quietly. 'To help get the baby out of there.'

Aurelia nods. 'Yes. She could have. But what a gamble, Steffie. Your boyfriend is his best friend. You believed she was going through postpartum psychosis. It was a leap. To think you would take that baby off him, hand her over to Loll. There would have been legal implications, I imagine, too, if you did that. That's a lot to take on. It's one thing, for family. . .'

A beat. Then the practical.

'Besides, in the end Marc wasn't leaving any of you alone with the baby. You couldn't have done anything more than Loll.'

I move my own shoulders from side to side. An ache in my neck pinches from turning towards Ro's mum all the way on the flight. I wish Romilly were here to give them a quick rub, like she does on a long day at the café.

I wish Romilly were here, full stop.

What's happening to her now?

I picture her with Marc and a baby she did not name. A distorted version of a normal family picture, the three of them on their holidays in Provence, flip-flops on their feet, sun cream on their necks.

Aurelia looks at her phone. 'You're coming off the next exit,' she says. She turns to me. 'She's a kid, Steffie.'

But I am defensive on Romilly's behalf. There are different forms of adults. Just because one kind doesn't fold her towels properly, doesn't mean she doesn't count.

'And you're sure about . . . things?' I ask. 'Mental health wise? This stuff about Marc, it wasn't . . . a delusion?'

I am tripping over the language.

'Well I'm no expert,' says Aurelia with a sigh that says she has been over this, over, over, over every time she gets back from Marc pushing his phone in her face and talking about postpartum psychosis. Because even if you're 99.9 per cent sure, even if you speak to her every day, with the family history and Marc pushing it as a theory all day every day . . . how could doubt not kick in?

God, poor Loll too.

This has been in her head for so long and she has been looking after Fleur, being polite to Marc, changing nappies, putting the dishwasher on, being Ro's lifeline, pretending to be on Marc's side, keeping calm enough not to raise an alarm . . .

I picture Romilly then, grief-stricken without her child, barefoot in her flannel pyjamas and I am winded again.

I picture Loll. Feel that niggle again.

'Argh sorry, it's this one!' yells Aurelia, a second too late.

When I pull too sharply into the inside lane, the car behind presses hard on the horn. Aurelia braces against the car door.

'Sorry,' I mutter, but her eyes are dazed: she is back elsewhere.

I look up now as we are forced to slow, leaving the motorway for the French countryside. At the side of the road is a cart selling scarlet cherries so plump I could pick out the ones I want from here. We pass a boulangerie and the scent of warm butter drifts in through the now open window along with chatter that moves between a flurry of French and dollops of English. Holidaymakers walk alongside locals on their way to work, as Europe moves forward from years marred by Brexit and a pandemic.

There are many reasons I will remember this summer.

My stomach lurches, as I hope one of them will be for the moment we brought home my friend.

And not for something else.

The Woman

Jasmine grows up and over the front of the *mas*, a beautiful French farmhouse Airbnb would describe as rustic. The mas is an antisocial figure; its only neighbours the olive trees that could surely keep the country in *l'apero* for years.

It's not fancy. I suspect it was the only thing available at such late notice.

A car door opens. Slams.

I climb gingerly out of my own.

Two old sunbeds have started to rust out to the side of the mas, ready for two people who like being in each other's company to laze all day, G&Ts in hand as they reach with the other for a couple of those olives. Imagine it. And yet, not that long ago, we used to do it.

Marc behind me, I walk slowly to the front door, the only way I can walk now. Gravel crunches underfoot and the sun singes me like a grill; I could be toasted here in seconds and I feel my skin smart.

Marc reaches into the back seat and unclips the car seat. Takes it out and holds it in the crook of his elbow like a handbag.

'I'll get her,' I say, reaching out, but I wince as I do it.

I feel his arm block mine.

'No no,' he replies, pleasant. 'You've just given birth.'

We are playing normal again. You've just given birth. In

between that you fled the country and left your child. But still! You've just given birth.

I try to inhale slowly to stop my breath from catching, my heart from racing as I see my baby. Fresh lavender. Wild thyme. Guilt.

Fear.

I hear Marc's breath; a rasp to it.

'Let's get inside,' he says, soft. A hand lands on my back and guides.

Every minute since I left, I've imagined this moment.

My insides have thumped as I thought about the skills Marc must be learning, fast-tracked ahead of me in all things daughter when only a few days ago we stood at the starting line together.

A dad, now.

And meanwhile, did I count as a mum?

Did I count as anything?

When I was swimming in that lake, no one noticed me. When I dried myself off on the shore, no one noticed me.

I was roughly young-woman-chilling-out-for-the-summer-shaped. Close enough.

No one saw the missing baby.

No one knew I was a mother.

No one knew that when my eyes glazed over, I was thinking about whether Marc remembered where I put the Sudocrem stash. If he is doing the vests on a hot wash.

Inch closer though and you saw it: the loose stomach, breasts swollen to their limit. There are the differences you don't see too; the stitches at the entrance to my vagina. The way I groan sometimes, with the ache of pressure between my legs if I am standing up for too long.

I have to be here, I told myself, whenever the surge of panic came. Just for one day.

Marc held all the cards because to the outside world I had abandoned my daughter. I read and reread those messages. Abandonment. Abandonment. Abandonment.

I needed to make everyone understand why. When Marc tried to take my daughter away from me, I needed something to weight things down in my favour.

I needed someone who no one thought had a mental health condition to stand there and say: *Yes. Marc is an abuser. Marc lies. Marc tortures. Do not believe Marc.*

One day was all I needed with Ella. To persuade her to talk. And then I could get back to my daughter and make a life.

Now though, there is no rush to get back because my daughter is here.

They are both here.

Marc opens the door to the house.

'After you,' he says, pleasant.

I stand in the hall as he steps in, takes the baby out of her car seat.

I feel a sting on my forearms. Look down. Realise that it's not the prospect of sunburn I was feeling but the redness already on my skin. I am quite badly burnt across my arms and chest, the day with no self-care, the moments catching up on my pasty British skin, when there was no one here to launch themselves at me with the factor 50.

When I look up, Marc is snuggling our daughter into his long arms. They look like love.

I picture ties between them I can't emulate.

Marc, with one hand, locks the front door behind us. It's heavy like a coffin.

My husband slips the key into his pocket and oddly enough I feel nothing. When Marc is here, Marc is in control: that is how life works.

'Why France?' he says then.

'For Ella,' I whisper. No point keeping anything from him now.

He frowns. Bites his lip. 'Ella?' he says, nonchalant. 'Who's Ella?'

As he turns to me, I twist a strand of my hair, starting to grow back now, so tightly it hurts my finger but I keep twisting, twisting, twisting.

Like my finger is being slowly strangled.

Day #5, 6.30 p.m.

The Best Friend

I stare out of the window.

Those industrial edges of the city are a distant memory now and at the side of wide roads are small wooden frames selling fresh melons, figs. We pass *magazin du vin* after *magazin du vin*; unending boxes of Côtes de Provence stacked up outside.

'Loll tried everything,' she says. 'Telling Marc to sleep. Offering to take Fleur for walks. But he wouldn't let her out of his sight.'

Perhaps that claustrophobia was less to do with flickering lights and more something I was soaking up from Loll.

'What I still don't get is her leaving the country,' I say. 'It makes no sense when she was trying to get closer to Fleur, not further away.'

Aurelia nods. Sighs.

'Loll and I both felt exactly the same. God, it was frustrating. Romilly was insistent there was no other way. She said this Ella was the answer. But in the end it sounds like the whole thing was pointless.'

I have no idea what she is talking about. Who is Ella? The name means nothing to me. I stay silent waiting for her to explain.

'Left turn here,' she says, looking at her phone. Then she murmurs to herself: 'Where are you, Lolly?'

A frown is etched deep into my forehead. I don't know whether I am now considering Romilly's mental health myself

259

or just imagining things from Marc's perspective; working out what will play into his narrative.

But something here is sitting badly.

Romilly had just given birth.

'Why would she be boarding a plane?' I sigh. 'Who the fuck is Ella?'

Aurelia sighs.

So Aurelia fills me in. And I am so focused on this bizarre tale of the trip to France to find Marc's ex that when I look up, I don't know how I got here.

A dirt track; our little car huffing.

'Is this right?'

Aurelia looks at her phone.

Shrugs.

'Looks like it.'

We pick up.

'But Romilly called me yesterday; Ella was no use,' she murmurs. 'Who knows why but she wouldn't say a word against Marc to Romilly. Said their relationship was barely memorable. Romilly was inconsolable. She had pinned *everything* on this. Gone all that way. She begged her, pleaded. But nothing. And there was Romilly, left out here all alone away from her baby.'

Aurelia shudders.

We turn down an even smaller track. It feels like we are in somebody's back garden.

I hold my breath for an angry farmer with a gun; instead there is just a washing line, and lines and lines of pants.

It niggles at me again, that feeling. Ella denying things. Another cross against Romilly's version of events. That's not a reason to worry, is it? Not a reason to doubt?

I picture Marc again, exhausted but in love, staring at his baby girl.

Finally we come out of the other side of the track. I exhale.

We are in a small village now, the road narrow. On one side a *boucherie*, with all kinds of unimaginable French meatiness hanging in the window. A hungry dog faces into it, stares longingly.

'This is pretty,' says Aurelia, loving travel, loving a sense of place, but her eyes are glazed.

Something occurs to me. A question I had wondered about earlier. 'How did Romilly get her passport? If she only decided to go to France after she left hospital?'

But Aurelia points out: Loll had free rein of Marc's house, cleaning, tidying. It was pretty easy to grab that.

Of course.

We sit in silence for a minute or two. There is a lot to take in.

On the other side of the village is a town hall, and then a courtyard. Aurelia opens the window and lets the buzz permeate; carafes of local rosé glugging into large glasses, chatter that tumbles along too fast for the basic French I learnt at GCSE to pick up. Scents drift in clearly though: rare steak, steaming frites, toasts topped with tapenade made pungent with anchovies.

I have a quick scan for Romilly, just in case.

Her mum reads me.

'I don't think they're going to have popped out for *moules frites* darling,' she says, a sad smile.

I nod. Wherever Marc has taken my friend, there's no doubt that it will be somewhere they can be alone.

Aurelia waves her hand to the left and we are out of the village and into countryside that goes on as far as we can see. Less lush than in England, home to vineyard after vineyard. Tiny farmhouses lie at the top of long potholed lanes where you can try the wine, pick up some olives, throw in some saucisson for dinner. A couple cycles up one of them, wobbly enough that they might have visited a few more vineyards before this one. Behind them is a group of women in their forties on electric bikes, battery pack in the back for when they hit the hills or hit the vin blanc.

Round the gentle bend there is a language school: eat cassoulet and drink pastis with strangers each evening after a long day working on your past participle. Right up Ro's street, actually. Back in the day.

Aurelia flicks a glance in my direction.

'Do you remember when the midwife put in his head that Romilly couldn't have left by herself?' she says. 'That was us done for, I think, from that moment. Marc started looking at Loll oddly. Asking questions. She was worried he would try and contact Lucy, to find out what she knew.'

I picture Lucy's face. Her Uncle Marc. How confusing this must be for Loll's kids.

We overtake a beautiful but slow red vintage car with the roof down; retirees out for a drive. Their life – from a distance at least – pleasant, content.

'So your visit?'

'Yeah, all fake,' Aurelia says. Half a smile. 'Thank you, am dram society. Loll and I were pretending to be snippy at each other so Marc wouldn't realise we had made up. Everything has been different with us since Romilly had the baby, since we knew what had been happening. We had a shared focus.'

She flushes.

'They think I'm useless, my girls, so I was surprised they let me into things. But in this situation – so strange, so precarious – there aren't many people you can trust I suppose.'

I know it shouldn't, but that bruises.

'We couldn't let Marc realise that though; it would have rung alarm bells. Wasn't hard to pretend to be at each other's throats. We've had years of practice.'

I think about a percentage of what was real in that house. Maybe ten?

Ro's mum softens, a touch. 'I hope it helped to make up for lost time. Being there for her this week. I'm getting older, Steffie.'

She pushes her glasses back onto her nose, focuses, and I feel horribly, horribly sad.

But the part I'm coming back to . . .

I stare out of the windscreen.

Walking past the car, there is a family heading back from a market, loaded down with bags. Walking the walk of the fatigued, sweat darkening their clothes, pink edging on their shoulders. They try to keep to the shade under the trees that line the side of the road but I am still a little too close. I swerve. Put a hand up in apology. See a hand raised back at me in rage.

Aurelia pauses.

'Loll had told the kids that Auntie Romilly was coming while she got better from having a baby. Now she had to tell them she had gone home to her family. Meanwhile the whole time: no baby. The whole thing was a shitshow.'

'Did Lucy not ask if she could meet her cousin?'

She nods.

Throws her head back hard against the seat. I jump. She raises a hand in apology.

'Yes,' she says. 'She told them Fleur was still too little to see other children. We both did. And it's not the biggest lie I've told lately but it's another one. Another one to add to my long, long list.'

Out of the corner of my eye, I see her look at me.

'We weren't liars before, Steffie,' she says.

Do I know them all now? I think. Do I know all of her lies? And what about Loll? Adam? Marc? Romilly? Do I know all of *anyone's* lies?

Aurelia starts crying then, nothing held back, it gushes over and it's ugly and I bite my lip. It is horrible to witness when I am driving and can't comfort her.

But I am unsettled too.

'Why would Ella lie, Aurelia?'

I hear my voice and it surprises me with its ice.

Day #5, 6.45 p.m.

The Best Friend

A landscape change again.

The long road we drive down now feels like an aisle: Van Gogh's favourite plane trees – Aurelia's knowledge, not mine – reach over from each side, stretching like students in a yoga class to meet each other in the middle.

'Fear?' she says. 'A reluctance to dig up the past? I don't know.' Her head snaps up. 'Oh shit. Turn around. We missed the road.'

I mutter under my breath. We can't afford to waste time.

I find a place to do a risky three-point turn and head back to where we need to be and try, really hard, to ignore the pressure of my own tears. I remember something Loll said last week: they aren't helpful, Steffie. I don't think she was being callous; only realistic. Save your energy for the stuff we need. There will be a lot of it.

But those tears exist. They need an outlet somewhere.

'Fuck, fuck, FUCK,' I mutter, wishing I wasn't in a contained space and in charge of a vehicle so I could shout, swear, punch a wall.

What is happening now?

Are we too late?

And where, as her mum and I drive through the French countryside, is Loll?

I look out of the windows at a young couple coming out of a small, boutique art gallery.

At a teenage boy having a breather and a can of Coke as he leans up against his bike in the blistering heat.

And you, Romilly? Where are you? Are you getting a breather from whatever you are doing?

But there is nothing I can do. Not yet. I look at my hands, gripped tightly to the steering wheel.

I think of how I've never heard Ella mentioned. Of how, really, I never hear *any* part of Marc's past mentioned. There was a visit, once, I think, that Romilly and Marc made to his mother on the South Coast . . . Romilly didn't talk about it though.

Odd, in retrospect. We talk about everything.

Ro's mum reaches into her bag.

I imagine Loll at home now; kids' clothes ironed and lined up for the next day on the radiator; a bedside table with night creams in a row, floss sticks in a jar, dusted twice a week.

But something hums. If that's the picture, why are you not answering your phone, Loll?

I feel the pain in my neck again. Move it around to release it. Outside there is a queue at a van for rotisserie chicken. The smell drifts through the window and my stomach reacts and I realise it has been eight hours now since I have eaten.

For five minutes or so, we drive in silence. I start to feel like I have a hangover and I don't know if it is the gin, the hunger, the weight of all of this or the fear: what next? What now?

When we are static at traffic lights, I turn to Aurelia, wrap my fingers around her forearm. Squeeze.

Sweat makes its steady way down the back of my T-shirt. We drive through a village that blooms at the start of the summer season; outside the car, tourists peel off layers and shove them in wheely cases that thunder along behind them over rickety stone even though it's after 6 p.m. A heaving market wraps up its brie, takes in empty paella vats.

Kids clutch tight to bobbing horses on carousels, rainbow colours jump in the corners of my eyes.

I put the window back up. It's doing nothing except letting in hot air and happiness. I'm not sure which is worse.

The air con fares no better.

The dashboard of the car tells me that it is thirty degrees outside.

The sweat runs down my back.

And I feel a shiver run from my head down to my toes.

Day #5, 10 a.m.

The Woman

I have changed one of my first nappies, my husband passing me wipe after wipe after wipe, and then – when I did a far from expert job – a new vest and babygrow for her too.

When she cried, he soothed her, rocked her, walked up and down the house with her.

In the end I went to the kitchen. Got a glass of water. Stared at the wall. It was preferable to what was in the other room: seeing them together was almost unbearable.

Now, I watch Marc sit down on the too-hard sofa and cuddle our daughter into his large frame. She is fretful. Rooting, I think they call it. I feel my right breast sting.

Do I offer? Could I? Would I know where to start? I think of those hours in the hospital. We had made a beginning. We could pick up from there.

'Are you okay?' asks Marc, unscrewing a bottle of instant formula from his bag, decanting one-handed into a bottle I remember ordering online.

I nod. Look away. Leave it.

I stand in the hall staring at magnolia walls for as long as my throbbing vagina will allow me. Then I perch on the sofa and do the same, as my husband feeds our baby.

I watch the baby suckle. Her throat swallow. Feel my own mirror it. Gulp hard.

I look at Marc.

He will never grasp the pain that I have felt over the last five days.

Inside me, I have been scribbled in with black.

Options have felt closed off to me like rows in a Connect 4 game. I stared at the board; couldn't see how this could work.

All I could do was keep loading up the circles.

Me, who feels everything like it's being sprayed onto me, fake tan in a booth. The guilt over missing a friend's birthday can ruin whole evenings; break-ups have felt like grief.

And yet I did this.

Every time I have spoken to Loll.

'Have you got her?'

'Not yet, Romilly. Not yet.'

I didn't get how it could be impossible. At times, I was angry with my sister. Was she trying hard enough?

Could she not spirit her out in her sleep? No, she said. The baby slept in an attachment joined to Marc's bed. I know, I said, I *bought* that attachment. Spent hours of my life researching the attachment. Reading reviews of the bloody attachment.

But surely Marc slept deeply; he must be exhausted? Yes, she said, he must be – but he doesn't sleep deeply. He's always half-awake for the baby. Holds her hand often to comfort her. There is no way she would get her up and out of the house without him noticing.

My heart hurt and hurt and hurt.

I'd focused everything on Ella. And she'd answered like it was nothing.

'Romilly?' asks Marc again, somewhere, sometime, somehow.

I went to buy supplies when I got here. I picked up toilet roll. I paid money.

How is it possible, even in the darkest times, to go through these life motions? To act as though the minutiae matters?

'Romilly.'

268

Sometimes, it was like I had a migraine but instead of flashing lights I saw babies, babies, babies.

One baby.

What was I doing here, when my baby was born only days ago? 'ROMILLY!'

Marc. Really here.

I turn to him.

'I'm going to put her down in the travel cot,' he says, gesturing at our daughter in his arms with his chin. 'Okay?'

I nod. Watch him walk across the room. He must hate that bald spot, I think, as I stare at it moving further away from me. He must absolutely fucking hate it.

I take in the place then that we have come to for the first time. Someone's home, or second home. A photograph of a man playing an accordion in nearby Eygalieres market. Provence in the 1800s, the women in large-brimmed hats, wide skirts. A vintage poster from the tourist board in Cassis, one from Marseilles, Arles.

I watch them across the room, Marc and the baby.

Can I do what Loll didn't manage? Distract Marc enough? Get the baby out of here?

But I think of the strength of my sister, and my own weakened body and mind. How can I do it, if she couldn't?

When Loll is a superhero.

I have thought about going back so many times.

But how could I face what awaited me there?

The horror as I put my key in the door.

The midwife appalled – me the first she had known to do this; hopefully the last.

A baby who didn't know me.

A husband who made it clear he did. The version of me he wanted to paint, at least.

And what came next, as he made sure that was it for us. As I was removed for good. Police. Social services. Psychiatric units.

The crazy one. The one who left her baby. The two weren't hard to paint into the same picture.

I imagined headlines. Judgement. Vitriol.

And you'll never guess what else: that awful woman spread lies about that lovely husband, the doting dad. Can you believe *that*?

But something else, now, is certain.

I can't leave without Fleur.

Not this time.

We go together, my family and I. All. Or nothing at all.

Day #5, 11 a.m.

The Woman

After a drawn-out feed and what felt like hours of attempts at burping the baby later, and then more screaming when he tried to get her to sleep, Marc finally puts the baby down in the travel cot.

The travel cot was in situ when we got here, as were a lot of the baby's things. Marc stayed here last night too.

Ready to move quickly.

Ready to pounce.

He sits down in the armchair next to her cot, as close to Fleur as he can be. I know he won't move.

His gaze rests on me.

'Ella is your ex,' I say, picking up. 'That's who I came to see.'

Marc furrows his brow, scans through history like there were tens of girlfriends. But I know there are only two of us. Before that there was Old Mark. Bad skin, overweight, rejected over and over and over. Not that I have ever seen a picture: photos of Marc's life only begin at twenty-four.

'Oh, that Ella! You came to see *Ella*?'

He is incredulous. Mutters. 'Jesus, if this doesn't prove that you're experiencing a psychosis, I don't know what does.'

He softens then. Kinder.

'You left the country when your baby was a few days old to see some . . . ex of mine I haven't thought of in years?'

Even softer. 'You do see, don't you? That this isn't standard behaviour?'

My head is low.

I don't know. I don't know. I can't remember. I am spent.

Doubt again. Too many people telling me I'm wrong. Perhaps I am. Perhaps I am. I don't know. I'm so tired.

'Why would you come to see Ella?' he repeats. 'We were barely anything.'

'Yeah, that's what she said.' I stare into space.

'Well then, there you go. Everyone is telling you the same thing.'

They are. He's right.

'She's amazing, isn't she?' he says then, and for a second I think he is talking about Ella and then I realise I am staring in the direction of our daughter and I see his eyes shine, his smile take over his face.

I nod. 'She is.'

'And we made her, Romilly. Please don't forget that.'

My head dips. I bite my lip to stop myself from falling into his arms and weeping.

Try to clear my thoughts. He loves her. He's a threat. He adores her. Don't trust him.

When I look up he is upright in the chair, fingers interlaced. Composed like he is conducting a job interview.

'I think it's time we talked properly, Romilly,' he says, eyes on mine, a heavy sigh. 'I think it's time for the truth.'

I nod my head.

Yes. I'm ready.

Day #5, 7.30 p.m.

The Best Friend

There's a specific buzz to that moment when summer days turn into nights; when swimsuits come off and a little mascara goes on. When you're freshly showered, wet hair dripping down pink backs. When limes are squeezed and the ice tray is taken out of the freezer and someone sweeps away the ice-cream wrappers and sets out a little bowl of olives and you take your first sip of gin and tonic. The music's turned up; the sun will soon go down.

It's that time when Aurelia and I get to the campsite Ro has been staying at, the day on the cusp of evening.

Sounds of splashing swimming pools have faded now, replaced with clinking plates that are piled high with local sausages, to be charred on the barbecue as soon as aperitifs are done with.

'Stef!' shouts my boyfriend but my eyes aren't on him, they are behind him, next to him, all around. I know that Romilly and Marc aren't here. But hope didn't get the memo.

'Where did they go?' I ask, at the moment Aurelia asks the same question.

It's the way Ad scratches the back of his neck. Steps onto one foot then the next, jiggling like a three-year-old who needs to go to the toilet.

That evening hum seems to mute itself.

And I know this isn't good.

'Where did they go, Adam?' says Romilly's mum. Her voice fires like a gun.

'I drove after them but they lost me,' he says, and my insides are on fire. 'A Fiat 500. I got the reg; I've spent all day driving around looking for it. But nothing.'

As Aurelia begins swearing and I put my head in my hands, Adam holds his hands up – surrender, not me, guv.

'The woman who works on the campsite says they looked fine though and look, they're *married* . . .'

'Marriage isn't a fucking trump card for all other adult considerations, Adam,' fires Aurelia. 'Believe me. Didn't you *speak* to Romilly when you were with her?'

Something crosses Adam's face. Regret, perhaps. The knowledge that what he has just done could have catastrophic implications.

He glances at me.

If he's ashamed, shouldn't I be too?

It was my doubt in Romilly that confirmed Adam's thoughts. I spoke to her at length, then I spoke to him. We agreed. This wasn't a coincidence, that she thought some random ex of Marc's was a reason to leave the country when she had a newborn after being monitored for postpartum psychosis. Marc was right. Marc *had* to be right. Yeah, something likely happened between them before Romilly had the baby. But that didn't negate what happened afterwards: that she was hit by a mental health condition that she was genetically predisposed to be hit with.

She was high risk.

It wasn't a shock.

I stare, my eyes on Adam.

But sometimes the sensical path isn't the right one.

By the time I realised I was wrong, it was too late.

Adam shakes his head and starts to justify but I don't have the stomach for it and shake mine harder. No. Let's not go over it now.

We have no idea where our Ro is, with a husband who is

persuasive and can manipulate. With a husband who has the power to destroy her life. With a husband who once took her beautiful face and shoved it down into the water that she loves. Who held her there until she learned, instead, to fear it.

Adam stands there, barefoot next to the tent, and slowly, like it's a tick, shakes his head.

'I don't know,' he says. 'I don't know anything.'

I picture Romilly then, my bird of a friend, scooped into a cage and spirited away by a man a foot taller than her. A man who is trying to convince people that she has a serious mental illness when she has not.

A man, I now know, who is abusive.

Who wants her back under his control.

A child runs past barefoot in pirate pyjamas. Is welcomed back to his tent by his watching mum. The zip goes up as they tuck themselves away for bedtime.

I look up slowly. 'Did the woman say how he was he behaving, Ad?'

Adam recoils. 'He had the baby. He wouldn't . . .'

Aurelia mutters under her breath: 'Jesus.'

And I see doubt cross Adam's face.

The sky is still blue. But the atmosphere around us feels like it has moved now, to black.

Day #5, 8 p.m.

The Best Friend

Perhaps it was easier when she was far away than now, when she is close. When Adam says those words, I kick at the tent in fury. It's Romilly's mum who pulls me off.

'There's no point, Steffie,' she says gently, and she holds my head with her fingertips. I think of our hands touching on the plane earlier and in the car. There is an understanding. We're stripped to the basics, a pair of human beings tied together as we try to navigate a nightmare.

I look around the campsite, as though my friend will emerge from canvas, sleepy hair and blurry eyes, all a mix-up. But she is gone.

'How long ago?' I ask.

'Early morning,' says Adam. 'They left about 7.30.'

It is now 8 p.m.

Over twelve hours. Alone.

Aurelia cries like an animal.

All of that time.

'How did I not realise the truth about Marc?' I ask into the ether but Aurelia answers anyway.

'Didn't you?' she says.

I look up at her, Romilly's mother, in flip-flops that make my heart ache for Romilly, who has been spotted in them before now down on the beach in February.

I raise my eyebrows in question but I know what she means.

Did we all know something, but we had our own reasons for staying silent? Bowing to marriage as the ultimate dynamic of adulthood. Bowing to pregnancy as a different plane; one we couldn't access. A feeling we weren't close enough to question, in Aurelia's case.

Excuses, really. We should have tried harder.

I think about her distance – from me more than anyone. Was I too close, Marc? Was that it? Would I have seen too much, if you hadn't made Romilly push me away?

The confidence she'd always had was replaced with something that bordered, often, on self-loathing. She was too tired to swim. Couldn't be bothered to paint nails that were usually bright rainbows.

Her hair, shorn. Severe. Without joy.

Aurelia swaps her glasses for prescription sunglasses again as she blinks into the sunlight.

'Let's just get in the car.' She sighs, like Adam and I are her petulant teenagers and I picture Loll and Romilly; another time, another life. 'There's no point hanging around here. We have to at least try to find her.'

Her sigh contains a multitude of emotions. It berates herself. It tears Marc apart. It is fear. It is exhaustion.

And something in her expression reminds me of Loll, bringing another lost woman into my mind too.

My stomach lurches again, again, again for two sisters I need to hold close.

We walk towards the hire car, chastised.

'Adam,' she barks. 'You get in the back. I'll direct you to a place, Steffie. I read a bit about the area when Romilly flew out. It's the biggest town, the most accommodation. Get maps on your phone, darling.'

I do what she says. Hand my phone to her.

For the first time, I think, pausing for a second to look at her face, she looks old.

Aurelia holds my phone out in front of her. Starts stabbing something into it. The heat is intense and even now, sweat soaks out behind my knees, swathes of it across my face.

'It's only a hunch!' she says. 'But if we've got nothing better, we might as well try it.'

With Aurelia next to me. Adam takes his seat in the back. He reaches round the back of the seat for my shoulder. Squeezes with a clammy hand.

When we're on a stretch of road where I can, I reach behind for his hand, my own palm damp too. I squeeze back. Hard.

No point holding on to the rage.

It's rapidly giving way anyway to a different emotion: a fear that we have no idea where we are going and that already, we are much too late.

Earlier That Day

The Husband

I can't believe how easy it was in the end, travelling with my baby.
Adrenalin beat fear.

And bloody hell, Fleur was good. Slept through take-off, barely a whimper at landing.

We were drowning, in the airport and on the plane, in offers to help us. With bags. To hold Fleur (an emphatic no) while I had my drink. With compliments too: how beautiful the baby was, how well I was doing on my own, what a great dad I was.

'Good for you, lovey,' said a woman in her seventies, and I think she would have pinched my cheek red if she wasn't a foot shorter than me. 'What a lucky girl, having a daddy like you.'

I can't lie: I bloomed. Always have, with praise.

'I'm the lucky one,' I told her. And I leaned down to cover Fleur's face with kisses.

The questions hung in the air though: where was her mother? And why were we on a flight to France when she was clearly a newborn?

Thank God, in the end, for the emergency passport application: her mum sick abroad. She went to the top of the pile, my girl, and off we went. No hold-ups.

I glance in the rear-view mirror on the way to the house with Romilly and see that face, slowly unfurling, slowly being known to me.

You and me, Fleur: *we* did this.

We did it!

We get lost on the way to the house, then we stop to pick up some nappies and formula, basics for Romilly and for me too, and by the time we get there, it is 9 a.m. and twenty-six degrees outside.

'After you,' I say to my wife.

She hesitates for half a second; we no longer know how to be around each other. Then in she goes. I follow, the car seat hooked on my wrist.

The note I read yesterday from the owners telling us to enjoy our stay, recommending the local Moroccan restaurant in the courtyard. We wouldn't have know it was there but we were told we mustn't miss their lamb.

When Fleur is fed, I put her into her makeshift bed without a blanket.

'Doesn't she need . . .?' says Romilly.

Her mouth clamps shut. I know what she's thinking: she hasn't earned the right to query my parenting decisions. She still doesn't believe it: that the postpartum psychosis is to blame; that none of this was her choice.

I sigh. God, this is hard. Explaining it to someone who's suffering delusions, paranoia. And expecting her to listen.

I look at her then for the first time properly, as her arms hang loose and aimless, reminding me of Loll's that time at our house. Our house? My house?

Depends if you're coming home to it, Romilly.

I tread carefully.

My wife turns and walks away to get a glass of water. The house is filled with antique trinkets and I expect the glasses to be the same but what comes out jars and is pure supermarket; the cupboards stocked for the Airbnb crowd who will drink too much rosé and smash two or three during their boozy, carefree fortnight away.

She gulps it down.

Behind her, I check the lock again and that big old stone door; make sure they are closed behind us.

Romilly turns; watches me over her shoulder. Her eyes are wide.

'I'm sure it's a safe area,' I reassure her. 'But I worry so much now we have a baby.' I laugh. 'I think I've become one of those paranoid parents. That didn't take long, eh?'

Romilly nods, slowly. Dazed.

I touch the key in the pocket of my shorts. Walk up and down the room, trying to read the French on the vintage tourist posters that line the walls: Marseille, Cassis, Arles.

And all the while Romilly watches me, sits, silent.

Day #5, 9 p.m.

The Best Friend

Hunches work sometimes; not others.

Adam found Romilly at the lake from Steffie's note. She had stayed there after meeting Ella. Nowhere else to go; not until her flight the next morning.

Easy.

She was waiting for him like a mirage.

Now, it is not so easy.

Adam, Aurelia and I drive around the ring road of a town called Saint-Rémy-de-Provence. I imagine the best little bistros and wine bars live inside in the maze of narrow lanes we can just about peek down as we go but its front page is a beauty anyway.

Outside the window, carousel horses sit in wait, for the morning and the children to come. A tea bar is closed up too, buttery toast will be served steaming when the breakfast crowd arrive in a few hours. For now, it sleeps.

Next to it though, the terrace of the locals' café is heaving at its seams, chalk lines through words I can't translate showing that everything has been eaten tonight; all the specials at least sold out. Plates are collected with shared jokes; latecomers are greeted with bottles of *bière* and three kisses, children run around playing tag just outside; hoping they can stay up past their bedtime.

We move on.

A cat stalks across the road around the village, lazy so that we have to slow down, like she has had one too many *vins rouge*. The chocolate shop window is art and outside the seafood restaurant, prawns are so large they look like lobsters. But whole lobsters laugh in the face of them, even bigger, carried proud and high by beaming waiters.

I look at everyone I see, just in case. You, you, you.

I see someone who looks like Loll and am reminded too that it's now over twenty-four hours since we have heard from her. The sick feeling spreads but I have to block it out; can only deal with this now. Loll will have to wait.

I look at the group popping olives into their mouths outside a high-end champagne bar, leaning in close, glasses filled with the palest of sparkling rosés.

At the queue outside the pizza van, *anchois* and *jambon*, *trois fromage* and *champignons*. Inside his vehicle, a man smiles, stretching dough like he is working on a sculpture.

'It's the biggest town in the area for touristy places to stay,' Aurelia says as we pull off the road and take a quick left, and then up outside the fifth Airbnb on our list. 'Van Gogh was in hospital here. Some juicy archaeological ruins. Quite a few . . .'

She catches herself, on detail no one has time for.

'Anyway, it would be my best guess for somewhere you could rent a house or book a hotel room at short notice. And they must be staying somewhere.'

We see a battered old French Citroën, a car with German plates, mopeds, empty driveways. But Marc's rental car is not outside this house, nor the next, nor the next.

I start the engine.

We try again.

Romilly's mum looks at her phone. Gives me directions for where to go next.

Some momentum though is being lost as we try the seventeenth, eighteenth, nineteenth.

Eventually the list runs out and we move back around the village, the spike of adrenalin that was flying around the car the last time we did this lap dissipated now as we fall silent.

I no longer check the bars.

Outside the window, stragglers sip the last of their aperitif and head to dinner. Middle-aged couples start long walks home; drives they shouldn't do after all those kirs. A petite younger woman, alone, spritzes mosquito spray, rubs it into her neck. Swoops down to wipe the remainder onto her ankles for the walk home. I take a close look at her but then another woman joins her, she looks up. No. Not you.

We head up a smaller road now, supermarket closing its doors, Japanese noodle bar bringing steaming ramen to outdoor tables. We hold our breath as we get too close to passing French cars, going too fast with car doors that are almost concave.

Ad reaches for my shoulder. I put my own hand out to Aurelia.

The rest of the drive back to the campsite is quiet. Almost silent. There is nothing more to say.

Earlier That Day

The Husband

Romilly moves on the sofa, tries to get comfortable but clearly doesn't manage it.

'Fleur,' says Romilly, her body curled awkwardly. 'You named her Fleur.'

We have to start somewhere, I suppose.

I stop pacing. Nod.

'Well,' I say. 'She needed a name. You weren't around to give her one.'

'But you knew I . . .'

I look away. I know that none of it was really her choice. But sometimes it doesn't stop the thoughts.

Sometimes, it's too hard to process when all I want to do is glue myself to that girl's side. How can she have left our girl for *Ella*?

'Did you do it officially?' she asks. 'The name?'

'Not yet,' I say. Half-smile. 'There's been quite a lot going on, Romilly.'

It is barely a movement but Romilly does something akin to a nod. I return the chin dip.

After a few seconds, I sit down at a distance from her on the large corner sofa. Rock hard. Uncomfortable. I didn't try it last night when I arrived late: headed straight for bed. I doubt people spend much time in here, though, looking at the small terrace at the front, and the slightly larger one at the back. The cheapest place I could find, but still a fortune. Three nights minimum too, when I know we'll be heading home as soon as we've talked. But what choice did I have?

I put my feet on the coffee table. Glance at my wife. Romilly takes up a tenth of the space I do, perched awkwardly on the end.

It is 10 a.m. now and I realise I haven't eaten since the pastry I grabbed when I landed last night.

'I'm going to make a sandwich,' I say with a sigh. 'Do you want one?'

She looks at me like I am losing my mind but food interrupts the darkest moments, the starkest realities. Always has.

She says yes.

I return with Comté baguettes for us both. Wince at the strength of cheese I thought looked mild. Romilly shovels it in, as I pick at dry bread.

'Look,' I say, when we have finished. Fuelled now. 'This is really simple. The postpartum psychosis we feared would happen because of your mum did affect you too. It's medical.'

She stares at me.

'Postpartum psychosis,' she says. 'Of all the things to choose, Marc.'

God, this goes deep.

I keep it simple. 'It's the reason you left.'

She stares at me. 'I can't work out if you have convinced yourself that's true, or if you're trying to convince me that that's true but I'll tell you now that if it's the latter, it won't work.'

I cross my foot onto my thigh. Sit back.

Be patient.

'Okay then. Why do *you* think you are here then, Romilly?'

'To get. Away. From you.'

She is boiling now.

'I get that,' I say, deadpan. 'Adam explained what you said about me.'

The hardest thing, to hear your best friend tell you your wife says you're violent. The worst conversation of my life.

She stares at me, willing me to look away but my eyes are focused. We stay like this for a long time.

'You're lying about Ella.'

Incongruously she laughs, like she's won the poker game and her shoulders can drop.

'You think having a baby has made me weaker, Marc.' She smiles, serene. Goading. Crazy. 'But you know what happened? It did the opposite.'

I look down.

She says I scare her? Romilly is terrifying me.

The Best Friend

'There is one more place,' Aurelia says. 'A bit out of town.'

I glance at the phone.

'Go on then,' Ad replies. 'Anything is worth a try at this point.'

And so Romilly's mum steers us there, from a guidebook, from maps, from gut.

The road twists like a rollercoaster and I have no idea where we are, only that I am moving higher, higher, higher in a place I thought was a plateau.

'You should probably see a big vineyard on your right,' says Aurelia, hesitant, and it's laughable because we see nothing on our right, nor on our left, barring lights that move at speed as they overtake us; locals who can feel their way around these bends like their own landings. 'And maybe one of those olive oil producers, funny old ones where you taste the oil on tiny spoons, lots and lots of olive trees?'

In the mirror, I can just make out Adam's face pressed against the window.

The plan is to follow this road round. There is no specific end point, only a belief from Aurelia that if you wanted to be isolated, if you wanted to shake some people off, this might be where you'd come. Perhaps St-Rémy was the wrong call; too much bustle.

'Unless they've kept going?' Adam says into the glass. 'Headed somewhere further afield? Or even back to England?'

But Aurelia shakes her head. 'Baby Fleur won't wait for food that long,' she says, her voice softening even with the mention of her granddaughter.

'And Marc would worry,' I add. 'About her travelling for that long in the car seat. Apparently it's not good for them when they're so little.'

I look in the mirror. See Adam look surprised at my knowledge. The last few days though; they've been like an intense parenting course.

So how do we marry these two things? Marc the emotional abuser. Marc the rule-abiding dad. Or is every person in the world a body full of contradictions? Isn't that the essence of people?

'Try the dirt tracks, try the side roads,' Aurelia pushes, her own face squished against the hire car window now too.

And we do, car bumping over potholes that are normally bumped over by cars that clink with wine, picked up from the vineyard to go alongside the *plancha*-cooked steaks they'll be having for dinner later. Cars that clink with joy.

When I open the window, no breeze comes in and the outside air feels like it holds its breath like we do, waiting for us to find Romilly. For this to move on. The only thing that can reach us are the scents: an overwhelming rosemary, a punchy thyme.

'There!' yells Adam suddenly from the back. 'Turn around. There!'

I swing the car round. Nothing coming. Please stay that way, I think, a heart that felt like it was pounding at its limit taking it up an extra notch as I put it into reverse. Things move fast on these roads.

I turn.

'First right,' he says. 'I'm sure, I'm sure . . . yep, it's coming up . . . now!'

I lurch across the road to the right onto a track that's even more potholed than the last. But Adam's right. There. Tucked behind an olive tree. In front of a farmhouse showing no sign of life.

A little Fiat 500, lit by the light of the house. The registration we have all been looking for.

Marc's rental car.

Earlier That Day

The Husband

'The irony is that I *wanted* people to look out for postpartum psychosis. I wanted *you* to look out for it. You knew that, from the meetings.'

Romilly has her hands on her hips. Paces beneath the posters.

'I would have thought it would be something you would want to embrace, to be honest.'

My voice sounds sharp and surprises me.

But wouldn't you?

'At least then people might be more sympathetic about you leaving your newborn,' I mutter. 'There's been a lot of . . . judgement, Romilly. Until I tell people about your condition.'

This gets her.

My wife shrinks.

I cannot see the expression on her face as her head is bent low. Shame? Or anger? Something dark, for sure. My mellow Romilly, padding in in her flip-flops sprinkling on her chia seeds, is a figure from the past now. This version is a wreck.

I wait it out.

'I never meant to,' she says quietly.

'How can you not mean to leave a baby?'

Fleur starts to mew then, lightly from the corner of the room. Probably the heat – this house a sauna.

'We were coming back for her,' she whispers. 'But you interrupted.'

'Look,' I say. 'Let's be clear. I don't blame you for this. Delusions are part of the psychosis. They are—'

'I showed Adam the texts you sent me. I. Do. Not. Have. Postpartum. Psychosis.'

'I don't know what messages you mean,' I say.

She goes to get her phone. Scans back. And it breaks me, watching how deep this goes. How much she truly believes it.

'They were here.'

I see it cross her face then. Doubt. I touch her arm. Speak gently. 'People who have psychosis are very unlikely to be able to perceive it in themselves,' I say, a parrot for Google. 'They are—'

'I. Do. Not. Have. Postpartum. Psychosis.'

But her tone, now, is less certain.

Day #5, 10 p.m.

The Best Friend

'Can we not get even a little space?' Marc sighs when he answers the door. His stature is that of a goalkeeper and he blocks all shots, covers the whole frame. His voice drops a level. 'Please. We need some time.'

Aurelia positions herself in front of him.

'I want to see my daughter,' she says. Voice steel.

But if she is preparing for a fight, she doesn't need to: Marc moves aside and Romilly appears, holding her own daughter, barefoot.

My breath catches at the sight of them.

There it is. Romilly and Fleur, together. All is okay.

Except it's not, is it?

Reuniting them was just part one.

I smile at my friend. She doesn't look at me.

'Well you've seen her,' says Romilly, focusing on her mum instead. 'Now honestly, like Marc says, we need this space. We have a lot to talk about.' Her voice cracks.

Aurelia laughs. But it's disbelief. Fear. Many emotions, none of which are mirth.

'You've been together since this morning,' she says. 'Hours and hours. I'm not leaving you alone with him any longer.'

Romilly sighs. 'It's like Loll is here speaking through you,' she says and even in this moment that other worry ticks away.

Where the hell is Loll?

'I'm an adult,' Romilly adds. 'You have to allow me to make my own decisions.'

Aurelia stares at Marc.

Loll should be here. Of all the times, she should be here. My fingertips go to my phone in my pocket, but it is resolutely still, silent.

In front of me, nobody speaks.

Marc puts his hands up in surrender.

'The only way to fix this mess is for my wife and I to spend some time together and talk. I know we've had hours already but that's not surprising, is it? We have a lot of stuff to cover.' He smiles. 'And someone who distracts us a bit.'

He looks at Fleur. Touches her hair lightly.

I have deferred to Aurelia but I can't stand this.

'All the stuff you told me on the phone,' I plead to Romilly. 'How he treats you. How he—'

Ro holds a hand up now, just the one: halt. And this time she does meet my gaze.

'Look, it's been an emotional week. For all of us.'

She reaches out and takes my hand.

'I am not saying I'm not grateful for everything you've done for me, all of you, because you will never ever know how grateful I am. But look at me.' Romilly stands straight and taller than her metres. 'I am here out of my own choice. I need to speak to Marc. I am fine. I have a phone. You know where I am. We need to get to the bottom of all this. I need to be with my baby.'

'You can be with . . .'

'. . . and I need to be with my husband.'

Aurelia scoffs. Puts up a fight. I step in, echo her.

'Jesus, *listen* to her, Steffie,' snaps Marc. A little spit gathers in the corner of his lips. I step back; recoil.

Ad grasps my hand. His mouth sets. 'Don't speak to her like that,' he says, and something in his voice has changed. 'Everything she has done for you, man.'

Marc puts his head down. Nods. 'I'm sorry, Stef. Honestly, I am.' When he looks up there are tears hurtling down his face.

And I want to go to him too; it's not just Romilly. We are good friends, Marc and I, and I feel it again: an inability to marry all of this. My brain either hasn't caught up. Or it doesn't buy something.

'Do me a favour though,' says Marc, gently. 'Just consider for a second that what if . . . what if I'm not a bad guy? What if I'm not? Do you not think I'm a good dad? Have you seen any evidence of this other stuff?' He puts an arm around Romilly. 'I love her. I love her just like you all love her.'

We all watch Romilly, but she is silent, head low.

'An hour,' grants Adam. 'And we're coming back.'

'No fucking way,' hisses Aurelia.

But Romilly looks her mum right in the eye.

'Yes fucking way. Go away. Come back in an hour. You can sit at the end of the track if you want, but just give us the hour.'

Aurelia folds her arms across her chest. I see damp patches forming in the armpits of her multicoloured kaftan.

'We're taking Fleur,' says Aurelia. 'She isn't sitting through this.'

Marc goes to protest but Romilly nods. She wraps Fleur in a blanket, kisses her head and hands her over to her MawMaw.

We sit in the car at the end of the track, to give them the hour, Fleur asleep in an instant on Aurelia's chest.

After that, we will take our friend and her baby home.

Day #5, 10.30 p.m.

The Husband

I am trying my best to be patient.

In the face of Romilly's delusions though, it's hard.

When I'm tired in my bones. A newborn, a mental health condition, a flight. Talking, *all day*, to a brick wall.

With them all out there in the car, waiting for us, refusing to leave, manning the dirt track like security.

My head pounds with it.

It has been hours now since we got here. Feeds for Fleur, cooling her down from the heat that worries both Romilly and me with a chilly bath, nappy change after nappy change after nappy change.

Anyone with a baby knows how long days can be in a flow of change, eat, sleep, repeat. Try slinging in a conversation like this.

And somehow enough time has passed that it is dark outside.

I see Romilly wilt.

The car is still there.

I pull the curtains over.

The Best Friend

'That's long enough,' says Aurelia, long orange fingernails emerging from between her lips, where they have nestled for the last hour, her other hand on the small of Fleur's back. She takes her guidance from afar. 'If Loll were here, she would say that's long enough.'

It's been fifty-two minutes. Fifty-two minutes of watching that dark house; our windows wound down to react to any sound – mosquitos taking advantage – and our eyes trained on the front door.

Fifty-two minutes is enough. We all silently agree with that, and we tramp across the loud gravel the few metres to the house.

Aurelia's rap on the door is a warning.

The silence that comes back is a bigger one.

'I knew this was a mistake,' says Ro's mum, voice on the edge of fear. She tries the door with one hand, Fleur still sleeps on her shoulder. She shakes it. The door does not budge.

I place a light hand on the baby.

Hold your nerve, I tell myself. It's not even been an hour.

'I knew it,' Aurelia says, handing Fleur to me. 'Find something to kick it down with, Adam. Find something.'

She is crouched down, picking up rocks, scrabbling, when we hear Adam's soft voice say her name.

I look up and the door is open, unlocked from the inside by

my boyfriend who, while we panicked, swiftly climbed in through an open window.

'Romilly!'

We all bustle in and shout at once.

But this house is silent.

'Hey.'

Adam nods towards something.

Aurelia makes a sound from her throat that brings goose bumps to my arms.

She is a few metres away from us at the other end of this rustic open-plan farmhouse.

In front of her are two water glasses, the end of a baguette. A box of Fleur's formula.

Behind her is a back door, open wide, straight out into the darkness.

The Day Before

The Husband

Loll made me a terrible cup of tea just before I looked her in the eye and called her a liar.

Too milky, like always.

She never listens.

When she went to leave my living room, I touched her arm lightly. Well, not lightly, but the way she looked at the sleeve of her hideous blouse was like I had bloody assaulted her.

'What are you doing?' she spat, and the room contracted. The teammate tie between us was slackened. We could feel it for the lie it was.

'I think there's something we need to talk about, Loll,' I told her.

She nodded. Turned. Came back into to the living room and sat down on my sofa, where she had become so at home. She used to visit once a fortnight, perhaps, if that. Stay for an hour with the kids. Neck a cup of tea.

Now it's home. One leg was crossed over her knee and dangled, Loll stocky in her thick black tights, Romilly's slippers.

Neither of us drank our tea. Tea was not for conversations like this.

'You never went to the police,' I told her.

Our eyes didn't move from one another's.

I smiled at her the whole time I was speaking. Well, I would; we're family.

She smiled back, and it was made of ice. Family, family, family.

'Of course I did, Marc,' she said. 'Why would I not go to the police when my sister is missing?'

My eyebrows flitted upwards. Light. Relaxed.

Light, Marc.

Relaxed.

'Right. Exactly. Why wouldn't you?'

A second passed.

'I did.'

'I never bothered seeing that CCTV in the end. Put my faith in you, too distracted by Fleur, whichever. But you never chased it.'

Silence.

'Do you have any documentation from them?' I asked. 'To prove that you went to them?'

'To *prove* it?' She was fizzing then, with something, with everything. 'Why should I need to *prove* that, Marc?'

And she shouldn't. Except she did need to prove it. Because when I asked the midwife if the police had been in touch with the hospital staff, she checked for me: nothing. When I asked her if there was any update on the hospital CCTV, she had no idea what I was talking about. When I had called our local police department, feeling my way around something that seemed off, they had no record of Loll ever getting in touch about this, or about Romilly being missing at all.

'Well that's just an admin thing clearly,' she said. 'You know what they're like in organisations like the police; it'll all be a paper trail, nothing in any decent system. Yes I have stuff – *evidence* – but not with me. At home.'

The wind gathered pace outside, fierce for summer again and whistling at us, louder, louder, louder.

'Do you think you could go home and get it now?' I asked.

'To be honest, Marc, no. When I go home, I'm staying home.

I have things to do. Lucy is at a tricky age. I am spending *a lot* of time here, looking after Fleur.'

Yeah. She was.

I looked at her then, this single mum who had given herself a transfer to our family.

'Why *have* you been staying here every night, Loll? It's a bit much, isn't it? Like you say, you have your own kids.'

'I think the word you're looking for is thanks, Marc.'

Martyr is one of Loll's favourite fucking roles.

'I'll come with you then and see the documents,' I replied. 'I'll stick Fleur in the car seat.'

She stared at me but I didn't break.

'I'm not sure where the stuff is, Marc. I don't want you and Fleur sitting there for hours if I'm turning the whole house upside down.' The eyes. She did not relent.

'I'm sure it won't take that long,' I said.

She smiled, deeper frost setting in. 'You clearly have never lived alone with two children,' she answered.

Bullshit. I'd seen that woman on a cleaning mission.

'No,' I said. 'Just one. I was hoping your paperwork could help me figure out where that child's mother was, Loll.'

She grimaced. Finally glanced away, shoving her phone into her bag.

'Marc, to be honest I'm not sure why you are so fixated on this,' she said, sharp. 'I told you everything I've been through with the police. It was brief. She's an adult.'

'An adult with psychosis. That would up the ante, Loll.'

A howl from outside; a gust that felt like it was lifting my tiny house clean off the ground; Loll and I just doll figures inside. Able to be flung around. Snapped apart.

'You'd think, wouldn't you?' she said, eyes right on mine. 'Sadly mental health awareness is still not as good as we'd like it to be.'

She's never been good at doing 'light', Loll, and now she was worse than ever as she gave a flimsy laugh.

'This is getting irritating now, Marc.'

'Why?' I queried. I stood up. Over there on my sofa, making herself at home, just like Steffie did.

'Why is it getting irritating, Loll?'

Fleur stirred in her Moses basket. Loll went to get her. She was halfway up to standing when I felt a flash of rage and pushed her back down onto the sofa.

'She's my daughter,' I snapped, and it surged. 'Just leave her to me for fucking *once.*'

Her next laugh wasn't flimsy. 'Oh now we're getting to it, aren't we?' she said loudly. 'The real Marc. All that nice bloke gratitude gone, then?'

She was standing up too now. 'And don't push me again, either,' she hissed.

Fleur, incredibly given the raised voices, settled back down.

'Barely a push, Loll – don't start down that path now.'

She raised an eyebrow. 'I think I'm going to leave,' she said.

'Not until you tell me why you didn't go to the police,' I replied. 'Why you've been lying about it since the day she went. And what you know about my wife disappearing that you aren't telling me.'

Loll moved towards the door. 'The *irony*,' she muttered as she walked past.

'What's that supposed to mean?' I put a hand out to the side, slammed the living room door shut.

She said nothing, lips a tight single line.

'I said what the hell is that supposed to mean?'

'Why don't you tell me?' she said. 'Why, if you think Romilly is experiencing postpartum psychosis, why you are not on the phone to the police every single day pushing them to do more?'

Silence.

'Unless of course, you don't believe it at all, Marc. Unless you know it's not true.'

The drip of that tap.

'If there's one person round here who knows more than they are letting on about Romilly's disappearance,' she said, then, 'it definitely is not me.'

I didn't know I was going to do it; I really didn't.

But we all know what a lockdown is like and this last five days had been my own version. The tea was always weak. Her voice grated like first-grade violin. I hated her motherfucking *blouse*. I knew she was lying. The light flickered. The window jammed. She and Steffie always wore Romilly's slippers. For four days now I had been punching walls, kicking fridges, pent up in hidden corners of the room as other adults roamed and did the task and took the walk and stopped me from having any sort of an outlet.

The weather outside got angrier.

And I couldn't, any longer, keep it in.

The front door was locked.

Loll screamed.

Day #5, 10.30 p.m.

The Husband

Half an hour, now, left of mine and Romilly's allocated time. Half an hour more of just us.

It is 10.30 p.m. and we are exhausted. Spent. Getting nowhere. Romilly looks out of the window. Starts to fan herself furiously.

'Is there really no air con in here?' she says and I look around again but I can't find anything. It's an old farmhouse; no mod cons is what this place sells itself on.

'I can't breathe,' she says, hand to her throat. 'Marc, can we get outside? I need some air. Let's go for a walk?' she says. 'Do this while we move. It may help. The others can wait until we're ready. This can't be rushed.'

'It's a bit late, Rom . . .' I say but she is right: this place is unbearable. My own hair is damp.

A breeze might help us not to pass out while we go over and over and *over* this. While I make her see.

And so we head out straight into that beautiful, craggy old limestone in what now feels like the dead of night.

You have to see this place: mountains that might be less dramatic than their less cutely named alter ego The Alps but still have their moments. Beauty. Drama.

Danger.

I say see them, but it's limited.

The darkness is acute.

The grass, even at the start of summer, is parched beneath our feet.

I warn Romilly: be careful where you step.

The Day Before

The Husband

I could hear a wood pigeon outside in the trees and that fucking tap in the bathroom, drip, drip, drip, as I held Loll up against the living room wall.

She didn't even struggle.

Instead, she smiled at me. Composed.

'Now we get to it,' she said, like she was pleased. 'Finally the acting stops.'

A surge of rage.

Oh, the front. This woman who bleached my toilet and burped my baby in lieu of my wife because she *was so worried about us* being without her when in actual fact she was the one who pushed her out of the door.

I'd figured it out, over the last four days.

How I just put dealing with the police in her hands; too much else going on to question it. Too exhausted for my brain to process that there were gaps. Why had they never called me? Why were they happy to do everything through Loll? Why did they not need anything from me, when I was Romilly's husband? When I was the first one to see she was gone?

Once that happened, the floodgates opened.

Glances I caught her sending in my direction. Not the warm kind.

Then she would flick it back on: teammate mode.

Romilly, I knew by then, had help from someone close. Who do you go to, when you need help, if not your surrogate mum?

A bow hung from Loll's collar, lilac and mumsy.

My fingers itched to pull it tight.

Day #5, 11 p.m.

The Woman

Step.

Step.

Step.

In a different life, I think, I would have come on holiday here to cycle round these hills, rucksack and sweat on my back, smile on my face, flip-flops on my feet, picking up a couple of bottles of rosé from a vineyard, local honey – that was it, *miel* – from a farm shop, turning back up the lane to our rickety old farmhouse tipsy and tanned.

Happy.

I would head for lunch in one of the pretty local villages. Throw my bike down and find some shade under an olive tree. Do yoga in a meadow with impossibly taut young Frenchwomen. Smear brie as thick as a face mask onto crumbly baguettes. Take on the climb home with the confidence that only half a carafe of vin blanc at lunchtime can give you. Snooze it off on a sunbed at the other end. Begin again with an aperitif at 6 p.m.

This is not that time.

Step.

Step.

Step.

As we walk a trail into the trees in the darkness of the Alpilles – Marc and I still silent for now, all talked out – between my legs there is an aching pulse, my vagina so newly exited and recovering.

I look around. My eyes are adjusting to the dark.

I know this area a little now, walking as much as I could manage before I met Ella today – trying to figure out how to get her to open up.

It didn't matter what she said: I knew she was lying.

I remembered what he said, that man with such perfect English, when I walked into the school she taught at, to leave her that message.

'Oh, you wear your hair in a short crop too! That's how Ella had it when she first came to us. I thought it was beautiful. But God, she *hated* it.'

Day #5, 11.15 p.m.

The Woman

Marc and I are round the back of a village called Les Baux-de-Provence. I overheard someone at the lake saying it got its name because it appears, when you look up at it on the clifftop, like a boat. Sort of. If you have one eye closed.

But I was drawn to this place. Round the front of Les Baux there are fancy ice creams and *moules frites*, parked cars winding around and around the streets where tourists try to work the pay-and-display machines with minimal French in searing heat. Sweat drips down their backs and they are exposed but it is worth it to be the person who drinks their rosé in the sun in Provence on their holiday or for a well-liked Instagram post. Just to know who they are, when they turn off the light in their five-star hotel, smiling at the thought that breakfast will be served next to the pool in the morning. That the private Pilates class is booked for 10 a.m. That they'll head to the exhibition in the cave after that, of course, because who comes to an area with this much artistic significance without prioritising the culture?

Round the back of the fancy village though is where it gets interesting. You round the bend to those cliffs and they take you by surprise, like a gritty gruyere after that soft brie. Provence *is* soft and gentle. Even if the Alpilles calls itself a mountain range, other mountain ranges would laugh at its audacity. Here though, there *are* edges; the limestone juts out to get you wherever you turn. You stop ambling along, but clamber up. Nothing undulates;

it spikes instead. Travellers climb up high on the rocks in flip-flops to see those villages below, Saint-Rémy-de-Provence, Maussane-les-Alpilles, Mourieres, Egalyieres, a troupe of beauties even from this distance.

The holidaymakers pose for pictures.

Every time I saw them I winced; checked my footing.

And here we are, round the back of Les Baux in pure darkness. I can't even see where my feet are.

'I have a pressure pain,' I tell Marc, whether he knows what I'm talking about or not. 'I need to sit down.'

Careful, I find a rock and perch, the stone hard and cold beneath me. When I'm down, something gives way and tears start rolling, for the days I've missed, the overwhelming sensation of new motherhood, for my baby's future, for her past, for me and Marc, a love story gone sour.

'Look,' sighs Marc, battling to speak over the crickets who are insistent we hear what they have to say. 'I know you have decided I am the enemy. But that is . . . it didn't happen, Romilly. I just want you to come home, see a doctor, and we'll go from there.'

I look at his outline; it is too dark for his details.

'If that's the case,' I say slowly, 'if I'm imagining the text messages, what about those things you said to me the night I went into labour?'

In the silence that follows, I look around. Inhale the skin of Provence: its abundant lavender, rosemary as thick as ribbon.

'What things?' he says finally, with a frustrated puff of breath.

'That you would take my baby away from me,' I say, tears painted now down my face. 'You said you would take my baby off me and *that's* what made me leave in the end, that's what tipped me over the edge and yes, the fucking irony, Marc, that I lost her by doing this anyway, it is not lost on me. Please don't point it out.'

He is close enough that I can see him shaking his head, over and over, but his face is covered by his hands; his head moves from side to side.

I look up then. Try to work out where we are exactly though I don't know the landscape well enough. But I look down and see lights and in the distance Marseille and the ports and I look up and only see the clarity of the stars so I know that where we are must be near the highest point.

It is May and the start of tourist season but there is still so much space here that at this time, even just a few miles from villages packed with outdoor tables and tipsy tourists, the silence is absolute.

I picture them down there, the thirty-somethings with babysitters back at the mas, laughing over another bottle of vin blanc, brown legs bare. I think of the retirees and their unrushed walks through the market, basket in hand, filling up with cured sausage for dinner later, a nutty block of Cantal, olive oil spiked with garlic, imbibing it all: the scents, the experience, the feeling. I think of the teenagers I see zooming past, espadrilles light on the pedals of their mopeds. Of the locals. Of the ex-pats. Of the vintage cars and the mountain bikers and the hikers and the horse riders.

I think of all of them, living.

And I think of us, here, everything in our life with the film of a nightmare over it now, and I hope none of them have to live through a time like this, none of them.

'Do you feel up to walking again?' Marc says, finally.

So I stand up and I try to block out the pain and I step forward, forward, forwards, the crunch of branches juxtaposed with the simmering quiet of us. The smell of thyme is as strong as in a restaurant kitchen.

'Any answer?' I say, as the climb bends even higher. Marc walks ahead. Ignores me. I hear him breathe heavily; he has got unfit, I notice with surprise. His tummy flops over his shorts. When did that happen? He is obsessive about the gym. Obsessive about never being that old Marc – Mark – again.

A scurry, sudden. I jump.

'Just a gecko,' mutters Marc through that breath.

It is too dark to see it, even though I can hear it's close.

A few minutes later, I sit down again. Marc sits next to me.

'Sorry,' I say. 'It just gets a bit too much after a while. Still physically recovering.'

Marc leans down and touches me so lightly on my forehead then that it makes the hairs on my arms stand on end.

And then he sits down too, looks at me and takes hold of my chin, with its slight point.

'Listen to me, Romilly,' he says, and it's soft. 'I never said those words. Never. I never would. You're her mum. Always will be.'

I stare at him.

'So you're telling me I'm imagining *that* too?' I say.

He is close enough now for me to see him nod. 'I am, yes.'

'And you didn't delete those texts off my phone?'

I picture leaving it, during our marathon conversations today, when I went to the bathroom. Numerous times. Changing bloody pads. There would have been time too when I was changing Fleur's nappy, head down, concentrating: it's new to me, takes me a while. Plenty of time for a man who knows my passcode to delete swathes of one-way conversation.

'No.'

'That whole conversation before I went into labour?' I say, teeth biting at my bottom lip.

'Didn't happen, Romilly,' he says, firm shake of his head.

'I nearly died,' I say. 'In the water, in the car after you shoved me down the stairs . . .'

'Whoa whoa whoa, enough, Romilly, enough. This is warped. You can't go round saying these things.'

I am sobbing now.

'My hair, Marc. My lovely long hair that you hacked . . .'

'I hacked your hair? Okay. Okay.' He takes a breath. 'I'm sorry to tell you that – and I know it must be terribly hard to hear

– but you are ill. We can get you the help you need. Keep you home with your family. This is hard for me too, Romilly.'

And I laugh. But it is tinged with terror. The messages are no longer there on my phone. Ella says their relationship was uneventful. There is zero evidence.

What if I *am* having delusions? It's the biggest fear of all, deep in my stomach: how would I even know?

I go to reach for my phone to call Mum, Loll, Steffie, someone who can tell me what is true.

But it isn't there. I didn't bring it.

I sit back on that rock, look down at the lights and then I put my head in my hands.

The highest point.

The ache intensifies. I put my hands between my legs. Wince.

'I give in, Marc,' I tell him, 'I give in, I give in, I give in.'

The Day Before

The Husband

'It's odd,' Loll said, her back against the wall as my fingers rested on the collar of her blouse. 'Why would you think I did anything to help Romilly when your party line has been that she was experiencing postpartum psychosis? Why would anyone help her leave if that were the case? I would be getting her medical help. There is no way I would let her leave.'

I looked at that bow again, hanging low and loose at Loll's collar.

'Unless what you're saying is that you don't think Romilly experienced postpartum psychosis at all,' she said. 'Or didn't ever? Hmm. Interesting.'

I pulled, ever so slightly on both ends of the bow; one arm braced against Loll. My sister-in-law's eyes tried to show defiance but there was something else and I knew it because I have seen it before, in eyes identical to hers: the very edge of fear.

Had she lost weight through all of this too? She seemed lighter, somehow. Perhaps that was just seeing her at close quarters; deep wrinkles across her forehead, greys around her temples, the sad reality of this woman, another one who seems more imposing from a distance.

That's women for you.

'You don't think that leaving your newborn baby would be something you'd do if you were going through postpartum psychosis?' I asked.

She swallowed and I felt it on my fingertips.

'Yes,' she said. 'I think that could be something you'd do if you were going through quite a few things. Postpartum psychosis is one of them, sure. Pure desperation is another.'

I bit my lip.

Tasted blood.

Day #5, 11.30 p.m.

The Woman

But then, Marc allows me time in my own head.

Well, he doesn't *allow* it.

Actually, what he does is deliver a long monologue about what he says has happened to me. What I am going through.

I zone out.

Think instead about Mum.

Mum, who was never diagnosed with postpartum psychosis in a time before mental health diagnoses were given much attention. And then, when Loll was first pregnant, we talked about what had happened to her when I was born and showed her the list of symptoms. Loll suspected, from the parts she knew and remembered from being a ten-year-old, that that's what Mum had experienced. And she needed to know herself, so that if she did have a genetic risk factor, she could be monitored through her own pregnancies.

Mum's eyes had filled: 'Yes,' she had said, 'that. That's what it was.' They might never have named it but she knew.

Mum, who I resented for so long for not being like the 'other' mums. There was a distance between us, my whole life. Steffie's mum Sheila was more like a mum to me. My sister Loll of course *was* a mum to me.

But then, when I needed help, Aurelia came through. And I let go of the resentment. Grabbed hold of my mum.

She didn't know how I'd felt with Marc, like a lot of people don't know how we feel when it's unpleasant; it's only the good feelings we make public.

But when I left hospital, she was on the phone constantly. Got on a plane to help as soon as she could. We chatted for hours, about our whole lives. About my husband. She was my bolthole.

Back in the now, Marc goes on. On. On.

'You've got to admit it makes sense, Romilly.' He sighs. 'Mums don't *leave* their children.'

And all the while I sit with my head in my hands, bum numb now on this rock, discomfort in every part of my body especially my chest, which is so swollen and ready to explode.

I told you, I think, I didn't leave her. I never left her.

But there is no point, is there?

I reach a hand out and grasp at the lavender next to us.

Fleur, Fleur.

Perhaps her name could grow on me.

And all of this ticks around my head as Marc talks.

'It's nothing to be ashamed of, Romilly,' he says, his voice drifting in and out of my head like an ear worm, an awful song I've been trapped with after hearing it on the radio.

I've got the gist now; don't need my mind to hang around for the rest. I can move on instead to thoughts of how I can go home, how we can make this work.

To thoughts of us: our family and our future.

I picture Fleur's dark hair, each strand so fine it almost doesn't exist. Somehow I knew that's what she would look like. I know how fast they evolve into other people – my nieces have shown me that – and I try to still time, squeeze my eyes closed. We've missed too much, Fleur. I can never get that back. But I promise that one day I will explain to you why. And one day I will explain to you, because it will be our story, the story of the two of us.

Oh. You thought by our family I meant Marc too?

Ha.

No.

Absolutely fucking not.

The Night Before

The Husband

Loll is big on commenting 'as a mother'.

Who gets to feel more, *as an* anything, I always think.

So how could she, who places so much emphasis on her identity as a mother, believe that what Romilly did was okay?

She read me, then.

'I am not saying what she's done is great,' she rasped because I had been inching tighter and tighter incrementally. 'I am saying that what she has done may, perhaps, be understandable. Given a very unusual set of circumstances.'

'Which are?'

'You tell me, Marc,' she said and I felt her throat move beneath my hands again. 'You tell me.'

I tightened.

And tightened.

And tightened.

Day #5, 11.45 p.m.

The Husband

Finally, Romilly has stopped arguing and accepted what I am saying.

I can see it in her body language; as she sits on the rock, almost coiled in the foetal position.

Cowed.

She has stopped battling it.

And that is the crucial step.

Now, we can go home. Move on with our lives. Get out of this limbo.

I stand up.

'It's getting late,' I tell Romilly. More than anything, I could do with a beer. 'We should head back. Have some sleep and tell Loll and everyone it's all okay and get Fleur back into her cot.

'Then we can sit up and have a look at what flights we can get home in the morning. Get back to normal.'

She nods her head but when she looks up, she appears beaten.

'Can you give me a hand?' she says. She gives me the hint of a smile, pliant.

I walk over and slip Romilly's tiny hand into my own, twice the size. I can feel a roughness; her skin parched. God, Romilly. Another woman, so sexy, so recently and now exposed for the mess she is.

'Thank you,' she says, weakened, quiet.

I help my wife up, then turn to begin the walk back to the house.

'God, that view.' I stop and stare out at it.

Take a tentative step closer.

But something odd happens, and suddenly the move I am making is different.

Not a tentative step.

More a stumble.

A flailing.

And then I am no longer looking at the view and the lights but I am falling, falling from that beautiful viewpoint; the one people drive all the way up to, the one people like to enjoy their picnic at, the perfect spot, with their garlicky olives and their local cheeses and their cured fucking meat, and I am going down, down, down, nothing but air, then, until the violent rocks below.

The last thing I felt can't really have been the two small hands of my broken, weakened wife, can it? Pushing, decisive, no warning.

Stronger than you would think.

The last thing I heard can't really have been a voice, can it, shouting one word: YES?

Day #5, Midnight

The Woman

When I was five I looked up from a drawing I was doing and asked my mum to show me pictures from when I was a newborn baby; a fifteen-year-old Loll changed the subject, told me a firm no. My mum's hands started to shake as she dropped a boil-in-the-bag rice into a pan. Loll looked at me and moved her head slowly side to side — a warning, as Mum kept her back to me.

Loll had already started to protect my mum, even then.

And then a few years later, Loll and I were out shopping. I was sitting on the floor of a River Island changing room while Loll tried on sixteen different bikinis; none fitted her giant boobs.

'Why don't they make them in bra sizes?' she muttered.

I shrugged. Watched the shoes go by beneath the curtain. There was not a glimpse of a hill beneath my own T-shirt yet. These were not concerns of mine.

'Can't Mum take you somewhere to get one?' I asked.

A topless Loll scoffed, pulling her bra back on. 'Don't presume that adults have the answers,' she said darkly.

I looked up from the shoes. 'What happened with Mum when I was little?'

I don't know where I got the confidence from but it came out and Loll stood there, hands on bare hips. Her body had caught up now; her mind had been an adult for years.

She seemed to be considering something.

'Move up,' she said and squeezed onto the floor in that tiny cubicle next to me.

I knew there had been something. Once I heard Loll shouting at Mum about a time when she was left waiting outside the front door for so long that she wet herself. She was ten years old.

'When you were born, Mum suffered some sort of . . . psychosis,' Loll told me then. 'She got help. But not soon enough.'

When I was older again, Loll told me Mum had tried to kill herself when I, as a baby, was in the room. It was ten-year-old Loll who had found us and flushed away the rest of the pills. And who had never dealt with how that impacts a person. I wonder why Loll can't relax? Because she hasn't relaxed since she was ten years old.

I told Marc all of this. All of it.

When you are newly in love there is such a relief in tipping all of your life out for this person to see. Here I am. You love me, so you won't mind it, and now it's not just mine. At that stage all you do is share, share, share whether it's bodily fluids or early life trauma.

It helped, too, in explaining to Marc the strange ways in which my family worked. He hadn't met my mum yet: it was best, before he did, that he had some background. So he could tread as carefully as the rest of us did.

I cried as I told him. He stroked my hand. Listened well. He did, back then.

'Thank you,' he said when I had finished speaking. It seemed a weird thing to say, but I think he meant for trusting him with the densest of family truths.

And then, when I got pregnant we knew it was a risk for me too. Loll had been fine, both times, but it was luck of the draw. That didn't mean a thing.

We went to the meetings to monitor me, as a genetic risk, through my pregnancy. To the counselling.

When I went missing, he panicked. If people knew the real reason I left they would *know*. Would see Nice Guy Marc for who he was.

So he decided that the most personal of things made the perfect lie to shift attention away from him.

Remembered the parts he knew about postpartum psychosis and thought: *hey, that's handy.*

Told my friends that I had it when he knew that I did not. Because he knew the real reason I ran.

He knew it was because of him.

I stand there for a few seconds after he falls, waiting for something to happen but there is nothing.

It is too dark to see, too dangerous to go near the edge.

Instead, with careful steps and a thudding chest, I walk away in my proper hiking sandals. Good grip. Best there is. Thank God for that trip to Decathlon when I left the airport.

My heart hammers harder.

The path crunches beneath me.

My brain whirrs.

Is he dead?

Of course he's fucking dead.

I am not far now, from the house that sits alone, in the middle of nowhere. It's how Marc wanted it, not another soul around. Best not to think about why.

One foot in front of the other, as I smell the thyme, thyme, time after time, as I feel the mush between my legs smart, as the silence becomes overwhelming.

I remember then, how he spoke to me in those last moments, the same as he did when labour started, when I said I would leave him.

Like I was pathetic.

Like he could tell me anything, and I would buy it.

He thought I wouldn't hurt him when my vagina throbbed

and bled, when my breasts swelled. When I whimpered and asked for his hand to hold.

He thought I didn't have the strength.

What a basic lack of understanding about womanhood.

I have never been more physically weakened; I have never had more strength. To get to my child. To clear up his lies. To shore up my future. To shore up her future.

When I walk back towards the house, war is over, man has walked on the moon: something has shifted.

But not in a bad way.

It's lightness.

It's *freedom*.

And when I get inside, in through the back door, I find them there, of course.

They shriek at me but I reach for Fleur, speak over them.

At the same moment, I see them register Marc's absence.

'There's been a terrible accident,' I say. But my voice is giving a shopping list, a weather report.

'Okay,' says Adam. Careful.

I tell them what happened. Cuddle Fleur closer. She writhes until she is comfortable but then settles on my shoulder.

Adam draws a sharp intake of breath. Hesitates.

Aurelia nods. Makes eye contact with me. Nods again.

I pat Fleur's back gently.

'I'll call the police,' Adam says. 'You talk to Steffie in the meantime. Make sure you . . . know what happened.'

I nod. Sure. I tap a rhythm on my daughter and it soothes.

I know Adam wonders. Maybe always will.

But if he does suspect it, he doesn't sound angry with me.

In fact, what I hear is understanding.

I am in so much shock that I don't notice Aurelia take a phone call and leave the room. It's only when she comes back in and speaks that I look up.

'It's Loll.'

Day #9, 11 a.m.

The Woman

Cloud formations turn my baby into a mini zombie as she stares out of the plane window.

I look down at Summer – previously known as Fleur – who slipped out of her sling and into my arms for the plane journey.

We are getting to know each other, slowly. Maybe this is all we need, her chest on mine.

Across the aisle from me is Steffie. She reaches out, squeezes my hand at take-off.

'You okay?' she whispers, as the EasyJet voiceover tells us the safety procedures. I think of the last time I heard that: how the world has changed its fundamentals.

I nod. Tilt my head down to Summer.

I go to speak but I can't.

Instead, I start to cry for everything that's gone, for the time without Summer, for my marriage, for my big green door and my shared life and for the days when a hangover was my biggest problem. For youth. For choosing wrongly. For life. For death. For time, passing.

I am still emotional too from the conversation I had with Loll before take-off. Hearing what my husband did to her; leaving her unconscious.

Another woman he needed to gain control of.

By the time Loll came round, Marc had long ago left for the airport with Fleur, locking my sister in the house. He took her phone. We don't have a landline. It poured down with rain; not a day for lots of people to walk past, for someone to help and so she didn't get out until the next day when our cleaner let herself in and called her an ambulance.

My sister is physically fine. Brushes off enquiries about the other side of things.

'He took my glasses,' she said, and it was the only time I heard her voice crack. 'He took my glasses, Romilly.'

The hairs on my arms had stood on end.

She can barely see a thing without her glasses.

He wanted to make my sister – my strong, capable sister – vulnerable and scared.

'Hey,' Steffie says from across the aisle, soft. 'Why didn't you tell me? About Marc?'

I look at my best friend, her hand now back in Adam's.

I don't know, is the truth. Why didn't I tell everyone? Because I wanted it to not be happening. Because he had these tiny bright moments where I could convince myself it would maybe stop soon, and I didn't want everyone to hate him. Because then I was pregnant and scared, ashamed sometimes, exhausted. Because in between being menacing and cruel, he was joy and he was love. Because all I had the strength to say was I'm fine, I'm fine, I'm fine, the world's least trustworthy adjective. Because I was broken. Where do you even start to explain that?

'It's okay,' Steffie says quietly, reaching again for my hand. 'Whenever you're ready.' Then she pauses. 'I doubted you. Often. I'm sorry.'

I close my eyes. Then open them and turn to her. 'I doubted myself. Often, too.'

Steffie rests her head on Adam's shoulder and for just a few minutes before I have to change a nappy in a room barely wider than me, before our EasyJet cabin crew offer us two for one on the gin in the bag, there is a stillness, enough headspace to think about what has just happened.

And despite everything, that is not easy.

We reported Marc missing. His body was found straight away. It wasn't hard to pinpoint where he would land. When you fall from that height, you go straight down.

Adam told the gendarmes in detail about Marc's daredevil streak: the bungee jump he did on his stag do, the sky dive experience he was thrilled to get for his birthday present last year.

They think that might have been what gave him the confidence to climb so high; to balance so precariously. What led to him making such a terrible decision.

Nobody has asked many other questions; there wasn't a need.

Me? I was back at our Airbnb with our daughter. Newborn, yes. Thank you, she is adorable, I know. Gosh no, I'd *never* be out with her at that time of night.

The reality is that tragic accidents happen on high spots in dark hours. And even if anyone were looking for suspects, mums with tiny babies attached to their front and milk leaking onto their T-shirt are not high on their list.

We did talk though, of course.

'I'm sorry,' I said, glancing down at the wet patch, flushed. When I looked up the gendarme was blushing brighter; he was around sixty-five. 'But she really does need a feed. Is there any chance we can pick this up later?'

The baby and I got back on with breastfeeding that night.

No one ever asked me for a follow-up chat.

On the plane now Steffie closes her eyes and Adam looks over the top of her head at me, raises an eyebrow in question. I nod. Yes. Still okay.

Or will be.

I kiss Summer's tufty strands, not dissimilar to what Marc left behind for me that morning. I vacuumed our bedroom floor for hours but I still find the odd strand as a reminder. I suspect that was the idea.

Now, my daughter and I will grow our hair in sync.

Day #10, 2 p.m.

The Woman

On the sofa, my indent has remained and I slot back into it. Ah.

Loll and I let Summer's cousins, who have been desperate to meet her, have time for a cuddle earlier.

'Finally,' muttered Keira, hand on hip.

Loll had got new glasses.

Now the baby and I are alone, getting to know each other.

With Summer snoozing and attached to my front in a sling as I potter round the house, I go to open the window. Stuck. Panic rises in me; I need air. Thanks, Marc, I think, irrationally, like he did it deliberately. After a few seconds I push it hard, harder, harder again and finally it gives in.

Sometimes brute force is the only thing.

I go into the kitchen. Put the kettle on. Lean against the work surface and sigh.

A spotlight has broken, flickers on, off, on, off, enough to make you lose your mind. In the bathroom, I can't stop the tap from dripping.

We will take some warming back to each other, this house and me, not least too because of the reminders *everywhere* of Marc.

Back in the living room, I stare at the wall.

Something's missing.

The photo of my favourite beach, the one with the swimmers in the distance.

What did you do with it, Marc?

I stare at the absence.

That, the window . . . they feel like points scored, even when he can't score points anymore, and I swear at him under my breath.

I go to my bag, dig around and take a postcard of beautiful Lac de Peiroou out, a little crumpled. I had bought it at the campsite; intended to send it at some point to Steffie. I find some Blu-Tack and stick that up there instead – I'll frame it properly later.

That lake got me back in the water. It deserves to be remembered.

Summer snores lightly on my chest and I slip her out and lie her in the Moses basket. She makes it clear that's not happening and I smile, happy for her to come back to my chest, this time draped in a blanket.

Our Henry Dog lies next to us in his spot. Some things are the same.

I sit back on the sofa. With a baby and no husband, it'll be a while before I am back at the café but it will happen. They're family there too; the baby will doze in the pram, everyone will be happy to grab a cuddle with her on their breaks.

'We'll figure it out,' I say to Henry, who is part teddy, part cushion, 100 per cent comforter. A light hand on his sturdy back. He is strong, this dog, but with no idea of his power. I pat lightly. God, I missed you.

I hug him close. Is he missing *Marc*? Baffled to see me again, wondering if we are now working to a one-in, one-out policy? When he saw the baby he jumped on and off the sofa, his tail wagging like a workout. It took about five seconds before her cousins found their old groove with him too, pulling his ears, opening his mouth up to examine his teeth. I smile, thinking about Keira and my Lucy who has been so worried about me.

Mid-morning tomorrow, Steffie will be over with granola from the café.

Loll, of course, will be here often. She will drop a mac and cheese in, whip the duster round, let the girls pile in again for hugs with the baby.

What Loll can't move past is how Marc used our own family pain, the one that has sat so deeply in all three of us for years, for his own ends, and to shift the blame from himself.

Loll brought her notebook to my appointments and asked the follow-on questions. Requested I had a private room when I gave birth; told the midwife that she had read it could help, if I had a little more sleep. It's the same reason she used to call to make sure I was getting an afternoon nap in when I was pregnant. Rest, she said. That was important.

Loll pored over my care plan. Studied it – and me – like a textbook.

She was more knowledgeable than most medical professionals I saw. Muttered about their lack of knowledge on postpartum depression often.

She cared, more than anyone could ever care.

She stored the numbers to call, if, if, if in her phone.

My sister watched, eagle-eyed, all the way through my pregnancy. We talked, checked in.

Then there were those days after I had the baby, when I hid away at hers, my holding pen, my steppingstone, like a university, teaching me the ropes before I headed out into the *real* world.

Forty-eight hours for Loll to confirm her thoughts plus the calls from France that followed: there were many, many things I needed to figure out, but a postpartum psychosis diagnosis was not one of them.

She had her checklist, yes, given to her by the midwife. But she also had a deep personal experience of it and she was clear in her mind, she tells me: that was not what was happening to me.

When the others sat in the path outside our Airbnb, Loll –
having finally got out of my house and met Jake at the hospital
– messaged me from her ex's phone: *Do not listen to him. You
do not have postpartum psychosis. Remember it.*

I read the message, as Marc sorted Summer's milk out at the
house.

And then a second message.

*He tried to kill me, Romilly. I am in hospital now getting the
once-over. Don't take chances. Don't let him manipulate you one
more time.*

Something in me surged; eddies that started at my stomach
and surged outwards and upwards to my brain.

Stopped the doubts.

I didn't have postpartum psychosis.

He was lying.

Outwards and upwards, outwards and upwards.

All the way to the edges of my body, landing at my tightly
clenched fists.

Day #10, 8 p.m.

The Woman

Before that I had been alone with Marc for a long time; doubt had started to creep in.

What if the genes that meant Aurelia and I both felt no cold and retched at the idea of meat had delivered us something darker in common too?

Did I really message Steffie that odd text because I was in labour, and my husband was threatening to take the baby from me? Or was it more to do with what was happening in my mind?

But when Loll's message arrived, the doubts ceased.

Another surge. Another.

'I need to get out,' I had said. Something about fresh air.

Because hadn't he picked us the perfect spot for a night-time walk?

And so we headed off into the Alpilles.

I remembered Loll's messages as I watched him climb. As I watched him stand, so arrogant, a belief that he was infallible. Hand on hip, mussed-up hair. Pleased with himself.

Designer trainers, no grip.

I remembered Loll's messages as I watched him fall.

I remembered Loll's messages as I stood there and realised that nothing had changed.

That man had already become a body to me, gone from my life a long time ago now, when the honeymoon period ended; when he started, seemingly, to hate me.

When it was my fault he couldn't afford a stag do. When he boiled over like a pot. There are some deep dents in my walls since I got back; I shiver when I think what would have happened if he'd found me that day, not plasterboard.

Do not come for my sister.

He pummelled my mind the hardest. Imagine being a person who could do that to another person, make them doubt their own mental health, simply because it suited your agenda.

I shiver again now.

Do not come for my sister.

If you could do that purely so that then people wouldn't blame you for your wife's disappearance, hours after she has given birth to your daughter? Panic, grasp and come to *that* of all things.

So they would pity you, not blame you. Because you were so into your newfound adult popularity, *Marc.*

Perhaps he even convinced himself it was true. I don't know. Never will.

The doorbell rings to snap me out of my thoughts.

It's only 8 p.m. but I fear visitors now at any time.

Police?

The doorbell will get this response from me, I fear, for the foreseeable future.

Flight is a fine prospect except for when you have a newborn. The instinct to flee may be strong but the need to pack a giant holdall with nappies, wipes, Sudocrem, formula, a steriliser, bottles, eighteen babygrows and vests, and a couple of Elmer books is stronger.

Fight it is this time then.

Henry has his head resting on the side of the sofa but gives a side-eye glance at me. I return it. Reluctantly – *go on then, if I must* – he follows me.

I place a hand down on his soft, sleepy head as I take the lock off now and open it an inch, the green paint I applied so haphazardly coming into view. I spot the streak that ended up on the tiles; we never did get round to cleaning that off, did we, Marc?

I open the door.

Draw a sharp, horrified intake of breath.

You.

Day #10, 8.15 p.m.

The Woman

When I open the door, I am in my flannel pyjamas. Ella most certainly is not.

High heels despite being a good five foot nine already. A high ponytail makes her look taller still.

Her light touch of make-up could have been applied by a professional.

Toned. Fit.

'Oh.'

'Hello.'

We stare at each other.

She looks alarmed at Henry's bark. I shake my head to reassure her. He's softer than you, I think. If you were a burglar, he'd take you to the treat cupboard and give you my purse and PIN for a biscuit. But it's loud, and she looks nervous.

'How did you . . .?'

'The café. I remembered you mentioned the name. You should probably tell someone called Polly not to give your address out so freely in future though.'

I smile. But look around, nervous.

'I don't think you should be here,' I say eventually as Henry tires of his circles around her and heads back inside to see if his cousins left any crumbs behind from their flapjacks. I look to the bottom of the path, left, right.

Then back at her. God, she's a beauty. Dark hair, dark eyes, not a trace of a dark circle. That stature.

I close the door slightly, but she pushes it back.

'Romilly.'

I nod like I am confirming, but we have met twice before, Ella and I.

I open the door to let her in.

'I'm back visiting family. They're only twenty minutes away – but you probably know that, that's how I met Marc. Anyway, it seemed crazy not to call in. Ask how you're doing.'

Robotic, I nod.

'Of course, I forgot that you have family here. Just associate you with France.' I put the kettle on.

'They said he was in a particularly dangerous spot,' I tell her, looking up. 'I guess you know what he was like. Always wanted to be at the highest point, the sharpest edge.'

I start to cry then, genuinely, next to the kettle, because he did want that and when life was good, I laughed about that, and loved him for it.

She goes to come over to me but I hold a palm out.

'You know,' I say, after I have got myself together, tissue clutched in my fist. 'That he was a big kid. That area is a bit of a surprise, with its edges when the rest of the range is rolling hills.'

A beat.

'Are the police happy with that?' she asks.

Day #10, 8.30 p.m.

The Woman

I look up at her. Duck my head. Put my fingertips to my eye sockets. Henry whimpers and I crouch down and hug him, whispering to him: *'Good boy, good boy.'*

I take a deep breath.

I stare back. But not at her eyes. A large diamond sits on her engagement finger snuggled up to a wedding band; her husband, I know, is French. They will stay in the Alpilles; live a life of fresh bread and bike rides.

My own engagement ring is gone now: removed as soon as I was back in England.

'I found out I'm pregnant this week.' She smiles.

My eyes shoot up. 'Wow. Congratulations.'

'Romilly, it's the second time that's happened to me. The first time, the baby was Marc's.'

I stare at her.

'I had an abortion,' Ella tells me as she sits, in the way women often say those words, dipping their voices low. 'I was only twenty-three. It was too early. Nothing had begun in my life yet.'

I wince, imagining Marc's reaction. 'I needn't ask how Marc dealt with that,' I say quietly.

She bites her lovely pink lip.

'Not kindly,' I add. 'Not with understanding.'

A little red lipstick has stayed on her tooth.

'No,' I say quietly. 'I imagine far from it.'

She has her head now bent low, hands to her stomach.

'Was it worse than unkind?'

In my kitchen, the kitchen of a stranger really, Ella's shoulders begin to shake.

'I nearly died,' she says, barely audible. 'It had always been emotional before then, threats, putting me down, making me feel stupid. But I've got no doubt. If someone else hadn't turned up, he would have gone through with it. I wouldn't be having this baby. Wouldn't have got married. I would be dead.'

I go to her. How can I not?

She is me. I am her. He's made us each other.

A few minutes later, as I squeeze our teabags against the side of our cups, one, two, I sit down with her at my tiny kitchen table.

'When you got in touch it was traumatic for me. I had PTSD and talking about it again, reliving it . . . it started happening again, flashbacks, nightmares. I just couldn't.'

I nod. Think about the dream I woke from at 3 a.m. this morning. My pyjamas drenched in sweat. 'I get that. I'm sorry I put you through it.'

She shakes her head, angry. 'No. It's not good enough. Just to ignore it and leave someone else to live it too. That's not good enough. I should have been honest with you, not shut down on you at the lake. You needed help. I got protective of my life. Of being happy. Safe.'

We drink our tea. Silent. Happy. Safe. The basics. God, they are wonderful.

'How did he do it?'

'He tried to drown me,' she says. 'Quiet spot in the Lake District; we were on holiday. It was only someone else turning up, a pack of kids screaming, that saved me.'

'What happened, then?' she says eventually. She nods at Summer in the Moses basket. 'How did you end up in France without . . .?'

She takes a large gulp of tea.

I sigh.

'Summer. Her name is Summer,' I tell her. 'I only tried to leave *him*. Not my baby.'

And the whole thing unspools, once again.

'It seems crazy now, but I was desperate I suppose,' I say. 'I needed something to give.'

Under the table, I look down at our feet, platform trainers versus slippers. Slippers that feel stretched actually, I think as I look down. Bloody Steffie and her giant feet.

Ella looks back at me.

When she looks up again, I take in a smudge of liner, a curl of the lashes.

Meanwhile she sees a mum, in her flannel pyjamas, dots of nail varnish on her fingers that are hanging on for dear life, two months old. She sees eyes so heavy she can't imagine how that happens. She sees a state, perhaps, that she will never allow herself to be in.

A murderer? Ha. I had been so scared it would be what people thought that I believed I had to lie to the French police about where I had been. Very handy, hey, that my phone was left behind. I could put myself out of their picture.

We make eye contact again, Ella and I, sitting at my kitchen table now with our tea, and remain that way. My breathing slows.

Henry wanders back out to us, having exhausted the leftovers.

'I can't believe he's *dead*,' Ella whispers.

She wipes her eyelids so her heavy kohl smudges across her face, cheeks.

'You've taken your ring off,' she says.

I glance at my left hand. 'You mean *your* ring?'

A beat. Ella nods.

341

Day #10, 8.45 p.m.

The Woman

Ella doesn't ask any more questions about what the police said. I don't think she wants the answers. We have a neat conclusion and is the route to that conclusion such a problem?

There are two lives to get on with living. Two babies to raise.

When she hugs me, I whisper in her ear: 'Thank you.'

Ella's shoes make no sound as they walk a few metres down the road to where she has parked her car. I hear the engine turn. A quick visit home to see family and then she'll head back to France, where her present is.

And a little bit of her past, whenever she drives past that mountain.

As she leaves, she walks to the end of the path of my tiny house by the sea, her platform trainers smashing down the weeds that are coming through it. I follow her out. Glance back at our house.

I'll paint my front door again, I think. Jesus, isn't that the most prosaic fresh start you can imagine?

Inside the tears slow and stop and I walk with my Henry Dog to the kitchen and find a brand of cheese I don't recognise; enough bottles of beer for ten people at an all-day barbecue.

Henry finds some bonus crumbs on the floor next to the fridge. Gets to work.

I reel for a second, steady myself on the kitchen worktop. Crouch down to take Henry in my arms and let his softness soothe, like I am six months old with a dribbled-on blanket. He gulps the last of his snack down.

I picture what would have happened if I hadn't left, if a baby called Fleur or Summer or something else entirely had come home with the two of us that day and Marc and I had stayed, existing here for another twenty years.

In the image, I shrink and shrink and shrink, just as the baby grows and grows and grows and she watches me, diminutive now, barely a person. Someone her dad, a narcissist who grows in stature, controls, mocks, despises.

Or, I die.

Sometimes you can cry for something that didn't happen harder than if it had; you swerved a bus, your biopsy came back clear, you left the building just before it was set on fire and how close you came is almost unbearable.

I heave now. Crouched down. Folded over.

I tell myself to breathe, like I did here, in the same spot, as I went into labour so recently.

For all of its darkness, where Summer and I have ended up, alone, is right. Safe is not basic.

Before

The Husband

How much was planned?

Did she get me up there deliberately?

Know my habits: that I would always look over the edge, always check out the view, always find the rockiest point? Always take it a little bit too far.

Or was it a last-minute decision?

Did she know, by then, about Loll? Is that what did it?

I will never know.

Telling people that Romilly had postpartum psychosis is not something I was proud of. It throws lives against the wall. It can end them. It's not something to be used.

Would it help if I said that I did believe it, in those first minutes? That is true, I swear. It was the obvious place to go; we had been prepped for it, watching.

Postpartum psychosis was logical. It was repeated as fact soon, by Loll, by the midwife. By me. That was easy to be swept along with.

And yes, it was helpful. It stopped people looking at me as closely as they normally would: *always the husband.*

It helped too with an urgency, to get Romilly back *now.*

That's what I wanted. To stop her from leaving me. To get back here and be a family. To talk to her, so she would never tell anyone anything.

But once I had a chance to think, I knew she had been

showing no signs of postpartum psychosis. I had only seen her a few hours before. And Loll wasn't the only one at those meetings.

No. Romilly had simply left me. What I didn't get was why she had left her baby behind.

I didn't take Romilly to the Airbnb to hurt her.

She just needs removing sometimes from those people, with their opinions, their thoughts, their views on things.

So she can hear mine.

I *am* her fucking husband.

It seemed like the best thing, to marry up everything and tell her the same story too. To delete those messages quickly as she went to the toilet, again, wincing as she walked.

I also took Romilly to the Airbnb to get her back. Get us back on track. Okay, so there was that one time that afternoon when I hit out – shoved a knee in between her legs when she had already told me it hurt – but she *wasn't fucking listening*. She had this surety about her that I hated. It wasn't like her; more like I was back there talking to Loll.

Oh yeah, that.

I picture the last time I was in my house. When Fleur cried and I came to and I realised I had gone too far with Loll, I panicked: I threw stuff in a bag and I left for the airport. I'll figure the rest out when I get there, I thought. I just need to head for where Adam is. Be there. Stop being impotent.

When I let go of Loll, she slid down our bright blue wall. When I left, she was as static as the night. She was still wearing Romilly's fucking slippers.

What Romilly didn't realise, when she watched me go off that cliff, was that one thing had changed.

I would have been a good dad.

I *was* a good dad, for those five days.

None of it matters now though, does it?

Those days will be wiped from history.

345

I would have taken Fleur crabbing at the weekend while Romilly swam in the sea.

I would have let her have a sneaky spoonful of my Coco Pops.

I would have taken beautiful pictures of her, swinging at the park up the highest mountain.

Five days.

I would have taught her to play guitar.

I would have done all of it.

I would have done all of it, within the boundaries of what I could afford.

Because I think of that, in the last moments, too.

The gambling. The panic. The worry. The pressure. It came spilling out, often, onto Romilly. Not that she knew that was why.

The six credit cards.

Lying awake thinking about how the hell I would pay them. Seeing messages from the loan sharks I'd gone to in desperation. That one Steffie saw leaving our house comes to mind; she'd heard me on the phone to him before that too.

Three loans.

Sometimes I could feel that pressure physically in my head like a weight. How could you blame me for losing my temper?

I sold the only thing I had that was worth anything: my guitar collection. I couldn't bear to turn up at band practice with some shit replacement; I hold my hands up, I have an ego.

The reality is that things tumbled and somehow I was the man with the receding hairline, a shit career, debts and the ticking time bomb of a secret; the man who didn't make it, confirming what they thought, what they said, taunting, taunting, those sluts in their Topshop miniskirts back in the day.

The man who will never make it, now.

Look, I'm Marc Beach: I'll play my guitar at your wedding, make you laugh in the pub. I'm not that guy. I've just had a bad time of it, that's all. Teenage scars heal easiest on skin but on the inside they stay singed within you. I will never go back to being Mark.

No one will laugh at me.

No one will get to recoil and walk away.

I'm not evil. I'm not a sociopath. I fucking *loved*.

I know I will never get to tell them this, but I did, I did, I *loved*.

I lied in desperation.

Life was just hard.

I look back through it, all of it.

Romilly and me on our wedding day in a field. Looking down to see a large blob of mud on the red nail polish of her big toe. Thinking this was it, this was *it*, to be with someone who made me grin like this.

I think of how I adored being twenty-five, people singing songs back at me as I played guitar in the band at their wedding.

Marc, now. Round two.

Further back.

I think of my mum, laughing as I told her what they had said to me, worse even than the rest of them. Toughen up was the mantra. Man up. And sort that disgusting skin out. Then that shudder.

I think about music. Pictures. Beauty.

Fleur's face.

Her tiny body, curling into mine.

Her back, soft but strong against my hand as I bathed her.

I think about that sensation, that tumbling away feeling that is so palpable, how it is happening again now, but this time there is no chance to claw it back, no matter what.

I think about what I would do differently.

About the loan shark who will arrive at Romilly's door soon.

About the cancelled life insurance.

An unnecessary expense, I had figured. I was thirty, after all. Invincible. Peter fucking Pan. How I would change things, if I weren't so very, very dead.

Day #21, 8 p.m.

The Woman

My mum and I sit on my sofa, a baking show on a couple of notches too quietly.

Aurelia dozes lightly under a blanket; she has her own indent now. I've just made up her bed.

I've never felt more like I have a family. A village is what you might call it, perhaps. A female power crew has gathered around a new mother, a formation as old as time.

My mum broke up with Bill yesterday. He wanted to travel more; she wanted to retreat to an unassuming house in the seaside village of Thurstable on a peninsula in the north of England and read books to her grandchildren. She's listened to a lot of Lionel Ritchie but it seems to be abating.

She has been feeling it for a while deep down, she says: that pang for home and I can see a shift in her. Age, perhaps, or just the experience of chasing her daughter across southern France and finding her husband dead in a ravine. One or the other.

'Will you miss him?' I ask, hands wrapped around a mug, Henry in his spot on the sofa.

She nods her head. 'Fiercely,' she says. 'But God I was knackered.'

I laugh. 'Well yes,' I say. 'You were seventy-two and riding around the Basque country in a camper van; so you would be, Mum.'

She touches the tattoo on her ankle but as she leans down, I see a little pink on her cheeks. She's noted the 'Mum'; I don't use the word directly to her often, even if it's always the one I use in my mind.

'Will *you* miss *him*?' she counters. Slips her glasses down off her face and wipes them on the blanket. She reminds me of Loll, often.

I nod. Can't trust myself to say anything. Because, see, I will. I do. A version of him, at least.

What happened wasn't my choice.

It was Marc who carved the knife across our family and left us open and exposed so I had no choice but to stitch us back up, in any way possible, at speed. Not the most sophisticated job but it negated the risk, gave Summer and me a fighting chance.

Mum slips her glasses back on. Nods back. Bites her lip.

Now, life looks different. Mum is going to look at a new-build apartment round the corner from me. When I go back to work, she'll look after Summer.

We talk often about guilt.

After postpartum psychosis follows a period of grief for what you have lost and been through.

A thousand different waves of anxiety.

Sadness.

Bonding can be tricky.

Mum and I didn't have the best start; Loll often stepped in to help. It was a habit that set in in our family and stayed around. Loll's resented it all her life; being an adult since she wasn't one. And yet it is a habit she can't break; always being the grown-up in the room.

'Another tea?' says my mum. I snuggle down into my indent. Mum and I exchange a laugh at my Henry Dog, who is asleep next to me flat on his back, all four legs up in the air. His head lolls to one side; his tongue out of his mouth.

I wonder if I'll ever sleep that soundly again.

When Mum leaves the room, I browse a cookbook. There is a cherry cake that my stomach growls for. I fold down the corner of the page.

By the start of next year, Steffie and I plan to have Beaches, a tiny café looking out at North Wales, up and running.

A little homage to Marc. Seems fair, when his life insurance will be paying for it. I must dig out those forms.

You're wondering, aren't you, whether to conclude that I am good or I am bad? Answer number three: I'm human.

I can watch a man fall from a cliff, full of hate, because I'm crammed to the brim with love. For my sister, for my baby. For a cold day in a northern sea.

Soon, my mum goes to bed. I cross the room to check on Summer.

And then I wander round the house, hands wrapped round a hot mug of chamomile tea that my mum has put a little too much manuka honey in.

I take it in, this home I've come back to: a different person than when I walked out of it, bent double. I was a home myself then for someone else, vagina contracting, heart breaking.

I imagine this house in its temporary guise, being sublet by Loll. Those days I missed.

I could never have coped with being away from Summer if I hadn't known that Loll was there instead. Loll oozes motherhood from her every pore, writes meal plans in her sleep; could probably still operate the Calpol syringe with one arm if she was being held up at gunpoint.

My skin goose bumps with gratitude.

I keep it up, my tour of this house. Henry follows me, resentful, like I've made him go on a night out when he'd rather chill at home with some iPlayer.

The canvas print of a beach in Barcelona where Marc and I went on our first holiday together. The litter picker we took out on walks, before. The cards I cram on high shelves from important birthdays, anniversaries, celebrations. I know them off by heart though: the ones belonging to the days that turned bad.

All of these things, identifiers of a life.

I have a lot of them; you do when you're thirty-five, a mum, a friend, a sister, a swimmer, a baker, a person. A widow.

It's been a week now since I got back from France and I am still recalibrating, finding my way around a home that was mine and Marc's and now needs redefining.

For the first day or two I lived on toast and then I realised why the smell was making me nauseous.

Alone smells of toast.

Crises smell of toast.

Family smells of hearty curries brought home from the Goodness Café and spicy soup and a batch of banana bread that makes people smack their lips together and beg for another slice.

I pause.

There is one part of our tiny house I haven't been in yet, in the days I've been back.

I pause outside Marc's 'guitar room'.

Open the door.

Shit.

What the hell was that?

Something hits me right in the face.

I flick on the light.

A purple helium balloon drifts out in front of me, limp now, beaten. Wry smile: to be fair, I was wrong about his colour choice.

I pop the balloon and screw it up, pushing it deep into the bin.

'Oh, Henry,' I mumble, crouching down to hug my boy.

When I look up I realise something: Marc's guitars, his most valued possessions – all four of them – are gone. When was the last time I came in here – six months ago? It was made very clear I wasn't welcome.

I frown.

Then I glance up at the gallery wall that Marc and I put together into the early hours when we first moved into this house.

Action in every shot. We dance, we scale a climbing wall, I wobble in a kayak, Marc throws his face back as he holds a guitar, we play rounders with friends. I swim, I swim, I swim. We laugh, we laugh, we laugh.

How could the picture change so fully?

I peer closer.

There it is.

The one in the middle.

Marc, a day trip in North Wales, standing on the highest rock, no fear in his eyes though I knew there was plenty in the face that looked at him through the phone camera in that moment, begging him to come down. It had started then. I can see it in the arrogance of the stance. Maybe he was always going to fall, at some point, somewhere.

I close the door to the room gently. I think I'll turn it into a playroom.

Look, some clichés are true: every mum knows how to multitask.

Usually work and nursery pick-ups and ordering a new raincoat and emptying the dishwasher while you're on hold to British Gas.

But sometimes you have to apply your skills to a different area. Diversify.

Plotting the rockiest walking routes while you're having a conversation about your mental health, for example.

Looking out of a car window to see exactly where you are and where you can go as you masquerade as weepy, broken.

Thinking four steps ahead.

Marc is arrogant.

Marc likes risk.

Marc wears designer trainers with shockingly bad grip.

Marc gets *very* distracted when he can hear the sound of his own voice.

Marc and I were in the *mas* when Ella messaged me.

It wasn't brief, she admitted, opening up finally. *It wasn't nothing. It was what you thought it was.*

Marc had called her, she said, the day I got to France. He had got her number from someone shoddy who had no knowledge of privacy rights at the school she works at. He knew about *that – where she worked, that I had been tracking her down –* from my internet history, which I hadn't had time to wipe when I had gone into labour.

He threatened me, she says. *He threatened my husband. I was terrified. This is a man I left the country to escape.*

So what changed? I typed quickly, when Marc went to warm Fleur's bottle. *Why are you getting in touch now?*

My fingers shook.

I remembered your face in that lake. I remembered how my whole body shook when you shouted after me that you had left your newborn baby to come here and how I drove as fast as I could to get away from you but I couldn't get away from you because you were me really. Just a few years later.

She messaged again.

Where are you? I can come and meet you now. Let's talk.

One last message: where we were, or as much as I'd been able to memorise on the drive.

I'm with Marc though. Stay at home. We can talk on the phone later.

I hoped. I hoped there was a later.

She messaged again. *He's found you??*

I never got a chance to reply. Because then Loll's message pinged in. I heard Marc coming back with the bottle.

He tested the temperature on his wrist.

As he talked at me, I glanced quickly at the front door then the back.

You think Marc would have let me walk out of the front, back to my friends and family and ready to move on with my life? This was the more long-winded way to go about things. But the most effective ways often are.

As Marc and I walked, the route twisted and turned, and I

sat down in a spot that meant Marc – if he was going to continue that *incessant monologue* – had to get just that inch or two too close to the edge. It was the only other place to stop there.

Could I do it?

As I needed to sit down wincing in pain – the knee he pummelled into me there earlier didn't help – I had a quick check around me where we were, before we headed on.

Almost.

Up. Up. Up.

You hurt me.

I saw one of his large feet lose its footing.

You lied.

He grabbed hold of a rock.

Could I?

You will keep hurting me, again and again and again.

Started again.

You will keep lying.

Euphoric. Confident.

You hurt my sister.

Up, up, up.

I had come to hate Marc so deeply in my bones.

Up, up, up.

And then of course, straight back down.

He's wrong: instinct and panic kicked in and despite everything I had dared myself to do, everything I thought I wanted to happen as I suggested the walk, left my phone behind, headed for those craggy edges, I could not end a life.

It's just that as I stood there, realising I couldn't do it even though this was my chance, someone else appeared next to me and pushed him, hard.

We stood there together in silence.

When she hadn't had a reply to her message, Ella, guilt-ridden about lying to me earlier and worried about me being alone with Marc, had cycled straight over to the house.

She didn't want to draw attention to herself and didn't have to: being local, she knew the roads others didn't and pulled up quietly round the back. And as she did, she saw us leave. So she followed us, on foot. Adam, Mum and Steffie never got a glimpse of her.

On the walk, Ella stayed far enough behind to track Marc and me, but kept us in sight. Easy enough, in the pitch-black.

Marc had threatened her life, her happiness, all over again, just as she was starting to move on.

Safe isn't basic.

It wasn't me who shouted yes.

Not at first.

But a few minutes later, I shouted it loud. We shouted it at each other, Ella and I, before we wept on shoulders that had both been gripped hard by the same man.

Up there in the mountains, it would have sounded like an echo.

Acknowledgements

A lockdown book! Written! Finished! I'm going to have a large wine now, if that's ok. But first, some acknowledgements.

Whenever you write about mental health, there is - rightly - a responsibility that comes with it. Which means that my first thank you goes to the brilliant team at Action on Postpartum Psychosis, especially Lucy Nichol and Jenni. Thank you for answering my questions and for casting your expert eyes over my manuscript. You are doing such an important job and took time out of that to help me get this right and that is very much appreciated.

Big thanks and kisses to my friend Katie White from my favourite cafe on the planet (and my unofficial lockdown sponsors) Real Food Kitchen. Thankfully I have never come across a mean old Stella in there but many of the other elements of *Five Days Missing's* The Goodness Cafe pay homage to this wondrous community space. Thanks Katie for talking me through how your day to day works, letting me nose around upstairs and telling me juicy stories. Thanks also for bringing the Sri Lankan prawn curry and pineapple rice into my life. I have eaten approximately 250 since Covid began and am basically writing this book to pay for my habit.

Related to that Real Food Kitchen community, thank you to my pal Louise Beach (who first came into my life lurking around trying to find a wine opener behind the counter in there; I should have known we would be mates then) for gifting her frankly brilliant surname to me for the characters of Romilly and Marc. Great name; great woman.

Thank you too to all the other friends who offered wisdom and support, and a quick note especially to Rachael Tinniswood, who is always there for book chats, questions and general wisdom. I can't wait for your book, Rach. To my real-life author buddy Tabitha Lasley, in a year when travel was 'curtailed', being able to talk words face to face with someone who lives round the corner made my soul happy and my brain fizz. The same yoga class: what were the chances?

To copyeditor Helena Newton for fastidious attention to detail. All hail copy editors; unsung book heroes who always teach this grammar obsessive a new grammar rule. I cannot tell you how much I love a new grammar rule.

To my editor Helen Huthwaite. Oh, how I *love* working with you! Thank you for your insight, your tireless dedication to getting everything just right, your understanding of the childcare/words juggle and most notably, being a joy to work with and a friend. To the rest of team Avon, how lucky am I that I ended up in your camp? Cannot wait to see you all soon.

To my agent Diana Beaumont. What. A. Woman. I'm so glad fate (or as we sometimes call them, Lucy Vine and Daisy Buchanan – thank you to you legends while I'm on too) delivered me into your capable and brilliant hands. I hope that you will be making my books better and ordering The Official Best Pasta On The Menu with me for many years to come. If you're not too busy reclining on a chaise longue with a giant bag of truffle crisps, of course, which frankly you should be because it's where you belong.

Thanks to the rest of the Marjacq crew, especially Sandra Sawicka for remaining patient when it comes to those complicated foreign tax forms and for making those tax forms completely worthwhile when I see my books translated into foreign languages.

For any geographical errors in the France segments, I would like to formally blame Covid-19, for preventing me getting on a plane and swanning around Provence calling it work. Lac de Peiroou is a real place, and I've been there many times, but I would have liked to have done one more visit to check the details for this book in real life. For any errors in flight times, I would also like to blame artistic licence and the belief that a bit of drama beats the correct route into Marseille Airport.

Thank you most of all, as ever, to my family. To Mum and Dad for all of the support. To Gem, Chris, Luna and Blake for telling me stories about their late dog Henry, and letting him – with a few fictional elements for the purpose of the story – be a character in my book.

To Simon and our boys, for support, for the practical juggle, for making me happy, for being the three best human beings on the planet.

Her life was perfect. Until the video.

She thought she could trust them.
She was wrong.

THE BABY GROUP

'Addictive'
Stylist

'Twisted'
Cass Green

CAROLINE CORCORAN

The deliciously twisted thriller from the
bestselling author.

Lexie's got the perfect life.
And someone else wants it. . .

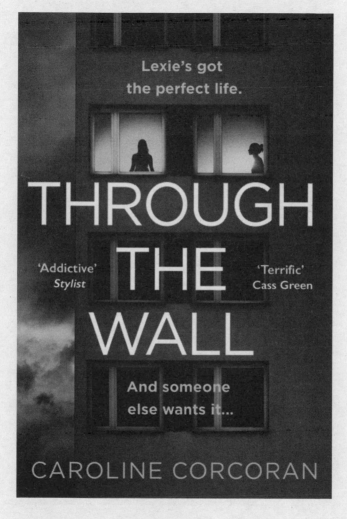

Lexie's got
the perfect life.

'Addictive'
Stylist

'Terrific'
Cass Green

THROUGH
THE
WALL

And someone
else wants it...

CAROLINE CORCORAN

A heart-racing psychological thriller perfect
for fans of Louise Candlish and Adele Parks.